THE NEW DARK LORD

BOOK TWO

THE NEW DARK LORD

BOOK TWO

Ian B. Urns & A. C. Erinle

Podium

Cover design by Art of Neight

ISBN: 979-8-89539-359-8

Published in 2025 by Podium Publishing
www.podiumentertainment.com

Podium

THE NEW DARK LORD

BOOK TWO

Prologue

The old king ran, and his lungs burned. They burned because he was an old man, as well as an old king, and had been forcing his body into a sprint for far longer than was comfortable. They burned because the air had grown hot and putrid with undead reek around him. They burned because his panic was turning to a fearful flush under his skin, and each breath felt sharp and cramped.

Around him, his palace was a ruin. Walls fractured and caved inward like helms struck by war hammers, floors beset by cracks spanning the width, sometimes even the length, of the corridors themselves. The old king was careful as he ran, for each way he turned there seemed some new tripping hazard where mortar or stone had been driven up and displaced by the fighting.

From outside he heard what was left of his men, either dead or dying. They were good warriors, the best. Knights, all of them, and a cut above their peers to have been selected as personal guards to his palace. It was all worth nothing. The old king had seen the invaders' monsters, and undead of that caliber could scarcely even tell the difference between knights or mere men. The ruin they made of bodies seemed unaffected either way.

A tremble ran through the building, and the old king stumbled, almost fell. One of those spells, he realized. The mysterious, impossible ones this dark caster had started unleashing, that engulfed the world in a fire so brief and bright it felt like a second sun was touching the earth within the span of a single eye's blink. A moment later, the sound reached his ears, like mountains crashing together. The old king hurried, pace increasing and carrying him through to the safe room.

They were all there, thank God. His sons, his daughter. Not a one of his mistresses was present—that much needled him—but he barely noticed such trivialities next to the sight of royal blood unspilled and well-preserved behind the safe walls of his retreat. He hurried in, hearing the door driven shut behind him and finally letting his aged lungs exhale in relief as the foot of solid steel lining every surface of the room fully enclosed them.

"Folami." He gasped, hurrying to his eldest son and embracing the boy. More a man now, and the old king felt as much in his grip. Strong with size and bodily maturation, invigorated by youth and made tightly desperate by the fear of their situation. He squeezed back, as best as his withered muscles would allow, to offer what meager reassurance the gesture would.

"Father, how goes the defense?" his son asked.

"He wouldn't be here if it had gone well," Ado noted, not meeting either man's eye. The old king resisted the reflex of chastising her, finding himself too weary and too beaten to bother correcting such improper things as her razored tongue now of all times. What use would it do her to speak more appropriately? She would not charm her way out of their situation.

"Quite right, my dear," the old king breathed, pulling back from his son and taking one last look at his face, etching the sight into his memory. He closed his eyes, sighed, and got down onto his knees.

Prayer. It was all he had left, all anyone had left. If God himself would not smite the attackers, then there wasn't a force in all the world that could.

The old king did not commune with God for long because soon enough the impacts started. Weak at first, barely audible through the layers of stone and steel. They grew quickly, soon intensifying in noise, then in force as even the metal was buckled and dented, bulging out in great mounds as it deformed before the strikes pounding against it from beyond.

He turned, watching the ruin progress and clutching his children tight. It didn't take long for the door to fold inward, smashed apart, jagged lengths of metal falling away from the ripped opening like so many sword blades mangled by hard use. There was little dust or debris in the air; such things were typical of holes made in stone rather than steel, and so the beasts responsible were seen almost instantly.

Monsters, there was no other word for them. Like great machines of meat and bone, bowstring tendons and support-beam limbs, bodies covered in articulated plates that looked to be made by a genius armorer and moving with an unseen musculature of impossible strength.

But it was not the mere mountains of flesh that drew his eye; it was the abomination atop them. The caster was a creature unrivaled among any other of his kind the old king had ever seen, a beacon of magic to engulf the greatest of court wizards and the eldest of magi. He was tall, taller than man height, standing easily eight or nine feet, and lithe as a fencer. His body was covered with plates of a similar composition to those that protected his creations, though more finely worked and made by far. Atop his head, a crest seemed to grow from his skull, protruding in such a way as to resemble a grand crown. His body was wrapped in a great robe, and it was that that the stories had spoken of the most.

It moaned, that robe. Groaning and weeping with every movement, low hums of agony that seemed unrelenting in their projection and heightened by every fractional movement. The caster came down from atop his mount, drifting slowly to the floor and making his way to the group.

"You resisted," he said. He had a soft voice, almost deft in its touch against the old king's ears. It was like the hand of a surgeon, but it still sent a chill down his spine all the same.

"How could I not have?" he asked, trembling, feeling a humiliating tear roll down his cheek. "You demanded total surrender. What king would simply *give that?*"

If the caster was moved by his despair, he betrayed no hint of it.

"Clearly a wiser one than you."

The old king couldn't argue with that. How could he? It was right. He had been a fool, a stubborn, proud fool. And now his people were slaughtered, his nation in tatters. Everything he cared about ground up as food for some dark magus's machinations.

He opened his mouth to speak, perhaps to plead or persuade, but fell silent as his eyes caught something more behind the caster. A towering figure, though still far shorter than the caster himself. A figure he knew better than almost any other. King Galukar.

"You." The old king gasped. "Galukar, what . . ." For one moment he feared that his old comrade had been killed, that he now gazed upon some reanimate. The Godblade dispelled that fear. It was still there, by his side, and still brimming with the divine light it always did. No undead could have held it; none could have even tried.

Galukar looked up at him for a long second, then turned his gaze away. Shame or regret, the old king couldn't see. It did not, he supposed, make a difference.

"Surrender now." The caster spoke up, commanding suddenly, voice hardened and edged. "Or I will further my already wreaked destruction."

It wasn't a choice at all. The old king simply heard his words and nodded.

"I surrender." He scowled, shaking with humiliation and regret. "By God, I surrender. My kingdom is yours, my people yours. Just spare them more of your barbarity."

The caster did not reply at once, waiting until the old king had raised his gaze to meet the man's eyes before he did so.

"My barbarity?" he asked, voice level, quiet. "You sit atop a feudal pyramid, subordinating your people with delusions of divine sanction and birthright. You leave geniuses idle and unutilized, treat magic as a secondary concern at most, and work only to hoard what you already have rather than create yet more and innovate. You do all this and dare to call me the barbarian? I am the liberator. I am the hand of civilization caressing your savage empire. An enlightened man would be thanking me for what I intend to make of your world."

He listened, more for fear of what might be done if he dared interrupt than any true fascination with what was being said. The old king had expected madness when he heard the dark caster speak, but what he heard now was worse. It was blasphemy of the highest order. He spoke of providence as if it were some foolish delusion, called God himself a liar.

This is the beast I am to deliver my people to, he realized. *A cruel heretic, caring only for power.*

The old king was deflated, all his strength slipping away in a single hard breath as the realization finally sank in that this was truly the end. Nothing now existed that might save him, or perhaps even that could.

Better the Dark Lord than this, surely. Better anything.

The caster eyed him for a second, then sighed.

"I should not bother. Your kind do not understand the truth of House Shaiagrazni. It must be drilled into you from childhood for your limited minds to grasp it. I am simply wasting my effort." His gaze grew cold at that, and final. "I have your surrender. That is all I ever required."

The caster's hand raised. It was a simple gesture, sluggish and lazy, but it sent the old king stumbling back a step.

"What are you doing?!" he demanded, eyes wide and bulging, jaw tight with horror. "I surrendered! We surrender!"

It was fascination and surprise that moved the caster's face, not pity or hesitation.

"And I will, as agreed, spare your people. But you must be punished for your resistance."

The old king took another backstep, looking around the room now. There were knights with him, of course, and each had their weapon drawn and body tensed for activity. He had no illusions that they would serve to impede the caster.

"I am a prisoner!" the old king snapped. "Not a soldier, not a peasant. You cannot do this—"

"There are very, very few things I cannot do anymore," the caster cut in. "My armies boast a combined biomass in the thousands of tonnes, my own personal equipment improves by the day, and even your divine magic is now mine to wield. You have no power here, and your world has nothing to offer me anymore. I will do as I will, and never again shall I be shackled by your idiotic customs or diplomatic procedures. Superstition does not rule me, however much it rules you."

Trying to speak, to say anything at all, the old king found his voice had abandoned him. Lips moving silently, dry with stress and fear, throat convulsive and fist tight as the panic crept ever deeper into his wits. Finally he managed an answer, though it was barely any sort of answer at all.

"I am a king," he breathed, feeling his eyes suddenly grow very wet, his legs suddenly very weak. The caster seemed almost to smell the enfeeblement of his resolve, and relish it.

"We do not have kings in my land," he replied, calm as if he were commenting upon the weather. "Nor do we believe in anything so trite as providence or divine rule. All I see now is the man more responsible for this waste of resources than any other. If you will not bear the consequences of your role in it, then you should never have been a leader at all."

The caster's body changed at that, great tendrils of bone and muscle protruding from both shoulders and shooting toward the old king. He didn't even have the time to scream.

CHAPTER ONE

Ado had seen executions. She wasn't supposed to have—such things weren't the place for a woman—but she'd always been fascinated by all things forbidden, and so she'd snuck her way into watching more than one. They were gory affairs, as might have been expected, and she'd secretly prided herself on having that fraction more exposure to the darker side of ruling than any of her brothers would have thought.

It had, she saw now, been an illusion. She had not inured herself to cruelty or death, nor had she grown world-weary or prepared for the savagery of man. The fate of her father taught her that lesson well enough to never be forgotten.

The caster's creations, those long, flexing spears of meat, stabbed clean into him. One struck the center of his chest, the other his throat. In moments their work began. Her father's body seemed to . . . fall in on itself, as if its insides were suddenly gone, and all that was left was skin and soft meat with no bone to hold any of it up. Ado watched the caster's tendrils withdraw as rapidly as they had shot forth, and stared in silent horror as they began to caress his cloak.

She saw it all happen so slowly, so precisely. Tissues, gray and stringy, wrapped and compressed, made dense, compact, carefully stitched into the mercurial fabric of the garb. Skin came next, stark against the pink and beige colors woven around it. Her father's skin, dark as coal and writhing until it shaped his very face into the material. Then came the groaning. The moaning, the low, humming exhalations of an unspeakable agony. It joined with all the others, just as her father joined with the cloak. The latest contribution to a chorus of human torture.

Folami keeled over, his vomit sliding out in a volume that might have been impressive were it not so pungently grotesque. His skin was sweaty and ashen with sick by the time he finally stopped, sluggishly rising to his feet, staring at the caster—more particularly at his garb—with a horror Ado could only imagine was no less visible across her own features.

"You," the caster said, turning to Ado.

Her mind sort of spasmed at that. Thoughts scattered as thoroughly as if they'd been bashed from her skull with a war hammer.

It was all she could do not to piss herself then and there, holding as steady as was possible upon her trembling knees and forcing out the most dignified response she could muster.

". . . Me." Ado nodded. "Yes, what . . . What would you ask of me?"

She hesitated, considering the use of some honorific, then realizing she hadn't the faintest idea which—if any—would be preferred. Instead she just tried to keep her tone as noncombative as possible. That, always, was the trick to dealing with men. They wouldn't accept a threat, but they wouldn't so readily see one in a woman either.

This one didn't have that usual disinterested look to him though. He seemed to focus on her no less intently than any other, and without any of the typical scorn Ado would see. No more than he held for everyone else present, at least. It was like being watched by an undead, or a bloodhound.

"I do not ask," the caster told her. "I give voice to the way things will be, and then watch to see if the world requires any correction before conforming."

It was quite a typical sentiment, Ado found, for a magus. Certainly for one of his power—though her family hadn't managed to find any history of education or even activity for this one. Nor any bearing a resemblance to him. Ado hadn't either, and she'd taken her own investigation a step further by looking into any *other* magi who *didn't* resemble him throughout history, all too aware that a fleshcrafter might choose to simply make a new name and face for himself as any other, more invasive transformations.

None of those had fit either, however.

"I understand." Ado nodded earnestly. She knew nothing about this man—if he was even a man at all. She was not her father or brothers, Ado had never been gifted with Vigor. Her own body burned with true magic, inherited from her mother. And it was this that let her see the caster for what he was.

A volcano. A hurricane, a falling star. Something larger than a man, as if his body were merely some shadow cast on a wall. Cast short, by something far, far larger whose form she could only glimpse between mountaintops from the corner of her eye.

For all she knew, it was some pagan god standing before her merely wearing the skin of a man. However much the grotesque approximation of human form she saw now could even be called a man's skin anyway.

If her fear and wondering caught his notice, he made no mention.

"You will become the ruler of this kingdom," he told her.

Ado paused at that, taking a second to let his words sink in, not quite believing them.

"I . . . Beg your pardon?" she asked.

"I said you will become the ruler of this kingdom. You will answer to me, and I shall rule it through you. Or do you dislike this state of affairs?"

"No!" Ado hurriedly replied, finding her eyes glancing back down to the caster's cloak, where she found the face of the last person to convey such a sentiment. "No, I do not. I . . . Thank you, sir."

"Good." The caster nodded, then turned. "Follow me."

Ado paused, risking a single glance toward her brothers. Tears were most of what she saw, staining cheeks and running live rivers as so many eyes fell helplessly upon the barbaric garb their father had become. Some though landed on her. Pleading, judging, demanding. Ado forced herself to look away, following the caster sheepishly.

Her throat was tight as they stepped beyond the confines of the old king's shelter.

Fadaka was a proud nation, near as old as Arbite and the crowning jewel of a vast kingdom. It covered more than an entire horizon in buildings, many small and squat, but numerous others towering and proud. It broke Ado's heart to see the state of them now.

The caster's monsters had proved a terror in battle, great mountains of death that moved like vipers despite their size. Ballista bolts had glanced from their armor plates like nothing; trebuchet stones had shattered to pieces and barely even irked them. Even Rochtai, the court magus, had proved too little.

Rochtai, who'd supported Ado's mother when she'd pushed to act out her own people's customs and train her daughter in magic. Rochtai, who'd never so much as flinched at the thought of his student being a girl. Rochtai, who'd always laughed at her genius and told her she was the greatest talent he'd seen since Walriq the wind mage or Arion Falls.

She saw Rochtai now. A crippled thing, body sluglike and smooth, limbs dysfunctional and useless. He writhed around on the ground with everything about him ruined and deformed, save his face. Clearly he recognized her, for he made so great an effort to avoid Ado's gaze that it could only have been born from the deepest of shames. She avoided his likewise, as much from disgust and squeamishness as pity.

"You are disturbed by my work," the caster observed, eyeing it all with an apathetic stare.

His work was devastation. Buildings crushed, streets shattered, towers toppled, and outer walls left crumbled ruins. A horde of giants might have trampled through the city for weeks on end and not done such damage. There was no battle, Ado thought. Only a slaughter. It hardened her thoughts against the groaning mass of misery and regret her father had become. He had been a fucking fool to ever try standing against such monstrous power.

"Why did you have to do this?" she asked, surprising herself with the question. Surprising herself more with the lack of fear. She turned to see the caster eyeing her, as if she were some ant he had found demanding answers of him in his food.

"Who are you to ask me such things?" he replied predictably. Ado still wasn't afraid. Why was that?

The answer was obvious. He was simply too big a thing to fear. She might as well worry about the prospect of being struck by lightning or swallowed up by the ground as his rage. Such a being—such an event—was beyond the scope of petty human survival instincts.

"I'm someone you've decided to put in charge of a ruined city," Ado answered. "And if I'm to rule, I would know what the motives are behind my doing so. Does this place lie destroyed because you want it to, for example, or was there some other goal in the deed?"

He did not seem angry. That was something. Though Ado imagined that, had he actually been irked by her words, the first indication she'd have received was being killed. Killed or . . . changed. She suppressed the shudder that birthed just as the caster spoke.

"Very well then. I destroyed much of this kingdom because I ordered that it surrender without question, and was questioned. This ruin will serve as incentive for the next I encounter to more carefully heed any warnings I feel inclined to offer them."

Ado considered that. It wasn't such a surprising thing to learn. Certainly she could see the logic in it. In stark terms, at least, perceived from far away and held to a slight scale.

So long as she kept herself from considering the simple humanity of it all.

"What are your plans for us?"

This time, the caster did look annoyed. Slightly.

"To improve your petty excuse for a civilization and absorb it into House Shaiagrazni. In the long term. In the short term, I intend to continue my research. I have learned much from this world already, and begun to master your magics for myself. But only begun. I suspect that, with time, I will find ever more means of empowerment from among you."

"Like divine magic?" Ado dared to ask. "You mentioned learning to use that yourself. Is . . . Is that true?"

She'd have laughed at the idea a month ago. Even an hour ago, really, but laying eyes upon this creature had made the implausible and inconceivable suddenly seem horribly likely. If God could wield the heavens for his ends, then why not the devil? And if the devil had ever appeared as any creature in all the world, it was surely this one.

"It is true. I will not be explaining more than that, however; it is not my custom to hand knowledge out to those outside my own household. Impress me, earn my favor, and I may see fit to gift you with it."

Ado looked back out to the city, where one of the roaming abominations was starting to coil and sleep in the midst of an amphitheater. Its body was so great in size as to almost fill the arena and reach the seating areas, despite there being easily space enough for a thousand.

She wasn't sure whether the knowledge of such a creature's creation was something she had any business or want in learning.

"He's still conscious, you know."

Ado turned instantly to see the caster speaking to her once more, though not looking her way.

"Your father, I mean," he continued, casual as ever. "I was very particular about keeping the minds of all those trapped in my coat, ensuring they remain intact and capable of pain."

Her mouth was dry and acidic with sick at once. Ado barely choked out her reply.

". . . Why are you telling me this?" she croaked.

That, at last, had the caster glancing toward her.

"To motivate you into a high quality of service."

CHAPTER TWO

Of the necromancers Swick had met, all two of them, he had to say the Sphera woman was probably his favorite. Certainly, she was the best adjusted. Which wasn't hard. She didn't wear a coat made out of human pain, and that was more or less where the bar was.

All things considered though, he might have preferred Shaiagrazni as a companion. They were back in the Dark Lands, surrounded on all sides by pitch-colored dirt and dying air. There was a sinister touch to everything that made him remarkably eager for the most potent ally he could get at his side, and recent events had rearranged King Galukar's position on that particular pecking order, even in terms of single combat.

Ideally he might not have been there at all, and most certainly wouldn't have been were it not for two simple facts. The first was, of course, his pay. There were very few things Swick wouldn't do for money, very few things anyone wouldn't do for enough.

The second factor, possibly the larger, was that they were in the plains in search of repairs for his ship. The moment he'd heard that particular plan, he knew he'd had no chance of escaping it.

It had been quick work in retrieving the wreckage from where they'd crashed and having it hauled back to Kaltan, thanks to Shaiagrazni's monsters. Quick work, and borderline useless. Swick had been impulsive when he'd crashed it into the Flying Fortress, and more than half drunk. The speeds involved in such an aerial collision had left little to salvage.

Little, but more than nothing. The most important, valuable pieces were all functional, more or less. The inertial core and most of the flight magics at least. That meant little when most of the superstructure was destroyed, and much of the connective constructs allowing the entire vehicle to function as a holistic piece, but it was a big leap in the right direction.

It was by far the most irreplaceable aspects they'd salvaged, after all. And there was every chance of scrounging what more was needed from the various cities and towns around them. Thus the fucking trip.

"You haven't traveled with Master Shaiagrazni any longer than I have."

Swick blinked, having grown so used to the silence that it took him a moment to realize the necromancer had spoken. He turned, eyeing her, blinking. He hadn't had a drink in weeks, kept himself carefully sober and sharp. It was the most miserably agonizing experience of his life, like trying to lever his own brain out through the top of his skull, and upon asking the fleshcrafter for some help, he'd been informed that it was only the Vigor in him that had even kept him alive through the experience of withdrawal.

But somehow, Sphera still had him on edge. She had that sort of feel to her, like a big pile of knives waiting for the nearest back to turn.

"No I haven't," he grunted in response, studying her from the corner of his eye.

"But you're a man."

What? What was she on about? Swick had to resist the urge to just grunt and leave the conversation there.

"Well noticed," he grumbled. "What are you getting at?"

The woman hesitated a second.

"Well, I was wondering if he'd expressed any sort of . . . interests to you. In women, I mean. Preferences, that sort of thing."

Swick understood instantly, and decided that he wanted no bloody part in that of all conversations within the same moment.

"As far as I'm aware, he never has, and has none," he replied quickly. With a stroke of luck it seemed the necromancer was satisfied to leave things there.

"I don't like the look of that city," she breathed, changing the subject with about as much subtlety as her master's larger creations. "Rather similar to the one you all got ambushed by Venka in. Easy to approach with a big force and little warning."

Swick agreed, and chewed at a lip in thought. He glanced over his shoulder to the contingency he and the necromancer had arrived with. There were certainly stranger things in the world these days, but it was still quite novel to be taking reassurance from a mass of waiting undead.

Not such a great mass, mind. There were apparently limits to necromancy. A man like Silenos Shaiagrazni could haul out thousands of powerful reanimates potent enough to crush even a fomor. His apprentice was somewhat less impressive. The hundred or so at their back was a sizable fraction of her potential, and not a one would have been even a match for the lithe monstrosities which had caused Kaltan so much trouble.

But a hundred undead were a hundred undead, one way or the other, and these ones were still strong enough at least that their combined might was more than Swick would have even tried fighting. Just another reason to be very bloody wary of the insane woman controlling them.

"I say this time we bring some more muscle," Swick decided. She scoffed at that, as if he'd suggested they call for backup from Shaiagrazni himself.

"We're trying to remain covert, you realize?" The necromancer sighed. "Covert, not overt. A hundred undead of this level are the sort of thing you march to an army, not a shopping trip."

There was a certain logic there, Swick had to admit, but it wasn't enough to sway him because there was simply no actual logic behind his urge. Just a simple, vague belief—no, knowledge—that things *would* go wrong and that he *would* need an extra hundred axes swinging away at whatever problem emerged.

"We're almost finished gathering the supplies," he noted. "This will be one of the last towns we try for, possibly *the* last. And your master is building up his forces by the day. Soon enough it'll be a moot point whether we attract the Dark Lord's attention or not."

And the quicker they got their work done, the sooner he'd have his beautiful vessel back. And when that happened, Swick would be once more watching danger unfold as an abstract thing from high above, just as God intended.

"If you're so concerned with speed," Sphera replied, "then surely you realize we'd be a lot faster if we weren't driving everyone away from us in a blind fear of the undead horde marching at our back."

Swick had been worried most about hearing what she'd just said. A logical argument. He sighed.

"Fine, let's go."

It was a tedious search, long and thought demanding. The scrounging of skyship components often was.

For one thing, Swick needed bracing. Ordinary ship making would render you a sky vessel capable of making all the usual turns, at the cost of snapping itself in half. He didn't want that, for obvious reasons, and so he took the extra time to search for some arctenite. It was a rare material, made by the deepfolk—or perhaps only mined by them—and impossibly light. No good for weapons or armor mostly, but excellent in construction for how much could be used while only adding the same amount of mass. Perfect for anything skyborne.

Well, he'd been ready for a difficult task in tracking it down. Having searched every city he'd already passed through for the stuff, Swick was beginning to grow convinced it would never reveal itself to him.

Sometimes surprises came, and very occasionally they were actually nice ones. Swick found his arctenite after only an hour of asking around.

The stuff was held by some metallurgist, expectedly, and put on display only behind a thick wall of steel-braced glass that looked as though it might have resisted a catapult. Though refracted by the sheer thickness of its guarding display, he could still make out the metal's texture well enough. Lighter than iron, lighter even than steel. Almost a silvery coloration as if the lack of gray pigmentation to its sheen were some indicator of the stuff's lack of weight.

"A fine eye for quality you have there, sir." The owner grinned, clocking instantly that Swick had come for the metal in particular, and no doubt raising its price the very instant he realized as much. Swick sighed and did business.

By the time Swick left, he had gained around one ton of the precious metal he'd come for. And lost almost its weight in gold. It was a stinging swindle to be wrapped up around, but one that had its bite reduced by the knowledge of what it meant. Soon enough, he'd be a sky captain again.

Sometimes though, surprises came. And only very occasionally were they actually nice ones. He and the necromancer had not gotten even halfway through the town when they caught sight of a familiar group and had to resist bolting at that very instant.

All dressed in dark armor and uniforms, walking with raised chins and arrogant sneers, a coterie of the Dark Lord's thugs made their way down a street. There were a dozen in all, and behind them marched a half dozen more men. The latter group were not dressed in their clothes, so much as vaguely hovered around, and had the tattered features and states that Swick had seen so often in Venka's camps. The back men were manacled, the front holding their chains.

Slaves, he'd bet anything on it. He turned to the necromancer and found her staring daggers at him.

"You want to do something stupid," she guessed. It was a lucky hit on her part.

"I've seen too many slaves in my time. Not in a mind to watch any more carted away."

"Give it a few weeks then," she snapped. "They'll be taken back to the Dark Lord and make the transition from slaves to undead."

Swick's pulse spiked, and he took a moment to identify the blend of anger and surprising desperation now giving his heart such a racing pace. He forced himself into as close a proximity to calm as was possible before answering her back.

"We're saving them," he said sharply. Swick didn't try to think of his men, how they'd died in the crash. But their faces hit him all the same.

Apparently Sphera had a sense for when she wasn't going to be persuading someone because she only sighed.

"I can direct my undead to circle the town," she growled. "Hit them from one side just as they exit it. Hopefully leave some confusion as to what happened."

"Then let's." Swick nodded, already turning to follow the men—subtly of course—to the point of ambush.

It was not a difficult fight, and that was a nice change from the recent pace Swick had found in his conflict. Within moments, the Dark Lord's servants were either dead or surrendered, all of them well trained and powerful, but none the equal of such a battle as dropped onto them then. Undead were circling their kneeling forms when Swick swaggered over to make himself known.

"Alright, alright." He grinned with all the calm arrogance he didn't feel. "That's enough. Everyone can calm down now. It's over. Now, Sphera, would you mind having our friends here freed?"

An undead was already moving to obey when he asked, cutting free one of the bound slaves, then the rest. Soon enough all the men were standing, hesitantly flexing wrists and testing their bodies in the unaccustomed freedom now upon them.

It was not the most heartening sight. Swick had expected, if not gratitude, then at least some healthy joy at such an unforeseen liberation. Instead these men seemed even more nervous than before.

Something, he surmised, was wrong.

"You've changed nothing," one of the Dark Lord's thugs snarled, then groaned as Swick hit him. The man fell into the dirt, spitting blood and coughing at the shock of his strike. Swick turned to the slaves.

"What does he mean?" he asked. The men looked worried enough to know what he was talking about. He was willing to wager that whatever was gnawing away at their relief was likewise fueling their captors' confidence.

He was proved right with the first answer.

"You haven't heard?" one asked, looking more confused than Swick. "The Dark Lord's coming. This changes nothing. You haven't saved us, only doomed us to another bout of struggling."

None present seemed to disagree, but Swick had to see for himself. He got the details quickly: direction, speed, size. Then he headed off to take a look at the nearing army and confirm what he'd been told.

There were plenty of hills in the region, the source of Swick's fear of ambush just short hours ago. Now they were a boon because he was quick in scaling one to get a better sight of the horizons.

What he saw was a punch to the gut.

There was, indeed, an army approaching. An army big enough to rival, even exceed the scale Venka's had boasted when it had marched on Kaltan. He felt a chill as he peered through his telescope, better sighting the density and width, identifying individual undead within. Fomors, dullahan, plenty of lesser reanimates. There were lichs near the front and winged reavers circling overhead, as well as some even he had never encountered before.

And ahead of them all, leading the entire procession, was a single figure that he didn't mistake for undead for even an instant. Towering over most everything around it and clad from head to toe in armor too blemishless and pure in its dark luster to be the apparel of mere dullahan. Over his back there lay strapped a sprawling mace, by his side a short staff.

Swick counted himself lucky enough to never have actually seen the Dark Lord before that moment, but he'd heard stories and read accounts enough that he didn't take even an instant to identify the man. He was the scourge of the continent, perhaps the most dangerous creature alive.

And he was heading right his way.

With no hesitation, Swick scurried down the hilltop and scrambled back for the slaves. They had a while before the Dark Lord reached anything of note. Even the town Swick had just shopped in was a good ten miles or more from his army. Ten miles, with a force that size, meant maybe a day. Accounting for marching speed.

There was time to get ahead of it, to report, to warn, to plan. Granted there were only so many plans a man might make when the devil decided to insert a mace in him, but Swick was eager to at least get a start on the making. He seized one slave rather less gently than before, grabbing the man by his collar and hauling him off his feet to interrogate the poor bastard from mere inches away.

"Who are you, and what do you know of the army?"

He was a big man, this one, towering over Swick and well-built. He didn't seem half moved to be plucked so easily off the ground, only empty.

"Kaltan," he replied. "Soldiers of Kaltan, all of us. And that's where the bastard's going if his men were to be believed."

Swick tossed him aside, turned his focus to the Dark Lord's men, and started asking his questions more harshly still. The answer didn't change though. The truth didn't wilt.

The Dark Lord was heading to try Kaltan a second time.

CHAPTER THREE

Silenos felt a stab of anger at the tedium of directing his grotesqueries to simple reconstruction, when he might otherwise be spending his time rebuilding the arcane defenses once at his disposal. Then he remembered why. His cape moaned its agony, as if to an unheard cue, and he allowed himself to bask in the satisfaction of having punished the one responsible.

He saw King Galukar stiffen from the corner of his eye and smiled ever deeper. It had been a long time since that particular monkey had dared say anything about Silenos's methods. Evidently, even his dull mind had finally realized the obvious facts of their new stations. How long would he last were he to attack Silenos this instant? A minute, perhaps two. There weren't so many grotesqueries within immediate reach of them; it would take a while to call in the forces needed to properly crush him.

Silenos buried the thought, having better things to do than continue swilling the taste of progress around his mouth, and turned to the girl.

"You are to prioritize being seen conducting the reconstruction," Silenos informed her, watching her jump at being addressed in that satisfying way she had. "It won't do to have the impression among your people be that you are some simple puppet for my whims."

Quite apart from the fact that she *was*, and Silenos generally disliked being fully understood in his actions, it would damage the morale of the people if they perceived themselves as fully beneath an external force of conquest. Best to let simpletons think of themselves as free. They chafed at management.

"You will focus on minimizing further death to start with, and then once the city is properly stabilized, you will push further into rebuilding efforts using renovations and changes detailed in the report I had sent to you. It contains the plans for a city made in the image of House Shaiagrazni's, and I will see it followed to the letter."

"Of course," she replied, nodding with all the haste of one who had the image of Silenos's new coat fresh in her mind. But then she paused, swallowing, licking her lips nervously, and speaking again without prompting.

"May I ask you a question?"

Silenos braced himself for exposure to the depths of human stupidity and nodded.

"You may."

The woman delayed only a moment before finding the courage to do so.

"You made me your puppet here, put me in charge of your new vassal state. Why? Why not my brothers? You must surely know how women are perceived in these lands."

He'd known as much, of course. It had in fact been *why* he'd selected her. Better to have a vassal who was not entirely certain in her standing, and could not turn her back to her own court, than one who was confident and secure within the city he'd left them to rule. Silenos had no interest in facing a rebellion, nor finding out the Dark Lord or some other party had subverted his latest conquest out from under him.

But he did not say as much, instead keeping a cool face and meeting her eyes more openly.

"Because I saw a considerable potential in you," he lied. "You have a quick mind, a dynamic intellect, and a manner of considering things that I suspect will lead to considerably skilled leadership in the future. I intend to cultivate that and give it the opportunity to blossom. In my people's homeland, it was considered standard for women to receive all the opportunities of men, and refraining from such a state is mere waste."

Her eyes could not have grown brighter, even if Silenos had set the woman's brain on fire. He drew satisfaction from the sight of a manipulation well executed, then noticed her smile. It was a soft thing, wide and easy, unguarded. It reminded him rather of Ensharia's.

"Now begone," he snapped, gesturing her away. "You are consuming too much of my priceless time, and I have more important matters to attend to than you."

She seemed rather confused for a moment, but nodded dutifully and turned to take her leave.

* * *

Galukar watched the girl scurry her way out, frowning as she went. He felt a stab of pity for her. Losing a father and a kingdom in one day was bad enough. Finding herself under the thumb of Shaiagrazni . . . He shuddered.

But not so much. After all, he was under that same thumb now and found himself chafing at it far less than he ought to have. In his youth he'd no doubt have been killed already after heroically throwing himself at the caster, all roaring Vigor and flailing swings. Maybe he'd even have wounded him. Maybe not. He was too tired for such puerile indulgences anymore.

"Was there any reason in particular you decided to dismiss her so bluntly?" he found himself asking, not entirely expecting the caster to turn and reply.

"She must not learn to see me as anything less than a superior, not until my grip here is cemented."

"I see," Galukar replied, studying the caster. "Well, you've taken the kingdom, at least. Taken it well, and with the losses suffered, I doubt any among it will have both the means and inclination to seize it back. For now at least, I'd call this a victory. What say you to a drink? In celebration."

That had the caster turning around at last, affixing Galukar with a look that hearkened back to when they'd first met. All frosty and jagged, edged like some barbed thing of natural armor.

"I was not aware I had said anything to indicate that I might indulge myself in such primitive a pastime as recreational cognitive impediment."

Galukar understood even fewer of the man's words than was normal, but he was able to gauge the rough gist of what had been said. He felt himself bristle at the obvious contempt on display, but felt himself shift more at something else. Something hidden beneath the surface.

"There's no need for such hostility," he replied, trying again, despite himself. "This is a time for anything but that, surely. You did well; you made progress. Relax."

"The last time I *relaxed*, I found myself hurled through dimensional walls and into a realm of silly little ape-men forcing me to fight in their silly little wars out of sheer self-preservation."

It was difficult not to match the rage, but made easier by the recollection of those damned flesh abominations.

"These are hardly comparable circumstances—" Galukar tried, then fell silent as the caster snapped again.

"What is your motive in asking me these incessant questions?" he growled. "You have never been particularly curious before, not about anything and least of all about me. And you're far from friendly to practitioners of my arts. I would think you simpering for life alone, but I know you care too little about your own death for that. So what in the world is your motive in this petty attempt at subterfuge?"

Galukar was not a politician, really. He had always been a ruler more fit for battle than peace, and had left the governing of Arbite to his advisers and hands since long before any sought to turn against him. Even so, he was canny enough to realize when his pretenses had fallen away.

He gave them up with relish, never liking the sensation of hiding behind a mask of any kind at all. Not even to a fleshcrafter.

"Very well then," he replied, not flinching as Silenos Shaiagrazni affixed him with that demonic gaze. "You have changed, and not in the way you think. You were always callous, cruel . . . Always evil. But never so drastically as this. What you're doing, with the coat, with the cripplings . . . It's performative. Ever since Falls died."

Shaiagrazni's eye twitched.

"Falls is not dead" was all he said, in a brisk tone unreadable as any singular emotion at all, but certainly conveying something.

It would have been a small thing in a normal man, but Silenos Shaiagrazni was not normal by any stretched definition. His denial was obvious and uncharacteristic, something Galukar knew all too well was a sign of some deeper crack in his emotional stability.

Whatever the caster claimed, he was not some ineffable bastion of knowledge and logic. He felt, just as any other man did, and Arion Falls's death had him feeling. Feeling enough to deny that it had ever even occurred. Feeling enough to discover some moral line, at last, that he would not cross, and keep him from reanimating his apprentice.

Galukar keenly recalled the abominable constructs roaming around the city, feeling some whisper even then of the awe he had been struck by upon first seeing it. If the master of things like that were to lose his senses entirely, it might well spell the end of the entire world.

"If you're sure," he said slowly, carefully. Well aware that he was not speaking with the most predictable of creatures.

Silenos Shaiagrazni snapped, but not violently. His anger came out as a contemptuous scoff, and a sidelong glance edged to a skin-opening point.

"Begone. I am tired of this conversation."

It had been a long time since anyone had seen fit to order Galukar around like that, and just for a moment he was half tempted to disobey. But he didn't, climbing to his feet and taking his leave with only the barest reluctance. It would be foolish not to.

The relationship between him and Shaiagrazni had been rather dramatically rearranged, of late.

It was a strange sort of silence that followed Silenos after Galukar's exit, the kind that made room for contemplation and thought. The kind that made room only for the contemplation and thoughts that were most unwelcome.

His mind drifted to the past, the favored refuge of any rebelling cognition, and revisited recent victories. They had been many, and easily won. But perhaps not as easily as they might have been. The more he scrutinized himself, the more imperfections Silenos found in his past reasoning, the more errors stuck out at his appraising eye.

Many things had occurred before him, many horrors and atrocities, no small number of which had happened at his own behest. But none had ever disturbed him the way he now stood disturbed. To feel the treachery of one's own intellect was not of House Shaiagrazni, and he found himself hastily scrambling for long-forgotten lessons learned as a mere apprentice to rectify the issue.

The answer, in the end, could not have been mistaken. It was Silenos's brain. His rewired, mangled intellect made pliable and intuitive where it ought to have been mechanical and pneumatic. He had recrafted it for politicking and emotional prediction shortly after arrival, to better plan around the unpredictable nature of humanity, and in doing so had introduced something . . . new.

Rationality, on occasion, surrendered to impulse. Sentiment infested him like calcifying tumors, growing with tendrils dug deep and parasitic into the meat of his brain. It was distracting Silenos for one thing, but what was worse was how it *influenced* him.

He had felt a sense of annoyance, even regret, upon hearing of Arion Falls's loss. Silenos had intended to one day see the boy rise through the ranks of House Shaiagrazni, and had fully believed him to hold potential enough to become one of their finest—with enough centuries of honing and study. To see his great talent snuffed out the way it had been was . . . beyond wasteful.

And then there was the matter of Ensharia. She had been a useful ally, and his first in the new world. But it had been her own stupidity driving her away, not any error of Silenos's.

To let either of these misfortunes distract him as he had been was a fallacy beyond description, and would lead to disaster sooner or later.

Emotion.

That was Silenos's problem. That was his curse. The petty, unpredictable little synaptic spasms he'd unknowingly set upon himself by reconfiguring his cerebrum. Well, he knew what the aberration was now, and he knew just how to fix it. He raised his hands to gently touch fingertips down atop his scalp.

Then hesitated.

It would be a time-consuming work, but not one he couldn't afford to devote his attention to. What truly stayed Silenos's hand was the recollection of his work earlier the day, how he'd plucked at the strings of Princess Ado's mind to ensure she moved in accordance with his plans.

That was not the sort of thing one managed with logic alone. Like it or not, Silenos had found his skill in moving others enhanced by the empathic knowledge of how they were feeling and what they might be inclined to do. It was, after all, the entire reason Collin Baird still remained by his side.

Could he . . . But no, Silenos had already created a strong enough region, and that strength would be improved faster with his full, untainted genius directed to crafting yet more engines of war and infrastructure. His hesitation was folly.

Silenos's focus was broken by the opening of a door, and he turned to see Collin Baird hurriedly scrambling into the room. The boy had more than just his usual look of dull panic about him, eyes hot with frantic urgency and adrenal potence. Silenos got to his feet even as the words reached him.

"It's the Dark Lord," Baird gasped. "Another army, led by him personally, sighted heading this way."

CHAPTER FOUR

Ado was not unfamiliar with the work needed to govern a city; she had, after all, sat in on most of the decisions made regarding her father's rule for as long as she could remember.

Which wasn't to say she was an expert.

She'd been given plenty of exposure, but that was not the same thing as actual instruction. She was cleverer by half than any of her brothers, but Ado would have gladly accepted knowledge in favor of wits any day. Had she been working entirely alone, she would have been quite in over her head. Fortunately, she was not.

Whatever might have been said about Silenos Shaiagrazni from an *ethical* standpoint, Ado had to admit . . . The man was a better ruler than her. Better than her brothers, better than her father. Perhaps better than any other she'd seen.

His plans were unorthodox and bizarre—something she mistook for ineptitude only briefly—but implied a philosophy of design for her nation that might actually have worked in its integration, despite being entirely alien to everything else about it.

It was, of course, a gradual set of changes being prepared. No alterations as large and invasive as the ones he had planned could have ever been done quickly. Ado was to let her nation's culture and infrastructure slowly mutate over years, even decades.

She'd heard stories of vampires or demons, demigods and archimages sustaining their lives through many centuries and manipulating the world from behind the scenes with plans that outlasted an entire human life. Reading through the schematics prepared for her felt like being on the other side of those stories. The villain's side.

Well, that was fine too. Ado had grown up on other stories, stories of Grecascnia, from her mother. A land where women studied whatever they wanted and ruled when they were best suited for it, of learning and knowledge. It was hard not to see everyone around her as a villain with that sort of comparison. Silenos Shaiagrazni at least had plans to stop people starving in the street, peasants included.

Her thoughts, and her work, were interrupted by the same thing. A runner, hurrying into Ado's new office with sweat painting their face and exhaustion animating their chest. They spoke through deep heaves, clearly not one born with Vigor—most of her father's actually swift messengers had been shot from afar by that barbarian Baird during the invasion.

"Your . . . presence," the wheezing peasant gasped. "It's . . . requested by . . . by Master Shaiagrazni . . ."

Ado could see the physical effort he was putting into spitting out the rest of her new ruler's ridiculous title, and she spared him the effort with a gesture and a quick motion to her feet. "In the throne room?" she asked, receiving confirmation with a nod and hurrying to make her way there.

It was not a long walk. Just a month ago, it would have been. Ado's father had always kept his administrators and counselors relatively far from the throne room, feeling more comfortable with some appropriate distance between the merely powerful and the divinely ordained.

The contents of the throne room had changed too. All the old heraldry torn down, and the ancient throne newly crowned by growths of bone and sinew shaped around it by Shaiagrazni himself. Ado still felt slightly queasy looking at them, even after all the days she'd had to adjust. She felt queasier still seeing the caster himself standing by them.

He seemed to have gotten taller, and certainly fouler of mood. It was almost enough to distract from the statuesque figure of King Galukar, just a few feet from him. Or the weasel on the other side.

Ado had never met Collin Baird, but she'd heard descriptions and seen renditions enough to recognize the murderous rat. It appeared that he made a habit of sitting in on the occasional meeting of import, when he wasn't busy murdering her father's bannermen and knights from a horizon away.

The boy was already speaking when she entered, and Ado steeled herself to listen. Bracing for whatever seditionist nonsense would slop out of his mouth.

"They're a month from Kaltan, and closing fast. Big army, but moving like you'd expect of an undead force. Faster than you'd expect, really."

He looked worried, not petulant. That surprised Ado for two reasons. The first, of course, was that she was well familiar with the dull, smug arrogance inherent to all Kaltans due to generations of poor breeding and management.

The second was because she'd heard reports from just a handful of assassins and warriors who'd managed to close into melee with the boy, and not one of them had ever described so much as a nervous swallow. As they told it, even when he was staring down his own death, he'd been unflinching as a statue and sharp as a razor.

She didn't see that now, only a pale face made clammy with sweat.

". . . What is happening?" Ado asked, managing to just barely keep the words from escaping her as a girlish squeak, fear eroding what little composure and certainty she'd managed to claw back for herself since Shaiagrazni's conquest.

All eyes fell upon her, and it was a testament to the evident danger of her situation that not a single pair did anything at all to further scatter her wits.

"The Dark Lord is approaching Kaltan, and possibly our current location," Silenos Shaiagrazni replied, speaking with uncharacteristic . . . gentleness. No, not that. With uncharacteristic uncertainty.

"The Dark Lord himself," Ado whispered. He could have punched her and not done so much to inspire confusion and fear. "I . . . How? What sort of forces is he bringing to bear? What—"

She was interrupted in her questioning, but by an explanation. It was not a long one. Apparently there wasn't much known about the Dark Lord, though Shaiagrazni conveyed what had been confirmed so quickly that Ado almost struggled to keep up regardless. By the time he was finished, the conversation had naturally progressed a shade.

"What sort of forces could be mustered from the kingdom?" Shaiagrazni asked, gesturing to a map Ado had somehow missed, laid out beside the throne, just barely peeking from its shadow. It covered the city and the regions surrounding it.

He was indicating several towns and larger villages, all within a dozen leagues of the city. All wholly exhausted of able-bodied fighters during the desperate attempts of Ado's father to repel the initial invasion. She told Shaiagrazni as much, then winced as he raised his hand and gritted teeth in anger.

For a moment she was certain he would kill her, or change her. Instead he simply jabbed a thumb into one of the numerous moaning faces etched across his cloak, sneering as he twisted the digit deeper into the soft tissue and elicited ever-heightening pitches in the agonized cries it let out.

"Inconvenient," the caster said with all the emotion of a turnip. "But not unexpected. We have other options available to us."

Ado was so fixated on the effort of trying to confirm whether it truly was her father being tormented that she almost made the near-fatal error of letting Shaiagrazni's words breeze her by unnoticed. She hastened to rectify that particular mistake.

"I beg your pardon, sir," she breathed. "What, uh, what options exactly do you speak of?"

She thought back to the abominations that had stormed her city's walls and found herself wondering whether he was intending on making more from the noncombatants among their citizens. Surely not. It was people like that who would sustain the kingdom for years to come in times of peace.

"The dead of this nation are numerous, and many thousands are fresher than a single year. If we excavate them from the various mass graves and battlefields scattered around the countryside, I will be able to add to the undead already among my forces."

Ado was quick in speaking up, but not as quick as King Galukar.

"That is a guaranteed way to spur your new subjects into open rebellion, and that would make it impossible to muster any kind of defense against an external attack with your rule so poorly established. However many monsters you have, if a hundred thousand people fight from a hundred thousand shadows, they will be an inconvenience you cannot ignore or fully remove for some time."

"You'd know all about the *inconvenience* of rebellion," Collin Baird murmured, affixing dark eyes on King Galukar. The giant did not seem to hear.

Shaiagrazni paid no heed at all to the interactions of his subordinates, his focus apparently consumed with the problems at hand and the barriers encasing their solutions. His eyes were holes, leading to some immeasurable pit.

"I do not need to raise them as undead," he breathed slowly. "I could simply utilize their biomass. I need living, sentient matter to create a functional grotesquerie—but that is only for the core of its mind. I can expand the body by reshaping any tissue, even necrosed."

"That would be no better in the public's eye," King Galukar noted, and Shaiagrazni's jaw tightened ever further.

"Then I . . . I see." He sighed, face contorting with an orchestra of emotions. For a long moment, nobody spoke. Then Shaiagrazni broke the silence.

"We will expand to new territory," he said with finality. "Most rulers, I suspect, are not so stupid as this kingdom's monarch was, and his fate will stand as the warning I intended it to. There ought to be at least one nation nearby we can absorb without significantly weakening in a tedious conflict first. They will serve to bolster our strength, particularly if we begin negotiations before word of the Dark Lord's approach reaches them."

It made sense, though Ado found herself rather queasy at the thought of boxing in another monarch in so shameless a way.

"That might put you in a difficult political situation. If nearby nations see us as a growing power, and believe that you intend to continue expanding as a result, they may well view you as the larger threat than the Dark Lord. There is, after all, a great deal more distance between his territory and theirs than yours."

Shaiagrazni considered that, but it was Baird who provided an answer.

"So pick one who's already made alliances with the Dark Lord," he suggested, as if it were the most obvious thing in the world. Ado felt a stab of irritation as Shaiagrazni looked consideringly at the boy while he grinned away.

"You have such a city in mind then?" the caster asked, instantly vaporizing the smugness from Baird's expression and leaving the scoundrel to falter.

"Ah, uh, no, I don't. I've been a bit busy since arrival—"

"But I believe I can help you there," Ado interjected, seeing her own chance. "I was never groomed for ruler, but I made sure to study all the relevant details about my nation regardless, including our neighbors. You, I think, would benefit most from allying with the Staligans. Their capital of Ironbane is not so far from here."

Galukar's lip curled at that, face twisting as if he had something rancid on his tongue.

"Demon worshippers," he spit.

"So some of the rumors say." Ado shrugged. "Allies with the Dark Lord, in any case, and years old ones at that. You'll find no perceived threat among the locals should you choose to crush the Staligans. You may even be thanked."

Shaiagrazni eyed Ado for a moment, suddenly considering.

"Why did you go to such lengths in learning so much about your surrounding area? Were you, by chance, planning to overthrow your father?"

She had never in all her life answered a question so instantaneously, at least not without any deception.

"No!" Ado assured him, heart turned to a war drum within moments as she realized how close she was standing to an abyss. "No, I would never. You must—"

Shaiagrazni raised a hand in silence, and it silenced her. He sighed.

"I see. A pity. I had dared to hope you'd possessed the morals to recognize your duty of dethroning such an inept ruler. Never mind then."

Ado decided, then, that she was going to have a very tedious time in working out exactly what it was that drew the man's ire, and resigned herself to it. He was speaking again before she could dwell on the issue.

"Where is this Ironbane city?" Shaiagrazni asked.

"The mountains," she hurriedly explained. "Near a large natural crest to them, surrounded on all sides by peaks and sort of . . . sheltered, if you can picture it. They've never been a terribly *strong* nation, but they've never once been successfully invaded."

"Natural defenses?" Baird asked, demonstrating his idiocy once more with the sheer obviousness of his question.

"Yes," Ado replied patiently. "The city surrounded on all sides by mountain peaks has a lot of natural defenses. It's impregnable. And it's surrounded by vampires, which make crossing the few passes that might lead you to it treacherous. I would recommend at least trying diplomacy first. It is far more likely to succeed than an attack, however potent your forces."

Shaiagrazni considered that quickly, then nodded.

"I see. Then we must send envoys, small in number and potent in combative power."

Ado was nodding for almost a full second before realizing what was being implied.

"I—"

But it was too late. Shaiagrazni's face was already turning to Baird.

"You will accompany her. You have already proved yourself a skilled negotiator when it comes to the Dark Lord's servants."

The bastard didn't seem half so bothered by it as Ado, which she imagined made sense. Rats didn't worry about filth when they crawled over a human.

"Any questions?" the caster asked, and Ado slumped.

She had none that would change things.

CHAPTER FIVE

It took Ado some time to prepare herself for travel, and would have taken a lot more if the damned bastard she was moving with hadn't been so blasé about the whole affair.

She was concerning herself with representing Silenos Shaiagrazni, and by extension House Shaiagrazni itself. Whatever that was. She ensured to dress herself well, properly, to cut as fine and commanding a figure as could be managed, knowing full well that her sex alone would undermine any inferior efforts of diplomacy she might make. It was hard work, demanding hours seated and still while servants worked on preparing her, and Ado did not appreciate being hurried in its progression.

"You're wasting time," Baird said, as if he were speaking to someone less than a hundred steps above his station in the natural order. "Slowing us down. Time means more than making an impression."

Ado bit back her annoyance, forcing herself to explain things slowly enough for him to grasp. It was difficult to even realize where his confusion lay, with that ridiculous accent. Every syllable from his mouth sounded thick and swollen, as if his tongue were the bloated organ between a dead man's teeth.

"We are embarking on a diplomatic mission," she said slowly. "Nothing matters more than making an impression. Doing so will save our master—"

"Shaiagrazni isn't my master," he interrupted, and Ado hesitated, stewing a moment longer in her annoyance.

"Our associate," she corrected. "It will save our associate a great amount of resources and wealth."

He nodded, then shrugged.

"But it probably won't work, and the longer we waste trying, the more reckless we'll have to be in assaulting Ironbane."

Ado found her temper fraying further at that, but simply moved past the issue. There would be no reasoning with this one, she decided, and only a great deal of irritation to be found in the effort.

They set off soon enough, thanks in no small part to the rat's incessant whining about any given delay. Departing by carriage, they were dragged along the road through the muscular strength of a smaller one of Shaiagrazni's creatures, barely double or triple the weight of a warhorse.

She almost missed how laughable it was to consider such a thing smaller, but even that was quickly eclipsed by the pulling power of the creature.

It moved as if it were accompanied by ten more things of equal size, hauling the thousand-pound carriage along like it weighed nothing at all, accelerating to such an extreme velocity in so slight a span that Ado felt rather queasy for a few moments. It was like falling horizontally, an exponential rise of speed and momentum that lasted far longer than instinct told her it ought to have. Finally they reached a plateau for it, moving perhaps as fast as a sprinting horse might have unburdened.

"Not used to working with grotesqueries?"

Ado glared at the man seated opposite her, lounging back along the carriage's cushions and no doubt dirtying them with those mud-crusted boots of his. Baird seemed altogether too relaxed, and far, far too pleased with her disorientation.

"And I suppose you were perfectly composed in your first close interactions with them."

Ado saw the man hesitate a moment before his smile widened.

"As a matter of fact, I was. My first close encounter was fighting alongside them to crush a coup within Kaltan, and I can honestly say I adjusted within seconds." She felt there was something being left unsaid there, but she couldn't exactly place what it was. "They're really no more than just big animals, are they?"

In the way orcs were, she thought. Or giants. Or even dragons. Ado's temper was growing shorter every time this man opened his mouth, and it seemed he'd finally found the last straw.

"Baird," she replied sharply. "Your name is Baird. And you are a Kaltan. Is there any relation to Finlay Baird?"

Ado had wondered whether he might deny it, but he didn't. Seemed proud of the fact, even.

"There is. I'm his son."

"Then you're the son of a murderous lunatic," Ado told him. She'd not expected to actually gain any effect from the accusation, but had hoped to at least see *something* in the way of a reaction. He only met her gaze and shrugged.

"It's definitely what people say. Stupid people, that is, whose parents were brother and sister."

It was the disregard that finally burned away what was left of Ado's patience.

"And how about the people who lost loved ones to his murderous rampage?" she snapped. "What about—"

"Every single fucking one of them deserved to die, and I wish I was old enough to have seen it happen. I'm half tempted to ask Shaiagrazni to reanimate the stupid bastards so I can kill them again myself."

The burning vitriol in Baird's voice actually gave her pause, stunning her into silence as she felt those cold, cold eyes fall upon her. Ado was suddenly left very aware of the fact that she was alone with the man, and in too confined a place for her magic to be of much help against his strength.

"I suppose we'll just have to agree to disagree," she said by way of peace offering. He snorted.

"Until such time as I'm under your power, at which point I'm back to being a semicivilized moron who needs a firm guiding hand to keep from upturning the natural order."

Ado wasn't entirely sure how to react to that, so she chose silence instead. Their journey was prolonged by the lack of conversation, but it was shortened much more by the ingenious efficiency of their motion. Leagues disappeared in minutes, and their pace remained tirelessly consistent as the beast pulling them along moved without fatigue or falter.

But Ado hardly noticed because her eyes never wavered from where they rested upon Baird. She'd regarded him as little more than a simple beast before and saw now what a mistake that had been. He was the worst kind of creature she knew of. A thing, not a man. A weapon that killed on its own. Such individuals were seen in court from time to time. She'd heard tales of them because they invariably did things to inspire tales.

"Respect a man who can stomach battle," her brother used to say, "because only one in three have that killing spark. But fear a man who can learn to love it because not one in a fifty acquires that taste, and the ones who do will follow it far."

Baird had everything else about the other ones in fifty. She saw it all clear as day now even as he shifted in his seat to rebury the tells. Ado's mouth was dry.

What in the world was at the front of his thoughts, she wondered, to leave his gaze so dark and bladed in its focus?

It had been a while since Galukar had actually done anything in the way of ruling, and he'd almost forgotten what a damned chore it all was. There had always been a reason, after all, for his leaving Arbite to such a lengthy string of hands and councilors. He had always been a better king on the battlefield than in the court.

His thoughts were interrupted briefly by the opening of a door, hinges gliding apart with barely a creak, and rapid footsteps.

"I'm busy at the moment," Galukar muttered, forcing his attention back to the document before him. What the bloody hell even was requisitioning, in the first place?

Something shifted behind him, and the air hissed for a moment. He heard a grunt of exertion, the strain of wood flooring bearing a sudden redistribution of weight, then his shoulder itched. Galukar hardly noticed, so work laden was he, merely scratching the annoyance as he continued his mental exertions. It happened again, this time with a slight twitch at the back of his neck, and his slow mind finally stumbled upon the obvious.

Galukar turned, then frowned at the sight of a boy perhaps as close to ten as he was twenty. He was tall, though had yet to gain the breadth of manhood at his shoulders, and was holding a sword that seemed better sized for a man double his weight.

Two dents lay in the edge of the weapon, where, Galukar imagined, the steel had struck his flesh and surrendered before its hardness. Not magical then. He was not so resilient as to break magical metal against his flesh. He sighed.

"What is this?" Galukar demanded, in no mood to be bothered during his work.

"King Galukar," the boy snarled, as if the name were a curse. It was strange to hear so appropriate a reaction to himself. "You were . . . I looked up to you. My whole life you were my hero, and now you're just some fucking dog of Shaiagrazni's. Standing by while he kills my people, ruins my nation, steals my brother's birthright and hands it off to a damned woman! Were you always a coward, or have you just fallen from grace?"

Galukar waited for some rush of guilt or shame, but none came. None had come in a long while, not really. Not for what he was doing now. He let his exhaustion show, watching the boy raise his oversize sword as slow as anything and bring it down with all his insubstantial strength. It was halted by the force of Galukar's finger meeting his thumb, steel pinched between skin and almost snapping with the grip.

"You're right," he replied. "I am no hero at all, but I am afraid that I never was. You looked up to me for my deeds, I take it?"

Tears fell down the boy's cheeks, perhaps as much for the physical exertion he was placing into wrestling Galukar's fingers as the emotions at play.

"Of course I did!" he snapped. "Who didn't?!"

Galukar met him with as honest and open a look as he could manage, which wasn't saying much. One couldn't be an honest hero any more than one could be a righteous villain.

"Then I have never been anything but a coward and scoundrel for so long as you have heard tell of me," he told him.

It was that, at last, that stunned the boy into some semblance of coherence. He released the sword, letting it clatter to the ground as he stumbled back with wide eyes.

"You lie." He gasped.

"I am telling you the truth," Galukar corrected. "All the stories you have heard of my battles fought and won . . . They are true, for the most part at least. Those things happened. But I am not a hero for them. Just a powerful man prone to wanton destruction and killing. I became a hero when people approved of my murderous rampages. That is all."

The boy looked torn between disbelief and yet more hatred. Galukar decided not to try to sway him one way or the other, just affirmed the facts as they were.

"Find yourself a new hero." He sighed. "Or better yet, realize that they don't exist. It'll save you a lot of pain and save anyone under your command a great deal more, if you face the reality of things instead of wrapping everything in fantasy and wishes."

CHAPTER SIX

Ado Mortascia was not the sort of person Collin had *expected* to like. By her background, and by the way she'd spent all their time together glaring at him even before either of them had exchanged a word with the other, he had assumed that their relationship would be about as pleasant as the one found between undead and a bonfire. But, as was so often the case, she had managed to surprise him.

She'd been far worse than he could have possibly imagined.

Beyond snooty, or arrogant, and beyond merely abrasive. Ado Mortascia was less a person and more some grand, larger-than-life congealment of aristocratic values and traditions. It was all Collin could do to keep from strangling her with his bowstring.

It wasn't enough for her to hate Collin, oh no. She had to be *justified*. Had to prove herself right at every turn, and thus look at every word from his mouth or act from his hands through whatever lens was needed to render it yet more evidence against him.

Collin was the son of Finlay Baird, and thus a murderer. He was from a family only one generation removed from the peasantry, and thus an idiot. He was a soldier, which meant he must be sneaky for having *subverted* so high a rank in his military, and surely prone to drunkenness.

And of course, he was Kaltan. All Kaltans were known to be an inherently rowdy and uncivilized bunch, ever since they started complaining when made to starve in the street or live in their own open sewage. Fucking nobs.

Their journey was among the slowest Collin had experienced, or at least among the ones he'd experienced at a constant rate of thirty miles per hour. It took them less than three hours to close in on their destination, and yet those three hours felt like three years. There was an ice to the air, a static tension to the space between them, and every passing moment left Collin shifting uneasily as he expected some barb, spell, or fist to come flying at him. Mortascia would hardly even have been to blame—she couldn't help but hurt poor people. It was what she'd been selectively bred to do for hundreds of years.

It was a relief when Ironbane finally poked itself up ahead of them, and Collin found the effect only *slightly* ruined by the instant, visceral dread of realizing just how horrible a bitch it would be to try to attack en masse.

Ironbane was a city of tall buildings and broad foundations, built into shapes he could best have described as three-dimensional triangles. They reached high, foundations clinging sturdily to the ground in such a way as to make it clear with only a glance they would not be yielding easily.

There was an outer wall, of some sort, but it seemed a small and insubstantial thing compared to the mountainous peaks ringing the entire valley. Collin could barely imagine himself fitting a thousand men through for a coordinated attack, and the actual fortifications looked the equal of ten or twenty times that number at minimum.

Natural defenses, indeed.

"Edmari," Mortascia muttered. "This architecture, the stonework, it's like Castle Edmari. The Flying Fortress."

Collin blinked, frowned, then slowly nodded. It was, at that. Not the same—not at all—but similar. A sort of aged, ancient style quite unlike virtually everything around it. He remembered some vague details about a long-gone civilization and how they'd spanned a surprising scope of the continent, but no more than that.

"It'd be too much to hope that meant it's aged and vulnerable," he muttered, feeling a sudden urge to spout that most classic of philosophical musings among the soldiers of Kaltan: Why was everything always their job?

"It would be," Mortascia agreed coolly. "Which is why it's vitally important that we succeed in our diplomatic efforts rather than start an inevitably protracted and difficult conflict."

Collin wasn't sure about protracted. There'd certainly be losses, but most of Shaiagrazni's grotesqueries were best measured for body mass in multiples of an elephant's.

Hundreds of them storming the place would flatten it, but even just a few dozen would have good odds of breaching it. The only thing he found himself worried by—the thing he kept an eye out for—were those cannons the Dark Lord had unleashed in Kaltan.

He decided not to contradict her though, seeing no reason to drag her into another argument when they had far more productive things to be doing. The two of them set off, Mortascia moving calmly and with a diplomatic poise, Collin trudging along just slightly behind as he scrutinized their surroundings for anyone who might plan on suddenly murdering them from behind.

"You know of Staliga's relation with the Dark Lord?" Mortascia prompted, once they were halfway to the entrance ahead. It was a tall, squared opening in the walls affixed with a clearly modern portcullis and a towering gate that was only fractionally less so. Collin wondered whether King Galukar could have brought either down.

"They're cunts who sided with him." He shrugged in answer. The woman's face was drawn tight in frustration at that.

"If you head into this with an attitude like that, your oversimplification will jeopardize this entire mission."

"Which is why I have you," he countered. "To do all the talking while I scope the place out and get ready to do the murderous bastards when it all goes tits up."

Collin saw a flash of disgust across her face, quite possibly from his language alone, and then the woman inhaled sharply, continuing after a moment in a tone that seemed carefully measured for speaking with fools and children. Probably, it was her "lower-class" voice.

"You have served Shaiagrazni longer than me," Mortascia continued. "It is important that you be ready to—"

"I am ready," Collin cut in, biting back his sudden annoyance. "If you think my acknowledging that we're going to need to kill these fuckers means I'm not, then you're even dumber than they are. I parleyed with the man responsible for killing my father the day after his death. I'm not going to go berserk at this of all things. I'm just being realistic. Talking is fine as long as you're not the last one to stop."

Mortascia eyed him, seeming less convinced than she did . . . wary.

"You hate them," she noted, and he spat.

"Of course I fucking hate them." Collin had to resist the urge to laugh at hearing so stupid an observation.

"What's not to hate? They're cowards, rolling over for the biggest bastard alive just because he has more men. I did read up on this place, you know. They turned to the Dark Lord in a big fucking wave, barely any hesitation at all. He extended his hand, extended his territory farther east, and they were too busy pissing themselves to even consider whether it was right or not. The nobility didn't even wait a day."

Her eyes grew frosty and hateful in an instant, but not with the usual casual contempt he'd grown accustomed to.

"They were scared," she snapped.

"They were dictators," Collin snapped back. "You can choose to be scared, or you can choose to unilaterally control the lives of thousands. You don't get both. Either you have no human foibles and weaknesses, or you stay in your fucking place and leave the rest of us to make our own decisions too."

Somewhere along the way, he'd started talking to her, Collin realized, but he didn't back down and didn't waver. It all felt right. He'd been toeing the line for years, letting people look at him as some fucking rat, reminding him with those silent looks that no amount of pomp or privilege would mitigate where his family had been a single generation earlier. He'd swallowed it because he'd needed support for Kaltan and his father.

And that was over now. The world was changing, things were finally kicking off, and Collin would rather spit his venom every place he could than keep his eyes down and feet shuffling away. If any of the narcissistic babies ruling this world had a problem with that, he might just cut their fucking throats. That's what a king did when spoken out against. Why not a peasant?

Mortascia might have sensed just how eager he was for her to give him such an excuse because she bit her tongue at that, and the remainder of their walk was had in silence. That was fine by him. Collin was getting sick of hearing the words from children of incest.

The space behind Ironbane's walls was little different to the exterior, save that the ancient architecture was far more expansive in its influence across the area. Collin saw lots more of the curiously stacked shapes, though smaller than the largest, and others in more cuboidal dimensions. The place seemed almost multilayered, with paths cutting up and throughout the higher levels, adding an entire dimension to its space. It was oddly chilling.

Many more could be contained within than he'd first thought, he realized. Perhaps the diplomacy really was a vital effort. Soon enough they were at the central structure, and quickly ushered in once identifying themselves and their business.

Collin found a chill down his spine as he realized how tight the interior was.

Not a good space for a ranger to be in, not at all. He seemed to have been doing a lot of close quarters killing these days, and Shaiagrazni's physical enhancements were not so great a benefit that he felt any more confident in the fact.

"Nervous?" Mortascia asked, grinning smugly as Collin glared at her sidelong. How he loathed that, the way aristocrats could waddle around like dumb toddlers, so convinced the world would do nothing to hurt them. He kept his anger to himself and moved on, reaching the place's throne room within the minute.

It was a more expansive area than the rest of the structure, but not by much. Its ceiling was maybe twenty feet from the ground, its walls perhaps forty feet from each other, and the throne sitting back against the far wall was so big as to almost make the chamber cramped. They weren't alone because a score of knights stood at large pillars lining the place, and a tall, wiry man lay across the damned chair ahead.

He was thin, very thin. With a pot belly, an excess of chest hair, and oddly pale skin around his inner thighs. Collin knew all this because the man chose to receive them wearing nothing but a robe, cock dangling out for all to see as he lay back in his seat and grinned at them. White teeth flashed as a luminous contrast to his raven-black hair, while eyes that were bloodshot with pipe glinted in the warm firelight.

"Welcome!" the king declared as if he were not presenting his genitals like some posturing ape.

CHAPTER SEVEN

Silenos had called on his apprentice the moment he'd heard of her return to the city. She had, however, been late in answering his summons. Late by an entire minute, no less. Such a transgression was unheard of from her, and not a thing he had any intention of humoring. He made his way sharply to her quarters at the turning of the sixtieth second following her time of arrival, storming through the expansive building and letting his displeasure show to frighten servants and administrators from his path.

Her quarters were not far from his own place of work, and that much was by design. He had barely resisted the urge to dedicate an entire afternoon worsening the old king's punishment after discovering the unforgivably inefficient layout of his palace, and ensuring as many people of import were within easy reach of him at all times had been a priority in their restructuring.

Silenos knocked once upon the door, waited barely half a moment to be granted entry, then pushed his way in. The sight awaiting him inside was something even he had failed to anticipate.

Upon her bed, Sphera lay strewn longways. She was uncovered and unclothed, save for a few thin strips of fabric that clung tightly to the more intimate parts of her, chocolate skin on full display and eyes luminous in the dull light. She smirked at the sight of him, stretching legs and pushing her chest out in quite a deliberate way.

"Forgive me for not answering your summons, master," she purred. "I thought it more fitting to await you more properly like this."

Silenos held her gaze for some time, watching as the woman's face slowly shifted. First to uncertainty, then confusion, then worry. He saw the humiliation slowly bubble up, relishing its infancy before finally speaking.

"Are you attempting to seduce me?" he asked, deciding to leave the question simple. He could aim more particular points at her upon hearing a response.

"I . . . thought that I would . . . would show my gratitude, master, for all you have done . . ."

Sphera was sitting up, and not-so-subtly drawing in covers to hide her body. Silenos let the sight of her embarrassment stew a moment longer.

"Because you believed I was in any way attracted to you," he finished, watching her humiliation deepen. "Well then, let me clear matters up now and inform you that I am not. Some in my household continue to indulge the primitive stimulations of biological impulse, but I was never among them even before being taken on as an apprentice."

Had her skin been lighter, Silenos knew he would have seen the pink tint of her shame. Instead he sensed it only through the biological triggers as blood pooled and flesh warmed. Sphera did not meet his eyes, merely nodding.

"I understand. Apologies . . . Master Shaiagrazni."

"Good." Silenos nodded. "Now we have work to do. Stand and aid me while I assemble a new undead."

She climbed from her bed and made for a drawer beside it. Silenos realized that his apprentice intended to clothe herself.

"No," he said. "You will not waste any more of my time. Work as you are."

He could sense the embarrassment and fury in her as they walked, but none of it was directed toward him. The sure signs of a valuable lesson going well learned. Silenos was not certain what he'd have done if he'd detected contempt in her. He was not, after all, within House Shaiagrazni's territory any longer. And after . . .

Blinking, he turned his thoughts to more important matters.

Silenos's new laboratory was not so far, and it was no great thing. Back in his homeland, he had laid claim to a workspace so large that ten thousand people might have lived within it, fit to display even the greatest of grotesqueries and fit every millimeter of their volumes inside. He was making do with rather less now, but it was still far better than the open fields he'd conducted the majority of his new-world research in. Silenos found it oddly, disgustingly luxurious.

Today he was not working on any creature large enough to require such space, in any case. He needed something with a touch more subtlety. Ironbane, from what he had gathered, was a region protected by great walls and tight passes in the surrounding geography, which meant efficiency and ergonomics were vastly more important than maximizing sheer destructive potential.

Fortunately, Silenos had already surpassed anything he might have managed in the past. There were few advantages to finding himself in the new world, but none were so great as Vigor. That ephemeral, mysterious magic that allowed creatures like Galukar to wield the physical potency of a grotesquerie dozens of times their weight. If it could make a humanoid weighing mere hundreds of kilos so strong, Silenos suspected the true potential of it in a properly made body would be fearsome indeed.

But there were natural limitations too. Diminishing returns came in combining biomantic perfection with excessive Vigor—Silenos had found himself able to bolster Collin Baird's strength far less than he had Ensharia's, and found a negative correlation between the benefits gained by fleshcrafting and the presence of Vigor within a subject. Something made with both would always be stronger than was possible using only one, but the difference was additive, not exponential.

The second limitation was one Silenos suspected would prove less immutable, though for the time being he had yet to find a way around it. Vigor was difficult to handle, a power not native to his homeland or, apparently, his people. Silenos had no innate ability to manipulate it as he might ordinary magic, and even his Entity-granted power to *see* the stuff of the arcane only provided him knowledge, not influence.

He could not bolster Vigor, nor could he control, combine, or redistribute it. If he wished a creature he made to boast magically augmented tissues, he would have to make it entirely from organic matter that was already magical in nature.

His experiments to take a small sample of flesh from a Vigor-boasting creature and simply grow more of it through standard fleshcrafting proved futile.

Fortunately, neither of these limitations were things Silenos found himself entirely halted by. For one thing, simply knowing the presence and density of Vigor in any given sample allowed him to carefully mix it with tissues from others, keeping a roughly constant level as he grafted one set of Vigorous anatomy onto another.

Sphera could not see the magic, which came as no surprise. Rare as it was to possess such an ability even in House Shaiagrazni, Silenos would have almost been offended to see it manifest in a primitive. What she could do, however, was serve as an extra pair of hands. Albeit clumsy ones, still sufficient to ease the process of Silenos's own work and keep his genius fully free to manipulate the finer details.

It was a successful campaign in which Silenos took his new nation, and so few of his own forces had been lost. None among them had been rangers, but he had carried the hindsight to keep the corpses of those previously lost well-preserved. He ordered them brought through, each contained in a large flesh-crafted pod designed to stave off bacteriological cultivation and decay until such a time as he had use for them.

Collin Baird had taken some time to convince, but the sheer utility of reworking their bodies proved well worth the effort of twisting his hatred back toward the Dark Lord. Silenos decided to use only one ranger for each of his new creations, having only a few dozen to spare and wanting to maximize their efficiency.

He armored them, taking the time to make plates of the very same material his own body was protected by. It would not have been possible were he not leaving them with such light and thin amounts, but there were benefits to forgoing quantity. Once they had been encased in millimeters of the stuff, he moved to their general anatomy.

The human form was rather inefficient, locomotively. Silenos went about correcting it, finding no small measure of satisfaction from being able to finally exceed the simple limits of aesthetic normalcy imposed upon him when he worked on Collin Baird or his other subjects. He altered joints, improving angles of movement, adding additional elasticity to limbs and elongating tendons and connective tissue about restructured bones. He broke down neuronal tissues, diffusing them into clusters of rudimentary cogitators serving as relays between myosin-sheathed nervous pathways to allow for a near-instant processing. That, above all, was something he could not have managed in other subjects. The price was dispersing his creations' neurons so thinly as to leave their reanimated intellects more bestial than human.

More bestial, but not entirely. Silenos ensured he left a sufficient fraction of higher cognition to keep the creatures crafty and unpredictable, estimating by the time he finished that their intellectual prowess would have been comparable to Venka's.

He felt a flash of amusement at the memory of the imbecile continuing to scribble his lobotomized drivel out, blissfully ignorant to the damage each new publication did to his legacy.

The muscle fibers required no great creativity, merely some mechanical engineering in regard to which angles and dimensions would best generate an explosive strength of movement. Silenos compounded them with natural weaponry, covering his creations with blades of keratin and nacre, carefully hardening their edges and treating their structures to leave weaponry able to slice apart steel without so much as a nick to their faces.

He added tails too, deciding that the opportunity for added killing power was worth the added weight and recycling slain knights to make the limbs from slower, more powerful Vigor. If any defense proved more than a match for the talons and claws already tipping his smaller grotesqueries' limbs, Silenos estimated the great lances affixed to their tails would prove able to punch through all the same.

Silenos altered balance, enhanced sensory prowess, added sharpened instincts toward stealth and ambush fighting, and of course, bolstered their aggression as best he could manage. By the time the first creation was finished, it was unrecognizable.

None were *larger* than they had been as men, but their bodies were made lean and sinewy, almost serpentine in their lithe efficiency and hardened with armor plating and wire-dense muscle. Both upper limbs ended in scythed blades, and smaller gripping blades protruded from the feet where they might climb, or else disembowel a target via kicking. The tail was of particular note—every bit as destructive as he had envisioned.

He took a step back, then smiled in appreciation as he watched the creature exert itself in tests. It passed them all, and passed them well, with only a scant few flaws revealing themselves, all of which were rectified quickly.

"It is perfection, master," his apprentice breathed, seemingly so enraptured by the creation as to have forgotten about her own near nudity. Silenos hummed.

Once he'd worked with materials produced by others of his household, tungsten-based metals and steels of the strongest order. Once, he'd made creatures able to bathe in fission fire and live. This was . . .

"Acceptable," he decided. "Given my limited circumstances, but one creature does not make an army. Let us produce more."

Sphera blinked at that but solidified quickly with a more certain nod.

"Of course, master." She grinned. "You have some means of producing them more quickly?"

Silenos allowed himself a smile. She really was quick, this one.

CHAPTER EIGHT

I t is an honor to meet you, King Alfonso," Ado managed, finding it remarkably difficult to speak suddenly. There were many things she had been prepared for upon entering this meeting, and on that long list of nasty surprises and jarring offsets, somehow a man's bared cock and balls had failed to appear. Her mind was slowed, churning by as she tried to blink back her surprise and simultaneously recall all the carefully woven plans it had scattered from her thoughts.

If the king's intent had been to cause her distress, he did not seem to extract any satisfaction from the obvious sign of his having succeeded. He merely sat there, legs, if anything, widening slightly while she spoke.

"I am here on the behalf of Silenos Shaiagrazni," Ado pressed. "It is his desire to establish diplomatic relations with your people, and perhaps even have you join him."

Alfonso seemed more amused than thoughtful, which was never a good result when offering a proposition.

"Really?" he mused. "Interesting. And why would I accept? I'm quite well-off now, you know. I don't suppose Shaiagrazni has mountains of gold, or jewels, hmm? No secret trove of riches or ancient relics?"

Ado felt her irritation bubbling up. It was bad enough that she be forced to prove herself the superior of her idiot brothers—bad enough she work with the fear of being replaced by one hanging over her neck like a guillotine blade—she just *had* to get the stupid pervert as her first task.

"No," she replied. "But he has— Oh my God."

There was really nothing more to be said. The sight of King Alfonso peeling back the skin around the tip of his cock, scratching the flesh under it, and *sniffing* the fingers involved just about shook all the coherence from Ado's thoughts. She scrambled to get them back, even as he got to his feet and walked across the room.

"You know, I receive a lot of these offers," the king noted. "They're never very appealing though. Odd that. Everybody would *like* my assistance, but nobody is willing to pay for it. That's just poor negotiating if you ask me."

Ado barely heard him. He'd started smearing some strange jelly from a bowl onto his nipples and moaning.

"Can you take this seriously?!" she snapped, temper flaring. "Perhaps you'd get better offers if you didn't act like some . . . some . . ."

He eyed her, smiling still.

"Oh, no, don't stop on my account. By all means, speak your mind."

Ado blinked, trying to pick through the confusing mess her mind had become, vividly aware that she'd somehow lost control of just about every facet of the conversation within the span of a single minute.

It was Collin Baird who regained it for her side.

"You know, as impressive a display as this is, I'm afraid it's really not going to carry you very far here."

Ado frowned, eyeing him, confused. Alfonso just tilted his head fraction-ally, seeming more intrigued.

"I beg your pardon?" he asked.

"I mean," Baird pressed, "that I know what you're doing. Don't get me wrong, it's a fine strategy. Nobby nobs are plenty squeamish, and if this one was on her own, I'm sure you'd be running rings around her while she tried not to screech the word 'degenerate' as loud as she could. But I'm a Kaltan, and my dad was a peasant. I'm a bit less . . . prim. I know what it looks like to use that against an aristocrat because it's one of my favorite tactics too, though with a bit less . . . skin."

The king met his eye, staring long and hard while the dreamy smile remained plastered across his face. Then he sighed.

"Ah, bugger, very well then. It was worth a try." He shrugged, pulling his robe closed without a moment's hesitation and clapping his hands. A wash bowl was brought through, complete with soap. He used both liber-ally on his hands.

Ado was too stunned to say anything, but King Alfonso was far more talkative all of a sudden.

"Well then, let's just cut to the meat of things. I know why you're here. The Dark Lord is approaching, and you've realized that you need more meat for Shaiagrazni's monsters, and you figured the best way to get it is by absorbing a nation already proved to be morally flexible in terms of allowing such evil magics. And if that leaves the Dark Lord with one less ally in the neighboring regions than he expected upon arrival, all the better. That about cover it?"

She nodded, guard raising. He was sharp, very sharp, and well-informed. Ado was far more used to dealing with that sort than the perverted sex fiend she'd walked in to first meet, but she knew it was far more dangerous too.

"I think you'll find Silenos Shaiagrazni is the better choice, diplomatically speaking," she noted. "You've already heard of how effective his grotesqueries have been in crushing the Dark Lord's forces."

"I have, and have you heard of how defensible a location this is?" The king grinned. "It's perfect for running interference in other conflicts. Say, between Kaltan and Arbite. Breaking up supply lines, for instance, and starving the former out when they've just gotten through a siege already. That sort of thing brings a lot of favor and rewards. Why, General Venka was made one of the Dark Lord's commanders for less."

Baird's face twitched at that, a grin plucking at his lips.

"And have you been doing much reading on the general lately?" he asked. The king shivered.

"I admit, your master may have the Dark Lord beaten out in cruelty, that much is true, but the test of military might still remains against him, and by no small margin."

"But that's assuming you succeed," Ado noted. "Do you really want to risk drawing the ire of *Arbite* on top of everyone already against you?"

The king sighed. "My dear, half the world turned against me the moment my nation joined the Dark Lord."

"And the Dark Lord will be rewarding you only if you manage to disrupt Kaltan supply lines," Baird countered. The king frowned.

"And?"

"And," the mud-boot continued, "I think you should consider the practicality of doing that very, very carefully. Most of our knights died in the purges. Know who we have left? Sneaky fuckers, like me. Rangers. Fast, stealthy, accurate bowmen who can take a head off from one thousand paces and have recently started developing quite a disturbing fondness for Shaiagrazni's strange blasting fluids."

The king swallowed, thoughtful now, but not backing down.

"Are you suggesting that it's somehow impossible to interfere with Kaltan supplies?" He sounded cocky again, amused. It all bounced off Baird like arrows against steel plate.

"I'm not suggesting anything," the boy replied, smiling now. But not smiling like a man. His grin was too wide, with far too many teeth. Too hungry.

Like a wolf staring at the sheep pen. "I'm *telling* you that if you move against Kaltan, we'll send some nasty, horrible rangers to break into your city. We'll kill you, then we'll go looking for your family, all the women, all the cute little kiddies, and we'll cut their fucking throats in their sleep. Start on us and your entire fucking family dies. Maybe we lose after, but you lose first."

It was there again, the hatred. Like a blast furnace with its door left open. Ado had to resist the urge to wince and turn away from the glare of human malice on display before her.

"Are you threatening me, boy?" King Alfonso asked, sounding caught between the twin extremes of fascination and fury. Baird just shrugged.

"I'm telling you my boys'll kill all your children if you move on us. You can consider that a threat if you want. It's meant as a promise."

Silence, silence so thick it might have stopped a trebuchet stone. Ado felt a chill run down her spine, found herself half certain she was about to watch one or both men charge at the other in a maelstrom of sharp edges and violence. But nobody moved.

"Fascinating," the king breathed at last. "I'd heard that Kaltans were a contentious bunch, heard your father called a butcher, but from all my actual research, you always seemed a fairly cautious, even moderate group. More concerned with survival and sustaining your new little republic than actually killing your enemies. You though . . . You seem to be something different. What do you suppose the great Finlay Baird would think about you now?"

"Doesn't matter what my dad would think," Baird replied. "He's dead and rotting, and dead people don't know what the living ones are doing. If you think my father's memory is something I'll hesitate to cross, then you're dumber than the brainless moron who killed him."

More silence, which Ado reckoned was fair enough given the horrific exchanges that continuously interrupted it.

"As intimidating as you are, Mr. Baird, I really must refuse. It's not that I'm not afraid of your people, you understand. I'm just a great deal *more* afraid of my own." Alfonso seemed downright chirpy, despite everything, while Baird looked at him the way a cat might a cornered mouse.

"That's your final answer?" Baird asked. Ado didn't even bother speaking more, finding herself entirely lost and suddenly devoid of control in the conversation. This wasn't diplomacy, it was a threat of violence, and that was something she had no business in bolstering with her own tongue.

"I'm afraid it is," the king replied solemnly. Baird just kept staring.

"Then it's war," he replied, and Ado sensed no small whisper of relish in his voice. "I'll see you soon."

Ado half expected to be ambushed on their way out of the castle, and then again as they made it through the streets. They were not, but her anxiety was barely abated by the fact. It wasn't until they were almost at Ironbane's outer wall that she finally felt confident enough to actually speak, and her fury was too great to be hidden as she did.

"What the fuck was that?!" she demanded, glaring at the damned caveman she'd been assigned to. For his part, Baird seemed to consider her displeasure as important as he did everything else about her, meeting it with no more than a blank, level gaze that spoke of tedium and irritation more than regret.

"I saw things weren't going well. You were cocking up the negotiation, so I moved things into easier territory. That didn't work either, but it was worth a try."

"You threatened him in the middle of a diplomatic meeting!" she snapped, and he shrugged.

"Some people need a bit of threatening. Didn't pan out this time but you'd be surprised how often it does."

"Not with kings!" Ado almost snarled. They were past the gates now, and her need to control the volume of her lungs was diminishing with every extra step. "Never with kings!"

Baird eyed her, shrugging again. He seemed no more concerned than if he'd been told he ate with the wrong spoon.

"Now I know."

For one long moment, Ado found herself staring at him. It occurred to her that Baird's rage had been altogether too big to remain buried, and that now he had exactly what he seemed to have wanted from the start. A massacre with the Dark Lord's men on the other side.

Was it all on purpose? Had she been sabotaged by the bloodthirsty thug? She couldn't say, and that was more disturbing than a definitive answer.

They continued on their way, reaching the carriage soon after and taking off at the ridiculous pace that had carried them so quickly to the city. Ado found herself unable to appreciate it suddenly. Unable to appreciate much but her own failure.

CHAPTER NINE

It was not as long a journey to reunite with Shaiagrazni as Ado had made to actually reach Ironbane, for he met her halfway between the cities. That had been the plan, of course. She would go ahead while he prepared the forces and marched, and Ado felt a fearful shiver run down her spine as she laid eyes on them.

New, all of them, and numbering in the dozens. She shouldn't have been surprised. She'd seen the man create monsters big enough to swallow a bull whole, and each of the bladed abominations now lined up behind him could have had their weights combined without equaling a single one of his largest creations. Still, it struck her.

". . . Sir," Ado croaked, suddenly feeling the unseen blade of his displeasure hanging over her. "I . . . We have returned, and I am sorry to say that our mission was a failure."

Shaiagrazni eyed her, head tilting fractionally as if he were studying some bloody specimen laid out across a laboratory table. Then he sighed.

"It is no matter. I did not truly expect you to succeed in any case. There is a reason I spent so much of my precious time preparing our . . . contingency."

Her eyes flitted back to the creatures, and her blood ran cold all over again. They really were revolting. Like some bizarre cross between cats and snakes, all long and lithe, limbs jutting in bizarre angles and coiled with thin musculature that bound their bones as tight as ship rigging. The look of the blades protruding from their arms made Ado feel rather queasy. She knew full well how viciously sharp the edged weaponry of House Shaiagrazni's monsters was.

"We will be attacking shortly," Shaiagrazni announced, looking to the few humans alongside him. Among them was his apprentice, Sphera. Ado had tried to make friendly with her before, knowing how rare it was to find another woman—let alone another woman of foreign-black skin—so high in any order as them. It had not worked, and she looked decidedly *less* friendly now than she had before.

"You did admirably enough, in any case," Shaiagrazni continued, drawing Ado's attention back in much the same way any extinction-level event's speech would. "Consider this a mark in your favor. The very act of marching so fearlessly into such dangerous territory has proved you possess a degree of mental resilience not common to this world."

Ado felt a smile blossom on her face, surprisingly enough. She wasn't certain why, wasn't certain, still, that she didn't *hate* Shaiagrazni, and yet somehow his praise touched some part of her that had gone long ignored. Her eyes flitted back to his apprentice.

Sure enough, her glare had only intensified in its hatred.

Collin wasn't surprised to be called on by Shaiagrazni for a personal chat. The man tended toward compartmentalization when it came to his subordinates. Probably it was a legacy of the great, ever-underdescribed betrayal that had first left him stranded in their world.

He answered his call, standing before him and feeling his back straighten on reflex. Collin didn't know so many ways of interacting with a superior, he supposed, and the military ones seemed most appropriate here.

"You were inside the city," Shaiagrazni noted. "You studied the interior?"

"Course," Collin replied, almost offended at the fact that his ally had even asked. "Got a good look, nice and proper. Even peeped around the insides of the palace a bit while the princess was drawing everybody's eye."

Shaiagrazni nodded, not seeming particularly surprised or impressed, but certainly pleased. That was about as close as he ever got to either.

"What did you make of them?" he asked eagerly. Collin took a moment to gather his thoughts.

"The defenses are more primitive than the natural barriers around it. The place definitely lets its location do a lot of the heavy lifting. That said, it's not exactly run by cavemen. There are city walls, battlements, siege engines placed in defensive positions too. And the king struck me as a sharp bastard. Probably there's a couple of extra surprises he had stashed away and out of sight before letting us through. Expect a fight, a tough one."

The necromancer was impassive as ever, as impassive as he might have been upon hearing that his enemy's gates were guarded by drunkards. It was strangely reassuring to work with a man so adverse to the basic treachery of expression and tone.

"Any other observations?" he asked. Collin thought about it, then sighed.

"I may have implied we'd be coming for his family, the rangers I mean. So . . . You know, they might make a good intimidating aspect. I reckon his forces'll focus on anywhere they have reason to believe we are. Might come in handy for redirecting their strength before you hit somewhere."

That certainly pleased Shaiagrazni, and he nodded.

"Excellent. Then get ready. I want you commanding the human element to our forces. Rangers, knights, the humanoid undead."

Collin blinked, surprise well and truly unhidden across his features, then nodded.

"Understood. We'll be playing distraction then?"

"You will," the necromancer confirmed. "As I understand it, you have quite a successful record of luring opponents into fixating too much on particular areas."

He felt a smile growing.

"I do." Collin turned, heading off to locate his new men, finding himself eager as he went. It was always a good stroke, finding the chance to kill more of the Dark Lord's bastards.

The battle began without any great excess of ceremony, though Silenos heard war drums pounding behind the enemy's walls. Whether for communication or morale, he could not be certain. It didn't matter much either way; soon enough they would be silenced.

It was rather tempting to simply stand back and watch his creations work; Silenos had spent so many decades growing accustomed to indulging just such a luxury. It was because of that past, and not in spite of it, that he forced himself to take part. He was not such a fool as to learn hard lessons twice.

At the walls, Silenos saw enemies gathering. Most were insects, a few of notable strength. One, two or three were higher undead, lichs. Clearly they had been placed in Ironbane to safeguard it against the local savages—the linchpin of any defense they would take part in.

Silenos focused on them first.

His new cannon was perhaps the most complicated mechanical construct he had yet created, but also a contender for the greatest height of genius. Silenos began its activation by compressing the great organic pistons he had lining its back. They closed in, squeezing the air tight, tighter, tighter still until its volume shriveled and viscosity skyrocketed, and he held within him a space of gas forced to a water-like density. Then the shadestuff came.

Ordinarily, shadestuff would fall down and fill whatever container he tried to conjure it into—eating apart biomaterial just as easily as it did stone or steel. Not now, however. Now Silenos left it in the midst of air dense enough that it was simply held aloft, and like always it left the gas untouched. Shadestuff did not leave a popping vacuum in its wake, even if it boiled away water. That had been the observation that made this creation possible. Finally, he encased the mixture in a shell of hard, thin bone and started the firing mechanism.

His cannon had been tweaked too, and its projectiles made able to fly faster. Silenos had yet to perfect the secrets of hypersonic flight, and yet that was an irrelevance now. This new kind of projectile could not withstand such intense strain as was generated by that order of velocity anyway, and it hurtled for the enemy at a middling Mach 2.

It broke against a lich, sending the undead back a step. Silenos watched through his enhanced vision as the inky shadestuff burst out from its container, pressurized air blasting out the moment it cracked open and letting the liquefied death cling crushingly tight to its enemy. Within one second, the lich was panicking, scrambling, trying and failing to wipe itself clean. Within two it was coming apart, body surrendering to the unrelenting destruction of necromancy's greatest weapon.

By the third second, the lich was a bubbling pile of sludge just starting to run down the battlement. Silenos allowed himself a smile.

Had Walriq the wind mage reappeared, he would have no luck blocking Silenos's shadestuff now. A single shot would leave him just as molten as it had the lich. He'd have to seek out a better quality of enemy to more properly test his new device, but that was a consideration for later.

Something hissed in the air, an arcing flight that drew Silenos's attention just in time for his eyes to catch the trebuchet stone in flight. It was a remarkable shot, accurate beyond measure, to have been aligned so perfectly on a single, man-sized target like him. He had the blink of an eye to move, and knew he was not so fast. Instead Silenos conjured more shadestuff. The boulder crashed into a wall of it, was enveloped instantly and eroded to nothing before it even hit Silenos where he stood a meter farther back.

The event galvanized his wits nicely. There *was* a battle going on, after all. He could admire his own genius once it had been won. Silenos turned his focus back to the fighting.

Collin wasn't commanding as many men as might have been inferred by the phrase "all Shaiagrazni's humanoids." The simple fact was that the caster wasn't much fond of using anything even remotely shaped *like* a man, and had seemed actively irritated for him to request that his own physical enhancement not turn him into some sort of monster.

He was also, as always, rather generous with what constituted humanoid. The giant snakelike sword creatures certainly didn't fit Collin's definition.

If nothing else, they looked tough enough to go a long way in helping with his endeavor. Collin tried not to think about how there may well have *been* nothing else to feel thankful for, and got to work.

His role in the attack was easily described—fuck the enemy off. Now, a simple man might have taken these instructions and considered them easy, simple, even mindless. Collin though was a Kaltan. He knew full well the vast world of difference that stretched between an annoyed man and a truly, sincerely, incandescently fucked off one. It was his job to ensure the enemy became the latter. The pissier they got, the more predictable and the more fixated they'd be on him.

What helped this was that Collin had a large pack of, essentially, infiltration units. Human rangers and these new raboviax of Shaiagrazni's. Both specialized for scaling walls, jumping unexpecting enemies, and cutting open throats.

The exact sorts of things a careful, fearful commander would watch out for when Collin Baird was on the enemy's side. Even to the expense of the enemy's other forces.

It was all theoretical, which meant that it was very likely to get a lot of poor people killed, but it was about as good a guarantee as Collin was likely to get.

Other than the guarantee of being shot at, of course. That came with the territory.

He started for the walls, aiming to come within three hundred yards. It was a smaller range than his own maximum, smaller even than the range of his rangers, but perfect for letting the enemy know where they were—and if the proximity let them get kills in that much faster then so much the better.

It didn't take long for them to take notice. It rarely did when people started watching their knights' and lords' heads explode. Collin felt the satisfaction that always accompanied his work, bowstring singing and arrows whistling as the iron bolts shot through one skull after another.

Ironbane's army was better than *most* Collin had seen. Nothing compared to Kaltan's, of course—that was a natural consequence of Kaltan actually caring when its individual soldiers died—but clearly more used to actually contested battle than was normal for the local region. They reacted quickly, reports moving like wildfire through their ranks, orders moving back down even faster still. He wouldn't have had it any other way. The sooner Alfonso's bastards took notice, the sooner everything could properly kick off.

CHAPTER TEN

Things *did* kick off, and faster than Collin might have expected. Soon enough he spied trebuchets prepared around the walls ahead of his locations, turned toward him, bolstered as archers repositioned and defenses thickened. He saw the bombardment coming a full minute in advance, and knew he barely had time to move from its path himself—let alone his men.

He smiled and gave the signal.

As one, dozens of raboviax hit the wall, all leaping from bushes and tunnels, clawing apart dirt as if it were nothing but water. Their bladed limbs dug into the stony walls, and their climbing started with all the mechanical intensity he'd come to expect from Shaiagrazni's creations.

Their position was blocked from the enemy by two walls, one lengthways and the other widthways. It had been design, not luck, on Collin's part.

He'd known there was a very specific place best used to attack him on the ground, and sent the grotesqueries to attack it from the most vulnerable flank it had. Like usual, his guesswork bore fruit.

The raboviax came down like a scriptural plague, falling on their enemies and cutting, carving, tearing. Chain mail split apart before their natural weaponry, and even plate armor proved too fragile a defense to fully protect the knights wearing it. For each that died, a score or more enemies died with them. It was like watching rangers fight men, and Collin felt a curious sense of nostalgia.

Something about how they moved, how they fought. A particular deftness . . . Surely he was just imagining things.

He wasn't imagining their deadliness, in any case.

Collin watched archers die, then spearmen hurry in and try futilely to stem the flow of blood among their ranks. Then he watched the grotesqueries move on, sweeping across the wall to tear apart siege engines and clear them of defenses.

War had been harder once. More complex. Collin almost felt a shade unfulfilled to watch how effortlessly a victory had just been dropped into his lap. Then the feeling was buried as he let the triumph of having weakened their enemy's position wash over him.

Something touched his wits. A pressure, a heat. The sensation of magic flooding out in volumes the air was too slight a weight to keep its position against. Collin saw men wincing as great winds rushed over them and barely managed to force himself to look on at the source. Silenos Shaiagrazni was rising high into the air, body shifting and growing in all the ways he'd learned to recognize as features of a combat form.

By the time his ascent stopped, he'd already become a thing made of nightmares.

Flight was a curious sensation. Silenos had never noticed it before; he had never had cause to. It was not an unpleasant thing to feel—indeed, it was rather delightful. A thing of liberation and freedom, with not even gravity holding sway on him any longer. His wings beat in great cyclonic arcs, powered by musculature strong enough to lift thrice the weight demanded of them, and the ease with which he moved left Silenos to dwell exclusively on the tactility of it all.

Silenos was not sure how he felt about taking such pleasure in a simple physical impulse, and he knew that he did not care one bit for finding himself even consulting his *feelings* on much of anything at all. For the moment, those concerns did not exist. He had others of a more pressing nature to be focused on.

It had been some time since Silenos truly worked to synthesize any great volume of material, at least within a combative scenario. Indeed, the last time he'd emptied his mana so quickly it had been for the very same thing. He created nitrous explosives, letting it all cling to the insides of a great, hardened shell.

Silenos felt his reserves of power shift, dwindling just a hair. Then he felt the weight of carapace grow more in his hands as the interior filled. Finally it held enough to be ready, and he dropped the sphere of death, watching it fall. Letting a smile dance on his lips as he did.

Among House Shaiagrazni, the power of nuclear fission was a rarity. It was a perfectly understood *technique*, of course, but the ability to actually induce it by overpowering molecular forces was beyond all but the most powerful. Silenos was not certain he had the raw power needed, and even if he did he had never studied the fields of magic that would make it possible. His own explosive was no substitute for the atomic devastation unleashed by those who had.

But it was certainly resting on the second highest rung of that particular ladder.

The air itself ran away from the detonation, as if fearing the density of energy spit outward. Silenos watched chemical stores break down into heat, force, and light. To his enhanced vision, there seemed a significant second passing between the sight of it all and the sensation of overpressure breaking against his body where it hovered some hundred meters above.

Four thousand kilograms of sinewy, muscled war flesh was nothing compared to the sheer kinetic wall that met him, and he spent several moments fighting to retain his balance in the skies. Down below, the devastation was without equal.

From where it had landed, just ten meters behind the outer walls, the bomb cleared out everything. Buildings came apart and flew away as clouds of jagged shrapnel, stone, and dirt leaped high into the air and cleared a crater measurable in liters by the million. People died so quickly and so completely that they could not truly be said to have lived at all.

It took far too long for the air to be sufficiently cleared of debris, and Silenos had no patience to await it. He flew around, observing the aftermath from the side and studying the ruin he'd left beneath him for any sign of insufficiency in the bombardment. From what he glimpsed, nothing of substance had survived.

Around the devastation, things were moving just as they had been planned to. One of the lichs had been near the epicenter of his blast, that much had been by design, and the other had been too occupied by Baird's clearing of the far wall to provide any sort of defense for its peer against Silenos's aerial assault. Now one wall was cracked and the enemy's defenses mangled, the time was perfect.

He gave the signal, a shrill, air-splitting sound formed by so complex a structure of muscle and cartilage that he almost feared even his skill had made a mistake in its construction. The forces below received it as clear as anything.

Grotesqueries moved as a wall of keratin and meat, setting the ground aquiver as they stormed along it. Many defenses remained, Silenos saw, among the enemy's positions, and with the tight approach his creatures were slow to cross the distance separating them from victory. Ballistae spit bolts, trebuchets stones, casters magic. It was enough that it may have caused casualties, even in creatures as toweringly massive as his.

He swooped down to ensure it did not.

Silenos blew one enemy apart after another, focusing the bulk of his power on those who boasted the largest magics, or operated the particularly fearsome siege engines. His deadly work was sustained for a full minute of strafing attacks, keen eyes picking out movement from his own wake, powerful wings twisting his trajectory back around to leave it still with yet more blasts.

Close to ten minutes passed before his forces finally reached the walls, and Silenos finally allowed himself to simply watch the carnage. It was an impressive sight, even for one wreaked by the grotesqueries of House Shaiagrazni.

By the time he came down to plant his feet back upon the earth, much of the fighting was over already. Defenders had been dismembered or eaten, fortifications properly widened to make room for his grotesqueries. Numerous knights lay dead with familiar iron lances jutting out through their eye holes, or throats cut savagely from behind, and those remaining creations of the Dark Lord were boxed in. Silenos knew no magic to turn a summon or reanimate against its original maker. Such things were rare even in House Shaiagrazni. He had them all destroyed instead.

King Alfonso received him by bowing so low as to almost kiss the ground.

"My lord," the monarch whispered, eyes remaining affixed pointedly away from Silenos's. "I must humbly beg your forgiveness. I should never have tried to resist you. Your power . . . In my foolishness, I did not recognize its extent. I know of you, know of your famous cruelty against those who resist, but if you would give me a moment to speak, I think you will find it inopportune to punish me as you have others."

Silenos considered the notion quickly, then nodded. There was little to lose by hearing him out, and the man had already demonstrated considerable mental resilience by even remaining coherent enough to try to persuade him at such a time in the first place.

"Granted," he said at last.

"Thank you, my lord," the monarch replied, speaking with all the haste of a man who had studied Silenos's reputation before finding himself at his mercy. "Then let me first point out that Ironbane is a city heavily reliant on knowledge. Our pathways through these mountains were set out by genera-tions of study and mapping. All that work was burned when I first saw that your forces would begin to gain the edge in attacking."

Silenos felt his temper ignite, and it was all he could do not to change the man right then and there.

"You have more, I suspect, than simple spite to inform me of?" he asked, hearing the rage even in his own voice. The king finally looked up with eyes far less fearful than his voice had been.

"Of course, because all those ancient records still exist. I memorized every single page of them long before giving the order. If you want to know the best, quickest ways to navigate your new territory, you will need to learn them from me. And I am, of course, willing to offer them to your highness as trib-ute . . . provided I am accepted as a subject."

Silenos had to stop himself from smiling. It was a fine play, a very fine play. Clearly this one had made a very *deep* study of his reputation and gleaned that pragmatism was far more important to House Shaiagrazni than cruelty.

"And how do I know that you are not simply fabricating these routes, buy-ing yourself freedom on a false promise?"

"You do not, yet," the king replied. "But you will know the moment you have finished testing the first of them that I reveal, at which point I will have already proved myself a boon to your nation—and to House Shaiagrazni."

It was a proposition worth considering, and so Silenos did. If he allowed the king to go unpunished, he would be reducing the incentive of others to surrender without a fight in the future. Furthermore, the king's status as a previous servant of the Dark Lord would surely work against him. Silenos would be seen as giving favoritist treatment to him, and his diplomatic rela-tions with other nations would suffer.

The benefits were considerable. There would be ways of gaining the knowledge he spoke of *more* quickly, but if it truly did require generations of scouting to accumulate in the first place then Silenos had no delusions of replicating that in more than a few years at best. He found himself torn.

But not for long. The answer was clear.

"I cannot accept your offer," Silenos replied. "The consequences would be too great—"

"No!" the king snapped, then tempered himself. "I mean to say—apologies, my liege—but I have more, much more. Information about the Dark Lord's plans for this region, orders he sent to prepare me for them, and secrets. He needed my people, you see, to prepare for his next plans. I didn't learn much about them, but I learned enough. Enough to know he intends on doing something that will shift the balance of power completely to his favor in a single fell swoop."

Silenos eyed him, remaining silent. The king's panic did his work for him, dragging out yet more from his blubbering lips. Most men only had so much courage, after all. It was the critical failure of emotion.

"Speak."

CHAPTER ELEVEN

It was not particularly fun, rebuilding a city, not at the best of times. Ado liked to think she'd gotten rather good at it, on account of having inherited one that was more smoldering crater than buildings just a few short weeks ago. All the same, that did not make the process easy.

What made it vastly, exponentially more unpleasant, of course, was that for reasons she could only flailingly guess at, Silenos Shaiagrazni had paired her up alongside Collin Baird for its duration.

He was useless, of course. That much had been well within her expectations. He was a Baird, with as much sewage flowing through his veins as blood, and the art of building and repairing nations was a thing done by kings and queens. Ado supposed she ought to have been grateful not to find him recreationally killing the wounded citizens of their new territory.

"From behind," she breathed, seeing the latest of many dead knights. His arms were jutting out, clearly flailing in the moments before his death, throat torn open by motions more crude and savage than skillful. She'd learned to recognize the sight of a man whose throat had been cut from behind, and it still sickened her.

"Problem, sweetheart?" Baird asked, looking over with those empty, corpse-like eyes and letting his voice carry a quiet challenge. Ado swallowed her disgust and let the anger come.

"Not too fond of murderers," she replied, eyeing the knight sympathetically. Baird only grinned.

"Funny, so it's noble heroics when they wrap themselves in protection a hundred times more expensive than their enemies can afford, but dirty murder when one of those enemies learns how to sneak well and puts a knife in the gaps."

Ado just ignored him, finding herself in no mood for the savage bastard's grunting politics anymore.

She tried to focus back on her work, but the day had been long, and her attention was slipping. Baird was by no means helping, sat there grinning away like he just knew for a fact he was better than her.

Well, he damned well *wasn't*, and if he thought she was some dull peasant girl to be drawn into a rut by that arrogant smirk or those veins twisting along his arms, he had another thing—

Movement, fast movement. Almost faster than she even knew movement could get.

Ado had studied magic, and she'd studied it well. She had that same, deeply ingrained reflex that all who walked the path of a magus eventually learned. Cast first, think later. Her hands were up, and her power was building before the sluggish muscles under her skin could even begin twitching. By the time her fingers flexed, the air was already seized and conducted to her will.

Water built, froze, solidified into a wall of ice then hardened as magic infused it. It all took so little time that Ado wagered a trained man could not have seen it happen had he been studying the entire process. It was barely fast enough.

She'd seen arrows move slower than that; she'd seen ballista bolts and trebuchet stones soar more sluggishly through the air. Ado felt her heart leap as the blade dug into the ice, smashed through, then finally stopped just inches from Baird's face.

The ranger was already moving by the time it did.

Ado had not actually seen Collin Baird fight, only heard stories of it. He proved to her in an instant how true those ghost tales were as he vaulted the ten-foot wall of ice she'd made with a single motion, nocking and drawing an arrow within the same move, then had his iron projectile soaring out the very instant he had line of sight to his attacker.

It was a woman attacking him, bizarrely, and more bizarrely still—she seemed almost as quick as he was. The arrow barely grazed her shoulder as she twisted to one side, then rushed back in as Baird landed to attack again.

Before Ado could help, more movement caught her. A new wall of ice was all that kept her from being crushed as another attacker came, this one close enough for her to make out more than just sex and speed. He was pale, tall, with dark hair and eyes as red as pooling blood. The man wore clothes of gray, brown, and black, and seemed a part of the dusk around them.

There was an unnatural grace to his every motion, and it was that that finally had Ado's heart sinking with realization. The vampire twisted back, landed a dozen feet farther away, and snarled as more of its kind emerged from crevices and crannies around them.

One, three, five. Six in total, including the one attacking Baird. Three more pulled away to charge at him while two focused on Ado. Any other time, she might have taken offense at the disparity, but nothing could have made her regret having fewer enemies then. She concentrated her magic, shoving out and letting her wall shatter into a spray of jagged death as the shards of ice lanced into undead flesh.

Vampires were durable, incredibly so. Unlike most undead, they bore humanlike intelligence as well, but there were few things able to match a magus for destructive power. Ado watched one of her two enemies drop down, shielding itself futilely with arms that were growing more badly mangled with every moment the ice continued cutting deep. Stripes of flesh fell down from its torso as bloody ribbons, ichor mixing with the dirt to make it clotted sludge underfoot.

But the second had avoided the attack, and closed in faster by the moment.

Ado didn't have time for another wall, and her physicality was to the vampire's as a toddler's was to an adult, so she focused on something smaller. She let a long lance of ice protrude from the air and braced it against the ground, forcing the vampire to twist aside, then turning to put the construct between them. It took precious moments clawing through—Ado used them to liquefy the lance, blast it over the vampire as a covering, and freeze it with a touch.

She watched the slowness take her enemy in an instant as every motion was suddenly restricted by close to a finger of ice encrusting its joints and body. The state bought her precious moments, and Ado used them well. By the time the vampire had reached her again, she'd conjured well over a ton more ice high above it, and watched as the mass crunched down atop the creature with force enough to drive it a handspan deep into the ruined cobbles of the road.

The first vampire she'd wounded was stumbling up, still gushing out the contents of its veins, while the second twitched and groaned in the newly made crater. Ado took a moment to conjure more ice, great javelins of it this time, and let them loose. The pounds of material hit with all the speed of an arrow, running through both of the monsters and ending things in an instant. Finally she turned to Baird.

It was no surprise to see him struggling, but Ado found herself jarred to see a vampire already dead on the ground with a head hacked almost completely off. Baird had forsaken his bow for the longknives he carried, and both were bloodied. Minor and larger cuts ran across the full length of his body as he danced one way and the other, somehow keeping ahead of even the supernatural speed his enemies were bringing to bear.

For one ludicrous moment, she considered running. Saw the ridiculous velocities the fight was taking place at, the way her enemy seemed to cross entire fathoms of space within the blink of an eye and barely even move at all before they were upon her. Then Ado recalled Silenos Shaiagrazni, and the consequences of his displeasure. She steeled herself, raised her hands, and searched for her moment.

Thankfully, it came soon enough. A swing at Baird that looked dangerously close to landing, blocked as the prepared wall of ice emerged in the weapon's way. The ranger did not hesitate in taking advantage of the opening; with one slash of a dagger, the vampire's arm was opened up, its hand splitting as the ligaments all frayed apart. The next dagger was a thrust, and it found one crimson eye with unerring accuracy. The metal tip did not fully penetrate its skull, but Ado swore she saw something bulging up under the creature's scalp at the back of its head. It fell, not spasming like she'd learned living things did when their brains were ruined. Just still.

Baird didn't waste any time after that, and neither did the vampires. Ado had exposed her presence by providing aid, drawing in one of the two remaining ones. This one seemed faster, faster by far, and it was almost on her before she'd even moved her magic outward. Baird's knife caught it right in the neck before it reached her, thrown so fast and hard Ado actually heard the wind of its motion just one moment later as a shaking, rushing thing. The vampire stumbled, righted itself, then flew back as she sent a frozen stalagmite to lance clean into its belly.

This one though really was made of different stuff. Ado broke skin, drew blood, but she did not impale it, and once the vampire finished flipping overhead, it came to land perfectly upon its feet, crouched and not even seeming to notice the wound at its gut. Baird sighed.

"You know, my dad always hated you lot," he grunted, nodding toward the vampire. "Had uh . . . a phobia, it's called. Used to set traps up in his room to keep one of yez from doing him in his sleep. All came back to this one fight, see. You've probably heard of it. The Skirmish on Rosar Hill."

Evidently, the vampire had. Its eyes narrowed, posture stiffened. If Baird noticed, he was not affected, simply continuing to speak as if chatting away to friends.

"A dozen of you against almost half a thousand men, and he was one of the only survivors. It was fire, wasn't it, that did them? Well, my dad learned that lesson well. Never let a vampire go unburned when he—"

It moved like death, like a whisper, like an arrow. Baird moved more quickly and explosively even than that. Just as the vampire was on him, he was low and rising, his dagger cutting a bloody chunk out of its neck, then coming down to take another. The severed head fell and rolled at his feet, then the body was burning all on its own. Baird grinned.

". . . Actually, what he taught me was vampires have a persecution complex . . . And that they get predictable when they're angry."

Ado just stared.

The ambushers came on like a swarm of flies—irritating in their speed, tedious in their ferocity—and it was all Silenos could do to keep from cursing aloud as he had his grotesquerie tear them to pieces. The fight was not long, but it had been well organized and dangerously planned. It told him something more.

Silenos hurried to the king's chamber, hoping rather hard that he was wrong.

It was not a long journey—his flight and native speed made it rather trivial—and Silenos was there within minutes. He forced open the grand doors, stormed inside, and found the chamber . . . A ruin. There had been guards, and now there were numerous pieces of those guards scattered every which way. There had been locks, which were crumbled and rent apart, and of course there had been King Alfonso.

There was no King Alfonso anymore, just an exsanguinated corpse with a woman standing over it. She was pale, crimson eyed, and altogether too smug as she turned to look at Silenos, grinning and flashing him a gesture so total in its impudence as to demand satisfaction on the spot. He raised his cannon to destroy her, cursing as she turned and surged back for the far wall.

A moment of confusion touched him, for the wall was many feet of solid stone, then Silenos watched as something congealed at her hands. It was familiar—shadestuff—and she made herself an opening with only a single arc of it. She disappeared out into the night just as his cannon cut the air, and Silenos stormed after.

By the time he reached the exit, there was no sight of the creature.

CHAPTER TWELVE

Silenos Shaiagrazni was not in a good mood. Collin could tell as much, and he was quite sure his apprentice and puppet queen could too. It wasn't any great feat for him to have noticed, mind. In all likelihood, the worms dozens of yards underfoot had noticed as well. He could've sworn the bloody ground was shaking.

Over the weeks, Collin had noticed the caster pick up a habit of pacing when his temper frayed, and today was no different. Their position in the center of Ironbane's throne room gave him plenty of room for the pacing, and he was testing its limits by marching wide circuits around its perimeter, fury dripping from him in great, acidic rivulets.

"Rebellions are popping up," Collin told him, deciding to just get it all over and done with. "A lot, more every day. The king really was the linchpin to this entire occupation. Without him, his people are starting to chafe. Particularly because half of them are convinced you went back on your word and murdered him."

It was, he thought, probably what their enemy had intended. Had Shaiagrazni just executed him on the spot, things would not be half so bad. Publicly promising his life and then killing him anyway was the worst of both worlds. Not a bad little piece of politicking, he had to admit. Collin made a note to broaden his own horizons and include such tactics. It was the sort of thing his dad would've done.

"It was perfectly timed," Shaiagrazni growled. "Clearly whoever did this was well aware of our coming ahead of time, and likely the motives for why. There is no other way they could have mustered such a force, even as a local power. And that force will have to have been within the city and primed to strike already when I spared Alfonso."

Collin considered that, and hesitated. It was the princess, Ado, who spoke up, however.

"Not . . . necessarily, my lord," she breathed. "Forgive me, but these were vampires who attacked us."

Shaiagrazni turned to her, his gaze as intense as ever.

"I am unfamiliar with those creatures," he replied frankly. "Explain what they are and why this changes things."

They exchanged a few glances, all of them. None seemed willing to take the princess's place in explaining.

"Undead, we believe," she said slowly. "But . . . different from others, strange. Their bodies are reanimated more completely, emulating life well enough to fool most who are not studied about them, and their minds are left almost wholly intact and independent. Vampires can't be bound by necromancy, like other reanimates, and they can propagate their own existences by draining the blood from others, then replacing it with their own. Blood, actually, seems a focus of theirs.

"They hold as much power over it as they do Necromancy itself, feed on it, subsist from it, thrive in it. There seems to be magical elements that only they can take advantage of in the stuff. Sunlight kills them near instantly, as will a shard of wood impaling their heart. Silver burns them and resists their strength, which is exponentially above the vast majority of humans."

As far as explanations went, it was a good one. Collin reckoned she'd probably studied them herself. If he remembered right, the woman had been trained as a magus, after all. Certainly explained that irritating, cocky way she had of looking at everyone. Different, somehow, from the other aristocrats Collin had seen. Demanding a challenge just for the pleasure of smacking it down. He felt a stab of annoyance again as she did that thing with her lips—

"I see," Shaiagrazni cut in, sounding no more impressed by the explanation than he was by most things. "Then there may have been no need for such careful preparation after all, if creatures of this caliber can muster so easily. This is . . . troubling. How would you all recommend we proceed?"

It was a rare feature for a man insisting on command to be so willing to accept counsel. Collin let himself appreciate it a moment more before speaking.

"I say we—" He faltered at the sound of an opening door and hasty footsteps on the stone floor, then turned to see a messenger scrambling in. The man practically glowed with terror, and for once it was not focused on Shaiagrazni.

"Apologies for interrupting." He gasped. "But there is a visitor, here to—"

The doors opened again, but this time a different set. The main pair, foot-thick stone designed specifically to demand its team of guards to force apart, multiton weight gliding inward as if moved by a dozen people at once. From the other side entered a woman.

No, not a woman. Collin recognized the inhuman glide to her step before she'd even taken three strides inside. A vampire, tall and lean, pale and twisted like the rest. He saw others make the same realization because Shaiagrazni's apprentice and the princess were both quick to raise hands with ice and darkness at once.

The fleshcrafter halted them with a single spoken word.

"Stop."

They did, the way any sane person stopped when commanded to by that particular man, but eyed him in confusion. Uncharacteristically, he gifted them some elaboration.

"If I am correct, our guest is here under a parley to speak with us peacefully," he noted, and the vampire nodded with a smirk. "So do not kill it, or it will become far more difficult to manage any kind of parleys at all in the future."

"Wise words, Lord Shaiagrazni," the intruder noted, continuing into the room. "I was hoping you'd see that wisdom in them."

"Spare me your flattery," the necromancer replied calmly. "I have no time for it." He paused, glancing around, thinking, then continued. "Out, all of you. I will have this discussion alone."

Collin saw no reason to disobey.

The vampire looked at Silenos in a way that no undead had any business looking at a necromancer of his caliber. Calm, considering. Like they were equals. It needled Silenos, but he did not let the fact show.

"You are here with terms from your master?"

As was common among undead, there seemed to be no subconscious twitches of the vampire's facial muscles. Silenos could read nothing of its mental state, and so he listened intently to the words with which it answered him.

"I do not serve the Dark Lord," it replied rather quickly. "None of us do. We are above such petty states."

Silenos kept his own features neutral, even as he stored the information. So rapid a response seemed, to him, to indicate a touched nerve. As far as he could guess, the undead was being truthful, and downright offended to have even been implied a servitor.

"We do work with the Dark Lord, of course," it continued. "For all the reasons you likely think; there are few other humans in this world willing to associate with our kind."

"The Dark Lord is human?" Silenos noted, as much for his genuine curiosity as to keep the vampire wrong-footed by steering the conversation. It hesitated.

"He is not one of our kind, nor a conventional undead, that much I know. Though I know of only Elves to wield the power he does, not even Archmagus Mafari did at the height of his power."

Silenos tucked the information away and answered it with a nod.

"I imagine it has not escaped your notice that I too would be willing to associate with your kind," he observed.

"It hasn't, nor have the Dark Lord's superior forces," countered the vampire. "I am, however, here to present you with an offer. Join him. Pledge your fealty and swear your loyalty. There would be a place for you as his second-in-command. After all you have accomplished, and with your forces and skills combined, the entire world would fall before you in short order. His words, not mine."

Silenos did not laugh out loud, but he certainly savored his amusement. The fact that he had even been handed such a ridiculous proposition was evidence of a deep-seated idiocy in both the Dark Lord and these curious *vampire* creatures.

He was a better necromancer by far than this Dark Lord, and had seen no evidence that the man was even able to fleshcraft. From what he'd asked of Sphera, he focused mostly on direct combat magic, which explained his effortless victory against King Galukar. A formidable foe, individually, but far from the strategic utility Silenos could bring to bear.

There was a reason he was receiving such an offer, and Silenos would have wagered it was to make the most of his magics, then kill him as quickly as possible to keep from being exceeded later on. Time was his ally, and his enemy's adversary. All he needed to do was win more of it.

But there was more to time, at that. It was a crucial component in the equation of distance.

"Your people live within these mountains, not just around them," Silenos guessed and saw the vampire stiffen. There were no instinctual twitches, but it seemed a psychological shock would still manifest in larger-scale body language. He noted that down as he spoke more. "I could scour them. Find you, eventually, and destroy you in retaliation for whatever ruin you may bring to my plans."

This time it responded calmly, unfazed by his threat, seeing through it with respectable speed.

"You could, but you won't. You have a single critical flaw, you know, as a leader. You're too logical. We've been studying you for a while, and it's been long since apparent that you aren't prone to acting out of a need for vengeance or retribution. Not when you have other matters that demand your focus, at least. We intend to safeguard ourselves from you by simply being less than your biggest threat."

It was, he had to admit, a competent play. Silenos was actually left thinking for a moment to try to circumvent it. Evidently, the vampire was enjoying its momentary advantage because it was quick in speaking more.

"You need to commit all your attention to maintaining stability within your newly stolen territory," it concluded. "And while you do so, your movements are restricted by pragmatism. Unless you would rather face the Dark Lord's arrival with a fractured territory. My Mistress advises that you do not attempt to."

Silenos eyed her, considered, then shook his head.

"You are a fool if you think you have trapped me, and I will not be accepting any of your conditions."

The undead stared but said nothing.

"That is all. Leave now," Silenos ordered, watching as it made its way to the door, then paused just before exiting.

"Think carefully before spurning my lady's advice," it tried futilely. Silenos did not even dignify the petty efforts with a further response, just waited for the thing to be gone. Once it was, he called on Baird once more.

If the ranger was as bothered to not have killed the vampire as he usually was at seeing the Dark Lord's associates retain their lives, he kept blissfully quiet about it.

"We need Ironbane stabilized," Silenos told him, in no mood to mince words or waste time. "And we shall do so through its royal bloodline."

The boy was thinking quickly, as ever.

"The king's uncle?"

"No," Silenos mused. He was an older man, well established and connected, there were better alternatives. "The king's brother."

Baird's confused surprise only reinforced how perfect a choice it would be.

"I . . . didn't know he had a brother."

"Many do not," Silenos noted. "But his existence is not controversial, merely . . . irrelevant. Until now. As I understand it, much of his time is spent in isolation, deliberately distanced from national politics."

"Making him politically weak, but socially powerful, and a perfect tool." Baird nodded, smiling suddenly. "You know, I'm starting to enjoy sacrilegiously abusing feudal inheritance for our own ends."

He was looking far, far too happy for Silenos's taste, and so it was with relish that he continued.

"Good, then you are to accompany the princess Ado in finding this new heir. And do so subtly. If he is still alive, it is because the vampires have yet to locate him. They may plan to do so by following you."

Baird looked rather quickly miserable at that revelation but nodded.

"Right, I'll be off then." He headed on his way, and Silenos called Sphera and Swick through to replace him.

"There are doubtless groups conspiring against us already within this city," he said frankly. "I wish for you both to root them out and if possible dismantle them."

They, at least, seemed far less irked by their own duty.

CHAPTER THIRTEEN

Swick was rather pleased to have been given the job he had, all things considered. It was one well suited to him.

He had, after all, a long history with rebellions and freedom fighters. In fact there wasn't a single uprising in the continent's south that he hadn't at least *betrayed*. It was simply among the best sources of revenue for an enterprising sky captain. Everyone wanted to know where their enemies were, everyone wanted their supplies yesterday instead of tomorrow, and the man with the flying vehicle able to cross continents within weeks could provide both.

And if that man was paid better to turn on the people hiring him, then that was hardly something he could be blamed for.

Well, Swick had found himself drifting from that way of thinking, in recent years. Some of the people he'd screwed over had deserved it; others hadn't. And he'd be lying if he claimed that fact had ever even been an influence on whether he did it or not. If nothing else, the long history of doing so had left him with a fair bit of familiarity in how competent rebels tended to operate.

It was that same familiarity that told him something was rather off about the ones Shaiagrazni had tasked him and the necromancer with hunting down.

"They're too organized," he breathed. "Too organized too quickly. Something strange is going on with them."

It hadn't taken too long to find some of the dissenters, and not much longer to find ones actually in the know. From what they'd observed in stalking them, the group was disturbingly well-connected and equipped.

"External funding, perhaps?" Sphera suggested. "Might be the king had them prepared as a last-ditch effort to keep us from holding his city, if my master had killed him."

Swick thought about that, but it didn't seem likely to him. From what he'd heard, the king had been fairly confident in his surrender, though that may have just been bluster. Shaiagrazni definitely had a reputation for brutality that might have encouraged such behavior.

There were too many unknowns for his taste. Unknowns got men killed more often than edged steel.

"I say we spook this one," he decided. "With luck, a group as tightly ordered as this will be careful about giving orders to report and refer any problems to their higher-ups."

She caught on quickly.

"You think he'll lead us to whoever he answers to?"

"Worth a try at least," Swick grunted. "It's either that or wait however long."

The necromancer thought it through quickly, then nodded.

"Worth a try," she agreed. "So how do we—"

"*Oi, dickhead!*" Swick roared, hurling a rock with just enough held-back strength to be sure it wouldn't seriously injure the man after clearing the two hundred paces separating them. It missed entirely, in the end, clattering from the floor and spinning him around to stare up in terror. Within an instant, he was running, and Swick dropped down to follow.

"You hang back," he advised, having carefully judged things to ensure only he was within line of sight during the display. "Follow me while I follow him. I'll pretend to lose him after a while, then you stalk him from the shadows until he's convinced he's in the clear and heads to whoever his bosses are."

She seemed rather irritated to have it all dropped on her so quickly, but did not protest. Swick began the hunt.

As he'd hoped, it wasn't particularly difficult to harass a single terrified rebel. Swick drove him on a merry chase around the city, pursuing maybe two miles before slowly letting him increase the distance, then falling back entirely. It occurred to him, then, that he had no real way of knowing whether the plan was actually working, and that he might be in for hours of waiting to finally receive confirmation if they'd failed.

Fortunately, Sphera was rather quick in reassuring him. Forty minutes passed before he caught the glimpse of inky black magic reaching high into the skies, visible for a single moment. Swick closed his eyes, concentrated, and translocated.

He did not reach her, but he got a decent fraction of the way there. Whenever someone he'd marked with blood was out of range of his translocation it would always take him as close to them as possible along a straight line.

Knowing where he'd been, and his distance limit, it was a simple factor to continue until he finally came to a rather large warehouse.

"Over here," came the necromancer's voice, and Swick followed it until he caught her in one of the shadows. Truly *in* the shadow as well because the stuff seemed half wrapped around her body, wreathed like a cloak and leaving her almost imperceptible against the dark backdrop. Necromancy, sometimes, just didn't seem fair.

"See anything of note?" he asked, hurrying up beside her, trusting in his own well-practiced sneakiness rather than any magical disguise. He couldn't see her expression behind the darkness as she answered, but he could hear an uncertain tone in her voice.

"Not yet, but I've heard a few things. There's lots of them in there. If they have a large number of fighters then we might actually be in danger trying to hurry in."

Swick realized only then that she didn't have any of her undead with her, and why. Most of them were poorly suited for shadowing a target. It was all well and good to leave them behind for stealth purposes, but now it rendered them a pair entirely specialized *outside* of direct combat. Suddenly Swick didn't feel quite so clever.

"Alright, stay here." He sighed. If everything went tits up, Swick had far better odds of escaping. Best to have her closer to their exit and farther from their enemy. "I'll go and see what's going on."

She watched him head in without so much as an *attempt* to dissuade him from his heroic risk-taking, and Swick was soon slipping into the warehouse and gliding along its floor. He heard voices within, which grew louder by the step, filling the building in their density. There *were* a lot. With luck, that meant they'd hit the mother lode of whichever group they'd managed to follow. Swick didn't want to imagine the implications of this just being a standard meeting.

Once he was through to stand just adjacent to the main body of them, Swick tucked himself away and peered out from behind a few crates. For the most part, nothing of actual organized import was happening just yet. It seemed mostly to be a restless discussion in anticipation for . . . something. What that was, he really couldn't say, but if it was responsible for the eager, expectant grins on all the rebels' faces, then he had no doubt it wouldn't be good for him.

It didn't take too long before he found out.

With more careful quietness than even he had entered with, the vampire stalked into the main room and silenced it using nothing more than her presence. Swick's breath caught in his throat as he instantly recognized her. The same one who had delivered the ultimatum to Shaiagrazni, no surprise there. Evidently her people were intent to try a few more styles of subversion than just regicide.

Red eyes practically aglow, she made her way to the center of the room, took a moment to peer around it at all the expectant faces, and then finally spoke.

Shaiagrazni had been quick in sharing what he knew with Ado, discoveries and inferences both, and she had to say she found them rather convincing.

The first thing he'd noted was the ease with which King Alfonso's killer had infiltrated the palace. Ado agreed that had been disturbing, and had chalked it up to the preternatural powers of a vampire. Shaiagrazni had had a different explanation, however. He believed there was a collaborator responsible for aiding them, and a short round of research and consideration left all largely confident that it was his uncle.

Collin Baird had been rather smug about that, vocalizing his opinion that royalty was simply immutably prone to murdering one another, and Ado had ignored him as best she could.

Truth be told, it wasn't so hard to find reason to suspect the king's uncle. Prince Dazarick had already started to consolidate his power, declaring himself the new king and promising to defend his claim by weight of steel. His residence was beyond the city's walls, for the time being, and easily located by the lines of marching men shuffling toward it in search of employment among his military. Ado saw them all, looking down upon them from above as she rode Shaiagrazni's curious airship. They looked like ants.

"Brilliant." Baird sighed. "I was worried we'd only be faced with a few hundred spears. Nice to see Lady Luck hasn't lost her touch."

"You thought a royal would have so few?" she asked, resisting the urge to laugh in his face.

"Of course not," Baird replied. "When you lot say jump, the world asks how high. I'm just getting sick of fighting outnumbered."

Ado turned away from him, suddenly exhausted with his prattling.

"We're leaders." She shrugged. "It's just natural. When we give an order, others rush to obey because that is the way of things. Your father might have mustered such armies had he not stolen his power from those with the right blood."

Baird's voice was jagged when he spoke next.

"My father *did* muster such armies, bigger than this one, actually, and full of men who'd eat these ones alive and spit the bones out. You'd be surprised what happens when you assign rulers based on ability rather than how violent their ancestors were."

"And your father was assigned on ability?" she scoffed, whipping back around. "He took his own throne by killing thousands. That's not assignment."

Baird paused at that, then shrugged.

"Which still makes him more suited than if he'd just inherited it from someone who did the same thing five hundred years earlier."

Ado turned back around and peered over the side without another word, finding no more patience left in her for Baird and his idiocy. Their journey drifted by, air frigid and cutting. It was curious, she thought, how cold things got as altitude increased, and how powerful the winds became. Ado had wrapped up warmly in anticipation at a warning from Shaiagrazni, but her thick woolen clothes seemed barely able to deter the frosty breath of the skies.

Fortunately, she was not left to suffer it much longer. They approached quickly.

Prince—or, debatably, King—Dazarick had clearly built his city with defense in mind, just as his ancestors had. Thick walls, tall enough that scaling them via escalade would be nightmarish tedium, and a surrounding area carefully flattened by magic and covered by rows of archers with unbroken sights.

"Not as bad as Ironbane," Baird breathed. "To attack, I mean. Still, best not to try it. We'd take heavy losses."

It was ludicrous to hear him refer to the sub-5 percent casualties of their last assault as heavy, after weeks of receiving word from her father about the devastation Shaiagrazni unleashed upon their armies. Ado supposed that was the simple perspective shift of standing by him rather than before him.

"Should we make a show of force?" Baird asked. "Let him just see a few grotesqueries, at least, to skew negotiations in our favor."

Ado was quick in shaking her head.

"Definitely not. That might set him off entirely. This is a man who almost certainly murdered his own brother for a throne taken by his nephew, and now he's seeing a second chance to claim it. We have no idea how eager he might be or how violent he could become if he thinks his claim is being threatened again."

Baird didn't seem to *like* the reply, but he didn't argue either. Nodding along reluctantly, pragmatically, and scowling at the city.

"You're thinking he'd murder the prince," he murmured.

She had been. If anything, Ado feared the boy was dead already. He was their real target, not Dazarick. Alfonso's rightful heir, and nephew to the newly emergent contender for the throne. It was not an unheard-of tale. There were always ambitious men in any family, and sometimes they had more support than those rightfully placed before the throne they sought. All the more reason to be quick in extracting their target before anything could befall him.

"I'll get the prince," Baird announced as they drifted down to the city. "I'm sneakier than anyone else I know. All I need is entry into the city and a lack of outright suspicion. Can you feign diplomacy enough to make them think we're only there to talk?"

Ado had started getting used to his way of addressing her, clipped and sharp as if he were barking orders at a row of soldiers. If anything it was rather more efficient than the rambling directions she typically received from others. "Of course," she said, nodding and hoping it convinced him. Because it certainly didn't convince her.

CHAPTER FOURTEEN

Ado was surprised to receive such a quick escort through the city. She had half expected to be shot out of the sky before they'd even landed Shaiagrazni's new vehicle, and the fear of being taken down some alley and skewered did not quite leave her until she was already making her way up the steps to King Dazarick's palace. She was, Ado realized, getting quite accustomed to being placed in front of danger. Every conversation with Shaiagrazni was one in which she took her own life in her hands, and Baird often seemed like he might fly into a murderous rage at any given moment. Ado needed a holiday.

King Dazarick seemed to favor more elaborate decoration than his nephew, for Ado found herself surrounded by an interior almost overdesigned with excess. Every step she took brought her past a new tapestry, sculpture, or painting. Every corner she turned revealed a new corridor turned display.

She wasn't sure what it told her, but somehow the sight was comforting. It humanized the man, in a way. Made him smaller and less distant. Ado could understand greed, or the urge to show off. She'd spent enough time among her family for that.

Dazarick was better guarded though. That much Ado saw shortly, as she was brought deeper into the keep and past thick doors, thicker walls, and large men clad in steel and wool. She shivered at their passing, finding an unpleasant sense of imminence hovering suddenly over her. A holiday, one day. But not soon.

At last she was ushered through a pair of broad doors and into a room just as exhaustively indulgent as the rest. Centered on it, seated in a towering chair, was a man she could only presume to be King Dazarick. He had a bathrobe on, legs uncrossed, and his cock on proud display.

One day, Ado told herself, she would get a fucking holiday.

Collin did love breaking into the homes of royals. There was just something so *satisfying* about it. Bypassing their defenses, slipping around unnoticed, making himself at home in the place they were most desperate of all to force people like him from occupying. It made him feel all giddy and warm inside.

There wasn't so much time for enjoyment, these days, and his father had always said it was important to appreciate the smaller pleasures of life. Collin felt the crushing weight of remembering him and knowing that they'd never speak again. His smile dropped, and he sped up his path through the building.

Clearly Dazarick was anticipating some sort of malfeasance—assassination, most likely, or else just spies. His palace was well guarded. Fortunately, Collin wasn't trying to murder the owner, yet, and had an easy enough time getting someone important looking on their own. The poor bastard almost pissed himself as he dragged him off to pin him against a wall in some remote storeroom.

"Hello," Collin breathed, smiling in that way he knew always left nobs fearing for their lives. "I have a few questions for you, and if you answer them you don't need to spend more than a minute in my presence. How does that sound?"

He was scared, this one, but not cowardly. An unwelcome surprise, as Collin saw steely hardness congeal in his eyes.

"I'm no traitor," the man croaked, throat tensing as his lungs prepared a more substantial noise. Collin interrupted them, tapping down on his chest with carefully measured strength to knock the wind from him, and just about leaving all the ribs intact as he did.

"Yes you are," Collin told him, taking his measure more carefully as he did. "Everyone is, particularly when their family comes into play."

He was a man in his middle years, and wealthy enough that it seemed likely he'd gotten himself a young wife. Sure enough Collin's guess proved right. He tensed in that way only family men could, fear suddenly returning, and far stronger than the courage.

"Okay," he whispered. "Alright, I'll answer your questions. I'm sorry. I—"

"The prince," Collin cut in before the man could start panicking. "Where is he being kept? What are his guards' positions and quality? What else might be relevant?"

Instantly the man froze, caught in a strange mix of confusion, reluctance, and horror. Clearly he'd not been expecting royals to be brought into the conversation. Whatever answer he gave now was likely to fuck him down the line.

Collin felt bad for the man, really. But not that bad. Poorer people than him were forced to make worse decisions every day, and nobody spared them any thought.

He left him there with a headache and a hasty binding that ought to have kept him silent and still until he was found, then tore off to find the prince.

Swick watched the vampire move, remaining stiller than he'd probably ever been in his life. He'd heard stories of them, and as of a day ago seen one himself, but even he was not a man able to claim himself an expert upon their kind. Vampires were elusive, dangerous, and above all, paranoid. One of the few mysteries the world still had left for him.

The quality of vampire hearing was quickly made rather *less* mysterious when it paused, tilted its head, turned its face, and stared directly at him. Swick had about half a second to make a decision, and he made it in one quarter.

"*Vampire!*" he roared as loudly as he could while dragging his thumb along the blade of his knife and flicking his hand out to spray the globules of blood. Something whipped through the air, black and jagged, and he translocated to the flying path of a fleck of his blood just in time to see the shadestuff splash over the floor where he'd been. It ate the stone away within moments, proving in an instant that Swick would not be getting far by relying on his bodily resilience for this of all fights.

The vampire stepped forward, closing in fast as a sling bullet, and Swick translocated again to bring himself at a sidelong angle to her. His lunge was wicked sharp and perfectly aimed, born from a lifetime of deadly combat, a body full of Vigor, and the monthslong lapse of so much as a whisper of alcohol. He saw the creature's eyes widen as his dagger dragged along its arm, snatching a drizzle of ichor out to run down the limb, sending it back.

Caution now shone from those crimson eyes. And the vampire started circling him. For one moment, Swick let himself bask in the satisfaction of having warded off such a predator, if only for an instant.

Then all the rebels around them started closing in with a vengeance.

Had Swick fought them all alone, he might have been in trouble. He was a Hero, after all, but not one specialized in direct combat, and not particularly armored or well armed. One hundred angry, blade-wielding people was fewer than he'd managed before, but never while fighting a vampire, and never easily. Fortunately, he was not alone.

The necromancer Sphera announced herself by barging in through a door and waving an arm out in an arc. Where her fingers flexed and dragged through the air, they gathered shadestuff, then flicked it out. An entire row of men dropped to the ground, headless, as the magical fluid ate through everything above their necks. One moment later, she was gesturing at the corpses, which climbed up to their feet and threw themselves at their former allies.

It was amazing, the amount of chaos a half dozen suddenly reanimated corpses could bring about by jumping into a mass of people. As far as distractions went, Swick had rarely seen better.

The vampire was focused though, its eyes remaining heavy and concentrated atop him as they circled each other. Swick lunged, the vampire sidestepped, and he translocated himself to a position just feet away where he'd left spatters of blood a moment prior. The vampire was quick enough to avoid most of his next swing, but still lost half the lobe from one of its ears. That, apparently, was enough to let it know that a purely defensive fight was not to its advantage.

Swick was retreating quickly as the vampire came on, blood coiling out from a newly opened gash in its wrist, thickening and hardening until it formed a great tendril akin to the ones used for flank defense on Shaiagrazni's grotesqueries.

It came at him, he translocated, and it came on again. An attack of infinitely dynamic length, trajectory, and speed, like fighting a whirlwind with teeth. Swick backed off, sidestepped, danced around, and winced as he saw the bloody limb gouge chunks of stone out of the floor, even rip a man in half on its backswing at one near miss. It was all he could do to stay ahead of it, all he could do to keep backing up.

More were emerging, pooling around the vampire, congealing and elongating. He had minutes, maybe, before they joined the first and overwhelmed him. Sphera interrupted that.

Two lashes of shadestuff, one barely missing, the other perfectly on-target. The vampire had no time to dodge, instead widening and spreading its blood outward into a broad shield and catching the necromantic attack. Swick watched the sizzling liquid drop down, eaten away in an instant, then he was running.

Behind him, the vampire drew more blood outward, this time from nearby humans and undead, working it rapidly into a devastating array of blades and bludgeons primed to strike out. He glanced over his shoulder, saw the first attack coming, then translocated just an instant before it landed to close in.

There would be no more defensive fighting for him than there had been for the vampire, he knew, and now he had Sphera's power on his side.

Swick went low, and the shadestuff went high. It boiled away a length of the vampire's gory weaponry just as Swick closed in to stab through the newly made hole, driving it back and into a bundle of reanimates. They fell upon the enemy, forcing its attention back around to batting them away while Swick himself leaped high, then translocated back to the ground. He opened the vampire's arm up as it raised to strike where he'd been, cutting deep enough that he might have nicked a tendon and drawing a pained snarl from the creature. Superhuman durability or not, undead flesh or not, that one had hurt it.

The vampire slithered back, pausing, thinking. Then it turned, breaking out into a dead sprint for the window. Swick hesitated only a moment before tearing after it, and he heard the footfalls of Sphera joining him. Human bodies fell away, scrambling into and over one another in their desperation to avoid the path of movement, and the vampire had quite the clear path toward the nearest exit. Swick translocated in just as it dove outward, both of them breaking down into a corridor leading deeper into the earth with a flight of steps.

He'd never chased down a vampire either, but their speed, Swick knew instantly, was no exaggeration of hearsay and rumor. It was pulling ahead with every extra step and disappeared down the far corner before he was even close to the bottom.

He swore, drew more blood from another finger, and flicked it out, translocating the distance away and redoubling his efforts.

This, he thought, was going to take up quite a lot of his time.

CHAPTER FIFTEEN

The vampire problem was one with innumerable nuanced issues all emerging from it, but a remarkably universal solution to most of them. Silenos's fundamental issue was that his forces were designed largely around battles, not skirmishes. The rangers had always served well enough in smaller-scale, tighter-packed conflict, and their dwindling numbers left them a poor match for any force that operated as the vampires did on so large a scale. He needed units able to contend with them in assassination, infiltration, and subterfuge.

Fortunately, he was not so far from accomplishing it. His newly made grotesqueries, built from rangers, had already come rather close. They merely needed specialization.

Silenos had spent much of his sixth decade around the oceans, while studying with House Shaiagrazni. He had no great fascination with them, merely suspecting that the extreme conditions to be found in the marine world would surely have produced interesting adaptive features. He had, of course, been correct. It was one of these he now drew on for his creations, derived from the cuttlefish.

Chromatophores were curious organoids found within the skin of the creatures, and several others. Containing careful balances of pigment, and controlled by precise nervous reactions, they could effectively change the color of a creature within a fraction of a second, going so far as to mimic patterns and textures in surrounding materials with startling accuracy. Silenos recreated them in the ranger-based grotesquerie he'd requisitioned for his work, and made some key improvements.

Some were made easy, even trivial. The higher-than-usual amount of neuronal tissue in the constructs meant that there was room for far finer control over the organoids, and Silenos was able to inure them to the more common weaknesses of temperature and pressure differentials through simply tweaking their surrounding tissues. Others were more complex. A critical flaw in the tissues was that physical impact could forcibly crush open the sacs containing pigments needed for appreciable shifts in color, and he spent some time wrestling with that particular problem before finally stumbling upon a solution.

With a care he'd rarely even been called on to employ to his work, Silenos crafted musculature around the pigment sacs and left them tensing and toughening in time with the nervous signals. It took a lot of trial and error, time dragging irksomely slowly, but eventually he perfected a layout that left the delicate tissues protected by layers of stiff, yet sufficiently flexible muscle. Upon hard impacts or great pressure, this would leave the sacs unbroken and protected, and when the time came for flexible movement, they could relax and become as dynamic as their surroundings.

It was not a perfect solution, far from it. In the moments where his creations were required to bend a certain section, their pigment sacs would be vulnerable to impact regardless, and of course any particularly potent blow might depress the musculature enough to rupture them anyway.

Silenos worked to reduce these shortcomings. He added a honeycomb network of micron-scale keratinous structures formed in similar patterns to the steel links used so abundantly in chain mail among the new world, fusing the rings at one another's edges to avoid the need for uneven distribution or vulnerabilities. With luck, it would add a degree of resilience and rigidity at all times.

Even so, it was far from a perfect mechanism. That fact needled Silenos, but he was forced to compromise once more with his surroundings. They would do, for the time being.

Silenos got to work on updating the rest of his creations with their new adaptations, and coining yet more.

Swick really didn't like chasing vampires. It was a reminder, with every step he took, just how many years he'd spent drowning himself in booze. This one was fast, or perhaps they all were, and it was widening the space between them every moment.

Which didn't mean it would get away, only that he'd have to get clever.

A man in Swick's career learned to get good at tracking exits, turns, and navigation just as a rule. One never knew when one would have to flee from guards, debtors, angry husbands—really, there was no shortage of unruly types who lived for the joy of attacking him entirely unprompted.

The vampire sprinted, tearing down the tunnel. Faster than a horse, faster than a thrown spear. Faster than a thrown spear thrown from the back of a damned horse, and faster than Swick. But he knew where they were going. He'd been careful to study up on the city's old sewers and catacombs, always a good habit to get into, going somewhere new, and he knew full well all the turns that would lead them down into a dead end.

They'd already taken one, which meant all he needed to do was ensure the vampire couldn't burrow its way out through the walls and into different tunnels once they reached it. To do that, he only had to remain in sight and close enough to be a threat.

His lungs burned. That might have proved harder than anticipated.

Sphera was far behind Swick, and growing farther. Necromancers were casters, after all, and though their reaction times and wits could increase as their minds expanded to channel the energies beyond, that meant nothing for their bodies. She was athletic and trained, which was why the number of yards separating them was still countable in only two digits, but he'd find no help from her until the enemy stopped.

With a nasty start, Swick realized that he'd likely be fighting the vampire on his own for a few moments before his ally arrived. Possibly a lot of moments. He buried it, having no time for cowardice—not now—and nicked another finger. He flicked the blood out.

Swick was ten feet closer, then twenty, then thirty. He saw the vampire throw a glance over its shoulder, eyes narrowing, lip curling. The fight was drawing closer even faster than he was; they both knew it. A corner turned, Swick bounced heavily off the wall to keep his momentum, then threw himself down.

Had he not been such a clever lad, he'd have died instantly. Swick had no delusions to the contrary. The volley of gory javelins that shot for him would have bitten deep and left him bleeding toward a convulsive death. As things were, they missed entirely, mangling the brickwork behind him and spattering the tunnel with arrow-quick globules of semihardened ichor that took further chunks out of every surface they hit. A few even caught his skin, stinging where they left cuts and bruises.

But Swick had expected something similar. It was just the sort of trick he'd have played, and rather than scramble to his feet, he just translocated up into the drop of his own blood he'd left in the air before dodging. He landed on his heels and bounced off them, lunging fast. Faster, clearly, than the vampire had been ready for. Her next barrage was still half formed, and her hand came up too slow to stop him, catching Swick's dagger clean in the palm.

Agony flared in the undead's eyes as the knife dug deep, deep, deeper. It was like trying to stab through iron, and his thrust exhausted its momentum just exiting through the back of the hand by an inch, but Swick had all the advantage he required. As his enemy raised her other arm to lash out, he twisted. Agony again, more now, and the vampire was twitching and seizing, body plucked from her control by the pain of metal against bone and forced into leaving an opening.

Swick didn't manage to do much with it, sadly. He punched her as hard as he could, but for all his skill and experience he was still, in the end, no warrior. His knuckles might have knocked down a baby tree, but they only sent the vampire back a step, cursing and stumbling as Swick followed the blow by ripping his knife free and lashing it out. It cut a nice gash over her brow, leaving blood to trickle down into the eye, but otherwise made no great leap in progress toward his victory.

The vampire wavered, caught between the instinct to flee and the knowledge that there would be no greater chance for escape than killing Swick now while he remained isolated. The hesitation bought him precious moments, and his own slight shifting, backstepping, and crouching preparation bought more.

Finally the vampire moved, drawing up blood, more than before. Volumes greater than it should even have been capable of holding, all of it becoming edged and hard as sharpened steel, an array of death glinting and twitching in anticipation of contact with him. Swick stared at it, waited for it to begin its rush toward him.

Then translocated to the drop of blood he'd smeared along the vampire while slashing her.

Swick barged into her, knocking the vampire down and hurriedly moving into a grapple. His arms hooked around her elbows and levered the joints, body tensing as he pitted every ounce of his strength against hers. Even with the position he had her in, it was barely within his capabilities to hold her in place. Like wrestling an elephant, with every struggle threatening to dislodge him and send them rolling apart along the sewer.

The vampire's struggles didn't weaken as Swick's did, and her blood thrashed blindly around, coming dangerously close to striking him on more than one occasion. He just held on. Seconds, a minute, an ever-closing end. Then footsteps reached Swick's ears, and he let himself roll free.

By the time he and the vampire were even halfway to their feet, Sphera was in the fight. Her shadestuff cut a notch from the undead's side, sizzling and devouring the necrotic meat, sending it stumbling away. Swick chased it farther with a knife swing, and then leaned back from a hastily thrown punch.

He saw no strength behind it, and noticed the vampire growing more sluggish by the moment. She backed away, shoulders hitting the wall, eyes narrowing with bitterness.

Then her hands raised upward in surrender.

Diligent as ever, Collin had been careful to scrounge up some of the palace's plans before furthering its infiltration. It hadn't been hard; bloody nobs hadn't the foggiest idea about proper security.

With them tucked safely away into his memory, he made short work of the path through its interior. He slid through it, darting around corners, avoiding sight. Rangers weren't as good in a close-up fight, but their speed and dexterity meant stealth was something they did even better than long-distance shooting, and Shaiagrazni had bolstered Collin's own abilities across the board. He felt like a ghost, avoiding glances before they even turned his way and slipping by every face he encountered, sometimes even by a margin of inches.

It was deep within the palace, his destination, but there were no real impediments to getting there. Collin was standing before the doors in under ten minutes, hesitating before he pushed them in. Then he stopped, and hesitated more.

A library. A huge library. It had surprised him to learn that such a place was the new prince's holding pen, and now it left him feeling somehow . . . on edge. Collin wasn't a great proponent of gut instincts, but even he couldn't quite ignore the pricking unease that was building by the moment in his belly. His mouth was drying, hands starting to tremble, body twitching and tightening with adrenal preparation.

Stupid, all of it. It was just a damned library. Collin pushed his fear down, the doors open, and made his way in.

True to what he might have expected, there were books. Some small, some thick. Shelved or strewn about, lining walls like decorations. Collin had never seen such a number assembled in any given place. The library of Kaltan had been opened for the public shortly after his father's revolution, but much of it had been destroyed in the fighting. A lot more had been destroyed when one particular cabal of nobles had realized it would be permitted for the dirty peasants and tried to ensure they couldn't enjoy it. Just thinking about that made his blood boil, and he focused on more immediately relevant things.

Carpeted floors stretched out expansively, warmly lit by chandeliers hanging high overhead. Expensive furniture littered the place, and he found an undeniable sense of *life* to it all. Collin's eyes were drawn more immediately, however, to the man seated at one of the well-carved tables.

He was a wiry thing, but tall. Delicate and thin, with a spectacled face framed by tousled brown hair, perhaps Collin's age. He looked younger. Before him was a book, and across his face was an expression of frowning confusion.

"Prince Nemo?" Collin asked, taking a step forward. "You need to come with me. You're in danger."

The boy's reaction was instant, and not at all what Collin had expected. There was no eagerness for a lifeline, nor indignance at being spoken to so by a man of his accent. He just frowned, backed up slightly in his seat, and licked nervous lips.

"I don't want to," he replied quickly. Collin's temper shivered.

"There's no time to argue," he snapped, closing in. "You're in danger, and a lot of other people are relying on your safety for theirs. Come with me now."

"No," he insisted again, standing now and backing away. "No, just leave me alone. You're scaring me."

It was like talking to some giant child, and that only irritated Collin all the more. *This* was the heir to a nation? Growling, he closed in more rapidly.

So rapidly, in fact, that he almost failed to notice the huge wall of fire sprouting up beside him until it was almost enveloping his body.

CHAPTER SIXTEEN

nd that's really the crux of it. My idiot nephew doomed our nation when he handed it over to the Dark Lord. Necromancy, I can understand. Fleshcrafting almost. But really, a *female general?* It's mad. There's just some things that aren't meant to be—aren't natural—you understand? You at least have the blood for it, even if you're just keeping the throne warm for your brothers, but that Sphera woman . . . Pah. Bad enough she studies magic, let alone putting her in command of the occasional army. Dark Lord indeed, hmm?"

Ado nodded, and did not strangle King Dazarick. It was an exertion of will on her part to manage either, let alone both.

It wasn't just the rampant bigotry, and it wasn't even the fact that he seemed to embody every kind of it at once. King Dazarick was gnawing away at Ado's nerves for the simple reason that he was a fucking imbecile, completely without self-awareness or introspection. Her truest, deepest, most awful realization of the conversation had been that the old bastard wasn't even mimicking his nephew's psychological tactics in exposing himself to her.

He was just a pervert, and Ado was stuck feigning patient negotiations with him. She was actually glad Baird had no idea of the particulars, for he'd surely have gone deliberately slowly just to prolong her suffering if he had.

"That's very interesting." She nodded, forcing the bile back down her throat. "However—"

The ground shook, and a moment later the sound reached Ado's ears. Distant, booming, almost like hearing one of Shaiagrazni's cannons going off. For one single instant, she felt nothing but relief to have been handed a larger concern than her diversionary task.

Then, of course, the implications of what she'd heard sunk in. Dazarick's eyes were wide, and a moment later the doors flung open as guards stumbled in.

"My king," one of them gasped. "It's the library. Something's happening there."

"The library," he echoed, then instantly turned to Ado.

She made her decision quickly, largely due to it being the only one Ado really had any option of making at all. Her magic was in her hands, power salting the air, and in an instant magi and knights were closing in.

"Alright, hold on, there's no need to get mental here," Collin tried, struggling enough to even keep himself calm, let alone the mad bastard attacking him.

Everything was on fire: the walls, ceiling, floor. One section of the room— quite a big, thickly built section—had been simply blown to pieces. Debris was scattered all over the place, a mix of broken and *melting* stone. Amid it all was the . . . thing.

It was hard to make out any details about its appearance because even looking at it hurt. It was hotter than a bonfire, brighter than a forge, and a single moment of lingering eye contact left pale spots centering Collin's sight. Around it, the floor glowed with secondhand heat, and the air was rippling and drying with every moment it remained in the room. It wasn't a *living* thing, he knew that much. No living thing could stand in the middle of such apocalyptic devastation, and yet undead feared heat and fire even more than people.

Was it . . . It surely couldn't be . . .

"**Burn**," the creature—the thing, whatever—snarled. Its voice was like a chorus, like a thousand thousand other voices chanting and groaning in unison. It ran through Collin, quiet and loud at once, almost threatening to send him stumbling with the sheer intensity packed into every syllable. The room shivered around them, wood straining at the pressure of its speech. Loud, then, apparently. It was loud.

"Hold on," he gasped, barely even hearing his own words over the ringing in his ears and the roar of flames too hot and potent to be a thing of nature. "Calm down. Relax. Let's not get crazy here—"

"Burn the human, burn him black, stuff his giblets in a sack. Take the sack and carry it far, send it up high bright like stars."

It was every nightmare Collin had ever had compressed into a single being, and growing closer with each word. He stumbled back, bow forgotten, all his old combat instincts leaving him. This was a demon. A fucking demon, made of death and destruction, an army eater. There'd be no fighting this thing, not with a dozen more of himself to help.

"Xekanis, no!"

The prince's voice, somehow cutting through the chaotic din of Collin's executioner. Remarkably, ridiculously, the demon actually halted. A face appeared in the flames, abstract and ephemeral of barely visible eyes and teeth, and turned toward the prince without a doubt. The demon's voice rang out again.

"It frightened you. It wanted to hurt you, to take you away."

"That's no reason to burn him!" the prince shot back, showing not the slightest scrap of fear as he stared down the demon.

Well, not stared down really. More pleaded with his eyes, appealing with all the same ways a little boy might to his friend. It was perhaps the most ludicrous thing of all that a person might try in moving something of its kind.

And it looked like it was *working*. The demon's flames died down, heat dissipated, and Collin found the stinging of his fleshcrafted skin abated somewhat as the ambient temperature started to plummet. To his amazement, not a single book had been so much as singed by the flames engulfing them.

"It listens to you," Collin breathed, struck stupid and slow by the impossibility of what he'd seen. Before the prince could reply, the doors were swinging open.

Several men stormed in, most big, all armed. Collin had snatched his bow back up off the ground before any of them had even taken two steps, nocked an arrow by the third, and put the length of iron clean through a man just as they swarmed him.

He recognized Dazarick among them, and the plated armor of knights in most others. Not an issue. Collin had killed creatures far deadlier than a group like that. From afar. He was in tight quarters now, and already too close for his weapon of choice. Discarding the bow, Collin switched to his longknives, swearing and slashing as they came.

Knife first he hit a knight frontally, then slipped around as his guard raised and hamstrung him. Two more were charging in behind, and Collin rolled between them before leaping back up swinging and slashing. A circle formed around him, patrolled by pointy steel as he drove the surrounding men back. Caution didn't last more than a few moments though, and he had no chance of winning defensively, not against weapons with their reach. Collin leaped on the nearest one.

A polearm came down for him. He sidestepped and stabbed into the wrists that held it. Before the metal tip was even clattering to the floor, he'd driven his knife down to the hilt in the man's neck, ripping it out with a spray of crimson and rushing onto the next.

This time they moved, last second. Collin's knife hit a pauldron, punching through and drawing blood, but not going nearly deep enough to nick bone or cut all the big veins. The knight reached out, hand closing tight around his wrist, and Collin barely escaped by taking off half the bastard's fingers with his free arm before a halberd came down. He rolled away, watching the floorboards smash to pieces where he'd just been standing.

Knights were strong. Rangers were fast. It was the way of things. Collin had been stronger than most knights even before Shaiagrazni's improvements, but these were clearly a cut above the norm. He snarled as he straightened up, knife torn from his hand and left in the shoulder. Prince Dazarick closed in on him.

"Spy!" he snapped, speaking in that slow, sluggish way nonrangers had when adrenaline was high and the world was dragged back to a crawl. His hands were closed around the hilt of some stupid fucking sword, almost half the Godblade's size and looking like it was made to be bolted above a mantel and bragged about rather than swung in anger.

It was swung though, and swung fast. Collin leaped back from it, ten hands of steel whipping by him, smelling of magic as it passed. Enchanted, brilliant. He needed to get himself an enchanted weapon, one of these days.

The knights tried encircling him, which further split Collin's attention. He tried to go for one on his right and keep them from completing their flank, but Dazarick closed and kept hacking away with strength enough that Collin had no choice but to focus on him. Chunks fell from his thick dagger with every parry, the supernatural edge to his enemy's weapon too much for mundane material to manage. Then the encirclement was complete, and the blows started coming down.

Shaiagrazni made good armor, for sure. Lighter, tougher than steel, something that would have changed war forever had he given it a few years to integrate even on its own. But there were limits to everything, and a half dozen greater knights swinging at once was one hell of a problem.

Cracks, creaks, flexive surrendering to the material as Collin abandoned offense and focused on just curling up to put his armored greaves between the enemy's steel and his own skull. It was done. A man didn't get out of positions like the one he was stuck in. He'd had a good run, but nobody's luck lasted forever.

"Enough!" came Dazarick's voice, and Collin sensed a parting to the metal-clad bodies before him. Just in time for the enchanted blade to come down and bite deep into his shoulder.

Collin had been wounded before, of course, and more than once. The agony of meat cut open in his body was a familiar feeling. That barely made it less debilitating though.

His legs weakened, body dropping, knees hitting the ground as he barely blocked another swing aimed for his neck. A greave surrendered this time, enchanted metal cutting him down deep into the muscle as he fell. Dazarick moved past him, disgust twisting his face.

"The Kaltan," he spit. "I should have guessed. Tell me, was the plan for you to attempt an abduction, or were you just unable to rein in your animal impulses long enough for the princess to finish her diplomacy?"

Collin had about a hundred retorts for the man, but none made themselves known to his hazy wits and swimming vision.

"And you."

The prince was speaking now to the other prince. Nemo, who stood cowering and trembling against a bookshelf with eyes left widened in horror. His uncle approached, sword still drawn, face tight with murder and rage.

"Conspiring with our enemies. Really, boy?!"

"I . . . I didn't . . ."

"Silence," the prince snapped, raising his blade to hover inches from the younger man's nose. He stared at it, cross-eyed through his spectacles and looking as if the metal were made from the stuff of nightmares. "I've had enough of you," Dazarick continued. "It was one thing to have you tucked away silent and unthreatening, but this is beyond the pale. You hear me?! *Beyond the pale!*"

He paused, inhaled as his eyes fell for a moment. Then looked back up, cooler and calmer, but no less deadly.

"Your father wouldn't have wanted this, but I don't care. Everything I've done was for this kingdom—everything—and I'll not have another sheltered brat pilfer it from me."

He raised the sword high, edge glinting in the lamplight, and Collin watched as it came down.

CHAPTER SEVENTEEN

Ado was on fire. It was all she could do to cool the air around her into a falling spray of slushy crystals before the heat burned through her skin and hair.

She hit the ground, scrambled back, and put an icicle clean through a knight as he closed. That was the third one killed, leaving only the magus. All the others had gone with the king.

"Fucking bitch!" the old man snarled, displaying a roughly typical attitude for one of his order. Lightning started building at his hands, and that was bad. Lightning was rare magic, not for the difficulty of conjuring it—for the alarming regularity with which the idiots learning to got themselves fried to death. It was pure destruction, and Ado knew better than to trust in a wall of damned ice against it. She used her precious moments well, freezing over the magus's fingers as he focused on conducting it.

The delay wasn't long, a second maybe as he desperately unstuck thumb and index finger. But long enough for his control to wane. The lightning went wild, and by the time it had finished dancing around the room, there wasn't anything at all left to recognize the magus by.

Ado took a moment, trembling. She really was getting into a lot of death matches lately, and this one wouldn't have gone her way at all if Dazarick hadn't hurried off to find that incompetent buffoon Baird. But she had a task to accomplish, and Shaiagrazni's displeasure was something she'd seen demonstrated all too clearly to risk experiencing again. She headed off briskly.

Fortunately, Ado did not have so hard a time finding where she needed to be. All she had to do was follow the heat and smoke. It was remarkable. The very air started to sting as she closed in on her location, as if someone had dumped a dozen furnaces' contents out into the palace and allowed the molten iron to flow out down its halls. Her sweat built, eyes teared, and fatigue grew with every new step taken to the source.

When, at last, Ado barged into the library, she found it rather less incendiary than she'd feared. Which was hardly an improvement. There were easily a half dozen knights present, and Dazarick was at the head of them. He had a ridiculously sized sword held in one hand as if it were light as a feather, raised high and ready to bring down upon a cowering young man she could only guess was Prince Nemo. The decision was not really hers to make, in the end. Ado had her mission, and no room for failure. As fast as she was able, she conjured the ice and sent it flying in a jagged streak.

Dazarick cursed, stumbling forward as the ice broke against his backplate and threw him off-balance. The knights turned all as one, and Ado barely had time to hit another with her power before they were moving. At such close range, and with all her might, the jagged icicle flew like a trebuchet stone and caught the man clean in his gorget. She winced at the sight of metal, then meat surrendering as blood touched the air, but Ado didn't have time to dwell on it for long.

Things would probably not have ended well for her had Ado been alone. Baird, however, seemed to have needed only a moment to stumble back to his feet.

She watched as he moved in behind one of the knights, faster than she'd have thought possible, and neatly cut his throat before moving aside to knife another beneath the shoulder. The moments of hesitation this bought let her send a third back with yet another blast of ice.

Near-death experiences were certainly not Ado's favorite thing, and she hoped she'd never adjust to them. This one though was over fast. Within a quarter-minute, she and Baird stood around six corpses, and King Dazarick was poised opposite them, blade torn from his grip and eyes narrowed.

"Go on then," he spat. "Do it, damned assassins."

Ado hesitated and considered the merits of trying to dissuade the man of their malfeasance now that he was under her power. That thought was dashed by the sound of rapid footfalls down the hallway at her back.

Knights, of course. Standard armsmen lagging behind the ten or so armored men fronting the charge, and a single familiarly robed magus at the back. Evidently Dazarick's household guard was somewhat more elite than they'd been led to believe. Ado felt her nerves fraying at the sight of them, raising her hands and conjuring a wall of ice before the door, thickening it as best she could before their new enemies could enter.

"You can't hold them forever." Dazarick laughed triumphantly. "You—"

Baird kicked him between the legs, harder than Ado had ever seen any man kicked by anything. He actually lifted up off the ground, rising a solid yard or two into the air as the steel plate around his groin buckled and folded, then fell groaning. The second kick, she thought, was probably not needed. The seven that followed it certainly weren't, but they served their purpose in leaving him incapacitated for the time being.

"We need to go," the Kaltan said, directing his words to the prince and projecting them with the tone Ado had heard on those precious few occasions where he'd left her truly convinced she might be facing down death. It affected the young prince as she might have expected, setting him to trembling with fear and uncertainty, tears running down his cheeks.

"Uncle . . . Dazarick," he whispered, not even seeming connected to the scene around him. "He . . ."

"There's no time for that," Baird snapped, empathetic as ever. "We need to fucking leave, and you're coming with me."

Something reared up before him, at that, and Ado took an instinctual step back as she felt the magic pouring out into the room. It was like standing before a volcano, almost hotter than the actual flames conjured by the source. Her mouth went dry, legs weak, mind liquid.

The burning monstrosity now just yards from Baird was unlike anything she'd seen since Shaiagrazni himself.

"You will not frighten him," it declared, voice like a chorus of screams in her ears. Baird only stared up at it.

"Oh, or what, you'll burn me to death? Good luck getting him out without me, idiot."

It probably said something bad about Baird that he reacted to the towering flame demon more or less as he did all other things, but Ado couldn't for the life of her muster anything other than relief to see it so openly challenged. Clearly, the demon itself was surprised.

"Prince, I know you're scared, and I know it'll be hard to leave your home . . . But please, you need to come with us. That door won't hold forever, and we don't have long."

As if on cue, the pounding began. Ado watched the thick oak doors shatter behind her wall, and then saw the ice itself begin to shiver before repeated blows from axes and polearms. It was stronger than normal ice, she'd made sure of that, but there were limits to her power. A wall of iron would have provided more protection, and she wouldn't have been confident in that holding for long against the assault she now faced either.

"Okay," the prince breathed, eyes on the ice now, and betraying no less concern than Ado felt. "Okay, just . . . Please help me leave."

Baird relaxed, sighed, and looked around the room for a moment. Ado realized only then that their sole only exit was covered with ice and barring the entrance to their death sentence.

"These walls look . . . breakable," the Kaltan breathed. "I think we could—"

"No."

The low, rumbling voice of the demon shook Ado to her core, more cutting for the abruptness of it than its nature. She turned just in time to see the entity grow back into a pillar of searing fire and make for her barricade.

One flash of fire and Ado's wall of ice was half liquefied, running down what was left of its structure in thick rivers, puddling at its base. It broke apart as the knights beyond continued their assault, letting the armored men storm into the library with weapons in hand. They barely had time for surprise before the next gout of fire washed over them.

The smell was by far the worst of it, like cooking pork. Ado felt sick rising in her gullet as she watched steel glow, collapse inward, and then melt, sticking to the charring meat below as bubbles rose and burst in the metallurgic fluid. She found herself looking away, eyes physically stung by the light's intensity.

Fortunately the display didn't last long, barely a few moments more.

"Cool the corridor as you go," Baird hissed, stumbling past Ado and speaking with the same irritatingly practical composure he always showed. She followed after, doing as he'd advised and reducing the ambient temperature of the hall as their group waded past blackened corpses and pooling steel. Her nostrils were stung by the acrid reek of smelting as they went, and even with her magic doing its work, she still felt as if it were a desert around her and not a corridor in a frosty mountain region.

That corridor didn't stay warm for long, and it certainly didn't stay empty. They'd barely turned the first corner before more of Dazarick's men were at their back.

"Not that way," Baird noted, bow out instantly and arrow flying. These were not knights, though they moved with the preternatural speed of Vigor. His metal bolt clove clean through the gambeson protecting one of them and even exited the man's back, dropping him like a stone to almost trip his allies. "Someone make us an exit," the Kaltan breathed, nocking and drawing another as if he were shooting on a practice range. "I only have about twelve arrows left."

It was a uniquely potent incentive, Ado had to admit, and not one she had any intention of wasting. Evidently, the demon had similar ideas.

Another gout of flame, this time aimed behind them. Ado felt her skin blister and hair singe as the flames splashed against stone, running over the wall behind them. It melted within moments, turning to a molten river that ran glowing out of the hall and hissed in the cold air exposed beyond.

"Outside," the demon ordered, dragging all of them along, as a demon's voice tended to do. The prince was hesitant to leave, until his demon carried him down, and Ado lowered herself gently to the ground below with a shrinking pillar of ice. Baird was out last, simply jumping the distance and falling sixty feet with nothing but the bending of his knees upon impact. Show-off.

"The escape's this way," he announced, taking off at a jog easily half again the speed of most men's sprints. Ado did her best to follow, but the fatigue was quicker in building than they were in reaching their destination.

Around them the ground was flat, for a mountain region, but it didn't take long for word to spread through the city. Within minutes, arrows were whistling for them. Baird was careful in guiding them to areas of difficult shooting and great distance from the largest guard concentrations, ensuring that no clean shots were taken, but even still more than one projectile came uncomfortably close.

"There," Baird grunted, nodding ahead to their vehicle. It was surrounded by men, of course, and in the process of seizure. It was all Ado could do to force down her exhaustion long enough to call on her magic.

Baird had three arrows in the air in two seconds, and each one found its mark in a man's skull. Their heads just came apart. Without Vigor to add resilience and durability, the bone and flesh making them up was too insubstantial a resistance against the unearthly force of his weapon. Explosions of wet meat sprayed viscera in all directions, then they were on the enemy.

CHAPTER EIGHTEEN

S ilenos allowed a curse to escape him. Vigor was remaining as stubborn a subject as ever, and the new knight flesh he'd seized in his conquest of Ironbane was proving no exception.

It was a remarkably tedious exercise trying to manipulate it. Silenos had no inherent power to do so, no more than before, and even his ability to reshape the body holding it was resisted by the same power that left it so resilient against all other harm. He could *see* it, at least, but that was of limited use. Better to fumble blindly and have the power to touch it than clearly perceive a substance that was denied to his influence, surely.

He leaned back in his chair, considering the problem. There were only so many avenues to approach it, but Silenos had to admit he'd been rather monomaniacal so far. Insisting on learning to master the magic himself and twist it to his own ends directly. Perhaps that was possible, perhaps not. There were certainly powers not within the abilities of a standard caster; he knew that much and had for years. Were there not, House Shaiagrazni would never have become masters of summoning and dealing with Entities.

Silenos considered the problem from a purely pragmatic standpoint, focusing exclusively on his desired end.

It was not, he realized, entirely necessary to directly alter the Vigor. Not . . . Not for sure. Vigor could, after all, change its own shape. People's bodies could grow and reshape without simply diffusing the amount of magical strength they held in them—a teenager with Vigor did not somehow leave it less concentrated in their flesh by reaching adulthood. So perhaps the solution was not solely in reshaping more finite tissue to create his works.

After a few moments to gather his thoughts and plan, Silenos began working on a new construct. This one was made of simple, mundane tissue, for he had no need of any supernatural prowess within it.

Silenos made it wide, tall. Large enough to fit a body, then larger still, and he began the careful process of leaving it fertile. He shaped proteins and worked them together, producing a nourishing fluid and slowly filling the cavity within his creation, then moved across his laboratory and withdrew a sample of particularly potent Vigor-infused tissue. Just a small amount, but large enough. He left it within the center of the fluid and worked it further still.

He keyed this fluid to recognize the structure of the tissue sample suspended amid it, then altered the organoids at the interior of the sac to slowly produce and diffuse yet more cellularly identical biomass to match it. Finally altering the tissue itself, Silenos made it into a growing thing.

A slowly growing thing, of course. He was not fleshcrafting more of this tissue—he couldn't do that while leaving the additional matter imbued with Vigor. This experiment was to see whether he could induce a state of growth within the stuff itself, using all the natural processes that turned an embryo into a fetus, into an infant. There would be no small time spent waiting before he saw any results, even if those results were a disappointment.

But that was research. There was a reason that the oldest of his household held so much more power and knowledge than the younger ones. A reason why Silenos himself was under half the age of most of his peers.

A knock shook his door and snatched Silenos's thoughts back to the present. He stood, turning to it and calling out.

"Enter." There was nothing particularly sensitive and in need of guarding on display, nothing that the savages of the new world could hope to comprehend, in any case. His apprentice was the first to enter, behind her Swick. Behind him, the vampire responsible for killing King Alfonso.

"Master." Sphera bowed, kneeling before him, eyes appropriately low. "We have done as you commanded and apprehended the vampire responsible for throwing your city into chaos."

As redundant as the explanation was, Silenos rather enjoyed hearing it.

"Excellent." He nodded. "You have both done well. Are either of you hurt?"

"Not much," Swick the Swift grunted, eyeing Silenos, and his cloak, wearily. Clearly he was not eager to have his body fleshcrafted, even for the removal of injuries.

"Then I shall begin the interrogation."

Silenos turned now to the vampire. He had hoped for some measure of fear in its face, but saw none. The undead remained defiant as ever, cold flesh untwitching, eyes hard and challenging. Was it immune to the sensation of pain? Silenos was rather eager to find out. He would learn a lot from vivisecting such a fascinating specimen. Of that much he was certain.

"I'll be . . . heading off, if you don't mind," Swick muttered, turning for the door with no scarcity of haste. He'd always been rather squeamish, a curious trait in a pirate but one that brought Silenos no great inconvenience now. The door closed soon, and he was bringing his gaze to full intensity upon the undead.

To his surprise, the creature's face was aimed down to the floor. As Silenos watched it, he realized its lips were moving softly, hands pressed together, eyes closed. Closed in prayer. He was halfway through a sneer when it struck him that he'd seen it all before. This was the very same prayer, with the exact same gestures, that he'd once observed his paladin companion perform, kneeling down in the dirt every evening and dawn.

It gave him pause, bizarrely. As if the sight were something substantial, something to be considered for even an instant before moving past.

"Master?" Sphera asked, sounding revoltingly uncertain. It snapped Silenos from his stupor in an instant.

He ignored her, addressing the vampire.

"That style of prayer," Silenos began. "It is strange. I have made a study of this land's religious customs. I've not seen that style of gesticulation much, even in the religious."

The vampire glanced up at his address, uncertainty no lesser to have been spoken to. Its eyes were pools of hatred, which was a comforting sight at least.

"It's how people from my city pray," the creature replied tightly. "Or did, at least, when I was human."

"And which city is that?"

The vampire seemed more confused than anything, answering his question shortly.

"Equiscia."

Silenos was not surprised to see his suspicions confirmed, merely relieved to finally be able to move past them and on to more important matters.

"I see."

Equiscia. It had been barely an eyeblink ago since he'd last set foot there. Not very long at all measured against the span of his fifteen decades. It was curious how suddenly distant the city felt. Silenos turned his focus back to the vampire, banishing the distraction with a swift jerk of his intellect.

The vampire was looking at him. That, in and of itself, was curious. Silenos knew there was fear in the creature—a fearless thing did not pray before their torture and vivisection—but it seemed devoid of the emotion's influence. Almost like those of his household who had refused to properly purify their brains of primitive emotion, yet transcended them regardless through sheer age.

Those ones, Silenos knew, were always the most trusted. As this vampire had been. Trusted enough that there might yet be a use for the vampire, one worth pursuing in any case.

"I have changed my mind," he declared, glancing to Sphera. "Take this one away, imprison it, but do not harm it. Have the deadliest of my grotesqueries guarding it."

His apprentice blinked, stunned by Silenos's order.

"I . . . beg your pardon?" she asked. Irritation blossomed in him like the mushroom cloud of an atomic genocide.

"Take it away, imprison it, but do not harm it," Silenos repeated. "Have the deadliest of my grotesqueries guarding it. Shall I prepare a second cell to teach you how best to listen when your master gives you an order?"

Her reaction was near instantaneous, propelled by that most unrivaled of fuels that was fear.

"Of course not, master." She shook her head urgently. "My apologies. You merely took me by surprise. I shall do as you ordered, of course. Please forgive me."

Baird had enjoyed their escape far, far too much. Ado was not certain when she'd first noticed it, but when she had, it had become unmissable.

He'd been smirking as their vehicle took off. Grinning as the attempts at pursuit started, and Ado swore she'd heard him *giggle* as the flying magi slowly catching up had started to fall back upon finding themselves impaled or dismembered by the impacts of high-velocity iron shafts.

Shaiagrazni's aerial carriage had been entirely filled with his ammunition, of course. Dozens upon dozens of metal arrows, each weighing them down by another pound, each proving its worth upon use. Ado wondered, watching the display, just how costly it was for Baird to do his business.

Then she recalled the cost of repairing mangled steel each time a knight's armor was tested by weaponry wielded by a warrior equal to its wearer. Compared to that, it suddenly felt rather modest. It was, after all, pig iron he was shooting. And largely lead cored at that.

Soon enough they were over the city's horizon, and their flight back to Ironbane was concluded without much more of note. The prince Nemo kept mostly to himself for its duration, merely seated and staring absently outward. His pet demon, thankfully, was even more isolated. It had reverted itself to a smaller form, an almost innocuous ball of puffy flames that danced and crackled where it levitated a few feet above the ground, never at risk of generating any real heat or burning anything of import.

Ado did not allow herself to be fooled for even an instant. The thing she saw, the thing she would keep seeing at night until the day she died, was still there. Just hidden, as demons were so fiendishly good at doing. When it saw fit, it would emerge once more. She could only hope to be far away when that happened.

"Your . . . leader. What's he like?"

Blinking, Ado turned and realized that it was Prince Nemo who had spoken, finally breaking his long-held silence. He'd picked a time for it. The city of Ironbane was just within sight, perhaps a few more minutes' flight away.

She considered the prince's question and quickly decided that it was not one she was best to answer. Particularly, not one she wanted to run the *risk* of answering. Ado turned, though it deeply disgusted her to do so, toward Baird.

"I believe the Kaltan has known him longer than I," she replied diplomatically. Prince Nemo's eyes followed hers to where the barbarian was testing the string of his recently abused weapon. He answered without looking up.

"A bastard," he replied. "Doesn't really value people, or their lives. All he cares about is knowledge and power, in that order. He'll cut you open as soon as speak to you, if he has his way, and every seemingly decent thing he does is out of pure pragmatism."

If any of that bothered him, he betrayed no hint of it.

"Do you really not care at all about what you do? What you fight for?" Ado challenged him. Baird didn't even bother looking up.

"Course I do," he replied. "As soon as Shaiagrazni stops fighting the Dark Lord, I'm ditching him and finding other allies that will."

Their flight continued in a grim silence after that, and Prince Nemo seemed by far the more disturbed for it. They touched down in Ironbane blessedly quickly.

The city had not changed as much as Ado would have hoped, and many of the differences she saw compared to when she'd left were . . . disheartening, to say the least. Rather similar to her own nation, during its final days.

She could only hope Shaiagrazni's would prove to have a more robust future. The walk to Shaiagrazni, at least, was not a long one. Ado soon found herself moving past guards and steeling nerves as they entered his commandeered castle.

Ado had begun to tell herself she knew the man, perhaps even that she could predict him. Despite the perpetual terror that proved innate to his very presence, she found the fear blunted as it came for her this time. That effect did not survive entering his throne room and finding him standing before a great pit holding several of his slobbering grotesqueries. Suspended above it, bound and tied by the ankles, was a familiar sight.

The twisted, ruined, struggling form of her teacher, Rochtai.

Below him, the grotesqueries leaped eagerly for their feast.

CHAPTER NINETEEN

Nemo felt like the walls were closing in on him, breath tight in his chest, ribs stiff. His lungs weren't working, refusing to expand, refusing to move at all. The air was just sitting dead and still where it rested within him. Only the pounding of blood in his ears forced him, finally, to take a breath, and he half hoped that doing so would break whatever sick illusion had replaced the world.

But it didn't because there was no illusion to be broken. What he saw was how things were. A waking nightmare, everywhere he went and everywhere he might go.

"You have returned," said the man beside the pit, towering so tall Nemo's eyes almost skirted over him on instinct, as if they were perceiving a piece of furniture. His clothing writhed and moaned as he spoke, animated in perhaps the most disturbing way Nemo had ever seen, and his eyes were terrible in the exactly opposite way. Lifeless, empty. Dead things that ought to be alive, affixed to the face of a man who wore a living thing that ought to be dead.

"I have, my lord," the princess replied, bowing deeply. Nemo could see her face tight and hands clenched, finding himself suddenly less sure of everything for the sight.

"And you have succeeded," the man continued, glancing now at Nemo. For one terrible moment, the caster's stare was all he felt, then Xekanis's warming presence touched the back of Nemo's mind and calmed him. He felt his breath steady, finally managing to exhale.

"I have." The princess nodded again, still keeping her eyes low. The man smiled, surprisingly. The expression was no warmer than his cool glare had been, no warmer at all.

"Excellent."

With a single gesture, the squirming thing held over the pit was plucked aside. Nemo watched it land hard beside the opening, then the caster was touching it gently. In moments, it transformed, changing to a naked, trembling man of wrinkled, pale flesh and unkempt hair.

"Rochtai!"

Instantly the princess was on her knees beside him, hands delicately coming down on the old man's shoulders as he sat up, trembles only growing. Nemo saw tears streaming down his face as he began softly murmuring to the woman and turned around before he further invaded the privacy of what was clearly a reunion long in the waiting.

"Your reward for your service and success," the man explained, as if what he was seeing was of no consequence. "Had you failed, I would instead have made it a punishment."

The princess stiffened, finally raising her eyes from the old man and looking up at the caster. Nemo held his breath as she spoke without defiance.

"Thank you, my . . . sir," the woman replied, swallowing, pausing, then continuing. "Might I please request that I be dismissed, if you have nothing more to ask of me for the moment? I would like to . . . reunite with my teacher."

"Of course." The man waved a hand, clearly seeing no great import in the request. "Do as you will."

She was out of the room quickly enough, taking her teacher with her and helping to cover him with one of the many redundant articles of clothing adorning her body. With her gone, and the mean bowman absent from the room to begin with, Nemo was left with no company at all but the man named Silenos Shaiagrazni.

He wasted no time in turning back to him, speaking as if the events transpiring mere moments ago were of no consequence at all.

"Prince Nemo." He nodded, face turning, somehow, to a new whisper of considering . . . respect.

"Uh, hello, sir," Nemo replied, unsure what more would be best to say. If nothing else, his choice of response did not seem to anger the man.

"Sir," he echoed thoughtfully. "Do you make a habit of deferring?"

Nemo didn't meet his eye.

"I'm just trying to be polite."

"I see." The man paused a second before continuing. "You are the most remarkably gifted esotericist I have ever met."

The compliment was marred, of course, by Nemo having no clue at all what an esotericist actually *was*. Fortunately the man seemed more than eager to explain.

"Your people, as I understand, have a different word for the practice. Demonology, done by demonologists."

Of course, it all made sense within an instant. Nemo swallowed, not meeting the man's eye, suddenly less comfortable than ever knowing what he was being praised for.

"Thank you," Nemo murmured.

It really wasn't much to be given credit for, just something Nemo had picked up as a child. Hours alone, in the library, kept carefully away from politics and the dangers of approximating succession had left him with few pleasures but books. And of those books, only the ones detailing forbidden magic had any emotional weight to him.

Those were the ones he'd always read with Al, when they were younger. Before the world had given his brother duties, and Nemo loneliness. At the thought of his elder, tears threatened to wet his eyes. Nemo suddenly felt the sting of his loss as sharply as if it had occurred just seconds ago, resisting a tremble.

"You must rule," the man told him abruptly. Nemo looked up at that, stunned.

"I . . . Rule?"

"Yes," he repeated calmly. "Your brother is dead; your uncle an ambitious, murderous fool. You must rule, or your people will suffer. You are, after all, the next in line. And unlike Prince Dazarick, you are neither a fratricider nor an idiot. Your innate mastery of magic demonstrates the latter, and the unrelated terms of your sole sibling's death the former."

Nemo felt like he'd been punched in the gut. Not that he actually knew how that felt, of course. He'd only ever read about it happening to others, but from what he could imagine of the experience it felt very much like what was happening to him now. And the man just kept on talking.

"I am speaking about saving lives, you understand. Every day your people are forced to live without the influence of stable Shaiagrazni rule, more perish from preventable illness, starvation, or misguided rebellion. Precious talent and potential are wasted by oblivion. You need not spill any blood at all yourself, merely accept the throne and take your place beneath me. I will guide your nation, as I already control it, and your uncle will have no choice but to accept it by weight of my overwhelming military superiority. The revolts will halt, and all will be well. All will be well, and all will be thanks to your decision, King Nemo."

No. Not that, never that. It was too much, too quickly. Nemo's head was spinning, the ground turning to liquid beneath him, his temples pounding and aching. He wanted to go home. He just wanted to go home, to his library, to his books, to his quiet life out of everybody's way where no one was getting hurt or threatened because of him. He just wanted to see his big brother again, just one last time.

"I can't do it," Nemo croaked, at last, hardly even thinking by the time the words left his mouth. Perhaps if he answered quickly and clearly enough, he'd be left alone that much sooner.

Apparently, the tall man had other plans. He grew more insistent, not less, as Nemo gave him his answer.

"Of course you can," he replied, rather more sternly now. "It requires no exertion on your part at all. Simply accept the role and do nothing. You may do whatever you please with your life after the fact, so long as you make the occasional public appearance as king under House Shaiagrazni."

Nemo shook his head again, feeling that tight, cramped sensation starting all over.

"I'm sorry," he replied. "I don't want to. I can't."

He couldn't. Not again, not another life with a bull's-eye on his back and a horror waiting behind any corner. Not after everything Al had done to get him out of the first.

"You realize what this means," the man pressed, growing more furious by the second. "You realize that people will die; people will be *killed* by your negligence. Or are you one of the moral cowards who has convinced himself that a degree of separation between action and inaction leaves you beyond culpability?"

Nemo kept his eyes on his feet right up until the man started moving forward. At that point he looked up and took a step back, suddenly more than just scared at the sight of him closing in with rage curtaining his eyes. He didn't quite reach him before another man dropped down from the ceiling, the one called Collin Baird, and placed a hand firmly down upon his shoulder.

"Enough," he said calmly, quietly, but as unyielding as a boulder.

The tall man's eyes came down on his now, but Baird didn't flinch a fingerspan at the intense glare he received.

"Are you defying me?" the caster asked.

"Yes," the ranger answered, defiant even as he did. "I'm not your subordinate. I'm your ally, and I don't think you're stupid enough to throw one like me away over your own ego. What, we're gonna fight now? Chuck each other around? Maybe I'll even draw a drop of blood from you before you kill me and deprive yourself of the best shot this side of the continent."

For a moment the tall man said nothing, face twitching. Then his gaze shifted back, terrifyingly, to Nemo.

"Leave, now," he ordered with all the barely hidden vitriol of a man finding himself upon the brink of doing something he knew to be unwise.

Nemo didn't need telling twice, scurrying out of the room as fast as he could manage.

Silenos would have to have the boy watched, he decided. For more reasons than just one. He was, of course, a natural flight risk, but the main issue at hand was his *magic*.

Esotericists were a rare breed in House Shaiagrazni. Any individual could become one, even if they had already dedicated themselves to learning as many varieties of magic as their age and talent would allow. The limiting factor upon it, of course, was the danger. Silenos could testify to that much better than most. It had been how he'd gotten himself trapped in an entirely different universe after all.

He himself had begun learning the art no later than his ninetieth year, calling on all his long decades of practice and experience. Even then, he had been cautious. One always needed to be when one practiced esotericism, for the predatory Entities it involved utilizing would punish the slightest lack, and often in a permanent way. As he had damned learned himself.

It was not impossible to hear of a man as young as Prince Nemo utilizing it, but to have successfully summoned and bound an Entity—even one as weak as the flame thing he controlled—was a feat. For that Entity to have been bound with only the book learning of a primitive, magic-frightened world to help . . .

Luck, clearly, had been at play. But a great degree of skill as well. Perhaps as much natural talent as Arion Falls himself possessed.

That sort of innate gift was something House Shaiagrazni had always prided themselves on finding and honing, in those situations where other circumstances did not keep it from use. Silenos could only hope Prince Nemo was not beyond being turned into a true caster. But that was a matter for later. His immediate concerns lay with the vampire.

Pushing aside the heavy door to her cell, Silenos made his way in. He saw the grotesqueries he'd ordered to guard it within, smaller things, barely the size of rhinoceroses and scarcely able to even withstand the primitive artillery of this world's people. They did their work well enough, all the same, keeping the undead cornered within its prison and warding off escape.

The vampire, to its credit, seemed to have fared better in such conditions than most humans would have. Silenos supposed that was one of the benefits it gained from its curious form of undeath. An interesting condition, that. Unliving, but emulating life through the imbibement of living vitae and bio-magics. He would certainly never have pursued it himself as an end. It was in some ways even more primitive than lichdom, but nonetheless . . . a worthy subject of study, when it was practical.

"What do you want?" the vampire asked, demonstrating its impudence as proudly as ever. Silenos took his seat without bothering to answer first, careful to secure the most comfortable position, and giving a reply only when that major priority had been seen to.

"I would like to meet your sire," Silenos informed it. "The creature that made you what you are. To discuss terms of surrender."

CHAPTER TWENTY

Nemo had been scared for so long that he barely even felt the emotion anymore. It had faded, fallen back into the hind of his mind like some casual thing. Wallpaper, unnoticed and insubstantial, too solid a part of his new normalcy to even be felt in any given moment.

He'd been sent away, but not from the city. Nemo's new home was not a library, nor did it seem to have much of anything in the way of books at all. It was a large room, though tucked deep within the bowels of the castle, unfamiliar and cold. Its walls were thick stone, furniture strange and unworn. Interior empty, save for him and Xekanis.

At the moment, his friend was in his standard form. Roughly head sized and vaguely ovular, hovering a few feet from the ground where he crackled and spit with embers. It was an illusion Nemo had long since grown tired of studying. There was no fuel within him to be making any sort of noise, nor, for that matter, to produce the heat. Where there ought to have been logs and kindling at the center of his fiery core was only air.

It wasn't that the form Xekanis now occupied was *fake*. It was as real, tangible and physical as Nemo's own. It simply wasn't constructed with the same understanding of natural law that was required of any functional organism native to the world. Xekanis had made his own body the moment he was summoned, and done a close enough job of it. Fundamentally though, it would never be more than mere emulation. An imperfect copy of a real thing, betrayed in its falsity by lacking all those concessions and flaws that were required of the things that played by reality's rules.

Nemo smiled at the sight of it. There was, in his opinion, nothing in all the world even half so beautiful.

"You're sad," Xekanis noted, humming the words in that curious way he had. Human speech had never quite been something he'd mastered any more than the laws of combustion. There was a melancholic note to his voice, however. Emotion he understood. Perhaps above all other things, emotion he understood.

"I'm a coward," Nemo whispered, curling up a shade tighter as his legs folded more closely and hands curled more painfully about him. Nothing ever hurt like the truth, after all. Particularly when it was a truth about one's self.

"That's okay," Xekanis replied.

Nemo blinked, turning to his friend. Usually, they did not speak about such things as cowardice. Xekanis had been summoned by Nemo to fulfill a singular purpose, and he'd done so perfectly for years. To be his friend. They played, laughed, joked—insofar as a demon's understanding of irony and subversion permitted that—and spoke of the endless stories Nemo had bound in the old books around him.

Serious conversation, of the sort that usually spawned discussion about cowardice, was rarely a factor in it. Nemo had rarely spoken of such things with Al, after all.

It wasn't that he hadn't expected Xekanis to answer the way he had, more that he hadn't prepared for it. Hearing the response out loud felt somehow more confounding than knowing it would come.

"People are getting hurt because of me," Nemo muttered, eyes growing wet again at the very thought. Wet, and impotent. His tears never helped people. They hadn't gotten him from that library, or saved Al; they certainly wouldn't be saving anybody else.

"That's fine," Xekanis assured him. "People get hurt all the time. It is actually very funny and good."

Nemo stared at him, almost without words.

"That's a horrible thing to say!"

For a moment, Xekanis paused. The only sound was that of air churning around him, and that ever-persistent phantom crackling that came from his body. Finally he spoke.

"I'm sorry. I've upset you. I didn't mean to do that."

Nemo sighed, turning away from Xekanis. It wasn't his fault, not really. He was a friend. His essence was to be whatever the little boy who'd half-accidentally summoned and bound him wished for. It was the boy's fault for not thinking that his friend ought to value human lives beyond his own while he was concentrating on making him happy and nice.

"It's okay," Nemo assured him, feeling the warmth touch his skin a moment later. Xekanis could never truly be cool enough to touch, and so such gestures had become their hugs.

"Do you feel better?" the demon asked hopefully.

Nemo hesitated, then forced a smile.

"Yes," he lied.

It had been a strange location Silenos had been given to meet the apparent vampire queen. Strange for several reasons.

Well within sight of Ironbane, yet rather far from its walls, the site offered no great comfort to either side of the negotiation—which was, perhaps, the point. It was an old place, covered with etchings as ancient as the sandstone pyramids in Silenos's new city, and reeking of a magic even he had only ever seen once before.

Most strangely of all, however, was that it was a forest. Silenos had made a more comprehensive study of organic matter than was physically possible for any singular human lifespan, and he was quite sure that such altitudes were far from nurturing for trees of the sort he now found himself surrounded by. It was almost as if the growths were there out of spite, towering purely to defy the world itself.

That thought struck him with the sudden urge to tear them all down, which Silenos did not come close to humoring. He did, however, think rather hard about the impulse.

His emotions seemed to be fraying more by the day. Why did he still suffer them? The moment he returned, Silenos would finally be rid of his pitiful cognitive spasms. Deciding as much struck him with a sense of finality and comfort, but it was not to last long. Movement ahead of him, deep in the forest, made all other considerations redundant.

More than just one body emerged from the shadows, of course. Silenos would have been horrifically disappointed had they not. All wore dark armor and moved with the twinned grace and strength that was found only in the bodies of uncommonly well-crafted undead. They came on as a single sweeping wave of darkness, faces hidden behind lowered visors, hands resting beside dark weapons. They carried with them such a terrible unity that Silenos almost felt as though he were watching constructs of his own house stride forward.

Amid them, one sole figure broke the monotonous blacks and grays of their coloration, and broke with them the invariable trend toward plated armor. She did so by approaching in a flowing dress of arterial crimson.

She was not a tall creature, but a single glance at her told Silenos how foolish a metric of power that would have been. She radiated magical energy as did an open furnace radiate heat. Her skin was pale and bloodless, eyes a deep scarlet, hair whiter by far than her flesh. She walked as if even the ground was beneath her dignity, seeming to glide over it through sheer force of contempt. In moments, she was almost upon him.

"Master Shaiagrazni," she greeted him, speaking in a voice twisted with emotions Silenos lacked the social context to properly identify. "I am here for your surrender."

It was refreshing to be dealt with in so efficient a way. Silenos decided, eagerly, to respond in kind.

"I have no intention of surrendering," he informed the creature.

She blinked, frowning. It was all a transparently deliberate gesture, he knew. Her kind made no involuntary facial twitches, which meant any he saw—she wanted him to see.

"I was under the impression that you called for this meeting specifically to *discuss* terms of surrender," the vampire replied.

"I did," Silenos confirmed. "Your surrender, however, not my own. I am rather uncertain how you mistook my intentions given the inherent superiority of my glorious power and unfathomable intellect over all others of this world."

The vampire tilted her head a fraction, perplexion worn openly—perhaps even intentionally.

"Interesting. You do not speak like a madman," she noted. "And yet you behave like one. Are you somehow ignorant of the Dark Lord's approach?"

"Not at all," Silenos assured her. "I merely have no particular phobia of rats or insects, and so see no reason to be concerned with it."

The vampire smiled, a tongue running along her lips for a moment. It was strange how slowly it occurred, the gesture taking almost unnaturally long. Emphasized, for some reason? Silenos made a note to investigate further when he could.

"You seem remarkably confident," the vampire observed. "Might I guess that you know something I am not privy to?"

"More than you could learn in a decade," Silenos informed her. "But in this case, the most fundamentally relevant piece of information you lack is that I have seized Prince Nemo, and am on the verge of taking over Ironbane and crystallizing my rule. Your mission to interfere has failed, and whatever favor you hoped to gain with the Dark Lord by executing it will have soured."

The vampire expressed no more than Silenos had expected, but his focus was upon her pause. A fractional thing, barely as long as most creatures took to react, but it was an age by the standards he'd seen set by the undead's quick wits so far. Clearly, his words had given her something to reconsider. A promising start.

"And you would have us defect to you, as an alternative?"

"What I would have is somewhat irrelevant," Silenos noted frankly. "As I understand it, you really do not have many other options. Your kind are viewed as abominations by most in this world, and those few who differ from the opinion are in no position to provide you any sanctuary."

"Unless, of course, you or the Dark Lord weaken the other so much that, even in victory, they are forced to accept whatever help they can—and thus provide more favorable terms in exchange for the protection and security that comes with an alliance to my people. We are powerful beings, caster, and old. I have walked this world for two thousand years. I know well enough how easily tides can change when circumstance does."

Two thousand years was, if a true claim, quite a considerable number of them. That would have made her one of the oldest things even among House Shaiagrazni, and Silenos suddenly found himself rather less infuriated to have experienced so competent an attack. It was like speaking with . . .

Yes, like speaking with one of his fellows from House Shaiagrazni. Refreshing, almost, and beyond stimulating. Conversation with an equal had been something Silenos had gone far too long without. He felt the great rust shivering free of his synapses as he turned them to the challenge.

"Which brings things back to the fundamental issue at play for you. I am wholly capable of destroying the Dark Lord if I see fit. I simply need time and chance to build my strength."

It was half a lie, at most, which made it a convincing truth. If Silenos had the time and chance he described, he would certainly have considerable odds against the Dark Lord, and if he won, he would likely do so in such a way as to remain potent afterward. The vampire, though, was too sharp for even such a deception as that to deter her scrutiny.

"Which only incentivizes me to ensure that whichever of you wins does so scarcely. I can certainly tip the scales to my own best interests, and do it with a great level of care. As you have seen already. The Dark Lord is the better bet. At worst, I shall throw my soldiers against yours and sacrifice some to save the rest."

Silenos had seen it, and he had fully anticipated the answer. His own was tailor-made to cut away the root of its merit.

"Which would foil my plans, and likely destroy me," he replied evenly. "And leave me with nothing to lose in seeking retribution by destroying all of you as my final act."

To her seemingly unending credit, the vampire appeared rather unperturbed by Silenos's promise. He would have expected nothing less.

"You strike me as a rational man," she noted. Silenos held her eye. "Perhaps too rational for revenge, and certainly too rational for so expensive a vengeance as that."

"There are very few things I will not do to avenge myself upon one who has so senselessly foiled my plans," Silenos corrected her. "Believe me, House Shaiagrazni's sense of propriety is more than strong enough to motivate such a thing as that. It is your own life, of course. I would just advise you to gamble it more carefully than you are."

"Threats won't work," the vampire first taken prisoner scoffed. Silenos turned to it.

So far, the creature had remained largely silent, seeming content to allow its leader to speak for it. Silenos could hardly blame the thing—House Shaiagrazni had just such a custom. Remaining silent in the presence of intellectual superiors was an excellent habit for any subordinate to learn. It was curious to see the undead breaking it now.

"Hmm . . ." the older vampire murmured, face turned to a slight frown as she eyed Silenos, not even bothering to glance at her subordinate. He supposed, in the absence of an immediate retributory maiming for its disrespect, Silenos could accept indifference as an almost appropriate reaction. Few beings were perfect, after all.

"He is not bluffing," the elder said at last. There was no particular fear or concern at the observation, none clear at least, but Silenos suspected his new opponent was rapidly reconsidering her situation. It was what he'd be doing, in her position.

"Now that we have established as much, I shall elaborate upon the terms of your surrender," he began. "You will provide your aid to my securing of Ironbane. I know already that you have considerable influence among its population. No doubt you have been seeding that for quite some time, and I deduce further that you were thorough enough to extend your powers into the city's nobility and wealthier classes. As such, you shall use this influence to stabilize the region. You will do so subtly, and keep your hand in it both unobserved and unattached to me. Then, once the city is irreversibly mine, you shall reveal yourself and take your place within House Shaiagrazni as a retainer."

It was the younger vampire that answered first, evidently emboldened by finding its previous outburst unpunished.

"Ridiculous," it spit, seemingly caught between the twin points of outrage and derision. "You're asking that we subordinate ourselves to you, forever I assume?"

"Yes" was all Silenos told it, finding the very act of debasing himself by even answering revolting enough. "Now be silent. I did not call for this parley to negotiate with you."

The vampire was clearly not happy about the retort, which only made it more satisfying to hand out. Silenos kept his quietude in anticipation of the elder's response, and was not kept waiting for long.

Her answer did not come as a speech, sentence, or even as an individual word. She merely lowered her eyes, bowed her head, and took a knee before him. Silenos remained silent, eyeing the genuflection and drinking it in. It had been so long since he had received such a show from one worthy of even considering; he had forgotten the satisfaction of doing so.

"Good," Silenos declared, finding nothing more worthwhile to comment upon. "Then our business is completed."

He turned, catching a satisfying glance of the lesser vampire's face as it stared in horror at the events. Silenos had taken only three steps before the elder's voice rang out again, pausing him mid-stride.

"Do you know what the people have started calling you, Shaiagrazni?" she asked. Silenos turned, letting his silence be its own answer, awaiting her elaboration. "They are calling you the New Dark Lord."

It was, he decided, only somewhat inappropriate.

CHAPTER TWENTY-ONE

The carriage was made beyond the limits Nemo had come to assume were in place for human craftsmanship. Its substance consisted largely of materials he'd not even seen before, outside of Shaiagrazni's other creations. Curious, almost bony stuff that flexed and quivered, but never demonstrated even the slightest surrender to its strain. Deforming wheels and flexing axles made for a remarkably smooth journey, and the sheer physical might of propulsion behind it was more impressive still.

A normal horse might, barely, have matched the carriage's speed. Briefly. Provided it was well-fed, well trained, and unladen by rider or harness. But no mundane beast in all the world could have sustained such a pace for long. At least none that Nemo had ever read about.

"Excuse me," he tried again as he gazed down at the creature. "Do you happen to know when we might be arriving?"

The carriage shivered, but gave him no response that might have found use. Nemo had suspected for a while that it was fully incapable of speech—though also that it could at least understand it enough to receive verbal instruction. Still, he'd asked his question a half dozen times already because there was simply nothing else to do. He hadn't brought more than the one book, and had finished that off within an hour.

Fortunately, his wait was not extended far past that moment.

Nemo felt the vehicle start to slow, then stop. He stepped out without needing to be told, finding hard ground unyielding and firm beneath his boots as he took to it and moved away from the carriage thing. The air was cold, very cold, and he hugged his coat tighter against himself at its touch. Ahead he saw figures centering a great, sprawling mass of life and construction.

Tents were nine-tenths of everything within his sight, fanning out in all directions like some great forest. Between them men moved every which way they could, carrying messages and supplies, or just forced to run laps as sergeants barked commands to do so.

All though were orbiting the same handful of people. Some he'd seen more than once; one was entirely new to him. Collin Baird, the Kaltan. King Galukar, a man whose legend was one to permeate even Nemo's cold library, Princess Ado, and . . . the vampire.

Nemo swallowed, having heard no small number of foul things about the undead called Lilia, and made his way to the group. He'd have given anything to be headed somewhere else, even to be back in his library. Anything at all.

And everything more just to speak with his brother one last time before throwing himself back into this new world.

"Ah, speak of the devil," King Galukar roared, looking down at Nemo and eyeing him curiously.

He really was tall. Taller than Silenos Shaiagrazni, for sure, and far, far broader. Like some great statue of a man, exaggerated to proportions moving beyond heroic and into the realm of ridiculousness, had been magically cast from stone to living flesh. Nemo found himself half expecting the ground to shake each time he shifted his footing.

"Hello, sir," Nemo replied, nodding and smiling as he knew was polite. The king took a moment before replying.

"Sir, how quaint," he murmured. "You have manners, at least, for a dark caster."

A dark caster, of course. Nemo didn't meet his eye. Fortunately, the conversation was not left there for long because Collin Baird spoke up next.

"Oh come off it, Galukar." He sighed. "He's a teenager. You're just embarrassing yourself by hurling all of this his way. If you care so much about principles, then why not vent some of them out in front of Shaiagrazni? At least then they'd be heard by someone with the ability to do something regarding them."

Kind Galukar's face twisted with annoyance, but he did not contradict the younger man. Nemo found himself suddenly disquieted again by the tension at play. The vampire spoke up next, breaking the silence.

"It is a pleasure to meet you, King Nemo." She smiled, holding out a hand. Nemo eyed it, trying to remember the appropriate turn of address in such a situation, and found himself entirely at a loss. Fortunately the woman did not appear bothered, merely withdrawing her hand with a knowing smile. "I welcome you to our war camps." She beamed, gesturing around them.

"You'll not be seeing any of *my* people for the time being, but King Galukar's, the Kaltans, and of course Princess Ado's own are all gathered."

For a moment, Nemo was confused at the vampires' absence, then he stumbled onto the obvious. Even Lilia, apparently the strongest of them by an indescribably vast margin, was shielding herself from the overcast sky with a parasol. He could only imagine the impediment her weaker descendants would face from it.

"My men are here too," Nemo whispered, finding the thought upon him suddenly. It struck like an unexpected fall, jarring his wits.

He was not the king of Staliga, would never be, but . . . he had not done anything to impede Shaiagrazni in letting the world think otherwise. All the Staligans present at the war camps—and Nemo thought he could spot at least one for every score of other soldiers—were here because of him one way or the other.

"Don't worry, Nemo, they'd all have died soon anyway. Human lives are hilariously short!"

Xekanis's efforts to comfort him were as counterproductive as usual, and Nemo was glad to find his friend's voice isolated within his own mind. He imagined few among his present company would have responded well to his words.

"They are," Galukar replied. "And they'll be put to good use against the Dark Lord. All our warriors will. Have you ever seen an army like this?"

As a fact, Nemo had never seen an army at all, but he didn't imagine that explaining as much would make for any great contribution to the conversation. He bit his tongue while the group split off to go their separate ways, soon receiving a guide in the form of a short, scruffy man who seemed vaguely cold and spoke with the very same sort of accent as Collin Baird.

"Lots of kings round these parts lately," Nemo's guide muttered, heading through the camp and weaving between tent lines as if it were second nature. Nemo, for his part, tripped rather more than that. It was like a jungle's canopy, so thickly did the bindings knot the ground.

Or, rather, it was like what he'd read about a jungle's canopy. Nemo had never seen one of those for himself either. Jungles didn't grow in mountain ranges, and they certainly didn't grow in libraries.

"This is the Staligans' section," his guide said at last, gesturing outward as they reached a relatively small, but still considerably large in gross terms, section of the camps. Nemo recognized much of the fabric and craftsmanship at work in the thousands of tents strewn about the place, finding himself awed by the sheer scale of it all. How could there even be so many people in all the world as he now saw sleeping rough or sheltered by hides?

"Thank you," Nemo breathed. "Uh, where will I be expected to . . . sleep?"

He didn't like the thought of trying out any of those tents at all, and was even less eager to sleep beneath the open skies as he now saw so many of his countrymen were. Fortunately, the Kaltan's snorting response did not inflict either fate upon him.

"Oh, you'll be staying in the command center. Our next stop. Follow me, if you'd please, your *majesty*."

There was once more a whisper of contempt to the man's voice that rather unnerved Nemo, but he found himself no more eager to make something of it than he had before. He followed him.

Nemo did not need it pointed out to him when they reached the command center. He wasn't sure anyone would have. As far as buildings went, it was not remarkably large. Certainly the castle in which he had grown up was several times its volume, but framed by a surrounding area of tents and bedrolls, its gigantism was exaggerated in every way.

The outside shared its bony composition with Shaiagrazni's other creations, and the entire shape was oddly . . . organic. Curved and smooth, almost like a thing that had been birthed and grown rather than built. That too was common to Shaiagrazni's work.

"The others should be inside already, I'd guess," the Kaltan grunted, taking his leave without any more to say on the matter. Nemo headed into the structure. He didn't exactly have anywhere else to go.

Outside, the air was cool and uncomfortable, almost shiveringly so. Nemo was astonished at the warmth he felt the moment he stepped in, almost as much so as he was by the *door*. It seemed to be some giant . . . mechanism, like the hinges on a more standard piece of architecture. Yet working by itself. The moment he closed in to it, he saw the walls shifting with muscular contraction, then the entrance parted for him.

The Kaltan had been telling the truth because Nemo wasn't venturing long before he stumbled upon a meeting of Shaiagrazni's commanders. Baird, the princess and king. The vampire too, of course. But now she was smiling rather more openly than before, while King Galukar's quiet discontent seemed to have turned into outright fury.

"I do think I recall you, actually," the undead was saying. "Your family, rather, sorry. Your kind live such brief, flickering lives I tend to get you mixed up these days. It was one of your ancestors I encountered a few centuries ago. He took it upon himself to try to end me, and . . . Well, he was not fortunate enough to be a wielder of the Godblade."

"Fucking parasitic whore," Galukar snarled. Nemo found himself two steps back just at the expression on his face alone, for he had never seen such a fearsome sight as the Godblade's wielder enraged.

Lilia though merely smiled. She looked more amused than anything, as if it were some infant scowling at her.

"Whore, is it? Two thousand years, and men are just as uncreative as they were when I still drew breath. How you ever came to dominate human society I will never know. Size and violence, I suppose."

One giant, plate-wide hand snaked toward the king's sword, then faltered. He hesitated, jaw tightening, and lowered his arm.

"It is fun watching you speak with someone whose head you can't twist off." Baird grinned, and before King Galukar could retort, the princess Ado addressed him.

"I suppose the idea of caution or self-restraint would be novel to you, wouldn't it?" she spit.

"Oh, careful, sweetheart. You'll hurt my feelings." The Kaltan smiled with a sneering, jagged edge to his mouth that made the expression seem altogether more fitting for the face of a wolf than that of a man. Nemo quickly looked away, wanting no part in it, or the attention of its wearer.

Princess Ado seemed to have no such compunctions, and yet her voice dropped down into silence as one of the doors slid open to reveal a new figure. Tall, lithe, seeming to slither across the ground rather than walk. Silenos Shaiagrazni was unmistakable, and his very presence silenced the entire room in an instant.

"You are all here," he said. "Good. Be silent so that you can better hear my glorious vocalizations."

The room fell silent, and he vocalized.

"The Dark Lord's forces are mere days away from us, and growing in strength as they travel. I suspect, however, that they will be taking longer routes than is strictly necessary. No doubt they intend to absorb the fighters of settlements they march through by forcing allegiance. Their end goal, however, is most likely Kaltan. This is where we shall move to impede them."

"Damn fucking right," Collin Baird added, looking personally affronted at the very idea of the Dark Lord's forces coming within a hundred miles of his home city.

Shaiagrazni did not appear pleased by the interruption, however strong its agreement, but he did not voice his dislike. Merely continued.

"Given your eagerness, you will no doubt be pleased to find yourself with a part in our efforts," he replied to Baird. "You are to deploy with the vampire

Hexeri and slow the Dark Lord's forces' advance across his other destinations, buying time for us to better prepare ourselves."

"So sneak around, kill the enemy, and fuck off before they can concentrate their forces enough to actually fight back." Baird smiled. "Just keep doing what I've been doing, then. Sounds fair enough. No point in fixing something if it's not broken."

Nemo found it surprising how little the man seemed to care about working with vampires, but then he recalled the expression on his face when they'd first met. Collin Baird was not a person with many scruples.

"It is entirely irrelevant how pleased you are with your assignment," Shaiagrazni told him. "Just make sure it is done."

Baird's smile turned strange, then, like milk just barely soured.

"So where am I heading first?" he asked the caster, giving no outward hint that anything had changed at all in his mind. Shaiagrazni, for his part, gave no hint at having seen even as much off about him as Nemo.

"You will be heading to the lands between here and the Whispering Hills. I have been informed that the region is home to a nation called Wudra. Your priority, if you have not yet guessed, is to keep the Dark Lord's forces from reaching it."

"Wudra," the princess Ado echoed. "I know that nation. It's old, powerful. Not loyal to him."

"Indeed," Shaiagrazni concurred. "Nor is it loyal to me, or fond of 'dark casters' as a general rule. Which is what you shall be attempting to overturn, princess."

The princess blinked, but her surprise lasted only an instant.

"Right, of course, my lord."

Nemo was surprised at the stark contrast in demeanor between her and Baird.

"You will be going with your brother," Shaiagrazni added. "So that his presence might soften the effects of your people's idiotic misogyny."

She did not seem to know how best to answer that, and remained silent.

"And what of me?" King Galukar asked evenly. Shaiagrazni turned to the man—it still felt strange seeing his head slightly craned to gaze upon *anyone*—and replied just as coolly as ever.

"Your task is a more purely martial one," he told the monarch. "I require you and Sphera to command King Nemo's forces, among others, and wage a direct assault upon the larger bulk of the Dark Lord's forces with a considerable fraction of ours, striking whatever of their armies are forced to disperse across the countryside for faster traveling and, if possible, luring them into fighting an offensive battle against you while you hold a practical position."

The king nodded with surprising eagerness. It seemed he could find common ground with dark casters, after all.

"Bleed them," he noted. "Sacrifice some of our forces to take away a great deal more of theirs."

"And give the rest of us time to consolidate a position here," Shaiagrazni finished with a nod. His lip curled. "The local terrain is not *ideal*, but it is a considerable step toward being so. While the rest of you work, I will focus on further terraforming it."

"Terraforming?" Collin Baird frowned. Shaiagrazni sighed.

"Further altering it to our advantage. I intend, by the time the Dark Lord arrives, to fight him with such a wealth of natural advantage as to crush three of his soldiers for each one we sacrifice. That is how House Shaiagrazni does war."

CHAPTER TWENTY-TWO

Collin's new bow was an interesting one. Maintaining it was almost a waste. Its elasticity and strength were sustained in the very same way his own body's were—natural self-repair. An organic thing, almost. With limbs akin to bone and a string seemingly made of tendinous tissue. When Shaiagrazni had first made a gift of it, he'd been hesitant to accept.

For all of a second. Then Collin had remembered the *other* things he'd created, and decided to give it a go. Perhaps unsurprisingly, he wasn't disappointed.

It wasn't just that it could store a ludicrous amount of tension with each draw—though, of course, it was no less than an equal to his steel-limbed original weapon in that respect. It was that it possessed a muscular strength of its own to add on to Collin's, making itself known both in the drawing and loosing of every arrow.

He put another of those arrows in the air, and watched it thud into its target. A post, solid steel, inches thick in every direction. Collin had marked the shaft of his weapon to track its depth in increments of quarter inches, and was pleased to see another one added to the average from his last weapon.

A small difference, perhaps, but he'd take all the advantages he could. The world seemed to be throwing him into a deadlier fight with each new one he entered, and Collin had no interest in finding himself rotting under the sun for want of a decent arm.

"Have a spare minute, my boy?"

Collin froze, then turned. He'd already recognized king Galukar, of course, by voice alone. His ranger's ears could have picked out as much from a quarter mile over the sound of howling winds and trebuchet impacts. It was the tone of the king's voice that sent a shiver down his spine.

He sounded *friendly.*

"What for?" Collin asked, careful not to speak in any way that might invite further socialization. The king seemed oblivious to his efforts, however, merely smiling at him the way an uncle might. Not that Collin had any uncles. They'd all died as children when people like King Galukar starved them.

"About what's going on," the king replied. "And what we're headed toward. Current events are rather . . . dangerous. For all of us—even for me. And you in particular have seen your fair share of battle already, haven't you? Why, I'd wager you've fought more at this age than I had by the time I was a decade older."

Collin wasn't one to turn down praise, but that didn't feel like what this was. The king sounded . . . *sad.* Regretful even.

"That's not strange for a Kaltan," Collin replied evenly. "Only difference is I went into it personally trained by Finlay Baird. Plenty of others have fought just as hard, and with a much harder start."

It was all true, and important to say. For all his talk of revolution and exploitation, Collin was under no illusions that his father hadn't paved a nice and easy way for him. He hadn't lived half as hard a life as the original Baird, let alone the other kids benefiting from his rule in place of the aristocracy's.

"And yet that changes nothing. You're still a young man. Still new to the life you risk so constantly" was Galukar's response. "You stand close to death, and closer each time you face down a new one, yet you have not even fathered a son of your own to carry on your family's name."

Collin couldn't think of a seamless way to end the conversation without sparking up yet more friction later, but by God did he give it a fucking try.

"I think I have bigger things to worry about at the moment," he noted. "We all do."

Galukar laughed.

"Oh, is that so? And yet I've seen you worrying about it plenty, eh?"

Dear fucking God.

"The princess Ado," he continued. "She's been catching your eye quite a lot, eh?"

Maybe if he just dived through the wall he could be out of visual distance before the king started sprinting after him.

"I can't blame you, my boy. She's a fine young woman. Healthy, of good blood, and with excellent breeding hips."

That, it seemed, was the limit. Collin stood up, clutched his bow tight enough to crush a weaker weapon, and started marching away. "I need to practice," he barked, a fairly truthful statement all things considered. He did need to shoot something.

Sphera found King Galukar apparently in the middle of terrorizing Collin Baird, albeit accidentally. She waited for their conversation to conclude, then closed in to speak with the giant oaf as the younger man scrambled away like a rat fleeing fire.

The king turned to meet her approach with his gaze, then his lip curled at the sight of her. Sphera paid it no heed. His lip tended to do that when he saw anything not strictly confined within the bounds of his rather mundane worldview.

"Necromancer," he greeted her, though really it was conveyed as more of an angry *slur*. Sphera met his fire with her own ice, finding that the most appropriate response in most such situations.

"King Galukar." She smiled, bowing the exact minimum amount she reasoned would be needed to convey a level of respect he would find pleasing. "It appears we are to work with each other for this next mission. I know we have our differences, particularly regarding that rather unfortunate incident with your sons, but I hope we can put them aside for the greater good."

She would not allow this grunting barbarian to sabotage things for her, that much was for sure. Sphera did not know even one-tenth—even one-hundredth—of all there was to learn about House Shaiagrazni. But she knew that it operated unlike any noble family she'd ever heard of elsewhere. If she excelled, if she did well enough, she would leave her position of mere retainer behind and join her master as . . .

Wife? No, certainly not with him. Sphera had learned that the hard way. Cousin, or sister, something akin to that. The particulars of their familial organization and relations were still lost on her, but in any case to become a named of House Shaiagrazni was to become an ostensive peer to Silenos himself.

Sphera would burn the world for that. She would burn it a thousand times over.

And of course she kept such things carefully to herself, for people like King Galukar so rarely tended to understand the glorious nature of grand ambition. If nothing else, he seemed to be considering her offer rather more weightily than she might have expected. Could she truly get through to him?

Galukar punched her. Sphera didn't see it happen; she didn't even really feel it in the moment of impact. Just knew she had been punched by the rushing wind in her ears and the throbbing ache in her skull. She flew back hard enough to smash into a keratin-woven wall, bouncing hard off the surface and landing in a heap.

Her body had been reworked by Master Shaiagrazni for resilience and sturdiness, and as such she now possessed skin able to withstand arrows, viscera with the toughness of hard stone, and bones many times stronger than steel.

That she felt such racking, convulsive pain after a single strike from King Galukar was a testament to the man's strength. Had she received such a blow prior to her reconstruction, Sphera had no doubt she would have been more than killed. She would have been obliterated.

"I will tell you two things, necromancer," King Galukar growled, striding over to stare down at her where she lay and gasped. "The first is that we have a long trek ahead. A very long one, so prepare your forces for such a march across relatively even, but occasionally hilled and silt clotted, terrain."

Sphera groaned. The pain was coming now. All at once, like a floodgate had broken in her mind. Everything hurt. *Everything.*

"The second," Galukar continued, heedless of her torment, "is that the blow you felt just now was not close to the limits of my strength. I held back to keep from permanently injuring a useful ally."

And with that, he walked away. Sphera took some time more to get back up, even after he was long gone.

She really did fucking hate Arbitans.

"This isn't fair," Folami growled, pacing around his quarters in the command center while Ado let herself remain rather less restlessly seated in one of its chairs.

It really wasn't a bad set of rooms, she had to say. Nothing compared to hers, of course, nor any of the living spaces afforded Shaiagrazni's highest-ranked retainers. Still, for a man yet to actually contribute anything to their work, her brother was living remarkably comfortably.

He should have been grateful. Grateful for the luxury, and more grateful still for the damned opportunity to prove himself worth something. Instead, he tantrummed.

"I am the king's eldest!" he snapped. "Me! I was raised for this, bred for this. It's my destiny. How can this Shaiagrazni imbecile just hand everything that's rightfully mine off to *you*? You've never even wanted the fucking throne."

As a matter of fact, Ado *had*. But she'd learned not to expect any actual acknowledgment from men of . . . Well, really any thoughts or feelings another might have. Particularly kings and their children. Life spent constantly thinking about a crown and what to do when it's *handed* your way tended to make one somewhat aloof when it came to dealing with normal people.

"It's not right!" Folami declared. "Nor bloody proper, you hear? Not at all!"

God, had he always sounded like this? Ado remembered a time when Folami's fury had been a thing to fear, right alongside her father's. Now . . . it was just pathetic. The impotent, mewling squawks of a tiny little boy whinging that a game was unfair once he finally started losing. How had she ever felt awed by *this*?

Lack of experience, obviously, she reminded herself. It was remarkable how fragile the authority of a crown felt when one saw a man create things with body weights measured in multiples of elephants. Silenos Shaiagrazni had been wrong about one thing: All forms of power were tertiary to the power of "can" or "cannot."

"Silenos will find a great purpose for you," Ado reassured him because that was what one did with children. Handle them gently and carefully so they didn't start squealing like stuck pigs all over again. In this case, it seemed, she had misjudged Folami's emotional resilience. The squealing started anyway.

"Easy for you to say!" he snapped. "I've been made your general. Your fucking general, a woman's!"

Ado felt her patience rapidly slipping away. Speaking to Folami was an exercise in recollection, and not anything that she'd have wanted to see swimming in front of her memory again.

"Instead of complaining about what you don't have, why not focus on trying to get it?" she asked, modifying one of their father's old quotes. As expected, Folami actually paused to consider that. Because if there was one thing capable of getting through to her brothers, Ado knew, it was a big old cock and balls dangling off whoever's words they were hearing. Imbeciles.

"What are you suggesting?" He frowned.

"I am suggesting that Silenos Shaiagrazni declares himself a man who cares only of merit, yes? Well show him yours. Show the world, for that matter."

Folami spat.

"You're far too trusting, sister. Think, would you? Why am I not already in my proper station as king?"

CHAPTER TWENTY-THREE

Y *ou are not in your "proper" station as king because you are a petty, childish, entitled fool who wouldn't know where to put a crown if it contained arrows and words reading, "Scalp goes here" around the edge. The only reason you are even a general is because Shaiagrazni was forced to acknowledge that your arbitrarily assigned title of birth gives you political weight, and by extension your subordinates, which does not exist for lower-born individuals whom he may promote to the same position. You are situationally useful for this single task, and once that has passed you will be put back where you belong. At the bottom of the fucking pile, you stupid, drooling cunt.*

She did not say any of that, of course, because telling powerful men the truth was somewhere between pissing on their shoes and kicking them in the groin on the list of things likely to elicit a positive reaction. Instead, Ado smiled soothingly.

"I don't know, brother, why don't you tell me?"

"I will tell you!" Folami snapped. "Because he has a bias against royalty, that's why. This damned wizard is nothing but a jumped-up commoner taking his resentments out on innocent people and stamping on primogeniture."

Ado did not tell him that, according to primogeniture, she would have been monarch before him anyway as the elder. That would have been telling a moderately powerful man the truth, after all, and the feelings of powerful men had to be handled carefully, like tiny little baby hummingbirds.

"Then prove him wrong, brother," she soothed. "Prove him wrong."

Hexeri steeled herself, as she had found increasing cause to do in recent times. Questioning her sire was always an exercise in . . . will. She would have had it no other way, of course, for only a creature as innately masterful of the vampiric glamor could so wholly deserve her fealty. Still, it made for inconvenient conversations. Bad enough to keep her focus just looking at Lilia, bad enough already by far.

The vampire queen was keeping to her own quarters, for now, and Hexeri took another moment to appreciate the remarkable fact of their very existence as she made her way down into them.

Silenos Shaiagrazni had not been given long to set them out; Hexeri knew that much. And he had started, as he started most things, with his grotesqueries.

She shuddered at the memory of them. These ones had been strange, half formed, she thought, and elongated in their bodies. Like giant warped snakes. Squatter, stronger, capable of tearing apart tons of earth with each passing moment and ripping open great furrows in the ground. It had taken them only half an afternoon to excavate the tunnel systems that would become her kind's sanctuary.

Of course, Shaiagrazni himself had made sure to reinforce the caverns as they were made. In his words, the very thought of a collapse offended his sensibilities.

It was this handiwork Hexeri strode past now. Hasty, she thought, but not hurried. Casual, but not lazy. She saw the support beams that had been first placed, and around them were the encasing layers of mineral structure. Fascinating things, those. Shaiagrazni had been persuaded to explain the mechanism by which his organic constructs could remain intact and whole while placed underground—where so many other things decayed with frightful speed.

He'd cheated, of course. Tweaking their biology to do a number of things she hadn't the knowledge to truly grasp, all of which culminated in . . . something. A new form of life, too small to see, that lived atop the surface of their catacombs' very building material and ate the minute organisms responsible for rot itself.

So far, the structure was too young to test the limits of its apparent imperviousness. But Hexeri was already impressed enough by its scale. She followed the winding pathways, heading down low, lower. The rooms were lit by strange, glowing growths from the walls. Bioluminescence, Shaiagrazni had called it. Yet another thing Hexeri couldn't hope to comprehend, and once more it was used for petty convenience. The stable glow of exotic organoids was more than enough for her undead eyes to make out every detail of her surroundings.

Walls, smooth and perfected. Thick keratin—added to the list of unknowns—protected them with sufficient volume to withstand siege weaponry, even if all the surrounding dirt were excavated to permit direct fire. The floors were similarly reinforced, and the ceiling, Hexeri had been reliably informed, would have withstood the entirety of Arbite suddenly materializing atop the dirt over their heads.

All of it was made of the same strange, half-bone-half-else substance Shaiagrazni made most of his armored materials from. Though different. It lacked the dark coloration that betrayed his most careful work. Hexeri had been sure to watch out for that. Were Shaiagrazni capable or inclined to wrap all his creations in material of that quality, they would have beaten the Dark Lord already. She imagined it took more time for him to make. A worthwhile hint.

But Hexeri was not left simply considering the limits of her ally for long. She soon reached her destination. One great, towering door with one great being on the other side. She did not even need to knock. Her sire felt her presence through the blood.

For her part, Lilia did not even need to instruct that she enter. Hexeri felt the command faster than any sound could have carried it to her and obeyed without the slightest hesitation. She stepped inside.

Silenos Shaiagrazni did not care much for indulgence or waste, which meant that it had probably been Lilia herself who had managed to secure such large accommodations.

It was no less than she deserved, of course, but Hexeri still felt a stab of disbelief at the sight. A dozen yards from one side to the other, and even deeper than it was wide, the chamber was lit by a *chandelier* repulsively grown like some natural protuberance of bone and generously covered with cultivated tissues displaying the bioluminescent effect Shaiagrazni described with a considerable intensity. They illuminated a chamber already filled with some of Lilia's possessions, but not all.

Hexeri suspected further renovation would come, eventually, or else her sire's faculties of research and development would be heavily limited during their stay in the war camps. However temporary that proved to be.

"My child." Her sire smiled, lighting up the room more completely than the growths within its chandelier, and fully obliterating any thought straight out of Hexeri's head for a moment.

Without hesitation, she dropped down to her knees, waiting for Lilia to gesture that she come closer. Fortunately, she did so quickly. Hexeri was soon mere inches from the Ancient and felt the comforting touch of her hand at the back of her head. So strange, that, always. To exist as a vampire was to exist in a world made for weaker, more fragile things. Stone was like dried mud, wood delicate paper, and even steel offered no more resistance to beings of their strength than did thick leather previously.

Hexeri, as an Elder, felt all of that and more. But now, with Lilia's hand resting on her, she was the fragile one. She was the delicate thing to be handled carefully. How much exertion would her sire need to crush the very skull she now caressed?

It was a morbid thing to consider, but so close a proximity to so great a power demanded such consideration. Fortunately, the ancient soon distracted Hexeri from it once more by speaking.

"You have come to me with concerns," Lilia noted. She spoke as she usually did, not *asking* so much as telling. In Hexeri, she had seen questions and uncertainty. In that much, she had been right.

"I have," Hexeri admitted, motivated in her truthfulness more by loyalty than practicality. Though she doubted any lie from her lips would have fooled the ancient to begin with.

"Then speak them. We are now settled, and there can be little done until night in any case. We have a few hours. I would spend them with you."

As always, the flutter of delight left Hexeri briefly speechless.

Briefly. She would never have been much use to her sire without the ability to actually formulate a sentence in her presence.

"It is about the caster Shaiagrazni," she replied. "I . . . I am uncertain of our alliance with him."

Lilia moved at that, drifting over to her throne and taking a seat. It was a large thing, carved of black bone extracted from a long-slain dragon, with its base specifically made to permit seating for its owner's numerous progeny. Hexeri followed her to it eagerly.

"You think he will turn against us?" Lilia asked, poignant as ever.

The question didn't leave much necessity for elaboration, so Hexeri just nodded. Her sire sighed. Apparently Hexeri was irritating her.

"I understand," she told her, and Hexeri looked up. Lilia's eyes were on her, and they were . . . sad. Regretful, even, but not uncomprehending. As she had come to expect, she truly did feel her sire's understanding. Just that alone was enough to melt back the ice of her worries, somewhat.

"You have suffered from the humans as few among our kind have," Lilia continued. "And you are still young. I understand that you are hesitant to trust any of them."

It still felt strange to be called young by anyone but Lilia. Hexeri supposed that was only to be expected. Her two centuries had been long and hard lived, but by the end of them, her sire was only one-tenth older than she had been at the beginning. The difference between them was one of ages.

And so she listened, carefully, like always. To miss even a single thing from Lilia's lips was to watch a precious treasure pass her by. Hexeri sometimes wondered how many vampires were denied their eternities by the simple failure to heed wisdom from one who had lived through more of it than almost any other.

"But Silenos Shaiagrazni is not like most of their kind. He's scarcely even *human* at all, I would say. His mind has been warped, partly through culture, partly through fleshcrafting. He will work with us for as long as he sees a benefit to doing so, and given our powers, I imagine he will never not see a benefit. The only thing that would change this is if we were to begin acting against him."

Hexeri did not miss that her sire had made a warning of that last remark, lowering her gaze and nodding. It was a fair point in any case.

"If you're sure," she replied. "Then I'll heed your advice."

"I am sure." Lilia smiled, patting her head. "And I appreciate your concern for me, my dear, but I will not end like your family."

It was a punch to the gut and a reassuring caress all at once. Hexeri spent one long moment recalling the scent of burning flesh, then nodded.

Lilia would *not* end up like her family, not if all the armies in all the world assembled to try to make it happen. She'd existed for two millennia in spite of humanity's best efforts. If they had it in them to put an end to her, they'd have managed it long ago.

"Thank you," she whispered and leaned into her sire's embrace as she gently pulled her face closer against her.

"Always," Lilia replied.

Hexeri was gone soon to seek out her job. The day was still burning outside, sun doing its best to engulf her in the foul light and strip away flesh and bone alike, but its vicious rays could not penetrate the opacity of Shaiagrazni's command center. In that regard, Hexeri was at least pleased to be working with him for the time being. Even Lilia could not assemble so expansive a shelter able to stave off the light, not as quickly as their new master at least.

Its size made finding Collin Baird somewhat tedious, but she managed it with only a brief delay in any case. He was easily tracked by scent. Hexeri had rarely ever encountered such a distilled hatred in any human as pumped through that man's blood.

"You're awfully lax," she noted as she came up behind him. "You know the last man who kept me waiting I drank dry."

Baird didn't even look at her, nor did she hear any circulatory jumps that might have indicated he'd been in any way surprised by her appearance. He simply replied.

"If you want to get a belly full of iron dust, then by all means, go ahead. That's all you'll get from my family's blood though."

He looked up then, meeting her eye. They both broke out into smiles at once.

"Ready to go?" she asked.

"I've been waiting on you." He grunted, getting to his feet. They set off together shortly.

CHAPTER TWENTY-FOUR

One day, Ado would grow accustomed to the visceral acceleration of Shaiagrazni's new carriages.

That day certainly had not been yesterday, nor did she think it would be any day soon. Every fluid in her body seemed eager to escape at the rush of movement assailing her. A phantom sensation, she knew. As Shaiagrazni had so kindly explained when asked for a less fearsome vehicle, he had precisely measured the acceleration to leave it well short of dangerous levels, and any sustained pressure or weight Ado thought she experienced was no more than a result of fear and uncertainty manifesting as false feeling.

As usual, she found a complete lack of comfort in the caster's reassurance. Probably that was his design. Silenos Shaiagrazni was not one to mince words or coddle a person.

Any person, for that matter, Ado realized. Man or woman. She wasn't some delicate child to be cradled and cared for in his eyes, just a person. A resource, with boons and flaws, uses and failings. To be assessed, employed, and if without further utility, discarded all without a moment's thought.

She steeled herself, opened her eyes, and sat forward in her seat. The sickness was still there, but Ado pushed it down, ignored the feelings.

"Wretched thing," Folami breathed, hand tight around the armrest beside him. "Dark magic, unnatural. What sort of madman would ever devise such a monstrous creature as this?" Ado found some measure of satisfaction at that. She tried not to think of how much worse she'd handled the construct during some of her earlier trips within one.

Unfortunately for both her and her brother, the nation of Wudra was not the short journey she'd grown accustomed to taking. That meant an opportunity to practice steeling her belly against the casual torments of inertia and angled turns, with precious little good but that.

The Whispering Hills themselves were not so hard to reach, but infuriatingly tedious to pass through. Lots of turns, curvature in the roads, dips in altitude, or towering heights on paths not designed for their speed.

They did not quite go so far as to tumble off the edges, but on more than one occasion Ado swore—despite Shaiagrazni's assurance that his creation possessed the innate sense to keep itself steady—that she was about to personally test the limits of its speed against the grip of gravity. Fortunately she was not left to fixate over their tenuous proximity to the pathway's ledges for long.

Soon enough, the city of Wudra came into view on the horizon. Ado was careful to get a good, long look at it. As much for the weight of its reputation as any practical advantage she thought might come her way from doing so.

Wudra was not the largest city Ado had ever seen, not in gross terms of area at least, but it held a considerable density of architecture between its outer walls. It seemed to have endeavored to fit the largest sum of humans physically possible within itself, and done a fine job of testing those limits.

At its center was the customary spire common to all truly holy cities of the faith, a spear cutting up through the ground and reaching high to demonstrate the distance between heaven and earth. Around it were the largest structures, homes for the clergy or aristocracy, and of course, the city's main palace.

The martial centers came next, and they were no less impressive in scale. If less luxuriously decorated and aesthetically considered.

Within the place, multicolored stones seemed to have been the common inspiration, and as Ado grew closer to the city she was struck by its scent. Human life, hitting her like a riptide.

Unthinking, she sent a glance toward Folami and found that her brother was staring at the place even more awestruck than her.

"This, sister, is a heartland," he whispered. "Do you think your dark caster could ever achieve such splendor as this?"

As a matter of fact, Ado was entirely certain he could. She'd heard of how Silenos Shaiagrazni had coated the entirety of Kaltan's great wall in bone, with only a few hurried days to work. It was simple prioritization and practicality that held him from creating such a towering structure.

For now.

Their vehicle slowed as they approached Wudra, for good reason. The pedestrians among the city would not have reacted well to an object so foreign and fast tearing through its streets, surely interpreting it as a threat, perhaps even as an attack. Nonetheless, they were notably swifter than a carriage as they entered through the towering gates and headed for the spire and mansions at its heart.

Through the window, Ado saw glimpses of the many faces turned their way. Some were tight with fear, confusion, others hate and revulsion. She supposed it would have been stupid to expect anything else.

Up close, the spire itself was more intimidating by far. For several reasons. Ado felt the prick of its presence against her arms, the hairs standing up on end where they sensed its static power. She swallowed, mouth dry, throat tight.

Of course, she had grown up on the tales. Everyone had. The slivers of divinity, wreaked from the stuff of primal magic itself and buried in the dirt by the first men. She saw no great mystery in its form. From her new proximity Ado could clearly make out the wrought iron for what it was. Dark and jagged, clumsily worked and crudely twisted.

But in spite of that, she knew it was a thing beyond anything modernity could muster. The Godblade, stretched a thousand feet high and a score of yards wide. It was a wonder the unholy magic of her carriage didn't combust on the spot.

"It's wonderful," Folami whispered, stepping out of the carriage beside her. Ado didn't reply. She wasn't sure whether it was wonderful. Great, certainly. And perhaps terrible. Wonder though felt an alien emotion these days. Was it so impressive a creation as Silenos Shaiagrazni's? No. Did it have even half the utility? Unquestionably not.

But there *was* something there. Something eerie and foreboding. It sent an icy finger running down her spine as Ado tried to articulate what it was. Something told her that she may well have been better without any specifics. Knowledge was power, her mother had said, and power was everything.

This though felt like the exception.

Fortunately, not everything around Ado was as confounding as the spire. She soon found her way to the palace of the city, announcing herself at its doorstep, and patiently awaiting the residents to make note of her presence. She was rather unsure what sort of reception she might receive.

An answer was quick in coming, as they were ushered inside with only minutes of delay. The interior might have impressed her once, for the finery of the church was more than any royal might have afforded with a mere nation's wealth. Ado had acquired a more pragmatic sense of taste, however, and found herself assessing the place only through eyes keyed toward utility.

Mostly, it was paladins they passed by. That made Ado feel comfortable, despite herself. Secure. The paladins had ever been an order more trustworthy than . . . well, any other. Certainly more so than her own family. And it helped that they cut impressive figures. Those who were not wrapped in plate armor of masterwork articulation and craftsmanship only made it easier to see their bodies, and each one was a vascular idol to the god of physical prowess. Watching them move was like seeing predatory cats stalking through undergrowth.

Ado's sense of security was befouled, however, by seeing the distrust, disdain, and dislike evident in so many of their eyes.

"They're glaring at us," Folami snapped, voice fortunately low. He had the sense not to advertise his petulance among the *paladins*, at least. "See now what comes of your association with that *animal*?"

Ado certainly saw a common closed-mindedness in them that she recalled from herself not too long ago. It was difficult sometimes to remember that she'd known Shaiagrazni for only a few short months. So much had changed, and not all of it had been external to her.

But that made it no less frustrating to see. Why shouldn't she have worked for him? Months she'd watched him use his dark magic, and it had only ever been for the betterment of their cause. She raised her chin, meeting the paladins with defiance, daring them to disapprove.

She wouldn't be judged by their kind, not anymore.

Finally, Ado was ushered into the throne room, or temple crux, or whatever the place was called. She found herself far less eager to internalize the terminology than she might once have been. It was a nonetheless grand room, large enough, she thought, that fifty men might have paraded inside with room to spare. Its ceiling sat atop thick stone pillars, painted and ornate with scenes of scriptural import, while its walls were decorated with long-hoarded relics and trinkets of sacred significance.

At the end sat the most important men in Wudra. They *were* men, of course. The king and the high priest, twin spheres of authority over which all else hung.

The former was a short man, and old. Of course he was old. His hair was gray, thinning, mustache prominent and carefully styled, chin and jaw shaved bare. He had cold eyes, scrutinous where they landed upon Ado. It seemed to her that he was trying to take her measure. She let him. At worst, he would learn something of her. There was always an advantage to frightened enemies.

On the other hand, she could not imagine gaining much of one from the high priest. He was fatter than the king, but younger, and bald as a baby with seemingly no grooming needed. His pudgy face contained a pair of small eyes, and his nostrils flared as he beheld her. Anger, Ado thought. A fascinating thing to see in one she'd exchanged not even a word with.

"Good afternoon," she began with a smile. It would disarm them, or anger them, or in any case tell her something about them, and that was always an advantage. "I have come on the behalf of Silenos Shaiagrazni, and I bring with me an offer of alliance against the Dark Lord and his forces. I have no doubt the both of you have heard of his approach across this region—albeit far from the Whispering Hills—and are wondering what might be done to curtail his next moves. Well, my lord is planning to do just that. In order to best heighten his chances, he requests your aid to bolster a force against the Dark Lord capable of sundering his army."

It was a temptation to prattle on, explain the costs and rewards, but Ado made herself stop. To speak too much would only convey weakness, and right now she needed them to see strength.

But they did not seem to, nor even did they appear to see *her* at all. Both sets of eyes flickered without a moment's pause to the guards lining the room's walls. The king's voice rang out, booming and acidic.

"Arrest this woman," he declared. "She has openly confessed to colluding with practitioners of the dark arts. I will not sully these halls by suffering her to stand free within them for a single moment more."

CHAPTER TWENTY-FIVE

It was interesting, traveling with Collin Baird. Interesting for several reasons.

He was not immune to fatigue. Hexeri knew that much. He may have appeared mechanical and tireless to *humans*, but her senses were advanced beyond such shortcomings. Even with his face still and his breathing forcibly steady, she could hear the pounding of his heart as it widened capillaries and pressurized arteries to compensate for the prolonged demands of his body. The men around him—rangers, all of them—were louder by far.

In this, they were all as fragile as normal humans. Vigor did much for the raw, explosive prowess of a creature, but it could never match the tirelessness of an undead body.

And yet they persisted.

Hexeri had seen some humans with a measure of the discipline on display now, but not many. They were rare, and all noteworthy. Stories told of King Galukar scything apart castle walls and grinning as bodkin-tipped arrows bounced harmlessly from his skin. They *should* have told, instead, of the sergeants responsible for rendering men like this from raw recruits.

In her experience, discipline was ten times the equal of strength. It was that, above all else, that made her kind so desperate in their fight for survival.

"Getting hungry?" Baird asked, snapping her from her thoughts with the abrupt question. "Or do you just find the sound of my heartbeat particularly satisfying?"

Hexeri grinned.

Always alert too. That was the thing Baird had that his men didn't, though all of them were cognizant of threats and ever ready to move if one came. It was that natural, perpetual, slightly paranoid awareness that truly made her feel a kinship with the man. Because that wasn't something native to those without vampiric blood in their veins.

It was something learned by those hunted for who or what they were. Neither of them needed to exchange a word to see that much in the other.

"Not at all," Hexeri replied, knowing full well that Baird was among the few quick enough to notice the minute fraction of a second her pause had already lasted. "I just find it quite amusing watching you pant away as we go, like seeing a child try to march uphill. Not used to walking this long?"

A few scowls and a few more choice words flew her way at that, and Hexeri smiled. Uphill, certainly, was a way to describe the near-sixty-degree angle they now scaled. It was a testament to each man present that he was still sustaining a quicker pace going over the jagged mound of earth than their forces still circling the base.

But it was necessary. Baird had insisted on that much. He wanted sharp eyes propped high in the sky to survey the landscape, and Hexeri found herself in agreement. It was increasingly common, these days, that she concur with him. He made a lot of poignant observations, for a human. She wondered what sort of things his native genius might pick up on with another century to mature in a brain not slowly rotting with each new year.

Hexeri recalled the other humans then, the ones who'd smiled and laughed right up until the burning torches and decapitating cleavers came out. Her grin dropped away to the dirt under her feet, and she crushed it with the latest in a never-ending line of crunching, thudding footfalls.

No, better not to wonder such things. Most human potential, after all, was in the threat they posed. And the less expected, the more severe. They were a weak species, but weaklings could kill if given a moment of relaxation to strike in.

It didn't take more than a few additional minutes to reach the hill's top, despite its height and steepness. Baird remained standing, which Hexeri had expected, but so did his other rangers. She could hear their fatigue, smell the lactic acid in their muscles, and yet they remained vigilant as ever. Perhaps *they* were the undead ones.

"What do you see?" she asked Baird. He glanced at her, surprised.

"You can't see better than me?"

Hexeri felt a stab of irritation at that.

"I can smell adrenaline and hear a heartbeat at twenty paces, but no. I can't see better than a ranger, not one of your caliber."

Not even so late in the evening, and that had been the most irksome realization of all. Hexeri's eyes might be the superior ones in the pitch black of midnight, but even then he'd have the advantage in pinpointing firelight to locate any enemies.

She really did prefer being around ordinary humans, far more satisfying.

Baird took a few moments to scan the area, and so did his other rangers. Soon enough, one of them spoke.

"Over there," he breathed, gesturing to a distant point to the west of them. "See it, boss?"

Baird narrowed his eyes, then shook his head. "No, point it out?"

"The ground," his subordinate clarified. "See that section of it? It's hard to make out, but—"

"Burns." Baird gasped. "Yeah, you're right, and the earth is disturbed, indented. There was a fire there. A big one. I'd make it a yard wide. Sound right, boys?"

"Five feet, I'd say," another cut in, but most agreed.

"So we're dealing with a few dozen, but no more. Otherwise they'd have needed several. Still, fair numbers. Could be a threat depending on what they are."

Hexeri followed their gazes, and *thought* she saw the point being indicated. It was certainly hard enough to make out though, even with her own vampiric sight. Rangers indeed.

"If they need fire, they're living things," she noted. "But if they're with the Dark Lord's forces . . ."

". . . Then they could've had numerous times as many undead around them that simply didn't need other fires built," Baird concluded. "Right."

He was quick in making a decision, as quick as he was in all other things.

"We need to operate on the assumption that we're not alone after all. Rangers, get into threes. I want you all moving ahead and checking the route for snares, sentries, anything else that might fuck us over when the main body runs into it. I doubt this is an army we're dealing with, but for all we know we're about to run into a pack of fomors."

They moved like the components of a carefully lubricated machine, all setting off on their separate paths near wordlessly and disappearing down the slope of the hill.

"Is that wise?" Hexeri asked. "Splitting up?"

Baird shrugged.

"Rangers aren't fighters, not really. We work best from afar, against enemies who don't know they're an enemy. Skirmishers."

"There were only a dozen of you to begin with," she noted. "Why not keep together?"

"Because twelve is a fuck sight easier to spot than three, travels slower, and runs the risk of all our rangers getting wiped out in a single fuckup. We don't have enough to spare for chances like that."

Hexeri understood when it was put like that. Numbers were not something a vampire often had issues with, but when it came to their own elites—the century-old creatures of night able to kill a hundred times their number of mortal men—they were even harder to replace than any human killer.

Besides, even the ability to turn more into their kind didn't make her eager to throw them away. A progeny was more than cannon fodder.

"What are you expecting to find?" Hexeri asked.

Baird hesitated.

"I'm not sure. The Dark Lord's forces aren't subtle, so hopefully we'll have an answer soon."

The two of them made their own way back down the hilltop, reuniting with the larger part of their forces. Conventional soldiers, these, spearmen and the occasional Shaiagraznian grotesquerie. Five thousand Kaltan veterans, bolstered with support and training enough that they could have equaled four times their number of conventional troops. It said a lot about what exactly they were marching toward that Hexeri felt little in the way of comfort from their numbers.

Of course, that wasn't just the Dark Lord's fault. Thousands of humans were good for one thing regarding vampires, historically. Protecting them was not it.

A day passed without any great incident, and the rangers were back by the end of it. All seemed shaken, not mollified, by their lack of any discovery. No snares, no pitfalls, and all the likely positions for enemies like them—those with Vigor put to improving precision and eyesight for long-range shooting—were empty and unused.

Hexeri understood their discontent. If they'd found evidence of some sort of trap, it would show they were fighting enemies who could be seen through. A total lack of that, however, may well have indicated they were the ones who would be confounded.

"Do we abort?" she asked Baird. He snorted at the very idea.

"Fuck no. We don't even know for sure these enemies are still in the region. They could've just headed off into an entirely different direction, for all we know. They . . ." He paused, swallowing. ". . . They could've been *behind* us, and set the fire ahead to distract us by relying on our scouting abilities to take note—"

The arrow hit the ground right by his feet, exploding a great crater of silt and shale out of it, sending fractals of stone to glance off every face in a dozen yards. Everyone present froze, for the arrow had missed their leader's head by inches. Deliberately, Hexeri thought.

"We have you surrounded. Move and you die."

Fortunately, nobody moved because Hexeri recognized the cadence infusing the voice. It wasn't one she was likely to forget.

"Our warriors will reveal themselves now," the dark elf told them. "Once more, remain still. Any movements toward weapons, or of deliberate speed, will be seen as precursors to an attack. We will halt them with lethal force."

Hexeri believed them. That was the way dark elves operated. Efficiently.

Sure enough, dark elf faces began emerging to match the voice. Hexeri scrutinized them for any she might recognize, but found none. It had been a slim chance, in any case. Her last meeting with their kind had been twenty years ago, and scarcely more to her advantage than this one.

They were a tall people, the elves. And the dark elves were no shorter, averaging a height of six feet or more—both men and women—and differentiated in build only by a breadth of shoulder and mass of muscle uncommon to their fairer kin.

All were dark-skinned, thus the name. Some in the way of humans like Princess Ado or her ancestors, others like corpses sometimes were. Gray or desaturated. All had crimson eyes.

It was annoying how often dark elves were mistaken for vampires because they really weren't much alike on the inside. Hexeri could appreciate their more superficial resemblance though. Seeing the elves move, it was hard to compare them to clumsy, blundering humans after spending so long among her own kind.

Theirs was a grace only typically possible among nerves made still by death and muscles precise by coldness. This grace saw quick usage now as blades were pressed to necks, angles of attack covered, bodies woven out among the men closest her.

All to ensure that dozens would, as the elves had said, die the moment any sign of attack was perceived among them.

CHAPTER TWENTY-SIX

Ado was shoved into the room, but without any great violence. Evidently, based on both that and the contents of her cell, her nobility was not being forgotten.

By the force of the push, and the harsh graze of her knees hitting the ground, neither was her association with Shaiagrazni. Ado forced her mind past the pain, which was no great detriment in any case, and hastily got back to her feet. Just in time to stare at her guard unimpeded by bars, for the fraction of a second he still needed to slam the door shut.

"How dare you?!" she snapped. "Do you have any idea who I am?"

The man didn't reply, just turned from the door and shifted to stand somewhere to its side, beyond the scope of her sight. Probably he was too bloody stupid to even *understand* her. It was hardly the rare, brightest minds among the peasantry who found themselves guarding doors, after all.

She caught herself before that particular unproductive spiral could fully ensnare her thoughts. Ado paused, turned forcibly from the door, and began pacing. She was pacing for a while.

Her cell was smaller even than she had initially thought, barely large enough for so much as thirty people to stand without touching within it. Its walls, ceiling, and floor were all diabase, as she might have expected. Magus made and colored like rust with the volume of raw iron naturally within the stone.

With all her magical exertion, she might have gotten through a yard of the stuff, and widened such a penetration as to fit her whole body through within a minute. But Ado had no way of knowing whether that would be all there was to her captivity. For all she knew, the diabase was *two* yards thick, or three, or more. She might have blasted apart a few feet of the stonework only to discover a blockade of pure steel waiting for her beyond.

Ado was not Walriq the wind mage, and she was certainly not Silenos Shaiagrazni. Beyond a scarce few inches, eroding through steel was beyond anything her magic would achieve, and if forced to do so *quickly* under the pressure of assault by prison guards, she doubted even that much was possible for her.

Which was all to say nothing of Ado's chances in actually *escaping* if she did blast through her cell. She didn't know this city's layout, nor where her carriage was located—or even if the barbarians holding her had destroyed it in a fit of zealotry—and she didn't fancy her chances of escaping by foot.

Even a stolen horse, which she *also* didn't know any locations for, would be a poor match for the speed of truly potent Vigor users. If there was anyone in the city with even a third—even a fifth—of King Galukar's prowess, they'd sprint down any mount she might find within minutes.

The more Ado thought, the fewer and more limited her options seemed to be. She supposed that was to be expected for a person finding themselves in a fucking prison.

She sat on her bed, which was lumpy and hard in all the wrong places. She strode around the floor, which was rugged in so thin a carpet that she fancied the floor's chill still hit her bare feet regardless. There were two seats prepared beside a bowl of fruit and breads, which Ado tried to distract herself by consuming. It didn't work. The only consumption happening was her own mind chewing at itself, working over the decisions she'd made, and how they might have been done less disastrously.

But the simple truth was that there really hadn't been much choice in the matter. Certainly keeping her carriage closer by would have been ideal, and insisting on a few guards alongside that might well have let her escape the city. But even that would have been risky, and a great escalation to her current troubles if failure found her regardless.

Ado's thoughts were perhaps a shade self-destructive, and certainly did nothing for her mood, but they at least kept her occupied. The time practically skipped her by before her cell's door creaked open.

She stood, and turned to it, affixing her foulest glare and preparing to make her demands. The plan fell through, however, when her brother entered.

Folami was alone, as far as Ado could tell, and he did not look nearly as petulant or furious as he had previously. Rather, a terrible smugness seemed to have crept over his features and given them a twist that was altogether vaguely familiar, and rather disturbing for it.

"Sister." He beamed, in much the same way a cat might after cornering a mouse. "I'm glad to see you unharmed. I had faith, of course, that God's chosen would not stoop so low as to injure a woman but . . . Well, you've always had an impudent streak, and I feared you might have left them little choice."

It was chilling. Folami had been an ass well after their reversal of roles, but there'd been no *bite* to it. He'd spoken petulantly, not confidently. Even he had known that she was the one with the authority between them.

But not anymore. Now he seemed secure in a way she hadn't seen since . . .

Since before their father met his end.

"What are you doing here?" Ado asked him. Folami replied by rolling his eyes, as if her question were some anticipated annoyance. As if she were a year younger once more, and dealing with little brothers who thought themselves her senior through masculinity alone.

"I am telling my sister that I've solved all her problems." Folami sighed, taking a seat without asking. "You have nothing to worry about, Ado. It's all well. I've spoken with the king, and the high priest, and I've coordinated a deal for you. All will be forgiven as long as you do what you *ought* to have done from the start, and simply renounce Shaiagrazni. Let the world see this little tryst for what it is—a momentary surrender to female weakness and insecurity."

"Female weakness?" Ado echoed.

It had been so long, really, since she'd heard anything like that. At least from a man she was under the power of. Oh, chauvinism had been far from uncommon within her duties as Shaiagrazni's diplomat, but being *controlled* by the chauvinists?

Her blood boiled.

"Undo it," she snapped. "You had no right to make this deal. Now reverse it this instant."

Folami smiled, as if he were amused by her antics. It was all Ado could do not to march across the room and punch him then and there.

"I am afraid, my sister, that you are not the one in control here." He sighed. "The authority of the true king is recognized in this land, you see. Not some jumped-up princess. A *king*."

Ado's heart felt like it had frozen in her chest. Even Shaiagrazni hadn't called her queen, and she was fairly certain as to why. Trust. Or lack thereof. He needed her under his power, needed her dismissable, if need be, from her own nation's authority. And so she was only a princess.

It was something she understood, and something she would surely have done herself—had she thought of it. But now she was seeing it spit back in her face, and it was boiling acid coming from the lips of a man like Folami.

"Get out," she whispered, and her brother sighed—again—and stood. He made his way to the door.

"Very well, sister. If you want."

Galukar was a good tactician. He ought to be, after so many decades of tactics. There was no native brilliance to let him intuit the complexities of battle— let alone warfare—the way the keenest minds might, but he had, through sheer weight of experience and time, become a cut above most.

And as far as he could tell, they were doing rather well. Granted, he could not tell very far. His weight of experience was of limited applicability when it came to fighting alongside undead, flesh abominations, and whatever else Shaiagrazni had stuffed into their army.

The Kaltans though were well within his scope. And they impressed.

"I'm not a commander," the necromancer breathed, glancing uncertainly at Galukar.

He arched an eyebrow.

"Your magic lets you summon undead to fight for you, and you're not a commander?"

"No," she snapped. "I'm not a commander, and trying to fix that, will you explain what's going on?"

If Galukar wasn't mistaken, the necromancer seemed to have gotten rather combative since their last conversation. He tried to recall anything he might have done to anger her, but focused majorly upon her request.

"Over there," he pointed, gesturing to a hilltop. "You see those Kaltans?"

Three thousand in all, a formation of considerable size. Sheer numbers forced the shield wall to a width great enough to engulf most of the terrain upon which it sat, and they held it admirably. A great wooden porcupine, bristles of steel quivering where they poked out from the oaken hide.

Shield walls, an unpopular formation. Beloved in Kaltan. Galukar had learned that they had advantages of numerous kinds. The obvious, of course. Ten men in such a structure could crush fifteen, twenty, even more attacking in many others. Mobility was limited, but he'd often found a strong back leg was more important than a swift front in battle anyway, and there was a certain magic to the mental effect it had on a man's courage.

But he had only understood the second, more terrible use upon observing it executed by the Kaltans. It was something to take full advantage of their rangers.

With Kaltan shield walls, constructed of well-carved wood and carefully banded iron, there was very little penetrating them. Heavy axes, perhaps, with a bit of luck, but they were damned sturdy things to be removed. Invariably, the enemy would turn to Vigor. They would send in their elites, whatever those were. Just as the Dark Lord's army was doing now.

Just as the handful of rangers still with them had been waiting for. They opened fire, ideal targets all conveniently bunched together well below the crest of their perch—a second hill higher than the one holding the shield wall.

It was no more than a vanguard, this force of the Dark Lord's. Galukar knew the enemy's strength would grow by the day as yet more of their landscape-burying army arrived to water the battlefield in blood. That first volley though set the pace.

Where plate armor was not defeated entirely, it was bypassed as bodkins slipped through gaps and chewed through mail. Spines, arteries, vital organs all surrendered to the skewering barrage and sent convulsive bodies dropping down to the dirt. Not undead, these elites, which was surprising, but a boon, nonetheless.

An undead didn't care how much steel was in its liver.

"We're doing well," Galukar decided, at last. "The enemy is trying to hurry this, which is their mistake. We're well dug in, and our flanks—our sides—are covered by natural defenses. Currently, the real struggle is that hill." He nodded to where the shield wall was still being battered, noting with surprise and satisfaction that even still, it held.

"What's special about it?" The necromancer frowned.

"Essentially, that's the strongest defensive position for miles. Currently we have it lightly held to lure enemy elites into ranger fire, but as the Dark Lord's forces arrive in full, I intend to move forward and bolster it and the surrounding area more fully."

It was a risky strategy, but Galukar needed an engagement. If the Dark Lord knew the full extent of his forces, he might send his own around them, while a small fraction merely engaged Galukar to keep him from distracting. All it would take was the enemy getting ahead, then all was lost. They could not outmarch an army of near-exclusively undead.

That risk, however, seemed to be paying off. The tide of bodies was growing rather than shrinking, far horizon turning dark with the shadow of marching men and monsters, all headed for Galukar's position.

He stood now at the head of the greatest army he had ever personally commanded. But it was a small thing indeed next to the Dark Lord's innumerable hordes.

"Numbers can be misleading," the necromancer noted, apparently seeing his concern. "Each of my master's grotesqueries will kill a score, a hundred—even a thousand. I'd say we're evenly matched."

It was, he decided, something she was saying for her own benefit rather than his. But Galukar had to admit there was a certain weight to the assurance.

He turned back. The Dark Lord's forces were fanning out, forced to widen their assemblies simply to close in with any real speed. Their numbers were working against them, for this left some men higher elevated than those in the same formation. It loosened them, leaving them all a softer target for the more tight, compressed Shaiagraznian ranks.

As he might have expected, the blood was flowing in rivers when they finally met en masse.

Arrows came down, bolts joining from crossbow fire. They thudded into shields, softening the enemy approach as they marched uphill before shield finally met shield. Ground was given, victory scrambled for. It looked to Galukar that it was well within reach.

Then the cries of horror rang out, and Galukar raised his eyes to see the skies themselves rendered apart.

CHAPTER TWENTY-SEVEN

In hindsight, it really, really had been impulsive to smash his ship into the side of that fortress. Swick had *almost* known it at the time, however deep his drunken rampage had been, and every passing day after the incident only made it more overwhelmingly apparent to him just how great an error he'd made.

Skyships were a technology beyond virtually anything else. Few could repair one, and virtually none could build a new one from scratch. Shaiagrazni had seemed to consider them primitive things.

Well screw him, because apparently he *needed* this piece of primitive technology. Swick just had to get it off the ground again.

"Your thrust is fine," the engineer told him calmly. "Better than fine, actually. Whoever worked on it last did a good job. But there's something off still."

"I know there's something off still," Swick snapped. When he'd tried to last take the ship off the ground, it had worked. For all of a second. Then the poor thing had started rocking, shivering, shaking. It had been all he'd been capable of just to plant it back down before it shot off in one direction and rammed another fucking building.

And he still didn't know why. Thus the engineer.

"I think it's with the vectoring," the man continued, apparently heedless of Swick's irritation. He was a tall man, taller even than Swick, and kept his face concealed behind one of those masked cowls so popular in the east. Nonetheless, the occasional flash of bronze skin was easily visible beneath the fabric.

"Vectoring?" Swick asked. The engineer sighed, but subtly. It was nice of him to hide his irritation at being forced to speak with a mere plebian, really.

"The, uh, aim, direction. For the thrust, I mean. Normal skyships automatically compensate for that in the air. They'd have to, or else they'd just start barrel-rolling after takeoff. Yours though doesn't seem to be capable of it."

Which, Swick realized, explained why it had almost started barrel-rolling after takeoff. Interesting.

"So fix it," he suggested. Another sigh.

"Do you know how to set something up so that it not only pushes off against a mobile mass like the air, but also compensates for that same mass *moving* in response to being pushed, as well as any tiny, sudden changes in direction caused by the wind hitting it from either side?"

Swick did give it a thought, as best as he could manage, before confidently giving his answer.

"No."

"That's a coincidence." The engineer grunted. "Because I don't either. As far as I know, basically nobody does. Which is a big part of why we can't make skyships anymore. You might've thought about that before breaking yours."

Had an edge to him, this one, but Swick didn't mind that so much. Years among pirates tended to leave a man inoculated against most forms of misanthropy, and this case was paired with a fairly promising level of actual practical understanding. There was very little he wouldn't forgive in exchange for that of all traits.

"Can you work it out?" he asked, made optimistic by the fact that the engineer hadn't just up and fucked off. As Swick might have hoped, the man paused rather than shooting down the notion out of hand.

"Probably," he decided, with no small touch of pride in his voice. Oddly high voice, Swick realized. There was a definite edge of aristocracy to it too. "But it'll take some doing."

"Then do it." Swick grinned, stepping back and deciding to watch the man at work. With a bit of luck, he might even learn a thing or two himself.

It didn't last long, that hope. Killed by a couple of factors working as one. First was the damned impossibility of actually seeing anything useful. This engineer, like most, seemed to much prefer working on the vessel by spelunking within its bowels, only rarely coming up for air—or, more often, a refill of his lantern—and then disappearing back down again to continue whatever unseen magics allowed engineers to shape reality as all other casters did.

The second was that those few glimpses Swick did see he had no bloody idea how to make sense of. There was simply no frame of reference in his life of experience for what was being done. Half of the components he saw, he couldn't name. The rest he couldn't describe. He felt like a blind man trying to study art by memorizing the sounds of brush strokes hitting canvas.

"You making progress?" he asked, eliciting another irritated grunt from the increasingly harassed engineer.

"It's hard to tell," he replied. "Do remember how unique this technology is. All I know of it is the basic theory and some anecdotes about its physical limits."

Swick saw no reason why that shouldn't have been enough. If engineers gained so little from all those years spent squatted inside hunched over books while their masters lectured away then it just made him wonder why they'd even bother to fucking do it. He decided that voicing the sentiment would not achieve much, however.

"Ah!" the man gasped, with excitement, not disappointment, infusing his voice. Swick stiffened, fighting back his own elation, not wanting to humor the emotion that had so regularly fallen into mere let down.

"You see something?" he asked.

"Yes, hush," the engineer snapped, moving farther into the ship's innards. Swick heard the sound of components displaced and rattled against one another as he fiddled with them, haste so great that it was being conveyed through the sheer volume of his work. He wasn't worried about any damage coming from it. Skyship internals were built to withstand jagged turns and swooping drops. He doubted someone without a plentiful infusion of Vigor in their muscles could damage it if they *tried*.

Swick watched, and waited. Eagerly anticipating some triumphant emergence from the engineer. Oh, he'd charge him everything he could in exchange for such a repair as this, but he'd pay it all willingly. Anything to sail the skies again, anything and more.

The smoke emerged thinly at first, then quickly congealed into an opaque inky cloud that stifled Swick's growing optimism just as completely as it did the light. He heard coughing, gasping, more coughing, and then a fit of swearing that demonstrated quite a considerable vocabulary.

He added to it.

Waving a hand and wincing at the mess, the engineer emerged. Swick deflated at the sight of him scrambling back from the skyship.

"Fuck," he gasped once finally clear of the smog and able to inhale without furthering the torture of his lungs.

Swick didn't bother asking what he could still do. He reckoned he'd already seen enough to know when a task was beyond someone. Perhaps these engineers should've hunched over a few more books before setting out to work.

"Captain Swick?"

The voice caught him quite by surprise, and Swick barely resisted his usual response to the calling of his name. He turned, rather than simply diving through the nearest window, and was pleasantly surprised to see a human, not a debtor, standing expectantly before him.

He was tall, hawkish, almost eerie. He spoke to Swick with the sort of recognition one gained through hearing a reputation, and those who spoke to Swick like that . . .

Swick's fingers danced toward the handle of his knife because those who spoke to him like that were generally bounty hunters.

"Can I help you?" he asked, ready to start slashing and stabbing at a moment's notice. The fight never came though.

"No, but I believe I can help you," the man replied. "I am . . . Well, names are irrelevant I think, I am hand to his majesty King Galukar of Arbite."

Swick eyed him, surprised but not disbelieving. He certainly matched the descriptions he'd heard.

"And you're offering me a hundred knights?" he asked hopefully. The hand didn't smile.

"I'm offering you a name: Bal the Treasure Hunter. You may have heard it before?"

Swick had done more than bloody hear it before, and he winced at the memory.

"Ah, that confirms it then," the hand noted. "I'd heard of your dealings together. The stories are true then?"

He reminded Swick of Shaiagrazni, always keenly watching, always catching the slightest hints that flitted past his vision and weaving them into knowledge.

Best be careful around this one.

"Yes," he replied, deciding not to bother lying. Better to save his lies for later. "Years ago."

Eight years ago, if Swick was remembering rightly. They'd been fellow outlaws, both clever enough to not trust the other. They'd worked together, briefly, for practical reasons, and their semivoluntary partnership had ended painfully when it outlived its usefulness.

Not a Hero, Swick thought. But uncomfortably close to one. Close enough to leave the eight-inch scar under his ribs that itched every time he remembered the bastard. A lucky hit, but most needed a lot more than luck to leave something like that on him.

Even if, in fairness, Swick had been drunk at the time. When hadn't he been, those days?

"That's convenient then." The hand smiled without it touching his eyes. "Because you'll be the one needing to find him. I have reason to believe he has just the component needed for repairing your skyship."

The dark elves were not numerous, but they compensated with sheer efficiency. One hundred or so, perhaps, and they took several prisoners each through carefully calculated lines of sight and well-prepared shackles.

And butchery. That, Hexeri knew, was the meat of it. Those whose bodies were strong, Vigorous, were taken for their use to a necromancer in fresh death. The others were disarmed, ushered away. And killed to keep from troubling the rest.

With weapons and commands, they might have offered resistance; with neither, the men either perished or ran. Most escaped, but the spilled blood of those few hundred stupid or slow enough not to was still a revolting thing. Then the march began.

Just like that, a force of thousands had been erased. Just like that, the Dark Lord had himself two Heroes and a dozen rangers as prisoners. Just like that, the fight was over, and a crushing defeat had settled into its place.

And the dark elves hadn't even needed to dodge a single spear thrust. The word "demoralizing" had not been coined for describing so harrowing a defeat. Not even close.

Naturally, Hexeri was split up from Collin Baird, and the two of them were marched under particularly weighty guard. She still heard him, over the other footsteps, having had ample time through their few weeks of familiarity to pick out his idiosyncrasies in stride, breath, and scent. For the better part of a few hours, she did nothing but occasionally check to make sure he still lived. Then, eventually, she froze.

Because Hexeri found herself hearing the sound of falling bodies and smelling the scent of blood. Then Baird was beside her, hacking through the steel of her shackles like thin rope. Both of them were free, and the fight came almost before she even recognized the fact.

Elves came in, three of them. They were faster than humans, faster than human knights even, and their hands held curved blades of metal Hexeri didn't even have a name for. She ducked under one, replying to its wielder with a punch that sank deep into their guts and *broke* something within the soft viscera. It fell, blood spurting from their lips, and Hexeri seized the ichor with her thoughts.

It became a spray of crimson fléchettes at the flick of her cognition, sent shooting for another elf like so many arrows. Faster than arrows, than crossbow bolts, almost faster than Baird's own projectiles. They dug through mail and lamellar, sinking into the meat below. Her target stumbled, fell, leaking more of their precious lifeblood out.

Hexeri appreciated the loss, for it gave her the ammunition to shred another two elves. Baird himself was killing away beside her, a human whirlwind of blades and teeth. Fingers came off, wrists opened, and every artery within nicking range was nicked so smoothly and sharply that his blades were probably a yard clear before the pain even started.

Seconds passed, then the two of them stood at the center of a dozen-strong litter of corpses. Some neatly switched off by pinpoint ranger-swift stabs and slices. Others ripped to piles of twisted meat by the less subtle touch of blood magic and vampiric strength. None were impeding their retreat anymore, and so they sprinted.

A dozen surprised dark elves was one thing; the ninety more readying to give chase was quite another.

Bolts of magic came after them, now that the shock of sudden violence was wearing off. Hexeri was already fifty paces away, and the jet of searing energy that sailed just short of her missed by a good yard. Even still, she felt its heat. A normal vampire would have been burned, even by that near miss. A normal human killed outright. Elfin magic was the stuff of legends for a reason, and the dark elves tended toward a more *overtly destructive* style than others.

There was nothing to do but run, and hope. They did.

Hexeri dragged the shadows beside them as she passed, pulling them up into a black mist at their backs. It would do nothing to impede such powerful energy—barely even enough to halt human arrows—but the obfuscation would hopefully keep them from being struck directly. It seemed just in time too, for an entire barrage of power shot through in moments.

The elves were slower in a dead sprint, at least. And they never did hit them. Hexeri and Collin Baird managed to disappear from the fight.

It was, in the end, all they managed.

CHAPTER TWENTY-EIGHT

It was a demon. Galukar recognized as much instantly. He'd slain men by the thousand—undead, perhaps, by the million. Killing, butchering his way across the continent for so many long, savage decades of murderous devastation. If any man in all the world's history could claim to have made himself a weapon, it was Galukar.

And he had only ever fought one demon, one time. Thirty years gone now, he and all his sons back before they'd been taken from him. There had been twelve of them in all, eleven near Heroes and one who dwarfed any other man in living memory to bear even that title. Plus the army at their back.

By the end of it, there had been only ten sons, and half the army. Galukar shivered at the memory. The Dark Lord hadn't summoned that one. He hadn't unveiled any when last he and Galukar had fought. He'd been taking things easy, Galukar realized, hiding cards up his sleeve.

And now he'd conjured the darkest nightmare of Galukar's entire memory to face Shaiagrazni.

He shivered because it was not a memory anymore. The demon was storm and chaos. Around it, the air was a gestalt vortex of deranged motion and fluctuating mass. It wasn't just that waves of heat rippled through it, like atop the ground of a desert. The world was *twisting*. Its very substance changed, warped. Surrendering before the madness inherent to its invader.

The demon's form was long and irrational. Almost serpentine, were it not for the incongruous bulges haphazardly situated across its length. Three great wings beat atop its back, each in a different direction. They seemed avian, at first, but Galukar soon realized that each one of their apparent feathers was itself a wing—smaller, insectoid, and composed of glinting black metal. All these smaller ones flexed so fast that his eye could barely follow.

Blood vessels ran visibly along the surface of the entity, sometimes even opening out through its skin to waste ichor as acrid rain, pouring down and searing great welts into the ground below where they ate at its substance. The stuff was dark gray, at odds with the violent pink of its carrier's skin. More at odds, still, with the demon's teeth. Each one was a rounded flexing mass that Galukar could make no reason from the composition of.

He shivered because this demon looked nothing like the one he'd seen all those years ago with its twisting form and its mismatched limbs. But they were identical twins in contrast to everything else. Two beings of polar difference, made undeniable kin by their stark defiance of all the rational laws and principles that governed physical anatomy in all other creatures.

Prince Nemo's pet had distracted Galukar, taken his mind from the world's true constants. There were the dark arts, and then there were demons. And the latter was closing on his army.

There may have been some facsimile of tactical cognition propelling it, or it may simply have been that the Kaltan shield wall holding their precious hill was closest. Either way, the demon chose that as its first target. A sound ran through the battlefield, cutting Galukar to his core. Crying children—screaming, even, in terror—and he knew instantly it was the closest thing this abomination could come to crying out.

A moment later, it was on them.

Tendrils of power tore down from its body, blasting through the oaken barricades and the meat of their wielders. In moments, the Kaltans separated, ranks frayed to pieces, panicked survivors sprinting away. Shafts of iron struck the demon where rangers fired on it, but they might as well have hurled beestings for all it did. Galukar was stunned for almost half an instant.

But his instincts were always more favorable to fighting than fleeing. He gave an order, the most important thing of all. Men did not run so easily when they heard an order boomed out regardless.

"*Hold!*" he roared. "*Casters forward! Target the demon!*"

Demon—Galukar almost regretted even naming it, but they all knew damned well what they were staring down. Nothing but the abominations from beyond the veil could do what they were seeing now. Perhaps not even Shaiagrazni himself.

Flames spit outward in the air as the great weapons—cannons, Shaiagrazni called them—fired. Five hundred yards from their target. Ballistae or trebuchets would have been wholly useless at such a distance. These projectiles though flew true. Galukar saw many flit closely by the demon, and several impacted.

Its body was not entirely mundane, not fully bound to the world. Raw strength and impact force could only do so much. Galukar winced as he saw it disincorporate partly, then weave its shattered form back together and streak across the battlefield for the source of its new attack. They'd gotten its attention, at least. Now they just needed to survive it.

"*Ready!*" he declared, glancing at the necromancer beside him. She wasn't freezing up, at least, but the woman looked far from ready for death. That was fine. It might make her fight all the harder against it. "*Cast!*"

Galukar's final command came when the demon was just shy of the range at which it had obliterated Kaltan's formation, and Galukar knew from long experience that it was far past the killing distance of most casters. Even trained magi. A good spell, thrown well and with considerable power, might reach two hundred yards and kill a man at half that. Accurately though it was unlikely to strike a human target beyond fifty.

The demon's sheer size saw a few of the attacks scoring notches into its esoteric form, regardless of it being twenty-fathom height skyward, but Galukar saw instantly the difference in power. Fireballs struck like pinhead embers from a flame, jets of water like raindrops. Enchanted thorns broke against it as if they were cobwebs, where hurled boulders seemed to crumble on impact like flecks of dirt.

Something was happening. The demon was registering contact at least, but . . . nothing substantial.

There was simply too little power within human magic to wound such a thing. Too little to even hurt it. How in the world had Galukar ever slain the one he'd fought before?

Help, distraction, and . . . a miracle.

God was nowhere near him, these days. There would be no miracle today. So help him, Galukar almost believed it before he saw the black streak that had spelled death on so many other occasions. He looked up just to see it land the luckiest hit he'd witnessed in years—splashing dead center in the demon's chest.

It was not half the equal of Silenos Shaiagrazni's, but the necromancer Sphera's shadestuff proved more than a nuisance if nothing else.

Another cry, children giggling this time. Galukar took a moment to realize the perversion for what it was. Pain was joy to a demon, and joy was pain. They'd hurt it. But one necromancer could throw only so many gouts of shadestuff, and now the demon's altitude had shrunk to its own offensive distance.

The energy built, and seasoned magi were blasted to limbs, viscera, ash . . . Then even that was scorched ever more, until it was reduced to nothing but clouds of pitch-dark debris swirling in the unnatural winds of too much heat concentrated in too small a patch of air.

Galukar roared, his impotence striking more than their deaths. He was not a caster, not a ranger. Magic could touch the thing, and he held more magic than any other in the battlefield. But it was a fucking sword. Within the reach of his Godblade, there wasn't a force in existence able to withstand him, but the demon was beyond it now. Hovering out of God's light, and delighting all the more in its savagery.

There had to be something he could do. There had to—

A cannon fired. A projectile tore a wing fully off, only for it to reform before gravity had even dragged it an inch downward. The idea came to Galukar before the screaming metal had even flown clear of sight. He glanced at the weapon responsible, at his sword.

No, that was stupid. He glanced at his legs instead, then flitted his gaze farther around the battlefield.

"Necromancer," he snapped. "Call the grotesqueries over and have them throw me, quick!"

The demon was running out of casters to kill, and it would not remain near to Galukar for much longer after the rest were dead. Fortunately, Shaiagrazni's apprentice was, after all, his apprentice. She understood fast, and the things lumbered over in moments. None were the fleshcrafter's biggest work—they would have been slower if they were—but the largest of them was still close to ten times Galukar's own height, and over a dozen times the average. In moments, he felt abominable flesh close around him, then the acceleration of strength employed with impossible abundance.

The wind screamed in his ears. Galukar screamed back, louder. He hit the demon like an arrow fresh from the string.

When Galukar had been a boy, he'd been taught to stab a man by bracing the butt of his blade against himself and charging in. Pinning it between their bodies, using his own weight and momentum to drive it through mail and meat. It was not a technique he'd used in some time. For one thing, it had been coined for smaller weapons. Longknives or shortswords. For another . . . it had been redundant. When swinging the Godblade, one rarely considered the prospect of finding it denied an enemy's death by durability. It either hit or the fight continued.

Galukar employed that long-neglected technique an instant before impacting, and he actually felt himself close to winded as his ridiculous velocity transferred between physical mass and the impossible angles of what his blade now kissed. Metal dug in an inch, a hand, a foot. Magic crackled and screamed. He felt taloned limbs close around him, gasped at the almost novel sensation of skin parting, muscle parting—*everything* parting almost like a normal man raked by normal claws. Then they were spinning, falling, thrashing. He dragged the Godblade out, grabbed a talon, and swung.

Iron sizzled and spit where it caught the not-flesh of its target, and there rang out a great sundering noise as light flashed and church bells seemed to toll around them. A gash appeared in the demon. The sort a normal sword might leave in normal flesh, but a damned start. Galukar cut again, severing one of the abomination's arms, then raising the limb up to clog its opened maw when gyrating teeth moved to clamp down on his head.

Blood hit his skin, gray blood. It burned, and Galukar snarled, then the demon dragged him closer as it spit out its own arm. Galukar wrestled the thing's strength, and realized it exceeded his own. More talons dug in, gouging, tearing. The Godblade worked back and forth—like a saw, at this close range, not a cutter—and both he and his enemy brought the other closer to death.

Like a normal man fighting a normal beast. Lion, bear, tiger. Death for the human, almost without variation. But sometimes, with a sword, will, and surprise, it was death for the animal too. An animal was certainly present, and Galukar heard it as his lungs convulsed into a long, snarling scream. He butted the demon to free his arm just enough to drive the Godblade upward and inward, digging down to where the neck veins would be in a sensibly designed body, then moving back to sawing.

Children laughing, a greater joy than he'd ever heard his own feel. The death rattle of a thing that shouldn't have been at all, finding the wrongness of its existence rectified. No longer were the talons scything, the jaws snapping, the unnatural not-muscles convulsing at odds with their motions. No longer was the demon doing anything at all but coming apart. Body to limbs, to viscera, to ash. Then to nothing at all.

Galukar had just the chance to smile, as widely as his enfeebled face could even muster the strength for. Then he fell back down toward the earth.

CHAPTER TWENTY-NINE

Ado's trial came quickly enough. The church's always did. She met it with as much dignity as was left in her, but that had been wrung out to a disheartening degree over her short stay in prison.

It was not, in the end, captivity that gnawed at her. It was Folami. Folami and his poisonous offer. Poisonous, not venomous. Because a poison's lethality came only when it was drunk, not injected.

She could live. To do so was surrender, desecration, betrayal, and defeat. It was to throw away everything she'd ever wanted, to turn on the one man who valued what she could do. To prove the world right about her weakness.

But it was to *live*. And living . . . Well, that was life instead of death. It was an argument just by the basic fact of its existence.

Ado paced, and thought. She slept, infrequently and for minutes at a time. Slowly becoming more and more bedraggled by her own discontent and fears. Slowly feeling death's scythe creep nearer to her neck. It was almost a relief when her trial came. Almost.

Folami was the one to take her to it, and for a moment she mistook his presence as a stroke of cruelty. The worry on his face though told her otherwise. Her brother hadn't been getting much more sleep than her, not much at all.

"Change of heart?" she asked, knowing full well he'd not answer in the affirmative. Folami's weariness disappeared quite quickly, buried beneath a new mound of bitter irritation.

"You always keep it up, don't you, Ado?" He sighed. "No matter what, that tongue of yours just can't stop cutting away. Even when it's cutting you."

She was almost impressed by the quick-wittedness involved in such an easy and seamless metaphor, but Ado was fatigued beyond such a petty sensation. She just sighed.

"What do you want?"

Folami sighed too. Apparently, whatever it was, it didn't inspire much in the way of hope for him.

"Sister, I don't know what you're planning for your trial. Please though, just . . . accept what's coming. Plead guilty. Confess your crimes. You know you'll be forgiven."

She did. She knew that very, very fucking well. Well enough to torture herself with it.

"And what will come of it if I do?" Ado spit. "Wudra will just hunker down and be destroyed. Even you must realize that."

"If they fight immediately," Folami breathed after a moment. "Yes, they will. There was a reason they did not send our father aid when Shaiagrazni's invasion first began. But that is not the plan."

Ado froze, stared at him, and then rearranged the events around her with that in mind.

"They intend to grant the Dark Lord passage." She gasped as everything clicked into place at once. "To send him forth and let him and Shaiagrazni fight each other, to watch their enemies destroy each other while they sit idle."

"And then to swoop in and crush the victor in their weakened state," Folami finished, grinning. "Correct, and so you see, sister, you don't *need* to continue this. Shaiagrazni is not the only way this world can be saved. You need not serve that demon of a man."

Need not.

They reached the room of Ado's trial, and it was, at least, no less than a man would have received. Large, pillared, sterile, and nearly pure in its construction of marble and steel. She saw galleries filled with glaring faces, and at the end of the room there was a seat held atop a podium, towered over by two more.

It was in those dual peaks that the king and high priest sat, waiting damnably for her entrance. Ado did not delay them any longer than was necessary.

"Princess Ado Mortascia," came a booming voice, ringing out the very moment her feet came down onto the top of her podium. "You stand accused of treason, subversion of the crown, and consorting with practitioners of the dark arts. How do you plead?"

There it was. How *did* she plead?

"Silenos Shaiagrazni is the only hope of defeating the Dark Lord," Ado replied, almost wincing at the sound of her own words echoing out across the room, let alone the reactions they drew. Hisses, glares, disgust. Rage. The sight of one angry man was something any woman knew to be very, very wary around. A hundred, as she saw now . . . It had every nerve in her body screaming for flight.

But she held, and continued speaking. Ado had precious moments before the room's shock wore off and her voice was drowned in protests and condemnation. She had to use it as best she could because it wasn't just her life hanging by a thread.

"I implore you all, please, think about this issue. Shaiagrazni did not send me as an envoy for no reason. He *needs* your aid. The Dark Lord is a threat to all—he wants to destroy this world to its very foundations. His armies kill and absorb, with virtually no exception. His people starve. *Starve.* If you are all right, and this does end with either of the Dark Lords weakened and finished off in their enfeeblement, then you have nothing to fear. But what if you're wrong? What if the victor is able to win against you, even still? You must throw your strength behind Shaiagrazni, for all the world's sake."

The silence that followed was a crushing weight upon Ado's chest, compressing her lungs into stagnancy. It made way for hope. A single, stupid moment of it.

Then the gavel came down, almost before the snarls and roars it was swung to silence. She turned to see the high priest glaring daggers at her.

"We've all heard enough," he roared. "Guilty. This woman is guilty. Bad enough to admit it so brazenly, she even tries to tempt others into her own charge with the time allotted to recant it!"

Cries of agreement ran out, pricking Ado from all sides like blunted needles. She felt weightless, suddenly, unbalanced as if the floor were spinning and rocking beneath her. Her head spun, ears rang. Hope crumbled.

"Ado Mortascia, you have pled guilty to all charges brought before you, and have shown no hint of regret in their face. You have left this court with no choice but to sentence you to death for your crimes against the human race."

What was happening? This couldn't be . . . What was happening? How could this be happening?

It all happened in a bizarre, elongated fugue. Ado was seized, dragged from the hall, snatched away from the hateful, spitting voices, and marched down a cold corridor. Mere moments later, her brother was beside her.

"What were you thinking?!" he spit. Ado froze. What had she been thinking?

"Shaiagrazni," she croaked. "People under him, they live . . . well. Long lives. They're happy. He kills aristocrats, nobles, strips them of power and displaces monarchs, but the people are—"

"Who gives a fuck about the damned peasantry?" Folami snapped. Ado stared at him. "This trial was about the subversion of a monarch and subservience to a dark caster. The only one to even mention the peasantry was *you*."

Ado didn't have the words to reply. She just considered his. And she realized he was right.

What had she thought of the peasantry a few months ago? Nothing. Literally nothing. They'd not even been a concern for her. Just things that did work and sent the rewards upward into their masters' hands. She'd been one of those masters. The happiness, contentedness—the basic damned rights of the ones responsible for propping her life of comfort up had all been less than tertiary. A nonfactor.

Somewhere along the way, between Shaiagrazni's lectures, Baird's arguments, and the simple, basic experience of *seeing* with her own eyes what the world was changing to around her, Ado had learned differently. And she'd forgotten what her people were truly like, what they valued. What they didn't.

What a fool she'd been, to try to convince nobles, aristocrats, and holy men that Shaiagrazni treated the common man differently than the Dark Lord. They didn't fight the Dark Lord over their peasants' treatment. They fought him to maintain their own hegemony. Everything else . . . at best was pretense.

"It doesn't matter now," Ado said finally. Her voice was fragile in her own ears, and sharp. It felt like wielding a needle of glass. She couldn't help but betray the bitterness wrapped around it. "What's done is done. There would never have been any persuading them, not of what matters."

Somehow, it was freeing to say that. Because Ado *didn't* matter.

"How far you have fallen." Folami sighed, staring at Ado as if he pitied her somehow. As if she were the mad one in a sensible world. "I tried, sister. I really, truly tried to save you from yourself. But . . . It seems you are intent on dying. It seems, no matter what, you will follow this path to its end. Even if that end is also yours."

"Perhaps the world would be a better place if fewer of its controllers cared about their own ends more than other people's," Ado replied, feeling a new fire taking her. "Think, Folami. For once in your life, think. Why exactly do you think Silenos Shaiagrazni has such an excess of allies in so short a time? Why do you think he was able to draw in Collin Baird and Kaltan, to travel for so long with a *paladin*, to bring in the vampires of Clan Liliai themselves? Why do you think each settlement he takes is so passive and calm after the taking? People are not loyal to us. A few are, maybe, those who truly drank in the dogma and duty we've spent so many generations feeding them, but for the most part they simply don't care for us. And they shouldn't. They should hate us because we *are* hateable."

By the time Ado finished, she was out of breath. And she hadn't even given voice to the most important part of all.

How do you think Shaiagrazni brought me in to work beneath him?

But Folami was not in the mood for discussion and debate. He only fell silent and bitter, rather than contemplative, after hearing her remarks. Ado watched him fall away from her side, letting the guards further escort her. With that, she was left to think all by herself.

She was going to die. She'd brought it on herself. Ado had practically suicided in that courtroom. And all she had left was the notion that it had been just.

Had it?

Ado recalled the sight of her father, her mentor. She recalled the countless thousands crushed to paste under Shaiagraznian grotesqueries. She trembled, but she did not falter in her beliefs.

Yes. In the end, with everything considered and weighed against all else, she had done what she'd needed to. The only thing she could have. Ado was competent, intelligent, and magically gifted. She had value, but she had none at all compared to all else that might come from House Shaiagrazni's rule.

Her hands clenched into fists. She believed what she'd said; she *knew* that it was true. And she pitied the fools now sending her off into a cell. Because their own people knew just what Shaiagrazni's rule could bring.

And they knew too that his emissary was scheduled for execution.

CHAPTER THIRTY

It was not Silenos's first time attempting to craft flying entities. Indeed, he'd done so on more than one occasion. Even gone so far as to imbue his own combat form with the power of flight. Today's attempt, however, brought with it a new order of practical issues he'd never been beset with before.

And it all came down to a matter of *weight*.

Shaiagraznian combat forms tended to be heavy things, of course. Four thousand kilograms in Silenos's case, and he'd known peers to go so high as triple that. There were simply natural advantages that came inherently to a great size and mass. Strength, resilience, yes. But *momentum* too. A resilience against the hurling effects of battle magics could be vital when war was waged in the hostile conditions his people had become accustomed to. Pools of shade-stuff, chasms running down core deep—there were any number of hazards that might slay even the sturdiest casters if they did not anchor themselves against shifts in momentum.

But it was a different grade of mass altogether that he was trying to provide lift for now. Lift and propulsion.

The fundamental task before Silenos was crafting a substitute for Swick the Swift's flying vessel. Such a thing was actually rather primitive by Shaiagraznian standards, which tended toward larger aerial vehicles of far more advanced armor plating and weaponry. Unfortunately, House Shaiagrazni achieved such creations with a far broader scope of power than Silenos had available to him.

Aside from his knowledge of biochemistry, he had no ability at all to create inorganic materials. If something was not an approximation of a substance native to some eukaryotic or prokaryotic life-form, then it was beyond him. Which meant he could not build the kinds of power generation or pro-pulsive technology that permitted such towering vehicles.

Naturally, that brought about his first concession. Size. Silenos had been intending to craft something on the order of many hundreds of meters' length, weighing thousands, even millions of tonnes. That wasn't happening, not unless he was content with a near-stationary vessel, and so he reluctantly scaled down his designs. One-third, one-quarter, eventually one-seventh. It was a painful lack, but if nothing else, it simplified his work. Not enough to leave it unchallenging, however.

The rest of it would have to wait though, for it was around that time that his door opened. Silenos turned to gaze upon the vampire Lilia, strolling into his laboratory as if it were hers. He decided to wait a moment, and obliterate her only if her justification was particularly subpar.

"Good evening," she began. "I see you're hard at work, as usual."

It always irked Silenos when the short-lived ordinary people outside his household insisted on the tedium of small talk, and his surprise at seeing similar behavior from a being as ancient as this almost outweighed his fury. He buried both. There was surely some order to her behavior, after two millennia.

"One of several vital projects," he replied. "But you have not come here out of mere curiosity. What is it that you want?"

The vampire smiled.

"Very well, to business then. You are centuries old, I believe."

"Not yet two," Silenos corrected. "But close."

It seemed to surprise the creature.

"Really? You carry yourself like one of considerably greater age. Interesting. Well, either way, you are certainly among the greatest experts of fleshcrafting and necromancy to set foot in this world."

"The greatest that ever will," Silenos corrected. The vampire did not con-tradict him, nor did she agree.

"As you say. And my visit here is to inquire as to whether you might use that knowledge to free my kind of our greatest weakness."

Ah, Silenos might have known. She had come to him for preservation from the sun. He would have done much the same. Vampires were an interest-ing breed, he had decided, and demanded further study. Certainly inferior to the purer forms of immortality his people had discovered—even within the sole bounds of necromancy, lichdom was by far the better choice. They had considerable power, longevity, and a degree of other advantages over even a caster already potent enough to become one.

But their reliance on blood, their bestial instincts. Their vulnerability to sunlight and enfeeblement during the day. It was all simply untenable. Yes, Silenos would be doing just what Lilia did now if he were in her position.

"You are aware that what you suffer from is a supernatural affliction," he noted, confirming the fact with a hasty glance from his arcane sight. Vampiric magic was strange, and . . . yes, abyssal in nature. Touched by an Entity. Clearly esotericism was at work in it. Whether Lilia knew that, he was not sure.

"Of course," she replied. "That much has been obvious for quite some time. You know, a man once tried to destroy me using magic he claimed to have been perfected in its ability to conjure the same style of light as the sun."

"Ultraviolet?" Silenos inquired. The vampire looked at him blankly, and he sighed. Expected, he supposed. "Continue."

She did.

"Well, to cut a long story short—at the cost of removing all the most entertaining parts—his false sunlight did me no more harm than might the warmth of a campfire. And then I drained his blood."

At that, the vampire's tongue ran along her lips as she spoke, gaze seeming to intensify as it fell upon Silenos's eyes. Was that some sort of simple tic? He decided to investigate the idiosyncrasy later.

"May I examine you?" he asked.

The vampire smiled.

"Of course. I would be remiss to deny such a vital step of the process."

She stepped forward, splaying her arms, and Silenos approached cautiously. With a single touch, he could feel the woman's millennia.

Aside from the raw, crushing power that came naturally to any caster whose life continued for long enough, there were certain tells of a person's age to be found within their magic. Skill, obviously, though that could easily be mistaken for raw talent. As could a simple weight of power for that matter. Indeed, the rate at which any two individuals accumulated magical prowess varied so much that Silenos had found, in his many decades studying it, there was truly only one way that even approximated a foolproof metric for assessing another's age.

It was the density of traps, pitfalls, feints, and misdirections wrapped around them.

He carefully navigated the labyrinthine preparations of Lilia's magic, allowing himself to study each one as he bypassed it, and consider them all fully. There was not a dual nature, as he had seen in the vampire's spawn Hexeri. Silenos saw at least three distinct kinds of magic. Blood and shadow, yes, but necromancy too. True necromancy, and . . .

No, four. Because he found a mastery over wills and minds among many of the defenses as well. Even in House Shaiagrazni, four distinct magic types was a rarity—the inherently exceptional ability of any caster to consort with Entities aside—that few could claim. Perhaps one in ten who shared Silenos's name did so, and almost all were over one thousand years into their studies.

Among all of his household, a scarce handful had ever reached the height of five. Even Silenos's own master, he believed, grasped only six. It was a chilling sight.

The purposes of Lilia's defenses were varied and inscrutable. Some were almost crude in their design, boasting techniques and measures made redundant in House Shaiagrazni before even the vampire's birth, while others involved techniques that actually exceeded even theirs.

It truly was like meeting an elder of his household. One who had acted independently from all the rest, and grown disparate in their knowledge as a result. Silenos would have been humbled were he not studying a necromantic subhuman automaton fit only for carrying out his glorious will.

He persevered in his examination, noting that each of the defenses was turned from him and laxed, but not deactivated. At a thought, the vampire might ensnare him in all of them. With their magic so interwoven, he would be destroyed instantly if she did. And so Silenos kept his mind focused carefully on ensuring that his own thought of breaking the connection came first.

"A waste," he murmured, deciding that distracting her was just as much a boon as focusing himself.

Fortunately, the vampire took his bait. Unless she was merely pretending to.

"What is?" She frowned.

"You," Silenos clarified. "Your power is breathtaking. Had you been inducted into House Shaiagrazni a thousand—even a hundred—years ago, you would be far beyond my own abilities now."

The vampire studied him.

"Most men would never say that, regardless of its truth," she noted. "Pride would stop them."

Silenos felt the disgust creeping into his cognition like grease in a whirring machine.

"Pride," he echoed. "An odious concept. There is no pride, nor is there humility. There is only the basic fact of one's excellence, and either an ability or inability to properly assess it. Everything else is illusory. When I speak of my greatness, it is a conviction, a description of what I shall will into being. Do not mistake that for pride."

He had not said those words in over a hundred years. He had not needed to, and they took his thoughts back a moment to his days as an aspirant. Young. So, so young. And foolish. Silenos had not yet been taught of the world. All he'd known of it was the burning fields of so many wars, and the simple, bare fact that those who could not produce such carnage were doomed to suffer beneath it.

"You really believe that, don't you?" the vampire asked.

Silenos was in the present once more, irritated for a reason he could not quite grasp.

"It does not matter what I believe. It is the truth. Pride serves nobody, least of all the people feeling it."

"But are you not pleased to be so potent a caster?" she challenged. "Delight and relish at knowing your magic to be so totally unrivaled. That could surely be called a form of pride."

Silenos was almost halfway to answering before he realized what he'd almost fallen for and paused. He decided to reply anyway. The information was far from sensitive.

"I am not the greatest caster I have ever encountered," he told the woman. "I am not even counted among them. Within House Shaiagrazni, there are dozens whose power, skill, or intellect surpasses mine—at least for the time being. My talent is unprecedented, but that is all."

Surprise did not appear to be in the vampire's facial arsenal, for she didn't flash so much as an instant of it.

"Fascinating," she replied.

They drifted to silence at that, and Silenos let his wits drift further. Finally, he broke contact.

"I have seen enough," he told the vampire, eyeing her warily now. "You know, I take it, where your magic comes from?"

She smiled.

"We call them demons here."

Silenos did not roll his eyes. Her power and knowledge was just barely sufficient to earn that courtesy.

"Entities," he replied, "are a common sight among House Shaiagrazni, for reasons I imagine you well know. Summoned properly, bound well, they are forces beyond the magic of any caster. Even ones of my order."

"Which makes them even more dangerous than they are useful," she noted. "And, of course, immediately raises questions about your ability to overcome the side effects of a curse born from their blood and power."

It did, and Silenos did not bother mustering any surprise to see Lilia's deduction either. He would have been rather disappointed to witness anything less.

"The Entity from which your power stems is more tightly woven into it than I have encountered personally. The magic is . . . considerable, and it is . . . Entity magic."

She considered that.

"It doesn't follow the rules both of us have grown accustomed to," Lilia guessed.

"It does not," he concurred, considering the problem. "It would be a considerable investment to put the necessary time into fixing this, even if it is possible."

The vampire smiled.

"And yet, as someone who has just seen both the weight and sharpness of my magic, you must surely realize that granting me the ability to walk unimpeded by day would be a greater reward still."

She had orchestrated it all on purpose, from the start. Silenos nodded.

"I concur."

CHAPTER THIRTY-ONE

Travel was slow without Swick's skyship, but he'd gotten enough time to adjust. It bothered him, but it didn't stun him. Not anymore. This was just the state he'd left for himself with his drunken maneuver.

The hand, at least, had been willing to use Shaiagrazni's provided transportation. The special carriages Swick had first used to reach Kaltan. They moved autonomously, grinding away at the earth and dragging their passengers along fast enough to clear dozens of miles within the span of an hour, slowing only when particularly difficult terrain forced them to.

Satisfyingly, the hand was rather perturbed by them. Most people were.

A life of living, fighting, and potentially dying atop the back of a skyship had probably inoculated Swick to the fears he'd seen so commonly directed at Shaiagrazni's carriages. In theory, they really weren't that different from his own vessel. Self-powered, automated, controlled via thought and instinct as much as steered through mechanical means. That tended to make newer crewmen uncomfortable too when they first found out. Had the ship been made from living tissue, Swick imagined the effect would have been a great deal more intense.

Intense or no, they'd have been idiots to pass up the chance at one. Anyone would. And Swick was reminded of that no more than when he rode on one of Shaiagrazni's genius carriages, and felt how *slowly* it moved compared to his own.

That movement took the better part of two days to take Swick and the hand as far as they needed to travel. Far from Kaltan, and almost as far back as Equiscia. Equiscia, the first city Shaiagrazni had set foot in. The birthplace of their latest ally. One of them, at least. Were Swick a poetic man, he might have had something to comment on regarding that. Instead, he just kept his eyes ahead and waited for them to reach their destination.

"Torib is a larger city," the hand told him. "A few dozen leagues from Elkatin, it was actually inadvertently saved by Shaiagrazni as the Dark Lord's forces attacked this region. Had he not made such a fierce defense with the paladins, the Dark Lord's lichs would likely have taken their time emptying its streets into more undead. Instead, they had to act quickly, to keep an enemy dark caster from bolstering his own forces."

Swick thought about that.

"You're not expecting them to be grateful to him surely."

"Of course not." The hand snorted. "In moments of fortune, people think of God. It's only in moments of ill fortune that they think of others."

That actually sounded about right to Swick, and he shifted his opinion of the hand somewhat. This was a man who did know *something* of others, at least.

"Torib," he murmured, thinking on the name and not taking long to draw up the relevant information. "Ah, city of outlaws. One of the bigger ones. It used to be a favorite spot of mine."

"Back before you lost the ability to travel the world without being arrested," the hand noted, and Swick scowled.

"Yes."

They sat out the remainder of their journey in silence, which was rather uncomfortable for Swick, but a great deal better than constantly being reminded of his little *accident* by everyone around him. Their carriage closed to within a mile of its walls before they stopped it behind a hill. It was not the black silt local to Kaltan's area, rather a more mundane dirt and grassy covering, but the obfuscation it provided would serve just as well.

"Best not to let our transport be seen," Swick explained as they began their walk. "It'd be nice to have it nearby in case we need to escape, but not worth the attention it'll bring. Even criminals don't tend to like fleshcrafters."

The hand nodded in swift understanding.

A mile's walk was nothing for Swick, but he'd expected to see some difficulty in the hand's own trek. Apparently, Arbitan men—even the chair-hogging administrators—were made of sturdier stuff than was common to other lands. Even well into his middle years, he kept a brisk pace, and the two of them closed in on the city's gates in under five minutes. Swick wondered how quickly they might have run the distance.

After so long spent around the most extreme of militarism, Swick had almost forgotten what a *normal* city looked like. Its wall, twenty feet high, seemed somehow petty and insubstantial, stony barricade striking him as pitiably thin and fragile. One hit from Shaiagrazni's cannons would blast clean through; one swing from the Godblade would sweep away an entire section. Even Baird's bow wouldn't take long to drill through, albeit with a smaller opening.

The hand seemed to share his impression.

"Lucky indeed that Shaiagrazni made so many issues for the Dark Lord in Elkatin," he noted. "Or else he would have a million more servitors shambling about in his hordes."

Swick was in agreement. He wasn't a siege fighter by any means, but one didn't serve as so prolific a mercenary as him without understanding the basics at least. If an army even one-twentieth the size of the one Kaltan had driven away were to attack this city, they'd be fucked.

The guards seemed to know it too because they kept their eyes down and their faces turned carefully away as Swick and the hand made their way in past the outer gate. It was a familiar set of behaviors—those carried out by dangerous men. Dogs that barked didn't bite and all that. Swick felt a mix of apprehension and familiarity to be walking through such a place.

Mud streets met them inside, embracing Swick's every footfall with a celebratory chorus of squelching deformation. He looked around. The buildings were wood for the most part, squat and grimy, the streets uncomfortably crowded. He felt fingers graze his pockets twice, and confounded both attempts with fractional leans too small to break his stride.

He was used to that, and he was used to the stares too. Fame was a problem sometimes, after all. And Swick's fame was never so strongly felt as in disreputable surroundings. The longer they walked, the more eyes he found tilting toward him with recognition. Some with avarice, others with the premonitions of violence.

The magic trick he'd paid the witch for stopped people from noticing him, but not from finding him if they were looking. There was a price on his head. He'd known that for years, and yet he'd not had to get used to wandering around relatively on his own until recently. His apprehension was soon vindicated.

A corner turned, a moment's delay, and the sound of heavy boots grinding against dirt. In moments, Swick and the hand were surrounded on all sides. Ten men, all big, all moving in that light, loping way men did when their bodies were twitching with unused Vigor. He forced a smile and didn't go for his knife. Better to draw it all at once in the instant he attacked and leave them all the more confounded about where it came from.

"Hello there, Mr. Swick." One of them grinned, revealing a copper tooth and a half-healed jawbone. "I almost didn't recognize you. Now wouldn't *that* have been a shame?"

"It would," Swick agreed, smiling back. "I'd have missed out on your wonderful conversation."

Eleven men, he realized, not ten. One was creeping on a rooftop, bow in a tight grip. The hand was shifting, fingers twitching for a shortsword. The men who saw that were growing tense. Things were drawing close to an incendiary escalation.

"You know why we're speaking, don't you?" the leader asked. "Just make this easy and—"

Swick's lunge came at the same exact moment as the drawing of his first knife, the dragging of his finger along its edge, and the flicking of his hand behind him. He'd already buried the blade hilt deep into the speaker's skull before even a single of his allies could move. Then he translocated to the flicked ichor as it splashed against one of the men who'd been behind him.

It had been so long since Swick had fought anything other than undead or superhumans that he'd almost forgotten the grade of power actually commonplace among mercenaries, even those with a touch of Vigor in them. The edge of his blade parted scalp and skull as if they were cloth, biting down deep to split the man's head down to his upper lip. He twisted the weapon out and spun, taking off another at the neck to mark his third kill. By then, others were moving.

The hand was as impressive in battle as he had been in the mile walk because he was the first to attack. His shortsword took a man at his shoulder, hacking the arm entirely off and continuing to open another's belly with the backswing. The noble just barely darted back from a nasty-looking axe and into the path of another that bit down into his back but bounced off the superior musculature protecting it. Then the arrow was flying.

Compared to Baird's arrows—or even any other Kaltan ranger's—the projectile was *pitifully* slow. Swick had all the time in the world to watch it shoot for the hand, carefully aiming his dagger before hurling it to smash the wooden shaft to pieces, then continue and stick into the chest of a fourth enemy for good measure. Before the man had even finished crumpling to the dirt, he'd rolled from the path of another swing and lashed out with his remaining knife to open all the big veins in the attacker's thigh.

That made five kills for Swick, and now only four mercenaries remained.

But that was no mercenaries, really, because the last few took one look at what had happened to their comrades in so tiny a span of time and turned to sprint away. Swick let them go, even as he saw the hand half wavering to give chase.

"Bastards," the noble growled.

"They are," Swick agreed. "You'll be seeing a lot of their types in my circles, given what a bastard I am too. Turn around. Let me take a look at that back wound of yours."

The noble grumbled but obliged. Swick was well used to checking wounds, and he was quick about it. The enemy had done him a favor by parting expensive fabrics to expose the injury.

Below the cloth, there was steel. Carefully worked into mail links that fell in fractals as he parted the ruined clothing atop. Beneath that Swick saw the blood, and he probed around in the gory mess for a few moments—ignoring the winces and hissed pains of the noble—to be sure of his assessment.

"You'll be fine," he told the man. "It's nothing. He would've cut wood deeper than he did your flesh."

Which was impressive. Swick found himself reassessing the man once more. Not a Hero, not even *close* to a Hero, but he was . . . something, at least. In physical prowess alone, he might have been almost a match for Collin Baird before Shaiagrazni strengthened his biology with fleshcrafting. There weren't many who could say that much.

"King Galukar insisted on a certain martial ability for all his council," the hand explained. "Even those without martial roles."

"Makes sense." Swick shrugged. "Captain needs to be able to deal with a mutiny, even if he's alone. Otherwise he's too easy to pick off."

The hand did not seem impressed by his feedback.

"Perhaps things are different on a ship than they are in a city, sir." He sniffed. "But I will bear you in mind if I ever seek the advice of one who's experience of leadership involves herding drunkards toward a common victim."

Prick.

Swick might have even said something about it had the voice not rung out and turned his eyes down across the alley.

"Impressive work, but then people don't get half your bounty without that sort of performance, do they, captain?"

He turned instantly, and his heart sank at the sight of the speaking men. Two dozen of them now, not eleven, and all uniformed. Uniformed with clothes emblazoned with etchings of long, red hands. The speaker was a towering man with hair, and right hand, just as red as the fabric on their clothes.

Eye patched and glaring. One-Eyed Red, the man whose brother had died when Swick had slammed his ship into a floating castle.

"Friends of yours?" the hand asked, not knowing even a tenth of what rabbit hole he was jumping down.

Swick did know them. He knew the Red Finger Crew like few others. After all, once upon a time . . . they'd been his own men.

CHAPTER THIRTY-TWO

One-Eye didn't gloat. He was cocky, or else the Red Fingers wouldn't have introduced themselves before attacking, but even he knew better than to give Swick a chance to act before the violence started. His men came in as a great wave, and all Swick could do was hurriedly snatch his knife from the dead man's chest to meet them.

It was a near thing too because Swick wasn't nearly as fast compared to these men as he'd been against the last. The quickest of them already had a spear at his face by the time he turned, forcing Swick to dodge into the path of an axe. He barely parried that, and while he did another bastard closed with a longsword that actually nicked his shoulder. Two more had the corpse he'd flicked blood on surrounded, ready to stab if he translocated to it, so he just danced away for the time being.

The hand came in at Swick's side, almost earning himself a reflexively thrown knife to the face, and parried a swing with his sword, grunting with exertion. Swick ducked another, hacking for its wielder's arm and feeling the satisfying touch of steel against bone. He wasn't able to even relish the sensation for an instant before more weapons came at him.

It was like trying to slice away the grains of a sandstorm, so numerous were the attacks. Each one Swick smacked aside was replaced. Vigor kept him ahead of them, moving twice or thrice by the time any of his enemies did once, but their numbers and coordination were such that he didn't have even a single free breath. Nearly all his wits were kept focused just on living, even as the hand fought at his shoulder to stave off those few blows he could.

Nearly all Swick's wits, but not all of them entirely. It was for this reason that his mind still clicked into place, just in time. He twisted, went low, and slashed, grimacing as the man who'd been sneaking up behind him fell back with a belly now spilling out slimy pink entrails. It was a classic Red Finger tactic.

It doesn't make sense, he thought. It was a strange idea to have bouncing around in his skull, given the circumstances, but strange ideas kept one alive in the long term, so long as they didn't distract a man too much from the short.

Swick felt a spear nick his leg, then slashed a man's face down to the cheekbone. Short term was . . . mixed in success, he decided.

The Fingers had plenty of reason to hate him, but not to be in this shithole of a city. Last Swick had heard, they'd been finding work far in the north and living the high life for its abundance. Something had dragged them south, and he imagined it was related to the heightened demand for his head.

The Dark Lord must've put a new bounty on me, one big enough to move even heavy hitters like them against me. Which means . . .

He was trying to keep Shaiagrazni from gaining control of the air with the repair of Swick's skyship. On the one hand, it was flattering to be considered such a threat. On the other . . .

An axe missed him by an inch, and its wielder screamed as Swick jabbed the bastard's eye out with a dagger, then twisted aside from a crossbow bolt that looked fast enough to bury its entire length in stone.

On the other hand, he really didn't care for the quality of killer that such a fear seemed to be sending after him.

A cry caught Swick's ear, and he turned. The hand was nursing a shoulder wound that hadn't been there a few moments ago, a stab, and it looked a lot deeper than the axe bite had been. Swick thought about his situation for a quarter second at most, then acted.

He cut a finger, splayed his hand outward, and splashed as many of the attackers as he could. All were familiar with his powers, a disadvantage. But familiarity could bite the one who held it if played right. While they were busy flailing, panicking, and trying to think of all the counters they'd practiced to keep him from translocating a knife into their guts, Swick turned to grab the hand and used his power to drag the both of them high into the air.

. . . Where he'd thrown his knife with the motion used to splash blood on everyone.

Swick caught the blade, caught the hand, and twisted as they both plummeted. They hit a roof, Swick's shoulders impacting first and smashing the fragile wood to pieces. He wasn't a warrior, not a knight or paladin. His bodily resilience was more akin to a ranger's than either of theirs.

But, despite how close he'd come to forgetting it over the years of boozing, Swick was a damned Hero, and that meant a level of raw Vigor that forced excellence in almost everything, regardless of specialization. They burst through the roof, ceiling, then a floor before finally coming to a stop at the bottom of the building amid a pile of debris and a cloud of dust.

For one moment, Swick just lay there and coughed. Interesting magic, translocation. He'd thrown the knife as hard as he could—hard enough to send it perhaps the better part of a mile—but that didn't mean that *he* had moved that fast. He hadn't shared his target's momentum, just its location. Which meant that when he and the hand had appeared beside it, they'd simply dropped right down. Good luck that there'd been a nice, soft house beneath them to break their fall because they'd probably been over a hundred feet up.

On the other hand, these finer details weren't something most people knew. Swick reckoned that more than one of the Red Fingers had seen his knife in flight, and they'd probably guessed that he'd translocated to it.

Which meant, if he was lucky, they'd be focusing on the area around its likely point of landing, had he not snatched it down with him. Thousands of feet away from where Swick himself currently was.

He did find it hard not to brag sometimes. Swick couldn't invent new magics or create giant monsters that spit toxic gas like Shaiagrazni. And he couldn't glance at two armies and predict exactly how their fight would turn out like Baird. But he could damned well trick a man, given half a chance. And that was good enough for the most part.

"What the bloody hell is wrong with you?!" the hand roared, snapping Swick out of his smug stupor. The noble thrashed wildly atop him, scrambling off of Swick, then coughing and spluttering his way to a stumbling half stand as he rocked across the inside of the room.

It was noon, thereabouts, and their surroundings were rather *exposed* thanks to the hole they'd left in the ceiling, but there was so much damned dust in the air that the light was scarcely even reaching the walls fifteen feet across.

Swick got to his own feet, sighing.

"You're welcome."

The hand glared at him.

"For almost breaking my neck?"

That, at last, actually irritated Swick.

"For dragging you out of a death match we couldn't win, sending the enemy a thousand yards off your trail, and breaking your fall with my own damned body. Or do you think twelve stone of asshole and another one and a half of chain mail is *pleasant* to feel crunching down into your chest skull first?"

Surprisingly, the hand actually paused. His lips thinned, nostrils flared, and then, slowly, he nodded.

"I . . . apologize," he said stiffly.

Swick waited for more, an elaboration, some *thanks* perhaps, but it seemed that was all he'd get. He might have even pushed the matter had his leg not flared up in agony at that exact moment.

"Bugger!" He gasped, feeling the limb threaten to collapse under his weight. The hand eyed him warily as Swick limped to lean against a wall, hastily pulling up his trouser leg and studying the wound.

It did not look good.

Swick hadn't even felt the injury, but that was no surprise. Sometimes the frenzy of battle would leave a man numb to the most grievous of wounds. This wasn't that. He was in no danger of losing the leg, let alone bleeding to death, but Swick could recognize a gnarly ruin when he saw it. Somewhere, somehow, he'd been gashed deep enough to almost reach the bone, and luck alone had saved him from an arterial wound. The muscle of his limb had been mangled, torn, or at best bruised, and he could feel its enfeeblement with every movement. It was a wonder he hadn't noticed his own slowness in the fight.

Or, rather, it was evidence that he'd taken the blow right at its end. The pain was increasing with every second, and Swick knew that it wouldn't stop anytime soon. He'd live, but he wouldn't enjoy it for a good while.

"You'll live," the hand noted, suddenly beside him. Swick looked up.

He wasn't delusional enough to think the noble was speaking out of concern. He just wanted to know whether his best chance of surviving the city would be likely to keel over. Swick could hardly blame him.

"I agree." He grunted, standing, wincing, forcing back the waves of throbbing pain. "But I won't be dancing for a while. Best avoid any more fights with people who can actually give us a run for our money."

"Agreed." The hand nodded, turning for the door. "It should be safe outside, yes? You mentioned throwing the enemy off our trail by a thousand yards."

"Probably," Swick replied, readying his knives just in case. "You never know, but my best guess is we're in the clear."

The hand seemed far from happy with that, which Swick also couldn't blame him for, but he was decent enough to get the door himself.

As luck would have it—or sheer probability, at least—they *were* in the clear. For the time being. Swick was under no illusions about their chances of evading the Red Fingers for long. He'd captained most of those men long enough to know they were sharp as well as tough, and the raw brute strength they could throw around as a fighting force meant answers regarding Swick-sightings would be all too easily extracted from anywhere in the city they cared to check.

Swick's count started the moment the first citizen saw him because that was when word began to spread. He hurried to ensure that he wasn't outraced by the deadly waves of gossip running outward in every direction.

As he and the hand shot through the city, Swick was finally able to test the man's true limits. As he might have suspected, they were not so great. A powerful ranger's strength, and a helping more than most knights', but his speed in mail was still worse than Swick's with a wounded leg. The two of them nonetheless made swift progress through the city, leaving gaping faces and snarling curses well in their wake as the wind carried them on.

"Everything always goes to shit," the hand whispered, seemingly to himself.

"Used to this?" Swick asked him, reckoning he could do with a distraction. The noble glared.

"The worst thing about today is King Galukar has almost been proved right. He insisted all his councilors learn to fight because that was what made a man. Well, today, that idiocy has saved my life."

Swick grinned. He could very much relate. More than once, stupidity had saved him too. It made men unpredictable, and an unpredictable man was very hard to catch.

Somehow, he got the feeling he'd best start getting clever, all the same.

Ado's cell was grimy. It was tight; it was tiny. Its walls were bare, jagged, untreated stone. Its cracks were numerous and wide. The ceiling leaked; the floor housed insect hives. By night it was torturously cold; by day it was torturously hot. Always it was isolating and mind-numbing, a constant crushing pressure on her wits that threatened to squeeze away every semblance of cognition as it compressed hours into minutes, to seconds, to no time at all.

In short, it was an actual cell. The sort she'd have been thrown in from the start had she not been carrying the blood of a monarch in her veins. The sort that would have awaited Collin Baird, whom she'd always judged for his low birth.

Just as the people who'd designed her cell would have done.

The third day—or, rather, after the third period of sleep that Ado had decided designated the separation between days in her timeless prison—was when Folami paid her his first visit. She might have turned him away, thirty hours earlier, but time in captivity had a way of gnawing away at all things. Will more than anything.

Her brother looked rather disgusted by Ado's surroundings, and she'd expected that. What surprised her was to see his disgust aimed at her own self too. Ado didn't have access to a mirror of course, but she had a nose. She knew full well how she reeked. Washing had been a privilege not much seen to in her confinement, and apparently it showed.

"Why did you have to speak out, Ado?" he asked, face splitting for a moment to let irritation and sympathy bubble out past the revulsion. It was worse, she decided. Worse by far.

"Because what I said needed saying," Ado lied. "And if you're only here to remind me of my poor decisions, then I'd sooner you just turn around and fuck off."

Folami looked aghast.

"And now you curse too. How far you've fallen. You were once so ladylike. So sweet, so inn—"

"Eat shit," Ado interrupted, and relished the look of horror upon her brother's face for the moments it lasted. "If you have something of substance to say, say it. If not, then just leave me alone. I already know what my mistakes were and weren't. I don't need you smugly reminding me. Run off and enjoy being king, your highness. For however long you last."

It had been petty of her, a reply Ado aimed to do nothing more than wound her brother as deeply and bitterly as she could manage in so limited a context. Still, she reckoned she'd earned herself a bit of pettiness.

"Shall I just go then?" Folami replied, thoughts apparently finished crystallizing and forming themselves into a structure of notably equal spite to Ado's own. "Because I don't *want* to be here, you know. I don't enjoy watching my sister fucking rot away over nothing."

Ado was so surprised to hear him swearing that she almost didn't register the *sincerity* in his voice. It was a harder, deeper-sounding punch to her gut than anything he could possibly have dreamed up as a retort. She could handle chauvinism and spite. Sympathy though . . . That was something else.

Folami held her gaze for a long moment, then started for the door in a storm of contempt. Ado let him get a whole two steps before her thoughts galvanized, and she spoke.

"You . . . This isn't all finished," she managed, needing to fight her own convulsive throat for every damned word it formed. "I know things look bad. I know my case is *poor*, but it's not *finished*. The king, he's sympathetic. More so than the high priest at least. I can reach him—I know I can. I just need to try in a private conversation, away from other people and their expectations."

It took a precipitously long moment for Folami to turn, and that told Ado more than anything else how close he was to simply leaving her. She wondered how much he *wanted* to. Things would surely be much easier for him if she died, and she'd seen herself how much pleasure he took from their roles. Whatever he said.

But still, he turned.

"Ado . . ." His face looked torn, pained. She half expected him to need more convincing and wasn't sure how she'd even go about it. But then her brother's eyes hardened.

"I'll do what I can," Folami breathed at last. "But I'm barely even a king here, outside of formality. You probably worked that out yourself already."

She had, at that. Ado saw nothing to gain by telling him though, and everything to lose, so she kept it to herself.

CHAPTER THIRTY-THREE

The king did not look bigger, now that Ado had been diminished in her power. That was curious.

She'd noticed long ago—or, rather, several months that *felt* long ago—how most of the men she knew were lessened in her current eyes compared to the towering beasts they'd once been. Ado had thought that might simply be down to the power they once had over her, and held no longer. Now she knew differently.

Whether anything would come of her epiphany, she didn't know. The king's voice rang out before she could much process it, dancing along the walls of his expansive study, reverberating through indulgent chandeliers and sliding across thick carpeting.

"How many last chances do you intend to have us give you?" the man asked, sounding more . . . weary than anything. There was the same look to his eyes that Ado had glimpsed before, but now it had evolved into outright pity.

She could understand why, at least, but that still needled her. She was *not* to be pitied.

"This isn't my chance," Ado told him. "It's yours."

The king frowned, his brow furrowing with a depth that only the perpetually worried could ever muster.

"What are you implying, girl?"

"I'm not implying anything," Ado replied. "I'm spelling it out clearly for you. This is your last chance to save your people."

Before the king could even sigh his exasperation, let alone have her escorted back to her cell, Ado pressed on.

"And I'm not talking about what the Dark Lord will do should he win either. I'm telling you what Silenos Shaiagrazni's wrath will be like. That is your real concern, believe me."

At last, that had him listening. Tentatively, perhaps, more from curiosity than urgency, but that was far more than Ado had been working with before.

"You seem to think he'll be licking his wounds if he wins, but I'm sorry to say that could not be further from the truth. Whichever side comes out victorious in this bout, they will have absorbed much of the enemy side's army. Hundreds of thousands of undead—in Shaiagrazni's case, exceedingly potent ones—and suddenly without their greatest enemy. And Shaiagrazni's sights would be set upon you, instantly."

The king's face colored, with fear or rage Ado wasn't sure.

"Why the hell would they?!" he demanded. God, it never ceased to amaze Ado how slow on the uptake the world's rulers could be.

"Because, as of this moment, you have unlawfully imprisoned a diplomatic emissary from his nation. Within a few days, you'll have executed her. Aside from this being a gross violation of diplomatic conduct—one that the rest of the world will not soon forget when considering negotiation with you—it is also an act of direct contempt toward House Shaiagrazni themselves. Tell me, how do you think Silenos Shaiagrazni is likely to respond to something like that? Because I've seen how he reacted to mere resistance. I will never unsee it, no matter how long I live. My father now lives, forever, as a part of his cloak. In agony, conscious and eternal. And all he did was fight back."

Ado could not have drained the color from the old king's face more quickly even if she'd cut his throat instead of speaking.

"You . . . How could you serve a creature like that?"

The question had no political aim at all. That she could see. It was pure confusion. Pure . . . Horror. Ado found herself considering it too. How could she?

Because she'd been ambitious, rejected by wider society for reasons beyond her control or merits, overlooked and scorned by all except Shaiagrazni himself. But that was not all, or at least not anymore. Somewhere along the way Ado had realized that Shaiagrazni had a *point* about it all. If she could be so easily overlooked, why not others?

"Because the choice I have been left with," she replied, "is between a cruel man and a world of fools. I will choose the cruel man. He, at least, can be reasoned with."

She was almost surprised to hear the truth from herself.

The king was silent for a long while after that, simply falling back into himself as if he were concentrating on some great effort of physicality. Ado knew better than to interrupt him. He was thinking, considering what she'd said, and if she just waited, there was a very strong chance he'd do the rest of her work for her.

He was afraid of Silenos Shaiagrazni, she knew. Utterly and completely. And the terror that gripped him was such that it pushed him away from the very notion of acting against the caster. No matter how wise it may have been—and Ado firmly believed defying House Shaiagrazni was about the least wise thing he could do—he'd be biased against the notion.

In this, she saw power. In this, she saw the genius of Shaiagrazni's deeds. The world would have hated him already, no matter what he did, simply for the justice of his cause. And so he had turned that hatred into trembling, seizing fear. Because fear could be used.

"You would have me free you," the king said at last, voice tight as a strangling noose, face purple as the man whose neck it was about.

"I would." Ado nodded. "For a start, that is. You understand you'll have a lot to make up for even after earning Shaiagrazni's mercy. And his mercy is in short supply these days."

The king's eyes were affixed on the floor as if someone had bolted them there.

"Even if everything you say is true, I am not the man to resolve it. My influence in this city is second to the high priest. Surely you know that."

As a fact, she did.

"Of course," Ado began, slowly, cautiously. "But, with so much at stake, you must realize . . . there are other ways to do what is necessary than the direct, lawful approach. Ways of taking power and placing it where it needs to be."

King Galukar must have fallen two, even three hundred yards. He'd landed hard, skull coming down upon a great boulder, dozens of stone in body weight and armor breaking the rock to pieces. For his part, he seemed to have taken barely even a scratch from the actual fall.

It was the demon's mauling that had so deeply savaged him.

Galukar was alive when they found him, but barely. Sphera had seen sides of beef less cooked than he was. His body was littered with wounds, inches deep and . . . festering. Some were rotting as any other injury might, remarkable only for the impossibly short minutes the necrotizing decay had taken to seize them. Others were aflame, hissing with steam or lightning. Even clutched by some dark multicolored substance that sizzled and spit like shade-stuff, and ignored all Sphera's efforts to examine it.

His blood was plentiful, and scattered out for a dozen paces around him where it had rained down. Black hair spilling out, eyes shut and tight with pain, bones nicked or cracked. The Godblade stuck in the ground just beyond his arm's reach. That, alone, was untouched. Its divine power was something Sphera had always been skeptical of. As far as she was concerned, Arion Falls had had the right of it when he called it nothing more than an ancient relic made by simpletons with more magic than brains.

But seeing it there, standing tall and unmarked where it erupted from a surrounding of molten dirt and stone . . . She could understand the reverence her men were showing as they beheld it.

There were other, more convenient times to indulge her awe, however. Sphera focused on the king.

"Healers?!" she demanded, looking around, frantic. "We need healers!"

There were not that many disadvantages to her master's approach of rule, but among them was that it was quite hard to convince people to import into his nation. The natural self-sufficiency of Shaiagraznian magic offset this, mostly, but one area in which they lacked was casters.

Healers, above all. A half dozen hurried forth, swarming around Galukar and blasting him with restorative spellwork. Sphera watched it all, mouth drier by the moment.

Everything had been hinged on King Galukar. He was their not-so-secret weapon, a man equivalent to tens of thousands all on his own, able to cross battlefields faster than any formation to either support a defense or crush the enemy's.

And now he was bleeding and convulsing in a pile at her feet. All because a single damned demon had shown up.

"Where's the demon?!" Sphera called out, suddenly remembering the creature—the *thing*—and thrown into a frenzy by the recollection. That was their biggest concern. If it had so much as a spasmodic death rattle left inside it, many more might well perish.

"Over here, sir," a soldier called, Kaltan, and all the more unnerving for it. His face was a testament to human terror, wrung like a chicken's neck and pale as a sheet. Sphera almost couldn't bring herself to follow the man.

She did though, and the remains she saw, Sphera knew, would haunt her through the rest of her life. The demon's corpse was beyond description and comprehension. But not beyond recollection. Life was far too cruel for that.

"Burn it," she whispered. "And burn everything within an acre of it."

Her voice sounded shrill, squeaky. It sounded like she was a child again. Because she was. And so was each and every one of the people now surrounding her. They were all stupid, blind, simple infants stumbling through the world without the slightest idea of what it held. And Sphera's glimpse behind the curtain left her wishing for the first time in her life that she'd never learn more again. Better to be an ignorant animal than subject her mind to a truth as dark as this.

Better by far.

Days passed, and King Galukar did not recover. Sphera knew the Godblade granted some measure of vitality to bolster the raw physical prowess of its wielder, King Galukar looking as youthful as he did at close to one hundred was proof of that.

Apparently, the miasma of demon-inflicted wounds was beyond even his capacity to weather. While he remained unconscious, she was left to maintain the army's cohesion by herself.

Her master had done a fine job of inspiring obedience, of course. Such was the bare minimum to be expected of a Shaiagrazni named, but it was still an uphill battle for her.

Men were scared, of course. And those few hundred who'd actually seen the demon up close were beyond scared. Sphera could empathize. When she wasn't dealing with the metaphorical nightmares of daytime command, her nights were plagued with terrors that shook her out of sleep a dozen times before dawn. Twice she shit herself, bowels loosed like a hanged man. Not once did the shame even register.

Nothing registered anymore, except the fear.

Within a week though, she had adjusted. The horrors were still there, but Sphera had come to terms with the simple pragmatics of what they meant and begun to work around them. She would not fail Master Shaiagrazni simply because she was cowed by the sight of some cluster of magic. She would sooner die. Marching became Sphera's newest concern, the mundane inconveniences of orchestrating a hundred thousand pairs of boots her new torment. They made progress.

Not as much as would have been possible under Galukar, however. Sphera saw it only now that the task had fallen to her, but that man had a way of moving men through sheer presence. It was the weight of the Hero, she supposed. Not something that could be matched by a necromancer, not even her master.

With the battle's result, there would be no more holding against the Dark Lord. His forces had been just as awestruck by the demon's death as

Shaiagrazni's had by its presence, which was the sole reason Sphera was able to march from the battlefield without being swamped by cavalry. That wouldn't last, however. And her men's terror would.

Galukar's infirmity already scythed away a great fraction of the army's combat power, and that was worsened by far as the harassing attacks finally began in earnest. Cavalry, yes, as Sphera had expected. But demons too. More of them.

Not a one was half the equal of the entity that had first attacked, but all bore a whisper of its power. Giant things with too many faces, or no faces at all. Formless and dynamic, esoteric and unstoppable. They came at night, mostly, and the Kaltans were well accustomed to that. But it made little difference. Their arrows punched through bodies of liquid, casters' fireballs sizzling out against the weight of magic infusing their enemies. Lives were lost, ground given, morale destroyed.

Day by day they marched, bleeding out more men with every new attack, and Sphera took to spending much of her time beside the bed of King Galukar. He didn't awaken, and his wounds began to smell of that sickly sweet death scent that betrayed a rotting body.

She almost expected their army to match that scent too.

CHAPTER THIRTY-FOUR

It wasn't a good plan, but that was to be expected. All Hexeri's good plans had gone out the window when her men were captured. And, at the very least, it wasn't an awful one either. Certainly, it was better than hiding behind a rock and waiting to be caught.

At least, she was somewhat sure it was better.

"You're ready?" she asked Baird, who grunted in the exact same way he had the other times she'd asked. He seemed to grunt a lot, on the mission, and Hexeri found the habit suddenly quite vexing. She made nothing of it though, rather too tied up with the prospect of her imminent death or capture to do so.

Collin watched the vampire sprint off into the night and took another moment to appreciate just how quiet she was. Rangers trained for years to move like that, but off she went.

Well, probably she'd trained for years too. With centuries of life—unlife—under her belt, he imagined she'd gotten practice doing most things just incidentally. Then again, Shaiagrazni apparently hadn't been in so much as a fist fight for most of his life, and he was barely younger.

Collin killed that train of thought dead, having more important things to worry about than the practice of his allies. Moments passed, quick and jagged as falling stalactites, then the distraction began.

Not easy, distracting dark elves. They were a diligent lot. One had to do more than just sprint through a sentry's line of sight to make them commit. That was why the vampire dropped down in front of one and neatly twisted his head off, then put her fist into the chest of a second. Quick, easy deaths. These elves were good, but they weren't inherently stronger than a human knight. Fragile things of wet crimson paper to the fists of a vampire as old as Hexeri.

Well that got their attention. Through the dark, Collin could clearly see as men and women—the elves ran a mixed-sex fighting force—leaped to their feet and came storming around to give chase. Hexeri was already sprinting her way from them, crossing a dozen paces before the first flash of burning magic could illuminate the night.

She really did look fearsome, in that light. Hair like coal, spattered with blood, eyes a deeper red than any of it. Collin had seen predatory animals interrupted from a feast with less gore and blunter teeth on them.

And that was a good thing, because the scarier a sight the dark elves saw killing their men, the more of them would be inclined to give chase.

She carried herself off at a surprisingly slow pace, and Collin soon saw why. Only twenty or so dark elves were after her, the rest standing warily guard around their camp, suspecting exactly what was happening. For a second, he feared the plan was doomed. Then Hexeri slowed, turned, and smashed into her pursuers.

It wasn't as easy a fight as it might have been, but it was over quickly. Shadows and blood dancing around at her command, shredding the dark elves apart in mere seconds.

More importantly, proving to the rest that this enemy couldn't be caught with half measures. More broke off from the camp to pursue her now, many more. Twenty, fifty, a hundred. Then more still.

Hexeri sprinted off into the darkness, magic flying all around her, even being clipped by one particularly close streak of lightning. She disappeared, then her pursuers did.

Which left the camp relatively unguarded. Collin made his move.

To begin with, he started simply. Taking out one guard, then another. He was careful not to draw his bow back its full length, ensuring that the arrows didn't produce the whipcrack signifier of supersonic flight and give away his position. Against enemies this fragile, four-tenths of their speed was more than enough.

One after another, the elves went down, falling as a singular corpse in some cases, blown apart at the seams in most others. Collin fell into the old rhythm of combat, barely thinking save to spot targets and run through the mechanical motions of loosing another arrow. His back and shoulders began to twitch with the low heat of muscular exertion, fingers numbing and burning at once. It was a manageable strain—another advantage to keeping the projectiles slow and weak. Soon enough, he'd dropped more than a dozen elves, perhaps a quarter of their defenders, and those who remained got clever.

Boots scraped together, shoulders meeting shoulders, and they formed a solid square around their prisoners. Bound and unarmed, the Kaltans were immobilized and unable to do anything but watch their captors' backs while Collin watched their fronts.

Magic flashed, shields rising up. He experimented with an arrow, which broke against the arcane barrier without penetrating. Collin was too far away for even his own eyes to recognize anything on the dark elves' faces, but he couldn't help but imagine smugness burning away behind their eyes.

Well, it wasn't the end of his plan. He'd suspected they might have a trick up their sleeve.

And Collin had his own.

He crept closer, gliding through the territory as quietly as he could, keeping low and out of sight. Fortunately he'd had the metallic limbs of his bow darkened, as was standard ranger tradition, and the rest of its structure was pure keratin, so there was no risk of his position being given away in a glint of moonlight. Collin closed until he was no longer confident of doing so without being sighted, just fifty paces from the enemy's formation. Then he reached into his pack.

Shaiagrazni was a bastard, but he really did make some powerful weapons. Collin held one of them now: an unassuming ceramic cylinder, completely filled with liquid. Even he had a hard time imagining it would do what he'd been told it would, but there was hardly any choice in the matter now except to find out. Collin threw it.

Inside, the liquid had filled as close to 100 percent of the container as Shaiagrazni was physically able to ensure. That had been the most important part of its creation because even the slightest bubble of air inside would have made it not only ineffective, but crushingly deadly to its wielder.

The cylinder—apparently called a grenade—impacted its enemy. Collin let his smile bloom at the sight.

He'd known, intellectually, to expect a large explosion. But he hadn't known quite how big it would get. The liquid contained within that weapon had been more powerful than the stuff Shaiagrazni's cannons used to propel iron balls the weight of small children across miles of terrain, and Collin was fairly sure he'd even used more in that device than he did in the usual cannon blast. The dark elves' shield shuddered, its entire length trembling and quivering as deep ripples ran along its suddenly visible surface. It held, but barely, and Collin saw the weakness clean as day.

Feeling generous, he helped it along to failure by putting a supersonic arrow into the part that looked most fragile.

The shield collapsed, the elves stumbled as their magic broke, and before they'd even righted themselves, a second of Collin's grenades came down on top of them. He really was glad he'd stashed them in so many wagons, rather than keeping them on him. Glad too he'd heeded his father's advice to always have a spare weapon hidden within grabbing range, or else he'd have snuck back to the site of their ambush and found nothing.

More than anything though, he was glad Shaiagrazni was so good at making weapons because the sight of close to thirty dark elves being blown into wet meat was satisfying on a level he struggled to describe.

Collin recovered from the display before the survivors, which he reckoned was fair enough. An arrow caught a skull between its eyes, ripping off everything above the jaw, and those six or seven left turned and fled without another word. Also fair enough.

But they had friends out there still, and Collin was in no mood to fight more dark elves than he absolutely had to. He took his time putting each one of them down before they could meet their allies, and enjoyed it as he went. It was a shame, almost, that Shaiagrazni's growing power was leaving him closer to the day where he'd run out of the Dark Lord's bastards to kill.

It was what it was, he supposed.

He reached the captives quickly, and got to work more quickly still. Plucking dark-elf blades from the ground, he freed a dozen and handed the weapons around with orders to loose more. They, in turn, helped to untie others. Soon enough, men were being unbound at a rate of hundreds per minute.

"Rangers?!" Collin called out, desperately sprinting among the men, searching for his chosen best. "Bring me the rangers. There's another fight coming, and we need every elite we can get our hands on."

But it was dark, and Kaltans—even the best trained—were not rangers themselves. Collin found only confusion among those he asked. Still, time was on his side. Hexeri must have been leading the rest of the elves on a merry chase because even with the passing minutes rapidly compressing themselves toward an hour, he soon found his men.

The rangers were in sorry states, half starved. Probably the dark elves had done that just in case of a breakout, as they were now facing. Clever bastards. Collin was quick about preparing, however. He'd not been able to drag many weapons from the place they'd been ambushed. Regardless of how many had *been* there, there were limits to what he could carry. A steel bow for each ranger, and a few dozen spears for those who weren't already armed in dark-elf weaponry.

It was a shoddy fighting force, outnumbered two to one by the enemy. But it was a damn sight better than they'd had before. Particularly with the rangers.

Half starved or no, they were still rangers. And they all moved quick and calm as they got into position before their captors could return.

Ado had not actually been sure what the first step of her plan would be until the moment she suggested it. She'd not much expected to even get so far as to give it voice before the king, let alone see him heed it. In the following night though, she was given ample time to consider her words.

She found no better alternative. Either she'd chosen well or foolishly, but no matter what, her strategy was the finest she herself was capable of.

Perhaps Silenos Shaiagrazni could have done better, or rather she was almost certain he could have, but she'd been alone, and she'd made her move without help.

Now all that was left was seeing whether it had saved her.

CHAPTER THIRTY-FIVE

The waiting was worse than it had been before. When Ado had first arrived in her cell, with nothing to look forward to but her own execution, the days had congealed together into a single, homogeneous torment. Now she felt every second as an isolated stab at her will.

She'd never understood, as a girl, how a person might go mad in captivity. Now she knew. When everything was so similar, when each hour brought entirely nothing new, it was terribly easy to grow lost within one's own thoughts. And the thoughts of a person finding themselves jailed . . . Well, they were things to induce madness without a doubt.

This time, however, Ado was not waiting so long. Or at least she didn't *think* she was. It was hard to tell, but she certainly slept less before being drawn out of her prison this time. Awaiting her outside was not a hooded executioner, but a more standard noble's escort. They took her through the palace and deposited her, once more, in the king's office. The man, if anything, looked worse than he had before, seeming to have surrendered an extra decade of his life overnight, and shaking as he poured himself rather more wine than he'd been drinking when last they'd met.

A good sign, Ado hoped.

"The high priest is dead," the king told her, his words direct, but his voice forced into a fearful whisper by his own tumultuous emotions. "Assassins sent by the Dark Lord. They permeated our defenses and slew him in the dead of the night."

Ado nodded in understanding. As far as explanations went, it was quite a pedestrian one, but she hoped that would only make it all the more sturdy over time. The king did not strike her as the sort of man who might maintain an elaborate lie, however better it might otherwise obfuscate their crime.

"I . . . apologize," he continued. "For not taking the true threat of the Dark Lord seriously enough, and I pledge my city's forces to Silenos Shaiagrazni. For as long as I remain in power after this."

He didn't expect to live? That surprised her. Ado had taken him for a true fool to have acted so obviously against his own interest without realizing it. Now she knew differently. He was just a good man, one who's own life was not the most precious thing to him. She felt herself suddenly moved by the display.

But she hardened her heart carefully. Emotion was a mental fault she could not afford to humor, now of all times.

"Then my own forces are welcome into the kingdom," Ado guessed, stifling the urge to grow confident at the fact. The king nodded.

"There will be rebellions," he croaked. "Blood will spill. So, so much blood . . ." The man swallowed. "Yes, they are allowed into the city. In fact, I will announce the high priest's death only once you have positioned your forces behind its walls."

Ado nodded, finding herself more and more convinced of the man's competence with every passing word. It was disheartening to know she had not come with any great weight of military power, but she had more than one Shaiagraznian grotesquerie. And one might almost have been enough on its own.

"Thank you," Ado replied, and was surprised to see the king's eyes grow hard and angry.

"I did not do this for you," he spit. "Don't thank me. Don't you dare. This is for my people, for the children of Wudra and the followers of God, understand?"

"I understand." She nodded, suddenly careful again now that she'd seen his temper give. It appeared Ado had found one of the lines one couldn't cross.

"Leave me." The king scowled, leaning back in his chair and looking suddenly . . . shrunken. "Please."

Ado left him.

Outside, she was not particularly surprised to find Folami waiting for her, and even less surprised to see a look of utter fury coating his face. Ado waited for the smug satisfaction or urge to gloat, but nothing came. She felt no victory looking at her brother, just a nagging sympathy.

You had everything you ever wanted, then had it taken away. I can relate.

Ado felt that sympathy, and she crushed it as completely as she was able. There was no time for petty emotion now.

"Are you happy now, murderer?" Folami asked, hatred reaching a new height as he spoke, voice trembling under its weight. "It wasn't enough to just aid a butcher. You had to become one yourself, is that it? Or do you somehow think the high priest's death is the fault of others when you as good as ordered it?"

It was fascinating how little his words reached her. Ado just walked around her brother, heading to her own rooms. They had been the ones she ought to have been staying in from the start, large and indulgent as any she'd ever set foot in. The rooms of a king—or a queen, in this case—and a conveniently short walk from the centers of Wudra's command.

Folami though followed her.

"Do you not even intend to defend yourself?!" he snapped. "Or do you not care about being thought a killer? Do you see no issues with that title? Damn it, woman, answer me."

They were in her quarters now, and Ado was pleased to see a pair of guards awaiting her within them. Big men, both of them. Doubtless, they had their fair share of Vigor pumping through every vein to have been assigned the task of watching her. They would serve perfectly for what she needed now.

"Men, beat my brother, but do not kill or permanently injure him."

For a moment, the room was silent. Then the sound of steel scraping on steel rang out as armored men moved. Folami stared, swallowed, took a step back, and opened his mouth with a face twisted tight into regal defiance as he made to speak.

His words were silenced by the first gauntleted punch slamming into his cheek.

His head snapped back, and he lost his footing near instantly. He was not allowed to fall, however, for the second guard grabbed him and hoisted him upward for a second blow to land upon his gut. Folami wheezed, folding over, trying to curl up as more fists came down on him. It was no use. Within moments, his skin was a canvas of bruising and his body was shaky with pain. Ado watched his half-dazed form dragged from the building and tossed out into the adjacent hall.

She waited to feel something, a touch of pleasure or satisfaction, but she was still just as empty as before. Ado had not hurt her brother out of spite or self-gratification. She'd simply done it because it needed doing.

Like Shaiagrazni himself. Rulership was not something she'd understood before his arrival. How could it have been? Her only exposure to it had been exclusively through the lens of imbeciles, and how vastly more gifted than any of them she was. Now she'd seen a true ruler do his work, however, and she understood the place of cruelty in it, just as she understood the place of kindness.

There was little place for the latter in this world though. Ado could be kind when humanity did not make itself her enemy. Until then, they'd need correction.

A knock took her door, and for a moment Ado wondered whether her brother had actually come back. But no, he was not a strong man—not strong enough to weather the sort of beating he'd just received and continue bothering her in spite of it. This was someone else.

"Enter," she called, not bothering to take a suitably regal position in her seat, just standing in the open and waiting to speak with her visitor. Ado hadn't known whom to expect, but Rochtai had certainly not been among her first choices.

The magus was looking better, which was to say he had put on some of the huge volumes of weight he'd lost and no longer had quite so pronounced a pair of bags under his eyes. The wear of his ordeal under Shaiagrazni was still apparent at a glance, but he kept it hidden with considerable skill. It was natural, she supposed, for a magus to hold his emotions tightly concealed. Even when they were as crushingly intense as his must have been.

"My lady." He nodded, respectful now. It felt strange. Ado had always seen a superior in Rochtai—a tutor. Now though, their stations could not be more reversed. Were she one of her brothers, she'd have been raised to expect such an eventuality, told as she grew up that it was her birthright.

Yet another entry to the endless list of ways in which they were fractionally advantaged over her, she supposed.

"Magus." Ado nodded, sensing a desire for formality in him and deciding to follow suit. It was only appropriate. Either way, a ruler could not simply fraternize as they saw fit.

"You managed to turn things around," he noted, smiling through his thick beard. "I knew you would. The moment we received the call to enter, I knew it was you. Mind, it came just in time. A few of our forces were eager to simply barge our way in."

Ado winced. That would have been a disaster. Wudra's forces were not as sophisticated as the armies of House Shaiagrazni, but they were still among the strongest of the continent's nations. Thousands of paladins, scores of thousands of normal men, and no small number of contracted magi from Magira in wake of recent events to boot. Her meager escort would not have lasted very long at all in a direct confrontation, let alone an offensive siege.

"Fortunate timing then, indeed," she noted. Rochtai nodded sagely, and paused for a moment, apparently struggling to say something . . . difficult.

"I am afraid, however, that your timing could have been somewhat *more* fortunate," he continued. "Because the Dark Lord has already dispatched rather a large force our way."

Ado swore. She should have known. The king had accepted her terms far, far too easily. Of course the Dark Lord was coming to crush them. He'd be an idiot to miss the chance of removing Shaiagraznian forces while they were isolated like this, and reanimating Wudra's armies after the fact . . .

It might well tip the entire war in his favor.

"How long do we have?" she asked abruptly. Rochtai was quick in giving his answer, as practical now as he'd ever been. Perhaps more.

"Days, at best. They drew incredibly close before being sighted."

That was what one might have expected without Kaltan rangers surveying the horizons. It would have been amusingly ironic to see Wudra fall for their own refusal to adopt such a useful tool were it not so pathetically tragic. Particularly if it were not dragging Ado down with them.

She would not fail. Sooner die than fail.

CHAPTER THIRTY-SIX

Hexeri had been chased by a lot of things over her unlife, which was not an uncommon boast among vampires. The usual, to start with. Illiterate, shit-smelling lynch mobs, paladins, that sort of thing. Over the years, she'd faced down a few more notable pursuits—two Heroes at once as she'd dealt with a few weeks ago had been the highlight.

One hundred and fifty battle-trained dark elves though might have been a new level of fucked, even for her.

Elves were humanoid, but not quite the same. There was actually some debate on which species came first. Predictably, both tended to prefer themselves as the progenitor race. The elves did seem to have certain advantages, however, in regard to making claims of innate superiority.

They were faster, by far. An ordinary elf of any kind made the quickest Vigorless humans look sluggish, and this exponential advantage remained even when both species trained to strengthen themselves. Hexeri had seen elves smack crossbow bolts out of the air, cross rooms before a human could even register their movement. Even, on one occasion, witnessed a particularly fast member of their species sprint across the surface of a lake.

Vampires were quicker, but only just. And there were a lot of dark elves after her now. Dark elves were among the more physically potent varieties.

Hexeri used every trick she could think of, dragging them through tough terrain, slipping in across passages that were easily wide enough for her but struggled accommodating her pursuers in their multitudes. The dark elves hounded her all the same, wise to her tactics from the first chase, and now not nearly as cautious in their pursuit.

There was no helping it. Hexeri had dodged magic as long as she was likely to manage. She had no choice but to turn and head back to the site of the prisoners. Either Collin Baird had freed his men . . .

. . . Or she was sprinting into the jaws of death. Funny how Hexeri just kept on finding her life balanced atop the hinge of human will. She supposed that was the consequence of living in a world with so damned many of them.

Her feet pounded the dirt into crushed debris, and the wind rang in her ears like icy fingers of air clawing down atop a mountain's peak.

Miles. Hexeri had to run miles. Had that ever been hard? It had, once before, when she was still a living thing of fragile meat and temporary strength. And now it was hard again because, though she crossed the span in mere minutes, every step she took was hounded by blasts of magic. Dirt shot up in great fountains around her. The air convulsed as heat diffused along it and whipped up great winds in protest. She felt her skin ache and blister with the temperatures, knowing that a mere human would have been incinerated in such conditions.

She ran, all the same. Because to stop for even an instant was to die.

Hexeri came to her destination, and her heart sank as she realized it held no assembled force of spearmen and freedom-drunk warriors. The dark elves continued their pursuit, now only dozens of paces behind her rather than scores, and the end drew nearer.

That was when Baird's first attack came, one of Shaiagrazni's explosive devices.

Explosions weren't a foreign thing to Hexeri—despite how they preached of their cerebral removal from petty human prejudices, magi didn't tend to like vampires any more than anyone else—but it still shook her to feel the concussion of one so powerful detonating so close to her. Every tooth in her mouth rattled, her ears throbbed with the pressure, and she almost lost her footing for a second. The temptation was too much to resist. She risked a glance over her shoulder to see what it had done to the dark elves.

Apparently, it had done a lot. A grizzly mountain of death met Hexeri's gaze, so mangled that she struggled to tell one corpse apart from another.

More dark elves were coming though. Spreading out, diffusing like dusk mist under a harsh morning sun. They were nothing if not rational, the elves, and scarcely hesitated to act in whatever way they deemed most effective. She watched them step over convulsing, dying comrades without so much as a glance downward and continue their assault.

By now, Baird's preparations were coming to light. His rangers were first among them, letting out a volley of arrows that tore into elves and dropped another dozen or so in sprays of visceral scarlet. She snapped out of her own daze, snatching the beads of blood from the air and sending them into surrounding enemies as jagged knives and thorns. They only got that one solid volley off before the dark elves closed in for melee.

It was not a long battle, but what it lacked in length it more than made up for with raw savagery. Baird had done a fine job arming and freeing prisoners because there stood perhaps a comparable number of spearmen to dark elves—even before the initial explosion. Still, they didn't last long. Defensive formation broken, bodies sundered apart, blood splashed out in all directions. Hexeri herself even felt slightly sick watching the mangling occur, but was far too occupied by her own killing to take much note of it.

Fortunately, dark elves were logical. Humans were not prone to unrelentingly fight until their force's numbers were entirely exhausted, and elves did not even feel the insane adrenal vigor that sometimes compelled their shorter cousins to battle so fiercely in the first place. They had to kill no more than thirty before the enemy fled.

But in killing those thirty, they lost many more. Virtually every spearman was cut down, and two rangers to boot.

Hexeri found Collin Baird kneeling before the slain elites, face low, hands tightened into stone-dense fists. There was a purer strain of hatred burning on his face than she had seen anywhere else.

"Friends of yours?" she asked.

Baird didn't look up at her. He just shook his head. Hexeri saw the tear glint on his cheek, despite the darkness of the night around him. A vampire always saw such things. It was as much a curse as their weakness before the sun.

Because one could not see and smell a person's thoughts the way they did and not understand them. Even while surrounded by hateful fire and sneering mobs, they understood them.

"My men," Baird breathed, a confusing mix of fury and misery in his voice. "Rangers. Been at it longer than I have. In fact, all the ones still alive have. I'm the only one left not in his twenties."

"They died well," Hexeri said stupidly. He glanced at her with all the scorn her reply deserved.

"There's no dying well," Baird spit. "There's living, and there's fucking that up. They . . ." He swallowed, closing his eyes and muttering something to himself as he stood. Hexeri listened in a moment, sharpening her ears with focus.

"First my dad, then the rest. One by one. They all die, and I keep living." His eyes opened, and now she saw a ferocity in them that put even her back a step. "And I'll keep on living until this is over, until I've gutted that evil fucker and watched the shit spill out of him."

Hexeri saw, then, what Collin Baird truly was.

"We've lost our chance to hinder the Dark Lord's forces," she noted, mouth dry. And Hexeri didn't see even a scrap of regret upon Baird's face, only that hatred. The bottomless, consuming hatred that seemed to blot out every other facet of his cognition. He did not smile, nor did he scowl. Whatever expression was on his face couldn't be described in terms as human as that.

He just showed his teeth.

It was almost fun, hiding in the city of Torib. It brought Swick back to his roots. The advantages of a skyship were numerous, of course, but there was something to be lost in the virtual untouchability and security it provided. How did a man keep his edge when he could actually afford to just drink himself stupid all day? How did a criminal remain swift, at all, when he had some magic vessel to provide all the swiftness for him? It was almost relieving to be rid of the thing.

Only almost though. Because despite all of that, the skyship had still provided *virtual untouchability and security*. God, Swick really shouldn't have plowed it into the side of that fucking fortress.

There were not many lifelines for them within the foreign city. Swick snatched up all the ones he could get and counted them carefully. First came the basic, obvious fact of their having a decent chance to leave sooner rather than later. So long as they could find the individual known as Bal.

More pressing than that though was that Torib was a *racket* town. Swick had spent most of his life in them, and that was no small thing. Racket towns were younger than most other kinds, coming into existence in response to the population boom that had struck the world over the last few centuries as magically augmented crop growth and infrastructure became more commonplace.

They were hellholes. Springing up simply by having the underclass of established cities emptied out into the world, ideally those guilty of criminality, but more practically just those who were considered undesirable by the rulers of their previous homes. Such people congregated, and the volatility of their new existences naturally bred just the sorts of things they were accused of partaking in to begin with.

Swick had been born in a racket town, he thought. He couldn't recall his actual birth of course, but he remembered his mother in those early days between her squeezing him out and her dying from one of the numerous diseases aging whores tended to contract. In any case, he had a familiarity with their general layout.

Each one was *different*, of course, but there were patterns. Trends. Things that emerged as a racket town did—through simple necessity—tended to conform in particular ways with other such specimens. The Red Finger Crew had been born in racket towns too, mostly. Which was where Swick's caution came from because it meant there'd be no navigational edge to be found against them.

Yes, the people you betrayed all come from the same scum pile as you, Swick. No honorable thieving for you! Only the finest, most undeserving victims in your treachery.

It did give him a leg up in navigating it quickly, and that may well have been the only reason they'd evaded capture so far. Particularly with the hand being dragged along.

"This is ridiculous," the man spat. "Who designs a city like this?"

"Nobody." Swick sighed. "This is a racket town, like I told you. It *wasn't* designed. Just built one home at a time by people who'd been chucked out of theirs."

The hand's lip curled.

"Criminals," he noted.

"Well they certainly are now, aren't they?" Swick snapped, feeling an unexpected irritation at the man all of a sudden. He'd been gnawing at his last wick for a while now, and the apathy was becoming more irritating with each word. "Now shut up and let me focus."

<h1 style="text-align:center">CHAPTER THIRTY-SEVEN</h1>

Swick did focus, and he focused long and hard for all it achieved. The problem was, familiar with racket towns or no, the things were still bloody mazes. And a single man in all of that was a very small matter to be searching for.

But doable, most of the time. He was Swick the Swift after all. The major concern—the only *real* concern—had been doing it with seemingly an entire city out for his head, and the enchantment upon his face no longer working.

Swick had added it years ago, and at no small expense to himself. Some touch of mind magic meant to banish others from taking note of him. It wasn't all-powerful—those who knew him, and those who were searching specifically for him, had low chances of succumbing to it—but for those who only knew him by portrait and reputation, it served as a powerful deterrent.

Not a small advantage, with the bounty he had on him. But it hadn't worked. That concerned Swick, and he devoted almost as much time to reasoning out why as he did to seeking out their Bal target.

The answer came to him on their third day in the city, hitting him between the eyes like a sledgehammer.

"Those mercenaries, the first group," Swick noted. "They were after you."

He directed his words to the hand, who frowned at them.

"What makes you think that?"

"They can't have been after me. My face repels recognition and memory unless a person has met me personally. The only reason you could approach me was because you didn't mean to have me captured. Which means the bounty they're talking about is on *your* head."

Instantly, the hand swore.

"Bugger." He spit. "Fuck. So . . . Fuck. That means it's the Dark Lord's doing, then. It has to be."

Swick had drawn the very same conclusion, but it still needled him to hear it. He'd been holding out hope that he was wrong.

"Best keep our heads down, more than before," he decided. "We don't know what else might be looking for us in this city."

The hand, for once, did not need any convincing.

Another day passed, and they heard whispered rumors of the one they sought.

Swick did most of the talking, now that they'd confirmed his magic still worked, and so information gathering went a damn sight quicker than it had before. They soon had a list of aliases, possible locations, and living habits to go by. Not a bad haul, he decided. Shame he wasn't charging his usual rates.

"When we find this Bal fellow, we need to take him by force," the hand noted. Swick glanced his way, baffled.

"Why the hell would we do that?"

"Because we can't afford to risk your skyship's repairs on him voluntarily saying yes" was all the man said, and his bearing suddenly seemed changed even as he said it. Back stiffer, face harder, hands flitting to a spot behind him as if they reflexively yearned to take some soldier's posture.

Arbite, Swick decided, was not the sort of place he had any intention of visiting.

"I'm injured," he pointed out. The hand rolled his eyes.

"You're a Hero, and I'm better than nine out of ten knights. If some bloody treasure hunter can hold us both off at once then frankly I'll be heading back to Arbite and stripping each one of the palace guards of their position."

He had a point, but still . . . Swick didn't like charging into fights. For all he knew, this treasure hunter *could* hold them both off at once. Or had a bodyguard who could. For all they knew, the Red Fingers had figured out why they were in Torib and were squatting around him ready to ambush Swick the moment he made his move.

Kicking down doors and cracking open heads was a fine strategy, sometimes. Make a habit of it though and one day you'd meet someone better at it than you were. And you only got to make that mistake once.

"Do you have any alternatives?" the hand asked. "This man has been perfectly hostile to kings and queens until now. How exactly do you think that will differ with Shaiagrazni?"

Swick had to admit, he had a point. He was still connected enough to all the old rumor networks to know that the stories attached to his boss were rarely the good ones. For every anecdote about him abolishing poverty within his conquered territories, there were five more about the pain coat.

Sometimes it paid to rule in such a way as to *not* make one's subjects think one was an insane murderous monster, apparently.

"Fine," Swick conceded, feeling his nerves fraying as he did. "Fine, bugger it, we'll do this your way. So long as you're aware of the risks."

"Oh, I am," the hand replied, fingers nervously resting on the pommel of his sword. "Believe me, I am, but I don't see that we have any alternative choices."

He was probably right there. Swick swore again, and then they headed out to find the treasure hunter.

The first two spots had been either bad information or just unlucky searches because they didn't find a trace of any Bal in either. The next though was altogether luckier. Third time being the charm and all that.

It was a warehouse, large and squat of the sort a magus might purchase in the hopes of converting it to some arcane workstation. There was no touch of magic to the air now, fortunately, but Swick still got the impression of strange and complex goings-on within the place. The hairs along his arms stood on end, and his mouth dried.

"Looks like a trap," he noted, and the hand scoffed.

"Looks like a bloody workplace. I know traps."

"You know military traps. A trap to you is something that stops a thousand men from turning around while they stand shield to shield. You have no idea about spotting a trap in the street."

The hand looked thoughtful for a moment, conceding the point with a nod.

"And you're not just being paranoid?"

Was he? Swick sighed.

"I *probably* am," he said at last. "But still, if I'm not . . ."

"Then it's a bloody disaster," the hand finished. "Damn . . . We don't have any choice. We have to get this man, trap or no."

"Trap or no," Swick agreed, and so they waited.

Fortunately, the treasure hunter named Bal was out of his workstation sooner rather than later. Swick's muscles had barely had the chance to cramp when he saw the door open and reveal a wreathed man striding out, without a bodyguard in sight. Tall, lithe, and . . .

Oddly familiar? Swick found himself frowning, trying to nail down where he'd seen the man before. It was no use. The memory would come back to him or it wouldn't, but he had no time to waste on simply dragging his heels in anticipation for it. Now was the time to act.

They paused only a few moments more, waiting for the treasure hunter to move across the street and draw closer to their perch. It was a good spot, relatively far from the street's center and high up—which meant anyone shorter than eight feet would have no line of sight to them. The hunter closed, closed more. Finally closed enough.

Swick lunged, slitting his thumb and filling the air with an arc of blood as his body raced it down to the ground. Clearly the treasure hunter heard something—his feet on the roof or his clothes dragging against the air— because he turned just in time to evade him.

He landed right where he'd been standing, and twisted aside from the blow he knew was aimed at his back. Swick saw the weapon miss him by inches—a damned bastard sword, and a big one—right before a boot crunched into his belly and threw him back. He stumbled, righted himself, parried a swing with one dagger, and slashed for the enemy's wrist with his other. He swayed back just in time to avoid him.

The hand was behind them, swinging too, but he missed the treasure hunter by a mile as he shot to one side, rolled, and sprang back up onto his feet. Circling now, cautious despite his power.

Swick's leg throbbed. Whatever was wrong with it had stayed wrong, despite the few days of healing, and the fractional amount of mobility he'd regained was too little for an enemy of this strength. He sent a glance toward the hand, who seemed to catch his meaning quickly. They split up, aiming to close in on the treasure hunter from two sides at once.

The treasure hunter moved first.

With a cry and a gasp, Bal raised his sword and just barely kept a swing from his enemy from reaching his gut. Swick moved to close and help, gritting his teeth against the burning of his wound.

He had to admit, the hand really was quite good. For a pen pusher. But his enemy was more than one, more than ten cuts above the knights he'd so favorably compared himself to. Even backing off and giving up the very notion of offense, he was failing to keep his body safe from the sword swings that seemed to close in almost a dozen times each second.

Swick sensed around himself, feeling his blood where it clung to the ground, decided it was worth translocating and tipping his hand. He appeared within eight feet of the treasure hunter, lunging with both daggers at once and clearly taking the bastard off guard by how he retained his head.

Not off guard enough though. Swick was still slowed by his leg, and the blade came up before his attacks could land. He felt metal screech on metal, stumbling back, hissing as his injury flared up again. The hand was already encircling their foe, however, squatted low and swinging for the belly.

A nasty wound, that, if it landed. It didn't though. The treasure hunter whipped aside and slashed downward.

Swords were bad against armor, at least with cuts and hacks. But there were limits to any rule, and apparently the hunter's strength was well past the limit of that one. Swick heard links of chain snapping apart as steel ate through steel, turning the air crimson where the hand fell back. He was moving a lot, and a glance told Swick the cut had been shallow. Lucky, nothing more.

He growled, sliced the back of his hand, and whipped it out in front of him. The treasure hunter moved, dodging, twisting, but just barely letting a fleck of crimson catch his arm. Swick translocated before he could even notice the failure.

CHAPTER THIRTY-EIGHT

The connection was a moment of glorious reaffirmation. Even wounded, Swick was still Swick. Even skilled as he was, this treasure hunter was no match for a Hero. His dagger bit through his shawl, then opened up the shoulder beneath. He pulled himself from it, cloth snagging on the blade and ripping itself open longways at his retreat to reveal a face beneath rains of tattered fabric.

Swick paused. The hand paused. The damned sky probably paused, for all the pausing that was going on. Because not a one present, save perhaps Bal, had been expecting a damned *woman* beneath all that flowing fabric and impossible speed.

Perhaps predictably, the woman herself did not pause. She came flying at Swick, if anything faster than before and far more ferocious. He was backing away again, parrying, dodging, trying his best to ignore the growing pain of his leg and aware the entire time how much slower he was growing. Every swing brought Bal's blade closer to him. Every parry was nearer to a fail than the one before. Swick winced as he saw his death coming.

Then the hand's words came out.

"Felicia!"

Finally, the woman paused. Only for a moment though because Swick's dagger caught her clean between the eyes in that brief moment's respite. Pommel first, given that he was a gentleman and she a useful ally, but with every ounce of strength he could muster. The woman shot back like she'd been fired from some giant crossbow, landing several of her own body lengths back from him and groaning.

Sometimes, in a man's life, he was forced to make a decision. To consider who he really was, and what sort of tales he wanted in his legacy. Looking down at his worthy opponent, seeing her grunting and stumbling to her feet with her sword lying yards away, Swick found himself certain what that was for him.

His dagger's blade came down to rest atop all the big veins in her neck before she got up, and she froze the instant steel touched skin.

"Don't go twitching now. There's a good girl," he breathed, suppressing the urge to wince at his damned leg all over again. "You made a good fight of it, but I don't think there's any doubting that you've lost now, is there?"

And there bloody had been until that very instant. Hurt or no, Swick would never have won against this woman easily. She was beyond strong.

Perhaps even a Hero, or close enough. The hand might as well have tried helping him with harsh language.

To Swick's surprise, the hand himself rounded on him rather than Bal. The man looked furious, and not entirely sure of where best to direct his rage.

"Be gentle with her, you oaf," he spit. "This is Princess Felicia."

In that single sentence, everything snapped into place within Swick's mind. The woman's way of walking, her posture. The sheer militarism of it all. The handling of that bastard sword of hers, and now other things too. With her body uncovered, and her hands no longer busied with his imminent demise, Swick was able to observe the woman's dark skin and darker hair, her tough, sharp features and the sinewy steel of her not-inconsiderable musculature.

And the look in her eye. Like they were orbs of flint, the pupils clumsily carved into them by a drunkard's chisel. He'd been a damned fool to have missed so obvious a resemblance to King Galukar.

"Treasure hunter." He frowned, staring at her. Well, it certainly sounded like a Galukar thing to do. The woman spat at her feet, suddenly seeming angrier with him than she'd been during the actual attack.

"What are you here for, you rat?" she asked.

For some reason—just basic association, really—Swick assumed the glare and harsh words were aimed at him. He realized only after a moment that it had been the hand whom Bal had intended to receive them. He drew his blade back, figuring the conversation would be a shade less awkward if she were able to actually move her head without fear of losing it, and *fairly* certain she'd not be trying to hack off any more limbs. For the moment, at least.

"I'm here for you," the hand replied.

"On my father's orders," Bal noted, phrasing it like a statement of fact rather than a guess.

Well, in her defense, it actually *was*.

"I am," the hand said testily. "But I see no reason why that should impact things here, because your father is acting on the advice of another."

At that, the woman snorted.

"Well there's a first time for everything I suppose." She sighed. "Shaiagrazni, right? Somehow it's typical that the first person to actually sway him on anything would be the second most evil creature this world has ever seen."

Suddenly, Swick found himself rather more confident in the decision to ambush her. Particularly knowing she was Galukar's. A drop of that man's blood would've made anyone harder to persuade than a mountain, and this one seemed to hold pints.

"This isn't about King Galukar—"

The hand's attempt at replying was crushed beneath the woman's answer, which came out in a great roar demonstrating such volume and potence of lung that Swick found himself wondering whether she might have killed a Vigorless man just by shouting.

"Everything is about him," Bal snapped. "Even now, a hundred miles away, everything somehow manages to be about him. So why don't you just get lost and let me put a few hundred more between us, see if that fixes things?"

The hand paused, clearly reassessing his conundrum and reconsidering his approaches. Swick could appreciate that. He didn't like the man, but he'd noticed his cleverness quick enough. And he saw it more clearly now.

"Then forget him." He shrugged. "And ask yourself this: How would you like to sit inside a skyship again? How would you like to *fly* one?"

It really was remarkable how quickly the woman changed her tune.

Or perhaps not. It was, after all, a damned skyship. Those were rather valuable when they weren't on fire and sticking out the sides of ancient castles.

"Conditions," Bal—Princess Felicia—began. "I'm not working for anybody. I'm a freelancer. I don't have to speak with my father either, and Shaiagrazni isn't going to come anywhere near me with his freakish magic. I also want a ton of silver. A ton, literally, as my payment. And I want an open position as the ship's engineer for me to come back to take and refill whenever I want it, no matter how much time passes after its repair."

Swick was slow that day because it took him quite a while to piece things together even despite the obvious hints.

"You're the engineer?" he realized with a frown. Bollocks, maybe he shouldn't have brained her between the eyes quite so hard.

Princess Felicia, apparently, was still rather annoyed with him for ambushing her. It showed in how she replied.

"Wow, you've recruited a genius, I see. Is this the moron who smashed his skyship into that building or am I to expect an even higher grade of stupidity in my future encounters?"

The hand sounded weary as he replied.

"This is Captain Swick, yes." He sighed. "I would ask that you show him . . . every courtesy."

She spit at her feet, and the man sighed again.

"That aside, your terms are . . . doable." He winced, even as he said it. "I do hope you realize a ton of silver is no small sum, even for Arbite."

"I do." The princess sighed. "That's why I'm asking for it. Completely reasonable thing to ask for a skyship, isn't it?"

Swick found himself grinning as the hand squirmed. He really did like this one.

"So we have an agreement," the hand tried, and the princess shrugged.

"Mostly I was asking that to see if you'd actually offer it."

The hand finally grew irritated then, which was a sight Swick didn't get to relish for long before his fury was covered up like so many other great treasures.

"This isn't a game," he snapped.

"Correct," the engineer growled back. "It isn't, and unfortunately for you, you're hinging everything on convincing a woman to make a return to her most hated place in the world. If I want to say no, I'm completely in my right, and if a ton of silver doesn't sway me then you have no right to judge me either."

Swick frowned at that. He wasn't sure about judging, but if a ton of silver didn't sway someone, he reckoned it made them a madman.

There were more pressing concerns than that, however.

"We should get moving," Swick cut in. "We were pretty . . . loud." He looked around to the street they'd churned up with dodged sword swings and thrown Hands. "And there are people after us. I don't like how easily they could catch us here."

The engineer scoffed.

"And that sounds like it's not my problem. If I want to stick my neck out for my father's thugs, then it'll be another ton of silver on top of it all."

"I'm serious," Swick growled.

"So am I," she growled back. "I still don't even know if I'll be working with any of—"

The arrows were in the air before she finished, and both she and Swick were diving within the blink of an eye. He hit the ground, rolled, came up to his feet, and turned to see the metal shafts sticking out of cracked stone in the walls and the floor. Bal had evaded them all too, if anything by a wider margin than Swick thanks to the crippling injury she wasn't suffering.

Unfortunately, the hand was not nearly so quick as either of them. He dropped with an arrow plunged deep into his shoulder, hissing and twitching on the floor where hot ichor poured out of him. Scraping boots caught Swick's ears from all directions, and he didn't even need to look up to know it was the Red Finger Crew closing in for him.

He fought of course, translocating around, slashing, headbutting. From the corner of his eye, he saw Bal doing much the same, though faring better by far thanks to not being nearly so strong a focus for the attacking mercenaries. Betraying a hundred elite fighters, Swick supposed, was bound to have its occasional disadvantages.

Come to think of it, he'd betrayed so many that it was a wonder he was only just suffering the consequences now. Swick stumbled from the battlefield, catching a sword across one rib—bad—and feeling an arrow dig into the small of his back—very bad. His Heroic flesh was like tough armor, but the weapons of men as strong as these were perfectly capable of bypassing that. He could already feel his strength failing.

CHAPTER THIRTY-NINE

S wick's flight through the street was not as long as he might have hoped. Whenever he tried something clever, tossing a blood-crusted object high to translocate away, it was blocked as a magus wrapped it in some shield to halt its path, or an archer shot it from the air using the same preternatural dexterity common among Kaltan rangers.

He was a rat in a maze, desperately fleeing toward some exit. And with every passing moment, he was becoming closer to being a *trapped* rat. Swick didn't feel any great weight of fear, but he felt no hope either. His chances weren't good. Anyone could see that.

And so it came as no surprise to him when one group of blade-wielding mercs drove him right into the waiting weapons of another. Thirty on one would have been manageable, at his best. Even when the thirty were each as good as these men. Thirty on one with his injuries, and reinforcements coming, was not. Swick gave up, and they were quick to bind him.

They didn't take him as far as he might have expected. Their base of operations apparently was located just a few hundred yards from Bal's. Unlucky, then. There'd never been a chance of them missing the sounds of battle.

He didn't bother trying to mount a resistance, just surrendered. Swick was done and captured either way. He reckoned there was no use in getting chained up with a few broken ribs when he could just pack in without a fight. Fortunately, the Red Finger Crew was not in a particularly vindictive mood because they let him keep the remainder of his health as they escorted him away.

Their base of operations was a fairly neat one, as far as disorganized rabble banding together as mercenary killers went. A big street that they seemed to have entirely rented out. They had a nice little perimeter set up, complete with wooden barricades to mark it separately from the surrounding areas and hastily constructed outposts where unlucky sods would keep watch. In the center, they'd erected a large pavilion that Swick imagined was serving as their main living area.

But there wasn't much imagination required to take note of that particular fact because he was the one who'd introduced the system to them all those years ago. He almost felt proud to see it surviving so long after the fact.

His former comrades shoved him into the pavilion, and Swick was quickly bound to the floor in iron shackles so thick that they might have held a building aloft, and certainly would have resisted the pull of his meager strength. It was overkill, even without his injuries. But Swick couldn't blame them for the caution.

It didn't take long before Swick met the man himself. Surrounded on all sides by overeager mercenaries, he was, if anything, surprised to live for the brief span One-Eye even took to arrive. He entered with all the grandiosity a common merc could muster. As much as Swick himself had, once, all those years ago.

A big man, One-Eye. Standing taller than the tent's doorway, and almost as wide as that of a common building, he ducked in as a great mountain of vascular solidity. His arms were bare and betrayed lumps of iron-dense muscle clinging to every inch of them, skin tanned and weather-beaten, tough and calloused. Scars crisscrossed it everywhere, save for the hand.

The hand was red. Pure red, as stark a crimson as Swick had seen anywhere but pools of fresh arterial blood, and revoltingly wet. He actually saw the tendons and tissues move as the fingers shifted, veins jumping, ligaments bunching. It was a study in anatomy, and a practice in holding one's stomach contents in place.

And it was Swick's damned fault, like so much else in the world.

"Alright, captain." One-Eye grinned, wearing the face of a man who was more than just pleased. Triumph lit his expression, bringing that rare illumination that seemed to stand in balanced opposition to all the darkness of life at once despite its fleetingness. Swick couldn't blame him. His was a grudge older than some adults. And it was more justified than most.

"I've not been your captain for a while," Swick noted. One-Eye smiled.

"And we drink to that lovely fact every night, believe me. Don't we, lads?"

A round of grumbled agreement rang out among the room, unanimous and downright eager. It would've been enough to hurt Swick's feelings were it not so completely understandable.

"Can't say I blame you." He shrugged. "Lots of folks I've fucked over less'd be perfectly fine to do much the same."

One-Eye seemed surprised, but not taken aback. It was a dull, scarcely felt sort of response akin to a man finding one more piece of beef in his stew than he'd expected. About as intense a reaction as Swick had ever gotten from the man.

Save for the time he'd hidden behind him to take cover from that skin-rending curse responsible for ruining his hand. Or the time he'd called that Kaltan's bluff, only to find he actually was a ranger and have it demonstrated with an arrow in his ally's eye. Or the time he'd drunkenly agreed to hold that pass in the Siege of Tibiltar, where One-Eye had lost a bollock to a stray trebuchet stone from the attackers.

Come to think of it, those occasions weren't nearly so rare as they ought to have been.

"Do you know why we're here?" One-Eye asked suddenly. His voice was soft, and it was all Swick could do not to piss himself the moment he heard it. One-Eye's voice was hard, gruff, pointy. Except for when he was truly enraged. That was when it got soft, like the muscles in a tiger's legs slackening the precipitous instant before it pounced. His heart was like a drum, and he had to fight against the instinct to gnaw off his own hands for freedom as he answered.

"That's a deep question, isn't it?" Swick smiled. "I've never been a religious—"

One-Eye's fist was not a Hero's, but he was a big man, and he had no small measure of Vigor pumping around in those corded veins of his. It knocked the wind from Swick, and he gasped for more. Eyes watering, head spinning, pulse pounding in each ear. All Swick could do was regret two facts: that he'd chosen to divert his power into translocation instead of sticking to the path of raw physicality, and that his former subordinates had so carefully scraped and cleaned all the blood from his battleground and hiding place after capturing him. There'd be no escape.

"Always were a joker, weren't you?" One-Eye said cheerily. More cheerily than before, come to think of it. It was almost as if he *enjoyed* beating the tar out of Swick.

"Sense of humor," Swick gasped. "Important—"

"For when everyone you know keeps dying," One-Eye finished, face darkening. "Aye, I know. I remember when you first told me that, the day we met. I think about that a lot. Think about how stupid I was then not to realize what it said about *you* that being your ally was such a dangerous task. But not as stupid as I was later, to stick around, eh?"

Swick could tell he was expecting an answer, but for once he couldn't think of one. He took a moment, caught his breath, bit back his pain. Spoke without bothering to think.

"You're right."

It didn't surprise him to hear his own words, but it sure as hell surprised One-Eye. The man might have caught a whole nest of wasps in his mouth for how long and wide it remained open.

"You're right," Swick replied. "And in more ways than you know. I'm scum, always have been. A cowardly, conniving piece of shit. I run from fights, I run from responsibility, I run from guilt. And when I can't live with all the running, I run right down a bottle to bury it. I got people killed. I got you maimed. I . . ."

Swick recalled the moments before the crash, the mix of horror and faith in his crew. How misplaced the latter had been. How One-Eye's brother had been among the men to believe in him.

"I killed your brother too," he whispered, eyes dropping under the weight of his shame. "I haven't had a drop to drink in months, haven't . . . stabbed a single back either. It took that for me to realize what was wrong with me, how both bled into each other." He swallowed, all humor dead and buried already. "Devrin," Swick continued, using his former friend's first name for the first time in a long time. "I'm sorry."

One-Eye paused, and so did the room.

The silence was thick enough to cut with a knife, then thickened even further until no knife in the world would have managed to even scratch its stony surface. Just when he thought the pavilion might erupt with the conversational pressure, One-Eye spoke at last.

"Aye, well, that's very big of you to admit, Swick. Really, I mean it. Congratulations. The hardest part with tackling addiction and dependencies is always recognizing your own problems, and it really is easy to get trapped in a cycle of reliance like you did without even realizing it. It's brilliant that you managed to snap yourself out of yours, especially after so long."

Other voices cut in, at that, all as eager and earnest as One-Eye's.

"Aye, good on you, mate," one merc said.

"Keep it up, lad," added another.

It would have been rather touching had it not been so bizarre. Fortunately One-Eye brought things back to more familiar territory before Swick could begin to further disconnect from what reality seemed eager to tell him was happening.

"I'm afraid that doesn't excuse the people you hurt though. Your problems were yours, not ours. And you let them affect you to the point of ruining things for everyone around you. That demands an answer, my friend. Blood asks for blood, and all that, aye? Some scores can't be settled with silver."

"Only iron," Swick echoed, licking his lips. They weren't dry. Moments from death, inches from ruin, and his lips weren't dry. Well, that wasn't a surprise. He'd stared the reaper down enough that it was almost mundane these days. And the years of boozing had dried his mouth out more than fear could ever have managed.

There came a time, a man just got tired. No two ways about it. Would he like to live more? Sure.

But that didn't look like it was going to happen, and Swick had come to terms with that fact a long time ago. You had to, growing up in a racket city. Because the end was after you from the beginning.

One-Eye moved. Swick didn't see how—he wasn't looking—but he heard the sound of a heel scraping on paved street as his mountainous weight shifted. It slowed the world, quickened his thoughts, brought the idea in an instant where before it might have taken slow, sluggish seconds.

You got used to staring down death, in a racket town, but if you ever got out of one, it was because you'd got even more used to sending it packing the other way before it could close in on you. Had to be quick, after all. Had to be Swift.

"You'll regret killing me if you don't listen first," Swick blurted out, wincing, fully expecting One-Eye to smash his brains out anyway. It would've been the smart thing to do, given their history. Swick had always been a good talker.

But the man hesitated, maybe out of sentiment, maybe because he was just that slow of a learner. Either way it was an extra few breaths.

"Listen," Swick repeated. "And listen well because I have a job offer you'll probably be interested in. And the best part is *I* won't be your boss."

CHAPTER FORTY

Ado was not a general, and far from an expert on the art of war. As something of a politician, however, she fancied that there was a good deal to be understood about the logistical aspect of battle, if nothing else.

And as far as she could tell, the logistical chances of each man in her forces killing one hundred undead each was fairly limited.

Perhaps that was an exaggeration. As far as she could tell, there were *only* a million marching toward them, after all. And it was far from the Dark Lord's finest. Venka's army had been a sizable fraction of that, from what she'd heard, with most of its composition being entities of considerable power. This was just . . .

Corpses, reanimated and thrown hastily at the enemy. Battlefields made empty and weaponized at random. It was the military equivalent of breaking a bottle over someone's head.

But ten men with bottles were more than a match for one with a sword, and ten-to-one odds were on the generous side of current numerical estimates. Her blood ran cold as she saw the forces close in.

There were many advantages to an all-undead army, but by far the largest was *food*. The total lack of it meant that the greatest limit on any gathering of bodies was effectively gone.

And, by God, was she staring at a gathering of bodies now.

Wudra's best were gathered, and that was no mean thing. Ninety thousand men at arms, all trained to a standard almost the equal of Kaltan's. They manned the ancient city's outer wall, for the most part, sheer numbers necessitating that they spill out of its more defensible fort. Besides, even if Ado had the space to concentrate them all within the center, she couldn't have done it.

Ordering the men to abandon the city at large would have gotten her lynched within the hour—not the wisest beginning to a defense.

And she'd not had much to do with this one either. She wasn't a warrior, and while her academic knowledge of war allowed for the occasional piece of useful insight, she'd been frustratingly reliant on Wudra's military minds.

Which, she suspected, were *total shit*. But that was aristocracy, Ado supposed.

Good Lord, I'm turning into Baird.

The lord paladin was out there, somewhere, Ado knew. On the outer walls, ready to meet the enemy first. She'd been told it was most effective to have him in the fighting as soon as possible, so that he could do his work in wearing the enemy down. Whether that was true, she had no way of knowing. She lacked the knowledge. Fuck.

Her thoughts were interrupted by the scrambling sprint of a messenger, whose face she had already turned to long before the speech came. Small boy, too young to fight, clearly, but by the speed of him he'd make a decent warrior one day. It sickened her a little to be thinking like that, and Ado buried the thought by listening.

"Gener— Uh, I . . ."

"Queen Mortascia," Ado gently corrected him, finding the scramble for proper titles far, far more tedious than she had shortly after first meeting Shaiagrazni and claiming her throne.

"Right, apologies. Queen Mortascia, Prince Folami is seeking an audience with you."

"Seeking?" Ado asked.

The messenger winced.

"He's forcing his way over here, and none of the guards are willing to risk hurting him by stopping him."

Figured. Well that was fine. Ado had been careful to surround herself with men who had rather fewer scruples than that.

"Send him on," she instructed, bracing herself for whatever was awaiting her.

Folami did not take long to bring himself before her, storming over at a hurried pace. Ado resisted the urge to swallow as she laid eyes on him.

"Brother, whatever this is, it will need to wait. I'm busy—"

He silenced her, instantly, by kneeling. Ado stared, stunned. Folami spoke.

"My queen, you must forgive me. I have acted improperly, treacherously, and deserved every response you showed and more. I ask for the chance to win back your good favor through deeds in the following battle."

For one moment, Ado was left scrambling for what to say. In the next she had it, and let the words leave her as a calm, cool stream.

"You have my permission," Ado said, at last. "Now go on and redeem yourself."

Folami nodded, getting to his feet, turning, and heading off to do just that. Ado watched him leave, still frowning. What had happened to cause this change?

Or was it just an act to lower her guard? She couldn't know, and had no intention of relaxing until she did. But either way, there were bigger threats to her—and others—for the time being than her little brother and his potentially troublesome ambition.

Minutes more passed, then the siege began.

As Ado had been told was typical, the Dark Lord's forces came on as a simple tidal wave of flesh. Almost climbing over one another to smash into the walls, and completely ignoring the retaliatory shots of trebuchet stones and ballistae, magi and archers. It was impossible to count them, and impossible to count those destroyed with each passing second. Scores, perhaps. Scores of casualties, thousands each minute.

She did the relevant mental calculations, and her blood chilled as Ado realized just how tiny a droplet in the endless ocean of their hordes that was. There would be no winning this. She knew that instantly, no matter what the paladins insisted. There would be no destroying one million undead.

They continued hammering into the walls, seeming to do it almost randomly at parts. Ado wasn't sure what the plan even was on their enemy's end, and even briefly wondered whether they were intending to have their primitive, rotting undead claw down the stone battlements with fingernails and teeth.

But the fighting continued, and their true purpose became terribly clear. Ado watched as undead began to climb undead, forming mounds of their own flesh to scale, drawing ever closer to the tops of the walls. Then jumping onto them.

Well, it made sense she supposed. In some terrible, revolting way, it damn well made sense. If one had the numbers for that, and cared more about seizing a city quickly than anything, *and* could replenish any losses with interest by actually taking it . . . it made fucking sense.

And it might well spell their ruin.

Burning oil tipped down onto the undead and achieved nothing as their deadened nerves failed to so much as spasm at the heat. Bolts and arrows ran through skulls, thankfully dropping them, but as fire was concentrated on the bases of those towering, fleshy siege engines, yet more bodies scrambled around them at the bases to shield them from harm. Ado scanned the horizons, trying to sift through the endless rivers of rotting meat for something resembling a leader to the chaotic mess of their enemy's assault.

She found none. Either they were hiding beyond the limits of human sight, or there were so many simple zombies in the attack that picking out even a large or clearly advanced figure from among them was impossible.

Probably, it was both.

"My queen, you need to get back from here!" Ado glanced over to find a paladin was speaking with her. She frowned.

"Shouldn't you be killing undead?"

"I— We're saving ourselves for the fortress, your grace. But that fortress will be the front line before you know it. The undead are breaching our outer defenses terribly fast."

"Ah, carry on then." She shrugged, watching the carnage unfolded and feeling somehow rather *fascinated* by it all. And not afraid.

That surprised Ado, and she found herself trying to piece together why. Had the fear just been driven out of her by an imminent execution? Was she just emotionally overloaded? Had she gone suddenly insane?

The latter, somehow, seemed the most likely. Particularly as she found herself chuckling upon seeing three undead at once lose their heads to one man's swing.

"That fellow over there"—she indicated—"I'd like to see him raised to—"

A scream cut the air as several more undead pounced upon the man, dragging him down and tearing him to a thrashing corpse with savage bites and punches. Ado sighed.

"Never mind."

"Your highness," the paladin urged. "Please, I really must insist."

"Well, that is a shame because I find myself needing to insist as well." She giggled. "Really, sir, I don't know what you think will keep me any safer here in the fortress. I'm far from the actual fighting, and at least here *my* men can look at me for a source of morale."

A trebuchet stone smashed into the base of an undead pile. Lucky shot, that. Very lucky—the bases had been carefully left beneath their lines of sight. Thousands of undead tumbled down, those higher up falling close to a hundred feet onto those below. Bones broke; thrashing stopped. It was rather a nice dent in the enemy.

Just a hundred more hits like that and we'll have actually thinned the herd.

"Besides," Ado added. "We're actually not doing that badly. Look for yourself."

She did hope it wasn't just wishful thinking on her part, but the rate of killing on her own side's end seemed to have increased as more and more undead diffused their ranks around the city. And walls were ever an advantage. Suddenly the idea of each defender killing no fewer than ten attackers seemed . . . plausible, if optimistic.

"All the same," the annoying paladin insisted.

"Oh, very well." Ado sighed. "I'll move away from here."

The paladin relaxed for all of a second before Ado headed to the front, magic building. It had been foolish of her to even wait as long as she had. Their defense needed magi, and as far as she could tell, Ado was the most powerful one in the entire city.

At least until the doors finally got kicked down, that was. God knew what the Dark Lord would be throwing at them.

Ado hurled ice in a way she never had before. There was nobody close to give her any sort of appraisal or examination, but if there had been she was fairly sure she'd have gotten higher marks for her magic than in any official test she'd taken.

The undead probably didn't agree, but then they were somewhat biased by being the ones she was blowing to pieces with it.

Icicles as long as arms smashed into bodies with all the speed of crossbow bolts, fully impaling them, then continuing on to hit even more. Fléchettes, as Shaiagrazni had called them, tore through a dozen in one volley, tiny finned darts that entered the body with far less fuss than they left it and painted the enemy's nonexistent ranks with rotting viscera. She conjured walls over the sections undead were leaping to, watching as numerous enemies simply bounced from the barricades and fell down onto their thrashing brethren below.

And that gave her an idea, after which Ado stopped *hurling* ice entirely and began simply conjuring great boulders and darts of the stuff to drop down onto the enemy below. Gravity did the killing for her, and the few times she glanced down to watch the results, it did it well.

But there was more fighting than what was happening immediately around her, Ado knew that much. A hundred other skirmishes were occurring at a hundred other points of the wall, and most were doing far worse than hers. Word soon came that one section had fallen, then another, then a third.

And after that, the order to retreat was given, and Ado found herself seized forcibly by strong hands and practically dragged back toward the central keep.

She shot a few glances over her shoulder and found her heart sinking at the sights. Fortunately, the undead were focusing on the defenders. Ado imagined it was to press their advantage, to keep the feral things from tearing apart civilians who might be made into yet more undead, or any other number of things.

Unfortunately, she was *one* of the defenders. And they'd already lost thousands in the fighting for their walls.

Siege engines kept the undead at bay just long enough for ninety thousand men to pack themselves deep inside the fortress and seal the gates, then a new kind of killing began. The kind exchanged between cold walls, without sight, fought on only the sounds of an enemy. Death was yards from her, and Ado knew nothing of it save the sound of its cool breath hitting the nape of her neck.

The undead didn't keep her waiting for long though. Undead never did.

CHAPTER FORTY-ONE

The castle was a cage. It wasn't as cold as Ado's cell, wasn't as dark, and the company she found within its stony embrace was so great as to contrast her previous isolation to an almost laughable extreme. But it was a cage. A prison, a cell. It was an unshakable, inescapably tight embrace. Its doors opened from within, locks obeying keys held at her will. But it was a cage because there was no leaving.

Anyone who set a single foot beyond its outer wall now was dead. The sounds of endless undead hordes smashing against its exterior made that abundantly clear. Even with the fighting taking up every entrance point that had room for fighting to occur, she could hear them over it.

For Ado's part, she was still involved with the slaughter. There was simply no choice in the matter. She had power, and she had the nerves to use it, which meant failing to do so would be tantamount to suicide. But her current conditions weren't quite as favorable as they'd been just an hour earlier.

Wudra's central fortress had been built for just such an attack, long ago, and Ado found no shortage of advantages within its walls. Each gate seemed to house a cacophony of native edges at one end, primed and perfect to turn any attempted assault to so many bloody ribbons as magic and metal rained down upon the invading enemies. Ado herself cast enough ice to freeze a river, watching time and again as her power blasted rows of undead apart. She stopped only when exhaustion made her, taking refuge behind conveniently placed cover until she'd recovered enough to continue the devastation.

But there were limits to any creature's stamina, and she was no exception. Magic or no, fragile undead or no, safely shielded by fortress walls or no. There were always limits.

And one million was a number almost beyond the reckoning of any.

First the paladins started dropping, their Vigor and training, armor and arms all proving an inferior match for the sheer multitudes staring them down. Some died as heroes, barring enemy violence from reaching other lives with their own bodies. Others went miserably. Dragged down, taken by surprise, simply giving in as their strength finally abandoned them and their will finally broke. All made more or less as much of a difference as one another, however their lives ended. Because each one meant there was one less elite warrior to crush the reanimated bodies coming on as a flood. Each one was that single deadly step closer to an end for every other life in the fortress.

And they were far from the end of it. As Ado held one of the main gates, she saw the king joining the fray to beat back a particularly savage enemy advance himself. He wore armor of resplendent silver, enchanted with a magic so fierce she could feel it even over the hum of necromantic power flooding the air so revoltingly. He swung a sword that looked more like a sunbeam than any construct of metal and mechanics, lopping enemies fully in half, taking chunks out of stone surfaces on his backswing. At his side were half a dozen paladins, seemingly invigorated by their king's presence, all doubts regarding treachery and coups forgotten before a snarling enemy and royal ally.

But the king too was nothing more than a mortal man. And he was not immune to the rare creatures of potency among their enemy. A fomor opened his throat up down to the vertebrae with a single swing of its great tendrils, and in one stroke, the royal line of Wudra was bereft of its patriarch.

The battle raged on around him, heroism made somehow inconsequential by the grander carnage unfolding in its proximity. Ado herself barely even glanced at the king's corpse.

Heroes, she had learned, did not truly exist. There were simply those who survived and those who didn't. Today, it seemed, there would be none of the former. She continued casting.

One stride at a time, they gave ground. The outer sections were taken at the steep price of many tens, even hundreds, of thousands of undead. The median points for a fraction of that. Each new area of their collapsing defense was bought more miserly than the one before it as exhaustion, fatigue, and death slowly sapped the fighting strength of Wudra's defenders. Ado herself found magic an increasingly stubborn familiar, her will and powers blunted with the overexertion hard fighting demanded of them. Fingers numb, eyes bleary, wits savaged, it was all she could do to even identify the great blocks of frosted water she sent smashing into enemy ranks.

Desperation set in quickly enough, always eager to pounce on any situation like Ado's and make itself known. This time though, there was a terrible, rational flavor to it. This time they really didn't have any other options save for the madness it was making look so appealing.

Plans were discussed to spearhead an assault *beyond* the walls, to try to take the head off the Dark Lord's army by killing its leadership. Plenty remembered the early assaults, when entire attacking forces had been rendered harmless and aimless by the death of the greater undead around which they gathered. And all knew they had no chance of holding the city conventionally.

Ado vetoed the idea, if only out of risk reduction. They were holding still, and holding well. There might well be another time to act brazenly and dangerously later, a time when they could do so more easily and safely. Estimations of their enemy's inexhaustible numbers failed now, but Ado's glances beyond the windows told her they'd been thinned.

By a hair.

So they would continue their defense until they'd managed to thin them by another. Every minute advantage made a difference, and they needed every one they could get. She got back to fighting.

A gate fell, then more undead were pouring in through yet another vulnerability. Arrows flew, bodies hit the ground, and they were forced back. For half an hour. They came back—they always fucking came back—and this time the defenders were low on ammunition. Divine magic churned the air with holy castings and appeals to the heavens, igniting necrotic flesh, restoring stamina, knitting wounds. A second wind hit the defenders.

They used it to hold for an hour more, mangling more of the Dark Lord's army until his attackers had to scale walls of their own slain allies before they could even reach the actual defenses. Even this did not slow them, not even by a shade. Ground started slipping from them again, paladins died, magi died, everyone was dying. Ado's brother.

He fought bravely, heroically. He died no differently for it, throat torn out and entrails spilling from him as the endless horde continued. Another casting of divine magic came seconds too late to save him. Ado would never know if he had been lying to her, or sincere. Her heart broke.

She gathered the advisers and paladins, spoke quickly. They prepared their spearhead.

Their assault began from a window, superhumans leaping or gliding down through the air as every defender still within the building unleashed all they had in a single controlled volley designed to batter the enemy and leave them briefly stunned. It worked, for seconds, and they all hit the ground killing.

Ado was among them because there was nothing more important she could be doing now than unleashing the power of a magus upon the battlefield.

They were a wall of Vigor and might, dozens strong and barging through the horde. Everything that came within paces of them died instantly, split or crushed apart, pulped, liquefied and allowed to fall at their feet. They closed slowly, inexorably on their target, and Ado felt a flutter of hope.

It was interrupted as the elves came.

Ado recognized them, vaguely, by species. Not the specific breed, but their tall, lithe forms and sharp, thin features were unmistakable. They moved like eels, seeming to disappear from the path of sword swings, bettering even knights in physical speed and dwarfing them in dexterity. They halted the advance almost completely, two scores of razor-sharp elites to engulf their hackneyed assassination squad and crush their chances.

There was no hope now—Ado knew that—and she was almost certain every man and woman fighting beside her knew too. But somehow that didn't have them fighting any less hard. Somehow, it only bolstered their fury. Maces swung, axes and polehammers with them. Magic roared out. Ado put an icicle the size of a man clean into an elf's face, watched his head just come apart like something crushed by a siege stone. His corpse disappeared under the thousand feet thrashing all around them, and another pace was earned. Paladins were dying again, momentum taken, but she didn't care. Because they could still bleed the Dark Lord's forces. They could still make him pay as dear a price for their lives as was payable, and leave his victorious army a ruined, crippled thing not able to take a single city more.

Her heart ached, and Ado thought of Folami. Her treatment of him, all her mistakes. She realized she was staring down into her last few moments alive. It was funny. Ado had always intended to die properly, dignified and aging in her bed, surrounded by family.

But a death was a death, and somehow she didn't mind this one as much.

The movement ahead caught her, eyes flicking up just in time to behold the sight of an iron bolt flitting through the air nearly faster than human perception. Ado froze, the world seemed to slow, and she traced the projectile's deadly path across the battlefield. That was an end. But whose? She found herself without an answer, and cursed the one responsible for sending her out without even knowing the enemy's army had so potent an archer as to fire it.

And then it struck home, and Ado's worries were displaced by a gaping, gasping confusion.

Collin had nailed the dark elf perfectly, and he allowed himself a smile as the head just sort of . . . came off. Neck surrendering to the momentum of his arrow, meat ripping, vertebrae bidding one another a tearful goodbye. The cranial missile disappeared from sight and bounced off somewhere among the thrashing undead. He'd already nocked and drawn another arrow by the time it did, eyes still on Ado.

The idiot was stunned, staring, pausing. Rookies. Collin really wouldn't ever understand why the human instinct in battle was so often to *freeze*. It was just asking to be killed, and he was almost tempted to put a bolt through her foot as a reminder.

Instead, he put it through another dark elf. The slightly more productive option, perhaps.

Around him, ten more rangers were loosing ten more projectiles, while Hexeri was doing horrible, awful things to everything that got within ten feet of her. Collin actually felt slightly sick watching her fight, a hilarious state of being, but perhaps a reasonable one. Combat with arrows and knives only did so much to prepare a man for watching a monster's whirlpool of blood liquefy whatever it touched.

There'd not been many places they could have headed and done anything of substance, so they'd all taken their harassing force—now rearmed after pillaging the spot of their capture—and headed off to help Ado.

It had been a smart decision because she damned well needed it.

CHAPTER FORTY-TWO

Another arrow, this one got a fomor. It didn't die, but its day certainly wasn't a very pleasant one from that point on as two more paladins smashed it down. Collin just moved on, picked another target, shot. He was going for the powerful enemies, the rarer ones who tended to actually hold fights like this together. Normal undead were stronger than humans, if only for the manic frenzy in which they fought, but their ability to damage a truly strong individual—like a paladin—was limited by their basic physicality. The killing blows in a fight like this would mostly be coming from stronger constructs that attacked those distracted by their lesser brethren.

So Collin slotted those instead. One at a time, killing twice or thrice a second, feeling his many quivers slowly empty of the hundred or so pounds of iron he'd been carrying. That was fine. He had backups placed right next to him. Collin was in a good spot, with plenty of sight lines, good defensibility, and a lovely summer breeze coming in from the east. The only thing that would have perfected his little rampage was if he'd had a picnic.

But life wasn't perfect, he supposed. Collin settled for just imagining one as he turned a dark elf's skull into several pieces of a dark elf's skull.

Up ahead, Ado was still fighting, but Hexeri had reached her. Even Collin couldn't hear the words exchanged, catching only the occasional one, but as far as he could tell she was doing her job of orchestrating the retreat. Good, they'd all die very, very quickly if they didn't get the fuck out of there. He was no white knight, and he'd not been able to find a conveniently located sunrise to emerge over when he'd arrived. This wasn't a saving of the day, just a saving of some of the idiots who'd survived its night.

Collin took a lich's arm off, and actually surprised himself that he'd gotten through its defenses. The momentary distraction sent a spell it had been weaving unstable, and it and everything within fifty feet was incinerated. Shame he couldn't count all the extra kills because that would've pushed him to the top of the scoreboard by a mile.

At a glance, he saw Ado and Hexeri were now making their way back. Hemorrhaging men, as people surrounded on all sides tended to do, but managing steady progress. Collin shifted to protecting them directly—interrupting killing blows, icing particularly stubborn resistance leaders, keeping them from losing any limbs or heads as best he could manage. They were a good hundred feet away, but at their rate he found them almost on him within a minute.

That was when Collin saw that he now was starting to become surrounded. Not quite as thickly, but certainly more so than he'd have liked. It was time to make a hasty retreat, he decided, and so he gave out the order for their last-ditch effort.

It had to be said, as far as diversionary ambushes went, several dozen fucking *vampires* was hard to beat. They just came flying at the undead— their fellow undead, Collin supposed—and started killing. Crushing skulls, punching off limbs, slashing apart several ranks in as many seconds, and making a nice, comfortable space for the spearmen to take formation. It was a good, careful, orderly retreat with everyone covering everyone. And that wasn't an easy thing to do. It took dozens of hours of drills just to hold a shield wall properly under the sorts of pressure they were facing now, scores more to properly move in one and keep it cohesive. And if these weren't Kaltans, Collin had no doubt the introduction of vampires would've had their formation coming apart.

Every single one of his soldiers would have been an elite in any other army, and by God did they kill their way off that battlefield. The thinned ranks still at their backs came apart like opened curtains, and Collin's rangers and Ado's coterie all packed themselves safely within the formation as they moved off.

Almost half an hour had passed in total from Collin's first arrival when they were finally, properly safe and free of the carnage. Everyone present dropped down and started gulping in oxygen like it was going out of fashion. Collin didn't blame them; he was too busy doing the same.

"Head count," he barked out, galvanizing his own thoughts only with a considerable effort. Grunting, groaning annoyance answered him, which was itself rather promising. Irritated soldiers had rarely suffered the worst they could have.

Officers headed out, speaking to sergeants, who tallied the men. Collin had a spare few minutes while that was done, so he attended to the matter closest to his heart.

No rangers dead. That was something, at least. He wasn't sure whether he'd survive another of them meeting their maker. Not without the Dark Lord himself keeping the unlucky sods company.

Night came on sooner than any of them would have liked, Collin most of all. The dark was always the enemy of most men. Ordinarily, he'd have appreciated it. Kaltan's rangers always did their best work at night, after all, when their enemies were blind and their attacks unseen.

But the rangers were a small sliver of his forces today, and they would be for years to come. Ten. It was pitiful. Sad, tragic. Ten fucking rangers left from a force that had once boasted hundreds. Collin took a moment to recall General Venka, then spat at his feet in the memory.

Shortly after that, the fires started. Undead didn't like fires, but they just couldn't help but start them up whenever they were unleashed on a city. Humans needed fire, after all, and so many houses were things of straw or light wood.

So many panicked people kicked over lanterns, or threw them at their attackers. And fire left unattended—like by a city claimed by death—spread like . . .

Well, like wildfire.

It was wild, at least. And it was awful. The flames started as a dull glow, like rays of dying sunlight peeking out over the crest of a horizon. Then they grew. Soon enough much of the city seemed engulfed in the conflagration, history and life consumed as one. Collin wasn't optimistic—stupid—enough to hope that the Dark Lord's forces were sitting on the pyre. They'd have been cleared out long before it swelled out of control.

But there'd be no more trouble from them; that much he was fairly sure of. Even with an army of unthinking automatons, it took a while to properly organize a march, and never longer than after a fight. Particularly a hard one.

So they could all sit back, rest, and watch the show. He glanced around, curious to see what would await his searching vision.

Well, there wasn't a surprise. That was for sure. Collin saw haunted fear, hatred, regret. Guilt, misery, defeat and horror and disbelief. So much disbelief. But mostly he saw hatred.

Good. He might have expected that much—this was, after all, a company of veteran warriors—but it was useful to have the confirmation. Fear was useless, regret a mixed bag. Guilt was better, misery worse, defeat a practical end to any utility he might have found. Horror was fear, writ more, and disbelief led to madness more often than battle.

Hatred though was good. Collin could work with hatred. He had worked with hatred. Hatred got things done; it turned men into killers, into soldiers, into winners.

And they would win. Staring at the distant blaze, wincing at the thought of whoever might still have been trapped within it, Collin promised himself that much. They would fucking win.

"Thinking about revenge?"

Collin almost stabbed the source of the voice, and halted just in time to avoid introducing Princess Ado to a pathetically ignominious end. She was beside him, waiting expectantly. Expectant of what?

An answer. His thoughts were still slowed by combat, trapped in that paradoxical state of lightning-fast cognition aimed everywhere, and at nothing in particular. Adjusting to conversation was like trying to cook with ice.

He managed it fast. Collin had plenty of practice.

"Lucky guess." He shrugged, though it'd been more of a safe one. She made lots of those, he'd noticed.

Without prompting, the young princess took her seat beside him, and Collin stiffened. He glanced over half anticipating hostility, but saw none. And that made him all the more ill at ease.

It wasn't that he had limited experience with women. It was that he had *no* experience with women who weren't whores or soldiers. A life spent killing was good for lots of things, but conversation with the smaller sex was not one of them. Fortunately she seemed to have more to say, lubricating their discussion conveniently as she did.

"My brother died."

As far as openings went, Collin had heard better. He shrugged. Shit conversation was about the only kind he ever had anyway.

"Sorry to hear that."

"He died badly," the woman continued, hardly seeming to hear him. "Painfully."

Collin shrugged again.

"It happens. He take any undead out first?"

She glanced at him, frowning.

"A few."

"Then it wasn't a waste at least," Collin replied. "That's about as best as you can really hope for. Anything else . . . all bets are off."

She studied him for a few moments before speaking once more, seeming to hold a greater focus now and letting it bear down upon him.

"Do you have any brothers?"

The question was a surprising one, though it shouldn't have been.

"No."

"Did you?"

Collin hesitated a moment longer this time.

"Yes," he said after a second. "I did. Three of them, all older. Dead for years now. One went in the uprising—my dad tore the cock off the man responsible. The other two . . . The Dark Lord's bastards got them."

And then they got all his friends, then they got his dad, and one day Collin's luck would run out and they'd get him. But he'd not die in a waste either. And he intended to kill a lot more than just a few before he went out.

"I'm sorry to hear that," the princess told him, voice sounding suddenly tight. "I'm sorry for . . . a lot."

Collin thought about that.

"Thanks," he said awkwardly. The woman smiled for a moment, and he wasn't sure why until she spoke.

"It's relaxing, speaking to someone who isn't a politician. You have no idea how stuffy it was in there. Or . . . Well, you probably do actually. I'd dared to hope my brother would be of some help, but he was even worse. Stabbed me in the back, went along with everything the others said, just dripping smarm and . . ." She hesitated. "And I had him beaten once I was back in charge, tossed around and humiliated. Even after he helped me. I was . . . so cruel."

The woman's eyes were wet, and Collin looked away. He was struck by the sudden urge to say something, and simultaneously by the sudden absence of anything that might be worth saying. His mind scrambled for long moments to coin a response before his mouth finally went off on its own.

"Bottle it," he said quickly. "Pack it up and cram it down deep somewhere. All that grief, that upset. Keep a hold of it, then use it. You'll know when. A fight, a chase, anything like that. Won't be long, in our line of work, before you find someone you don't mind splashing it all out onto."

Collin was rather eager to find one for himself, even just saying it. The princess though seemed to find the idea rather less appealing. She studied him like a leper, sympathetic and warm. It pissed him off.

"When did you first start doing this?" she asked. "Fighting. Warring. Killing."

He thought about it, and realized he didn't actually know. There'd always been cause to train in his house, even before the uprising. Collin had been very young when it had started—though already practicing even then. And once it was over . . . Well, half the cutthroats in Kaltan might have gone for the price he'd had placed on his head by disenfranchised nobility.

Then the Dark Lord had come and started a fight that dragged everybody in regardless.

"A while," he said at last.

"That must have been hard."

Collin felt his lip twitch, resisted the urge to snarl.

"It wasn't. It was something that needed doing, so I did it."

Ado eyed him, face an unreadable mask. "I think I finally understand the feeling," she whispered.

CHAPTER FORTY-THREE

Galukar had quickly exhausted his throne room's pillars in his fury, smashing apart each one with a single wrathful blow as his temper withered away and his fears grew sharper and more numerous. He'd thrown the rubble, watching stone smash into walls like sling bullets and splatter debris across the hall. He'd stamped his feet and sent cracks the length of infantry lines snaking out to every corner. He'd screamed and watched the windows shatter from the pneumatic power of his lungs.

He had tortured the world in every way his transcendental strength could manage, but none of it had brought back his daughter. Felicia was still missing.

She was not hiding in any of her usual retreats, nor had a more thorough search of the palace yielded any other spots that might have obfuscated the girl. So far as any of Galukar's spies, advisers, or guards could tell, she had simply vanished.

Galukar had been an inch from sending each and every one of them to the gallows for their incompetence before Shaiar talked him out of it, soothing him as she always did. It wasn't lost on him why. Their sons were watching his fury with fearful eyes, and that almost started Galukar's rage all over again.

First he'd lost a daughter, and now fate seemed to threaten him with a dozen more by showing his young warrior heirs as no more than sniveling cowards. Bad enough none had been deemed worthy of the Godblade—

But he had other concerns, and one was great enough to swallow every other thought in his head after mere moments. His damned daughter was missing, and the whole world seemed intent on conspiring to keep from returning her to him. Galukar had to fight the urge to go and seize his trusty blade from the vaults. A war would distract him, and if he could use it to search the lands of a nation most likely to have seized his daughter, so much the better.

For one moment, Galukar wished only to scream again. He stopped himself. Shaiar was still by his side, concerned and touching one arm in cold comfort. His sons stood less than ten yards away. None of their ears would withstand the extent of his lungs' capacity, and Galukar would not deafen a dozen family members for lack of one.

Hours passed, and his rage, confusion, and fear grew ever stronger. Solutions continued being suggested, tried, and failed. Galukar found new things to unleash his fury on. Soon enough, he was rending iron in his impotent, helpless anger. It was only after hours more than he finally received word of a hopeful variety.

"Your grace, there has been an update regarding Felicia. Your skyship— it returned mere minutes ago, and upon the deck we found—"

Galukar was sprinting for the vessel like a stone cast from the greatest of Abaritan's trebuchets, his footfalls cracking the smooth tiles of his castle's floors with each stride. In under a minute, he was before the vehicle, confirming the report with his own eyes. It did not weaken his anger.

Felicia was, in fact, beside the vehicle. Grinning. Among the older of his children, she was taller than any of her brothers or sisters and had yet to heed the lessons regarding her habit of showing teeth and tongue with too-wide smiles or laughter. She looked like Galukar a shade, though he saw no resemblance now.

"Where have you been?" Galukar snarled, the words escaping him in a scraping, grinding assault. If his daughter noticed the fury, she was content to not even mention it. Felicia just grinned back up at her father with pride.

Pride, for convincing an entire nation its heir had been stolen.

"I have returned, father!" the girl declared, speaking as if hers was the presence of some high queen and not an eleven-year-old girl with too much headstrong independence for her own good. "My voyage on the skyship has been a success!"

"Your voyage," he echoed, not confused as much as enraged. Felicia continued, seeming to grow hesitant, finally realizing her father's fury.

"Yes. I . . . I snuck on board before it left. I wanted to study it while it was in flight and learn how to repair it. When I grow up, I want to repair all your machines, Father, and I want to build new ones for you—like this skyship!"

Galukar closed his eyes tight, muttering a curse. This old obsession again.

"You stowed away."

The captain was beside them now, speaking with the fearful tempo of a man who feared death. He damned well should have.

"Apologies, my king, we were already a day into the journey before any of us knew she was on the ship. But . . . Princess Felicia has more than a passing skill with mechanics. She'd make a good engineer if you don't mind my saying so."

Galukar jerked his head up, affixing the man with a stare that left him withering into nonverbal trembles and hesitation. He held the glare for a long moment before turning it, finally, back upon Felicia.

She met it unblinkingly, as she always did.

"How many times," Galukar began, "do you need to be told that your place is not as an engineer, Felicia?"

His daughter glared back now.

"It should be!" she snapped. "I'm a good one. The captain himself said so—all the crew agree. I can help Arbite by—"

"*You can help Arbite by doing your duty as a princess!*" Galukar roared. "By letting us find you a good husband, by producing some heirs for him and showing him our line's fertility, by carrying Arbite's legacy across into other kingdoms and helping to bargain with your hand."

Felicia actually flinched now, finally showing the respect due to her father. It was too little, too late. Galukar started for the skyship, temper flaring again.

"I see what my mistake was," he snapped. "I've been too lenient with you, tolerated your oddities for too long. Well, no longer."

"Father, what are you doing?!" Felicia asked, a note of fear to her voice.

"What I must," he snapped, then struck the vessel with all his strength. The wooden hull, proof against siege weaponry, came apart into a spray of splinters and chips as a section of it the size of Galukar's own body was smashed inward. He punched again, destroying more, and more. Dozens of blows raining upon the precious construct of magic, each one leaving it that much less complete.

Felicia screamed and cried, but Galukar ignored her. Advisers protested and roared, but he ignored them too. Some things were more important than war or commerce. Within a few minutes, the corruptive vessel was nothing but a mangled pile of raw material. No more capable of flight than a boulder.

Perhaps he would find some use for it as kindling. Galukar turned back to the captain and his daughter.

"You, sir, are out of a job," Galukar snarled, eyes now flitting to Felicia. Hers were red and puffy with tears, fury burning on her face. "And you . . .

You need to start behaving properly, and stop being so damned troublesome. You are a princess of Arbite, Felicia, not an engineer and not a magus like that freak Mortascia's daughter. Start acting like it."

His eyes opened, and the first thing to strike Galukar, the first of all his innumerable sensations, was the density of physical agony.

It was everywhere, and everything. An acid pumping through his veins, a bolt of lightning dancing across his nerves. It scoured every other sensation from him as easily as sunlight did the flickering luminosity of candle fire, rendering all the other informational pangs of his body an irrelevance next to its bottomless mass.

Galukar gasped, and cried out. Then choked on his own sounds, lungs convulsing with their own torture, before finally falling into a weak, pitiable mewl. It was something. It meant he still lived. It showed he drew breath. It sent another wave through him to provide assurance that he still remained intact enough for feeling and thought, motion and deeds.

But it was torture, nonetheless.

"The king!" a voice rang out, high in pitch, exclaiming its shock and hope with that single sky-grazing note. It stung his ears, among the few body parts not already quivering with pain. "He's awake!"

Galukar heard scuffling feet as the message was carried off, and shifted where he lay. The movement gave him another shot of agony, but this one was blunter. Or else less surprising. He had chance and cognizance to examine his sensation and make a more articulated summary of his damages.

The back. That was where most of it lay: the skin opposite his ribs and down to his lower spine. It was raw and wet, where the demon had clawed his viscera apart like it was that of a common man. He could smell the wounds, taste them. There was a dark corruption to them that only a demonic touch could induce.

It was of no concern. Already, Galukar could feel it dying. Fighting a losing war with the divine magics of the Godblade that infused his body. The magic was being systematically purged from his anatomy like rot burned out of a mundane wound with flame. That it was still there at all, he thought, was testament to the entity's power. And perhaps explanation for his current condition.

Groaning, he sat up. More aches, more stabs, duller still than the last. Galukar was wounded, but not crippled and certainly not dying. Once the last of his slain enemy's power was purged from him, he would begin to heal at his usual rate. Within a week, he would be killing as well as ever.

But a lot could go wrong in a week, and he didn't know how much time he'd lost already.

"You're awake."

Galukar looked up, recognizing the voice but not placing it until he laid eyes on its owner. Sphera, the necromancer. She looked different. Worn down. Her youth seemed to have been destroyed by whatever span had passed in his unconsciousness, fatigue and stress etching deep lines across her smooth face where once there had been none.

"How long was I asleep?" he asked, fearing the answer now more than before. She sighed.

"Eighteen days. The army is in retreat, and has been for a while. You killed the demon, and the enemy was too disheveled by its destruction to chase us at first. But we got no more than a day's march on them. Even with our magi sabotaging the roads at our backs, they were able to threaten us with pursuit before we'd galvanized. That kept us on the move long enough for them to try to slip around. We've been giving chase, and are just barely shy of catching them now."

It was a damned lot to take in, Galukar had to admit, but it barely registered to him. One concern was stronger than any other.

"Where is my sword?"

The Godblade. As much as he hated to say it, as harsh a truth as it was, that weapon was worth more than any man. Any thousand. It was the very future of the world. In Galukar's hands, it had done nothing but evil, but in another's . . .

In another's, one day, it might well bring true peace. And if nothing else, it was the hope of that that left him worried for it.

"We have it," the necromancer assured him. Galukar exhaled.

"Where?"

The Godblade was sealed in lead, stone, iron, and ice. Galukar approved. Nothing less than that measure—however improvized it clearly was—could have done justice to the level of security inherently demanded by so precious a weapon. What left him questioning, however, was the fearful regard it received when finally back in his hand.

"It was hot," the necromancer explained, still eyeing it wearily. "When it fell out of that demon. Hotter than I knew things could get."

"Fire is hot," Galukar snorted, rather irked by so brazen a display of cowardice. The necromancer seemed more irked still by his response.

"Not like this. It was glowing. Like iron from the forge, but blue instead of orange. And brighter. So bright we had a man go blind from staring too long."

Galukar swallowed. That *was* something.

"How did you move it?" he asked after a moment. "It cooled down?"

"We cooled it down," she replied. "First we couldn't even go near. The men we sent forth got blisters just from reaching out to within a foot of it. We had to leave then anyway. So while the army was organized into a march, I had magi douse it with water and high-speed winds. By the time we could go, it was cool enough that a length of iron hooked around it from afar was able to hold and drag it behind us. We'd tried the same trick before cooling it, in case you're wondering. The chain melted on contact."

Galukar swallowed again, eyeing his weapon. There wasn't a blemish on it. Ancient iron seemed not even to recall that it had ever been resting within a demon's bowels at all. Damaged, perhaps, at a cursory glance, but no more so than it had been when he'd first laid eyes on it. Just chips and chinks born from untold millennia of history.

If anything in the world could destroy the Godblade, Galukar had never heard of it. Apparently the death throes of a demon were not a sufficient test to prove the limits of his relic.

Better to die than let such a thing fall into the enemy's grasp, he reminded himself. Better to die a thousand deaths.

"What are your plans now?" he asked. "Or, rather, what were they before my awakening?"

He saw a flicker of irritation in the necromancer's face, and recognized it easily enough. Galukar had seized command from others many times before and grown accustomed to the inevitable protests that came with it. They'd never bothered him in the past, and they didn't bother him now. Some things just needed doing.

"We're readying for a reengagement with the enemy," she said, sounding oddly . . . blunt. As if she'd carefully hollowed herself of concern or anxiety. Galukar recognized that too. And he approved. It was the mark of a disciplined mind, even in one as dark as her.

Disciplined did not mean well aimed, however. Galukar frowned.

"You can't be serious," he noted. "We had a chance to hold them once. We had the perfect ground possible and an army at full strength. Even that was doomed the moment they unveiled demons among their ranks. To try to force an engagement now would be suicide."

There was fire in the necromancer's eyes, however. Fire and steel. Enough to remain strong in the face of Galukar's disagreement.

"We have no choice. The entire strategy we've formed relies on an enemy slower and weaker than we've left them."

Galukar recognized that look. He'd seen it before. Seen it recently. It was the very same one that burned in Arion Falls's eyes.

"Girl, there are things in your life beyond throwing it away in service to something else," he replied, finding his own voice reduced to a shaky whisper.

"Strength is the greatest virtue and weakness the greatest sin," she replied mechanically. Galukar recognized the words well. They were Shaiagrazni's. "If I can further Master Shaiagrazni's plans then I will, whatever it takes."

He eyed her, finding his heart growing heavy.

"Yes, I suppose you will." Galukar sighed.

To lose a child was torture unlike any other that existed. Galukar ought to have known; he'd lost many over the years. All his sons, through violence, and more than one daughter through marriage or alienation. He doubted it was anything comparable to losing an apprentice, but that duty of care and culpability remained. If the sting was even one-tenth of one-hundredth of one-thousandth so sharp . . .

He hit the necromancer, almost before he even knew he was moving. Galukar was careful to hold back—he always was. He held back against knights, and he held back just a shade more against the fleshcrafted skull of Shaiagrazni's apprentice.

But not that much. She still left the ground, shot back, thudded hard against a thick wooden beam, and brought half a tent down by smashing through it, landing in a dazed heap and providing no further argument against Galukar. She'd been right, in a strange way. They really did need to delay that army. But she would be of little help compared to what she might contribute by returning to her master anyway.

And it had been rather satisfying to strike her again.

CHAPTER FORTY-FOUR

The necromancer was not pleased once she woke up, and Galukar was rather surprised by how long it took her. Ordinarily a blow to the head left someone unconscious for moments, if even that. Any longer and it suggested something had gone very, very wrong. She slept for hours. But it was just that, sleep. Galukar realized soon after she lost consciousness that he had not damaged the woman in any permanent way—simply made her succumb to what she'd been staving off for weeks. Fatigue.

She slept, and that was all. Genuine, true sleep born from nothing more complex or sinister than exhaustion. It wasn't until almost an entire day had begun and ended that she finally woke up.

More than enough time for a good army to manage twenty miles, and apparently enough for an army of Kaltan to march almost thirty. Galukar might have been impressed were they not dirty, disreputable traitors intent on subverting the will of God.

Their destination was not yet in sight, by then, but they had covered a considerable stretch of the journey. More importantly, Galukar was back in command, which meant the necromancer wasn't able to seize the army back around with orders, no matter how loudly she barked them. Days marching, distance covered, and morale slowly trickling back to some semblance of normalcy. Galukar was surprised to find he enjoyed more prestige, not less, for his near defeat against the demon. It might have been reassuring in other circumstances, but the awe he saw directed at him now only told him that the entity enjoyed a truly terrible level of fear from their soldiers. He couldn't be the man who did the impossible for killing one, not if they were to be convinced to so much as stand before another.

Galukar half expected to see the war camps in tattered ruins, so disastrous had their outing been. He didn't, of course. They were as far from the devastation of open combat as they had been at the start of the conflict, and unscarred as an infant. If anything, the assembly of tents had *grown*, diffusing and spreading across the landscape like some infection in a wound. It put into perspective how great a success Shaiagrazni had found in gathering forces for his budding empire.

And that, Galukar knew, was what it was. An empire. He had no illusions about Shaiagraznian conquest stopping once the Dark Lord was beaten. They were simply trading one for the other.

Which was fine by him because he'd seen the one.

Galukar saw the army break apart as they finally neared their destination. Men hurried out like scattering rats, running to what he imagined was a mix of wives, whores, and places with drink. In that order, he could only hope. His own path was different. Such indulgences hadn't held any sway over him for a long while now. He was surprised to find the necromancer trailing after him still, looking better but nonetheless wrung out after her ordeals during his unconsciousness.

That was fine. Galukar had no issue with her pushing herself behind the safe pickets of a war camp. He continued to the main command tent, stepping into the pavilion and searching quickly.

"Shaiagrazni!" he called out. "We have returned!"

Galukar searched with his eyes, first, then his hearing. There was no sight of Shaiagrazni, and no returning call of the caster to indicate he'd been heard. Instead another voice struck him, higher, softer, and twisted with amusement.

"Ah, you were rather quick," Lilia the vampire queen breathed, having taken a seat near the center of the room and swiveled to gaze upon him as he entered. "I take it all did not go according to plan, then?"

If she was concerned, the woman—the thing—gave no indication. Simply smiled away, as if the prospect of many thousands dying was of no consequence at all.

Galukar felt the words clogging his throat like snow piled up before a cart and had to force them out. They tasted bitter. Defeat always did.

"The enemy surprised us," he said at last. "Not in any ambush. They moved exactly as predicted—even had the conventional forces we'd expected to find. But they had more. A demon."

It was a rare pleasure to see the queen of vampires taken aback, a very rare pleasure. Galukar didn't find it in him to enjoy it, however.

"I see," she replied, voice suddenly a shade strained. He understood completely. "And this demon, where is it now?"

"Back in hell," he growled. "But there were more, weaker, but more. And I suspect we've not seen the limits of the Dark Lord's capacity to summon them either."

The vampire didn't answer instantly, apparently content to take a moment reserved for thought. When she finally spoke, her voice was calm, but far from relaxed.

"I see. And where were the Dark Lord's forces that you last saw?"

"Heading this way, perhaps a dozen leagues from us. With luck, they'll be here in one day. Without it, their attack will come at night."

The vampire nodded. "Very well. We shall handle it when they come then. It seems we're to fight a second defensive battle."

Galukar felt his anger grow then. The sheer *coolness* of this one was more than just unnerving; it was potentially disastrous.

"We need to act quickly," he snapped. "Urgently. Where is Shaiagrazni?!"

"He is busy," she replied evenly. "Far too busy, I think, to tolerate any sort of disturbance at all, even from me."

"Master Shaiagrazni has done this before," the necromancer pointed out, apparently feeling the need to speak at last. "During the siege of Kaltan, he locked himself away for days. I'll bet he's working on some new project to turn the tide against our enemy."

Galukar was inclined to agree, but he still recalled the long days Shaiagrazni had needed to finish his last. And how much smaller the enemy's army had been then.

And more than anything, he recalled the total immunity demons had to any kind of disease or plague. Even the kinds a fleshcrafter might produce.

But he said nothing. There was nothing to say, after all. He'd had a single chance to avert their current situation, and he'd failed the moment he fell unconscious from that damned sky.

Ado was beginning to think that Kaltans were not, in fact, human. They'd spent an hour marching before finally reaching the carriages Collin Baird had brought with him to rescue her, and though the distance and time were not nearly as long as some she'd seen crossed, they were long enough to make clear the difference between them.

There was a great gulf separating normal men from veteran soldiers, that much Ado knew. What was news to her was the still greater one between a mere soldier and the hardened killers of Kaltan, and that was to say nothing

of their damned rangers. At the pace they set, despite her carefully main-
tained fitness, her own lungs and sides were screaming in pain within a few
minutes.

It wasn't for lack of effort that she lagged behind. Ado was giving all the
effort she could have been asked to, and was motivated to do as much by the
sight at her back. A burning city, smoke still billowing from it, embers still
glowing bright. Brighter, really, against the ever-darkening landscapes.

She knew intellectually that there was little danger at risk of emerging
from the giant pyre. Intellect had very little to do with her legs though, and
the sight of such a momentous blaze seemed to compel them into movement
unlike anything else she'd experienced before.

Ado continued marching—almost jogging—until her mouth tasted sour
with stomach acid and her every breath was a chestful of burning coals.
Then she marched some more.

Fortunately, Ado was saved from pushing herself to exhaustion or death
by the carriages. They were rare things, rarer than perhaps any other variety
in all the world. So few, after all, were made by Shaiagrazni's own hands. And
none were faster.

The paladins took convincing, but in the end the argument was won more
by the vehicles' speed than anything else.

Of course their shock had more than a little to do with it, and there were
still those who insisted on trying their luck in the wilderness alone. Ado
didn't even pity them. She'd seen firsthand what religious stupidity could do
to harm others. She was rather satisfied to see it finally harming those who
actually owned the sentiments. The sensation of winds whipping her anew
certainly helped.

On a carriage—a real Shaiagraznian carriage—she was safe. Ado surprised herself by feeling the sudden certainty, even as she reveled in it. Titles,
authority, alliances, and promises of politics—all these things had shielded
her before. None had proved above the ravages of circumstance and convenience. But the sheer speed of these vehicles . . . That was something to be
relied upon. That was a simple fact of the world.

Baird did not seem to share her thrill. He did not seem to share much of
anything going on in Ado's head. As usual, his eyes were kept ahead, face cold
and still, everything about him denying the moments of fleeting vulnerability
they'd shared before.

Good, she decided. Ado would have squirmed at his very presence had
anything changed. What she needed now was consistency. Even if that consistency came from a cretin being cretinous.

But he never really was, was he?

Her thoughts bristled. Ado would have to apologize to him, properly. Eventually. But not now.

"Fuck."

Baird's utterance snapped Ado out of her stupor, and whipped her eyes around to fall upon him. His face remained unchanged. At first. Slowly though, the dawning horror thickened.

She stared ahead, scrutinizing the distance for any trace of whatever it was that had caught his notice. She saw none, temper fraying.

"What are you looking at?" she demanded, glancing back at him and finding Baird now turned to the head of the vampires.

"You see it too?" he asked.

"Of course," the vampire replied, both of them matching the other's tone nearly exactly. Dread, Ado realized, was crushing every other trace of expression in either mouth.

"See what?!" she growled, fear raising her voice's volume now. Applying a pressure at the back of her throat that demanded escape through frantic speech. Fortunately, it succeeded in drawing Baird's gaze back to her.

Unfortunately, his gaze was even more dark with focus and fear than before. Better to be skewered through the belly than affixed with a stare like that.

"The war camps are up ahead," he told her. "Ten leagues or so. Not very long at all by these carriages. But the Dark Lord's already on them. And his armies are bigger than ours. Exponentially bigger. It's like watching a lake try to fight the ocean."

Fuck.

The armies had gotten bigger. Galukar didn't think it was just through reanimative work on their route to the war camps. Something more was afoot. Doubtless they'd united with other forces on their way, bolstering themselves by concentrating strength and turning the great compound against them.

It was the very thing he'd been meant to prevent from happening. Everything really had fallen apart when that demon had rendered him unconscious. A twinge of pain flared up at Galukar's side.

He'd healed faster than he expected, and was now more or less combat ready. But for once that didn't fill him with any measure of confidence. Not staring at that force, and certainly not knowing what would be waiting among the ranks of undead and abominations.

"Hmm, more than I might have expected."

It was Lilia whose voice he heard, and Galukar turned to see the creature still wore her infuriating mask of confidence. She stepped forward, clothing changed now in style. Her broad, flowing dress was gone and replaced with more formfitting combat-appropriate apparel, hair bound behind her, leggings and boots protecting her lower body. The transformation was a stunning surprise, but it did nothing to instill confidence.

A woman with fashion consultants might have coined a similar transformation. That did not make her a warrior, nor did it mean this vampire knew the first thing about what they were staring down.

"You could at least take that smile off your face," Galukar grunted. "The enemy will cut it off you soon enough either way."

She grinned.

"Oh my, that does sound violent. I'll have to do my best to deter them then."

He noticed the vampire gave no hint about how that might be achieved, simply watched as their enemies closed ever farther in.

"We're doomed." Galukar sighed, watching the enemy's approach. Oddly, he felt no strong emotional response to the knowledge.

He'd not always known he would die in battle, but he'd certainly *hoped*. The Godblade's wielder wasn't immortal, just well-preserved. Within a few more decades, his weapon's capacity to sustain him would have failed, and he'd have surrendered to old age. Better to fall with a weapon in his hand and a mound of dead enemies at his feet than that.

The vampire, apparently, did not see things the same way.

"Relax." She grinned. "This will go better than you think, and Shaiagrazni is still preparing his latest project."

If she told him to relax one more time, Galukar might well start his final rampage with her. He growled, tightening his grip on the Godblade, waited.

Their position was good. Excellent, really. It was the total wealth of every force Shaiagrazni had yet mustered. They had magi hired from Magira and those nations who had been using such individuals. They had Kaltans, of course, and Arbitans to form the bulk of their military. Conscripts taken and carefully trained for weeks to as great a quality as was possible in so meager a time.

In any other battle—perhaps truly any other in all of history—they would have had the numbers. A quarter million men extracted from countless leagues of countryside. Today though they were outweighed several to one.

And they didn't have a fortress like they'd had last time.

Their defenses were hastily made things, walls of bone and that keratin stuff Shaiagrazni used so much, without even lacing from the iron that made his personal armor so fiendishly resilient. They stood thirty feet or so, and encircled most of their camps. Most. In truth, it was more of a giant wedge than anything else, a force multiplier to cut into the enemy's front lines and maximize their casualties for as long as the fight continued its infancy.

Once they were fully encircled though, that would vanish. There were defenses at the back, made to turn the sole entrance into a viciously deadly choke point more savage to traverse than any conventional breach. Still, the enemy today could get through with simple numbers.

Galukar started pacing, then stopped himself as he remembered the countless eyes that were doubtless scrutinizing him for such fear. He halted, turned back to stare at the enemy, fought the tremble that threatened to seize him.

"Relax," the vampire repeated as Galukar did not remove its head. "They're closing in now. We'll be able to do something soon."

Even as she said it, arrows started flying. Not ranger bolts, cast across a full mile to remove heads from mere pinpricks in the distance. Regular arrows, wielded by the bulk of their military. Three hundred yards, that was where they'd start from. Men could cover that much distance in scarily little time. Undead in even less.

Another minute passed with torturous length before the vampire finally sighed again and started moving forward.

"Well, I think it's about time we made a start on this battle." She headed to the front of their battlements, then dropped down below as if the thirty feet were mere inches and landed without so much as a bend of her knees. Then she continued walking.

The enemy was one hundred yards from them, now, and only ninety from her. They were closing like a black tsunami, and Galukar almost looked away. He was about to see the vampire torn to pieces.

Ninety paces from her. Then eighty, then seventy—and Galukar could start to differentiate the snarling voices from one another. Fifty, and he could see twisted faces behind helms and salivating maws stretched wide for her flesh. Thirty, and his heart was pounding as the vampire remained where she was and simply stared out. Was she frozen with terror? Was she petrified? Or was she just delusional?

He started for the edge of the wall, meaning to haul the bitch back by force. He could make it, Galukar thought. He could save her.

Twenty paces, and the vampire called out a single word. A word that ran through him cleanly, like the edge of a spear cutting through meat. Galukar froze.

"Halt," ordered the vampire.

And the enemy halted.

CHAPTER FORTY-FIVE

Two hundred thousand, or thereabouts. It was Lilia's record.

Not that she'd been counting much, recently. These days—these centuries—she'd been lying low. It was a good habit to get into, she'd found. Keep one's power to oneself, and it would always surprise others. Particularly one's enemies. And the greater that power happened to be, the more tempting it was to unleash upon the world at any given moment, the greater the surprise would come from it.

Well, two hundred thousand enemies enthralled within a single word was a greater surprise than she'd been banking on. One hundred and eighty would have sufficed; the extra twenty thousand was just a nice bonus.

There weren't many battle plans that withstood contact with the enemy. None, however, survived contact with one-sixth of the army they had been made for suddenly turned into frenzied berserkers and thrown backward into their own allies. On another day, Lilia would have preferred to save the move for a more *opportune* moment, to dismantle the enemy's organization right before an offensive.

But there would be no offensives today, not from her side. She was hardly surprised. Vampires were ever outnumbered when they came into conflict, and if anything, five-to-one odds were a damn sight closer than she was used to handling.

A twinge of fatigue caught her, and Lilia had to fight for a moment to retain her focus. Two hundred thousand. It was the very pinnacle of her power's limitations, and she was feeling it more with each second that passed.

Lilia was well accustomed to the pull of magic leaching from her reserves. She steeled herself, focused her will, and sent the enemy against itself. Two hundred thousand smashed into more than a million like twin earthquakes meeting, and she actually thought she could *see* the moment both sides came into contact from the shaking of the air.

It was an illusion, of course, and though the fight looked balanced from her angle, she knew better than to expect anything but what came next. Her controlled enemies—some human, many lesser undead—were simply torn to bloody scraps as they fed themselves into the meat grinder of their own army. Lilia was careful to march them quickly, making the most of her limited period of control.

An army that size—or a force that size in any case—could have held against the remaining eight hundred thousand invaders for ten, twenty minutes. With a suitably picked position and strong command, even close to an hour. But Lilia didn't want them to hold. She *couldn't* want them to hold, as she lacked the ability to control them for that long. What she needed was damage, as much as possible. So she sent her enthralled enemies into the rest as great jagged clubs, whipped them into a mindless, savage frenzy, and watched as they killed indiscriminately.

Their fellows were surprised, briefly. And that went a long way in maximizing the carnage she unleashed. Within minutes, the numerous lights of her magical control had been extinguished, however.

It was impossible to gauge the remaining numbers, but Lilia could only hope they'd killed a good hundred thousand or more before falling.

Perhaps, Galukar thought, it would be a good idea for him to look into learning magic. It was an impossible thought to avoid, seeing the vampire lay waste to so many thousands with nothing but a thought.

A smile caught his face as he leaped down over the battlements. Fat chance of that. Galukar wasn't a young enough man to run around learning new skills, certainly not of that magnitude. He was stuck with power and a nice big sword.

But then, that had always served him well in the past.

Undead, many of them. Uncountably many. Galukar smashed into their ranks like an avalanche and swung once. He cleared a space out everywhere within eight feet of himself as bodies came apart, but it was filled up within a second.

So he swung again, and again, and again. They were nothing, these creatures, mere space holders. If he could reliably fight nothing but them then he could slaughter each one of their million-strong army without any help at all.

But, of course, he couldn't.

A fomor reared up, half again his own height and three times his weight. Its body was a forest of barbed limbs whipping around, deflecting from the Godblade, missing Galukar's dodges, splitting nearby undead fully in half as they overshot their target and stopped too slowly. He took a moment to read the thing's tempo, then struck. Two arms came free with one swing, a third with the second. Galukar's final attack had no limbs to interrupt it and sank in deep through the torso, then erupted from its back. He flicked his elbow, cutting the creature in half as he freed his weapon.

Blood coated him, his enemies, the ground. More came. Galukar swung at them like the rest.

It wasn't his goal to personally kill every single enemy attacking the camps—that would have been impossible even for him. Merely to force a conflict. If the enemy knew the legendary King Galukar was going on a rampage at their center, they would concentrate units there to kill him.

Which would slow them down in redirecting those same units to encircle the camps, buy time before that happened. More time meant more arrows spit into their ranks, more stones dropped onto their heads, more of Shaiagrazni's cannons belching fire and death to punch jagged holes into them. Time, at this moment, was a commodity more precious than gold.

More precious than blood.

Fomors came in from all sides now, as expected, and Galukar jumped. He didn't land for close to ten seconds, hitting the ground like a falling star, impacting with such force that he actually saw the air shimmer as a concussive wave maimed and floored everything within paces of him. Then he was moving again, spinning, swinging. His sword was an arc of destruction, a farmer's scythe. Around him were not enemies, but crops. Galukar was quick in his harvest.

He had no way of knowing how many he killed. By the time he'd counted the corpses made by any single swing, he'd already completed two, even three more. Dozens died with each attack, that much he knew. And still they were galvanizing.

Just as planned.

Then he glimpsed *him*, and his heart felt suddenly close to bursting. Tall, taller than Galukar, and clad from head to toe in black metal. He wielded a flanged mace, its shaft long enough to be gripped with two hands, and his body burned with arcane power so dense that it was hitting the air as visible light. The Dark Lord.

The killer of Galukar's sons, just a few dozen paces away and staring at him. A roar escaped Galukar, and his destruction doubled in speed as he hacked a path toward the caster, all semblance of strategy purged from his mind by the sudden, irresistible killing need that was washing his thoughts.

Galukar forgot about how their last bout had ended, forgot he was standing within a few hundred yards of a vampire more powerful even than him, forgot everything in the world save the Dark Lord, what he'd done, and how he had to die.

Some part of Collin felt ever so slightly inadequate at the sudden, cataclysmic shift that befell the battlefield as Lilia turned her will on the enemy.

He ignored that part of him and stamped it underfoot. Such feelings were far too impractical for a warrior—let alone a general—and it was virtually impossible to even give them any true consideration next to the weight of relief washing over him. He'd always been good at counting—one had to be for any future in command—and as far as he could tell, there were around two hundred thousand undead being conducted backward into their own side.

That wasn't everything—only a fraction of their true numbers. But it was one hell of a fraction. It was a chance.

"*Come on!*" he roared. "*They won't last long! This is our only chance to help!*"

Soldiers were brilliant, really. With normal men, Collin might have had to give them a *reason* to charge into the mouth of death. Not with soldiers. Whether paladins, pikemen, Kaltan foots, or rangers, they were all the same. None of them needed telling twice, and all barely even needed telling the once. They had an enemy, they had an order, they had weapons and a defensible position that was nice and short of suicidal to try to hold.

And they had an opportunity to do some damage. They all rushed off like the glorious, self-destructive bastards they were, carriages tearing down to pour in through the back of the war camps and let them disembark from within.

King Galukar hit the wall.

He'd been a full hundred yards ahead of it, and it surprised even Lilia to see the speed with which he was thrown. Crossing that span in under a second, the king smashed into the solid construct hard enough to send blocks of splintered bone spinning away from the impact even as he himself hurtled over it and disappeared on the other side. The Godblade fell down after him.

One hit, that's all the Dark Lord had needed to turn away the greatest warrior humanity had ever produced. She smiled, as always, and felt a stab of genuine fear touch her unbeating heart.

She couldn't have done that. And neither could her sire.

A pack of fomors came for her, charging in one cluster, evidently eager to tear her apart lest she unleash more of the power from before. She didn't, but there were plenty of other magics Lilia had at her disposal.

Fomors were undead, but they had the trappings of living creatures. They held blood in their bodies. Lilia boiled this blood, instantly and with a single thought, in all three at once. She added her magic to the natural pressure of liquid so quickly turned to gas and watched as four towering bodies erupted to tiny slivers of pulverized meat.

A bit got on her shoes because it was just that sort of day.

From the corner of her eye, Lilia caught the Dark Lord's metal-masked face turned toward her. His head tilted in thought, then with a gesture so slight she almost missed it even with her preternatural senses, he directed his creatures toward her in force. A moment later, he was striding across the battlefield behind them.

It seemed he had recognized her as the true threat. Just perfect.

Undead came so fast they actually started forming mounds, physical piles that moved and shifted toward Lilia almost like they were falling. She blew them apart, of course. Contemptuously. Not even looking as she felt for the blood lying dead in their veins and dragged it out by force, then turning it into a hundred thousand razored fléchettes that she sent scything through the rest of the horde all while staring at the Dark Lord head-on.

Which of them was the stronger? Him, clearly and without question. Which meant she had every reason to leave him as uncertain of that fact as was possible, and confidence seemed the most obvious first step to doing so.

Lilia was almost convinced she might have fooled the caster, and then the demons erupted from all around him.

CHAPTER FORTY-SIX

They were a multitude and a minority, a horde and an elite. They were formless, shapeless. Made of matter, Galukar thought, but no kind he'd seen before, and endlessly dynamic. Their bodies shifted, melting, boiling, freezing from one shape to another. In one moment, the demons were animalistic, as if their forms had been welded together from the material of several lesser beasts. Then they were things of artifice, fanged boulders and taloned trees. He saw one take to the air as a string of numerals, another begin to glide its way beneath the ground, propelled by a subterranean wind of whispered prayers.

All of them though were powerful. He could feel that much. All of them were true demons, not familiars.

Galukar let his roar cut the air to ribbons as he charged past them, heading on an intercept for their commander. The Dark Lord was just halfway to the vampire when Galukar's Godblade came flying for his head.

To the bastard's credit, he was fast as ever. Perhaps faster. The Godblade whistled by him, and his mace was coming around like a Ranger's arrow. Galukar caught it, felt the strength disparity between them, and gritted his teeth. He slid back, heels digging trenches in the ground, body slamming into undead swarming behind him and reducing them to scraps of pulped meat with the collision.

Just as he stopped, the Dark Lord swung again.

Galukar had not felt a pressure like this since . . . well, the last time he'd fought the Dark Lord. It was novel, to be the weaker party. To feel his unyielding strength at risk of surrender, to gasp at the twinge of pain lancing down his bones as they absorbed impacts greater than their own musculature might have conjured. The novelty wore off fast, however. Soon all that remained was the fear of it.

The Dark Lord swung, and Galukar melted to one side. His enemy's mace hit the ground like a certain fortress Galukar recalled falling from, and he saw the dirt erupt as if thrown high by a volcanic blast. Everywhere within paces the ground disappeared, making way for a jagged crater littered with pieces of pulped undead and misting ichor.

It was, perhaps, the greatest testament of pure strength he had ever seen a man's weapon make. It was casual, over in an instant. The mace was after him before the dirt had even finished its flight. Galukar parried again, this time launched fully from his feet and sent to drop down hard atop a row of undead.

Fortunately, they made for rather a soft landing. If a disgusting one. He felt bones break beneath him and got up to the sickly sensation of ground viscera clinging to his back. Galukar ignored it, forcing himself to his feet and watching ahead to see the Dark Lord closing properly on the vampire queen.

He expected the fight to end quickly, even instantly. It did not.

Vampires were not made of the same stuff as humans, Galukar had to remind himself as he watched Lilia duck back, flit away, weave beneath and around every swing that came for her. She was faster than him, Galukar thought. Nothing near his strength of course, and not beyond his fleetness by any greater span than one would have guessed by their sizes. But fast enough for an advantage.

And with more than just speed to her name.

Galukar saw the vampire lunge forward and burst apart, illusion so life— undeath-like that it almost fooled him until the creator had finished preparing her next attack. Blood, a great wave of it as weighty and high as any that might churn atop the skin of an ocean. It smashed into the Dark Lord faster than a sling bullet, dozens, hundreds of tons of mass washing over him. Had he been a castle wall, Galukar had no doubt there'd have been nothing left but stony detritus stretching to the horizon, and a ground scraped clean of all structure.

But the Dark Lord was not a castle wall; he was tougher. The blood parted against him, sending him back a step and scything apart the ground around him until he stood at the tip of a great elliptical trench eroded yards deep into the dirt. Everything behind him was obliterated. He was unhurt.

The vampire didn't pause to stare, and that was what saved her. When the Dark Lord swung his mace, she was already leaping to one side, and the concussive blast missed her. It continued onward, punching a jagged, bloody hole in the ranks of undead at her back, then continuing on to drill through a gritty hilltop fifty paces back. By then, the Dark Lord had closed in and started swinging.

But then so had Galukar.

Their weapons met with a sound like lightning striking a boulder, and the impact ran along Galukar's arm with such intensity that he felt the hairs wither atop it as force turned to heat and ignited them. He turned the Dark Lord's mace aside, stepped in, then punched him.

It surprised Galukar, to find himself resorting to such a low blow. It certainly surprised the Dark Lord, sent him back a step even, and left a dent in his helm. A small one, barely even there, and a sorry reward for the throbbing of Galukar's knuckles.

But evidence, nonetheless, of a mortal enemy. Those thoughts were buried however by the attack of an immortal ally.

Her blood was not a wave, this time, but a streak. One that moved so fast it had already passed the Dark Lord by the time Galukar's vision caught it, a great, sustained jet of liquid that chased the enemy as he fled from it. A wise decision, Galukar thought, for such velocities would surely be devastating on impact. Still the caster ran, darting back, ever ahead of the attack, yet slowly finding his ground shrinking. Finally he stopped, planting his feet and raising his mace to guard it.

The attack passed through him, and Lilia appeared at his back. The real Lilia, not an illusion, and wielding a very real torrent of blood that she now cast out into a jet just as fast and dense as the first. This one though impacted directly.

A flash of light, and a rain of stinging impacts ran down Galukar's body. A moment later the sound hit him, sharp like a whipcrack. He realized what had happened only when he saw the Dark Lord sent flying, and smelled the acrid scent of cooked meat upon the air.

Impact, direct and unbroken. An impact so great as to send droplets of blood rebounding outward faster than the noise of their collision and flash burn the organic tissue as it smashed into metal.

The vampire was gathering more blood now, and Galukar stared at her while she worked. If it came down to it, if he had no choice, could he kill this creature?

No. Not with any certainty, damn it, he could not.

Galukar roared, swinging just in time to force the Dark Lord back. He watched as the caster wavered, drawing away from him, head flicking to the vampire. Body shifting slightly. Then the demons came.

They were a mist of matter, and even that descriptor seemed too concrete a term for the stuff they were made of. Talons came for him. Galukar ducked and swung blindly, his sword biting into something that wasn't, but felt like it was, and cutting apart the not-stuff with a paradoxical jerk of his arm. He rolled, came up, felt something hit him with force but no mass, then soared backward to roll, churn the dirt, rise again. He swung, swung, swung, screamed and swung. Retreating, ducking, fighting the whole world at once. The enemies were without number, without counting. They closed from every angle they could have, and all the rest as well.

Occasionally, Galukar caught flashes of other combat. Little glimpses. A ranger on the walls, a knight at a breach, and of course the vampire queen still locked in her hopeless battle against the Dark Lord. But mostly all he saw were the abominations swarming him from all sides, and the great edge of wrought iron he was using to fell them.

He felt his panic rising, fear growing, doom looming. There were too many for him to defeat, too many by far. And the undead swarming around them were keeping any of their magical units—casters and the line—from pooling their strength behind his to vanquish the demons. His body was accruing damage, losing strength. And faster than the enemy's abominations were losing numbers.

Galukar let out a roar of fury and frustration that seemed to shake the ground. No, not seemed. It *did*. Except it didn't stop as his screaming did; in fact, it even grew more intense. A trembling before long, intense enough that the undead were visibly rocked by it. Galukar had time to stare in incomprehension and wonder at it.

Then the dirt beneath him burst upward.

It was a creature of such size that, for several moments, Galukar's mind refused to even believe it was a creature to begin with. A worm, he thought, though larger than any he'd seen. Its body spanned the width of a castle gate, at least. Mouth extending outward far enough to swallow entire squads of men. Galukar saw as much when it did just that, undead disappearing by the dozen within its maw as it burst from the ground. Its body continued upward for a few moments, turning, arcing down, then landing upon a separate section of enemies.

They too disappeared. Swallowed instantly without so much as a struggle. Then more of its kind emerged. Galukar saw ridged armor around the creatures, deflecting magic and arrows like they were pinpricks. Thick musculature contorting as the creatures landed back down and propelling them back under the earth. He saw heat hissing off them, air rippling with the temperature of their gargantuan bodies, and he saw the hand of their maker as clear as day.

It seemed Silenos Shaiagrazni had finished his latest project. Galukar looked around for the man, even while the battlefield turned to mutilated chaos around him. It did not take long to find the caster. He had never been one for discretion.

Shaiagrazni flew high overhead, and he was in his abominable combat form. It towered, rippling with jagged muscle and armor plating, eyes a pair of bottomless pits, body adorned with a multitude of weapons. Some, through their travels, had made their purpose terribly obvious. Others were horrifically unknowable. All, he wagered, would tear apart the fortifications behind their creator in moments.

But he had another goal today, and he was staring at it with a monomaniacal heat.

"That trembling," the vampire Lilia called out, snatching Galukar's eyes around to find her lying prone and wounded before the Dark Lord. "I suspect that will be the last sound you ever hear."

Shaiagrazni charged.

CHAPTER FORTY-SEVEN

Then

Ensharia—the paladin—walked away. There was a multitude of things Silenos ought to have done in response. Variations of ending her life made up the bulk of them. She had disrespected him—challenged him—and left his service. She had made it clear her efforts would no longer be directed to aiding his ends. No longer was she a valuable asset; now she was only a nonentity. One who had defied the will of House Shaiagrazni.

Silenos watched her turn and leave, striding along the field of convulsing, choking orcs and shredded metal. He did not strike her down, did not seize her for some work of transcendent cruelty. He did not do anything at all but watch.

Turning himself, Silenos headed back for the ruined city of Kaltan. He moved his grotesquery to carry him with a thought, crossing the kilometers of land in under a minute, and quickly deposited himself within the city. He was not exploring it long before finding King Galukar, littered with wounds of varying severity, panting with exhaustion. The man's eyes were hard, and . . . strange. Sympathetic, Silenos realized. It was almost novel to receive such a look from a being so immensely beneath him. He might have derived amusement from the rarity were it not so immediately concerning.

"It's your apprentice," the king told him, eyes not meeting Silenos's.

With all that had transpired, with the carnage Silenos had walked through just to reach the inner fort, he would have been lying to claim he was surprised. All the same, the news irked him more than he had expected.

"Where is his corpse?" he asked.

King Galukar began to lead the way, wordlessly heading through the ruin that Kaltan had become. Silenos studied their surroundings as he followed.

Everywhere had at least some trace of the combat, and most places had many. Silenos saw barricades still half standing where they'd been hastily assembled and more hastily torn down, choke points clogged with arrow-riddled corpses, piles of limbs where defenders had been overwhelmed by their enemy.

Buildings were more rubble than structure for the most part, though those situated deeper into the city stood with less obvious a ruination. Silenos knew he'd find deep wounds in them, regardless, if he took the time to look.

He did not of course. The devastation was no concern of his. Barely providing sufficient visual interest to be worth studying as he walked, and affecting only the most irrelevant worms who had taken part in the city's defense. Still, he eyed it. A considerable level of destruction for a pack of orcs.

The greatest surprise was stumbling upon a slain grotesquerie. Silenos had known, intellectually, that his creations would be lost in the fighting. It still struck at the newly grown emotional centers of his cerebrum to see it with his own eyes.

"That one took a lot of killing," the king noted. "Saw it go down myself."

"How did they kill it?" Silenos asked, even as he scrutinized the carcass.

"Ballistae, a lot of them. At first. Then after a while, they started dousing it with flames using their casters. The armor started to blacken . . ."

Silenos sighed. It had been an obvious oversight on his part—he'd made the creature's armor resistant to heat, but not to the point of total immunity. Flames could carbonize and weaken it, simply slowly and without any appreciable thermal transfer to the meat below.

Now he knew the consequences of such a shortcut. It never paid to underestimate an enemy.

Well, Silenos was not left to dwell on it for long in any case. They were soon at the hallway. He looked around, noted the dissipating magics of several moderately potent undead, and his apprentice's corpse not so far ahead.

Falls had exsanguinated, clearly. His skin was paled by the loss of blood, eyes glassy and staring out into nothing. It was strange to see him in such a state. The boy had been a fool, but not lacking for *intelligence*. Merely sense. However brash his judgment, there had always been that underpinning cognitive weight behind every thought.

And now there was nothing.

"He died well," King Galukar said. "Heroically."

It was a ludicrous concept, good death. Death was death. No singular act could ever compare with the infinite potential a mind and talent like Arion Falls had possessed. Within a century, he'd have been among House Shaiagrazni's named. Within five, he'd have been one of their finest.

And now he was a corpse, body leached of its heat by the air. Inert as a rock.

"What did he say?" Silenos asked, surprising himself with the question. "Before the end. Did he have any . . ."

Last words? It was a laughably pathetic question, but Galukar was already replying before Silenos could recant it.

"He asked me to give you his apologies," the king replied. "He wanted me to tell you he was sorry he . . . couldn't be better."

"Leave me," Silenos said before he'd even realized he was speaking. The king hesitated, but only for an instant, and was soon gone. Silenos found himself alone. Alone with his thoughts, and for the first time since he could remember, they were making themselves hostile, bitter company.

Without even thinking about why, he approached his apprentice—his corpse—and leaned down to lift him from the ground. Falls was light. There was no surprise there. Body weight was a scant obstacle for his enhanced body. Silenos was in his laboratory within minutes, laying Falls down across the table. He began his examination.

The cold, mechanical realm of diagnosis and appraisal was something his mind was far more accustomed to, and the focus of it swept over Silenos like a cooling rag banishing desert heat. He probed Falls physically first, finding no trace of arcane malfeasance in his wounds. Then he turned to the purely supernatural examination.

That was always the harder. Magic was not natural to humans, not innate. Everything he understood about it was learned only through hard, tedious efforts to defy his own nature. But Silenos had done that for so long that it had *become* his nature. He persevered.

He had expected to find familiar sights in Arion Falls's body, a cursory examination merely meant to confirm his suspicions before the process of reanimation could begin. That would have resolved nothing, of course—his apprentice would be his apprentice no more. Robbed of the ability to grow, to properly learn, even, and forever stagnant at the power he'd held upon death. But it would have been one ally more if nothing else. A short-term gain, partly compensating for the loss of so great a long-term investment.

Silenos did not even get that, however.

There was interference about Falls's very essence—that deep, innermost point of magical and cognitive coalescence that primitives throughout history had called a soul. It was not a carefully made kind.

Not an attack—of that much Silenos was quickly sure. Had something managed to strike at so sensitive a part of his substance, it would scarcely have been left intact. And no traps awaited him that might have been left by a cleverer and more subtle enemy.

Besides, this world did not seem to have many, if any, who had mastered necromancy to such an extent. The Dark Lord certainly hadn't, and unless Sphera was merely a poor identifier of talent, no others could exceed even him.

Silenos probed the work more carefully, concern slowly mounting as he noticed its endless peculiarities. It followed no structure he had ever encountered, not House Shaiagrazni's, and none of the more formalized hedge casters his people had long since absorbed back in their own world.

If he had not known any better, he'd have guessed that it was some mere improvization. An attack, perhaps, that unexpectedly struck through Falls's defenses but . . . No, he had no such defenses against this order of assault. It didn't make sense.

The answer came to him all at once, a flash of inspiration that banished ignorance and calm both in a single stroke.

Silenos could find no trace of external attack because there was none. Falls had done this to himself.

With that in mind, he looked at the work through a new lens. Stopped searching for design and instead focused upon intent. The boy was a greater genius than he had suspected from what he saw, for only a true prodigy could have wielded necromantic soul magic even this precisely with only the barest relevant training. Could Silenos have managed that with Falls's experience?

He wasn't sure. It seemed increasingly likely that Falls's talent was greater even than he had believed.

And increasingly likely that he might be saved.

There were an endless number of things a necromancer might do to the soul of their enemy, but Silenos could imagine only one a panicking, dying man might think to try to do to his own. Sure enough, Falls had begun the delicate process of anchoring his spirit to his body and keeping himself from truly detaching.

It was that moment of transition that truly separated the dead from the living, magically speaking. House Shaiagrazni had yet to learn specifically why, but they knew very much about its significance. It made all the difference in the world.

And it was useless.

Silenos saw the fact quickly, but he kept looking. Not willing to allow so valuable a prize as Falls to disappear, stubbornly clinging to the notion that he might save him and wasting ever more time in the useless effort. But there was no saving him, and no salvaging what he had done.

In his genius, Falls had successfully kept his soul from undergoing the transition between veils. In his inexperience, he had done so by binding himself. And it was a clumsy, delicate thing.

If Silenos tried to forcibly extricate his soul from it, it would shatter. He would be dragged from his corpse and cast out beyond even the typical sea from which dead things were drawn.

There would be no bringing him back from that. No bringing *anything* back. That was a realm beyond the reach of even House Shaiagrazni.

Silenos's master had proved as much by her efforts to claim it, and the ever-present traceries of lightning scars that crisscrossed half her body no matter how many times they were fleshcrafted away even centuries later.

Entities dwelled there, and Silenos trembled at the very thought of attempting to pilfer what was theirs.

He did not realize that his fist was coming down atop the counter until impact had already shaken it. Silenos saw the stone crack beneath his strength, felt the vibrations run up his arm like the recoil of his cannon. Then he felt the pain. A distant, cerebral thing that nonetheless told him his damage's extent. Aching bones, burst capillaries, tortured muscle. The actual fist itself was by far the worse for wear. Knuckles caved in and gushing ichor, misshapen and deformed by their harsh strike into the stone.

Silenos stared at his hand, disbelief almost banishing his thoughts as he took in the sight.

What in the world was happening to him?

CHAPTER FORTY-EIGHT

Now

It had been a lot of work to properly prepare the local terrain for his new creations. A lot of work, but then so many of Silenos's accomplishments were these days. If nothing else, he had proved his power was removed from the crutch of Shaiagraznian influence.

Certainly, that of his latest grotesqueries was.

They were thin things, relatively speaking, bodies made eellike and slender to better burrow at higher speeds. Armored, as all his creations were, but more lightly. They relied upon ambush and the protection of their soily home to avoid enemy violence. And to that effect, they were quite a success.

It had been the eternal weakness of Silenos's other forms that they were simply too large and exposed a target upon the battlefield. Once, his fellow named had compensated for that, but those exotic magics were lost to him now. Only the Kaltan-made assassin forms had been exempt from that shortcoming, which was where he had derived the idea for this latest innovation.

In particular, Silenos wondered about their utility back in his own world. The idea of using ultrasonic vibrations to induce fluidity in granules of dirt or sand was hardly his own invention, but as far as he knew, no other in House Shaiagrazni had made it practical before him. Such an invention may well leave House Shaiagrazni beyond even the advanced modern weaponry they faced back home.

Well, that was a matter for the future. It was the present he attended to now.

Silenos dropped down, letting his wings fall away and reforming them into reinforcements for the anatomy of his combat form. This one was very much alike the others, save for a few smaller differences.

"The Dark Lord, I take it," he called out, dropping down before the caster and feeling the ground shiver at his four-thousand-kilogram mass. "I have been waiting to meet you for quite some time."

He studied the man, and found himself surprised. The Dark Lord was powerful—almost the equal of Silenos in terms of raw magical capacity. It was no wonder he had crushed King Galukar with such ease. He'd have distinguished himself even in House Shaiagrazni.

"Fascinating," he remarked. "You really have no excuse at all for such pitiably amateurish necromancy."

The Dark Lord moved without saying a word, which almost made Silenos regret bothering to add vocal cords to his latest war form. His enemy held a mace, a great thick one that likely weighed more than most men, and yet flew like a feather in his preternatural grip. Silenos had prepared for such a weapon—making sure to get a comprehensive report of how the man fought from Galukar long ago.

He raised his arm, keratinous weapon meeting the dark metal and letting out a sound like cannons firing. Within a dozen paces of them, undead were knocked down by the impact.

Silenos's combat form was physically stronger than Galukar, but not by much. Mere fleshcrafting could never have withstood the Dark Lord's strength. So it was fortunate then that his experiments in cultivating Vigor-infused tissue had been such a success.

His strength held, and for one moment they simply remained locked in a contest of physical prowess. Such things were unbecoming for a named of House Shaiagrazni, however, and Silenos put an end to it promptly. He raised his other arm, transfigured into his flamethrower configuration, and filled the air with white-hot death.

The Dark Lord moved before it landed, dodging admirably fast. Forced to keep the muzzle velocity modest to avoid his burning liquid being dispersed uncontrollably and made ineffective, Silenos realized quickly that the weapon was a poor choice for so swift an enemy. Even at point-blank range, he could avoid it.

Silenos found his enemy's counter coming before his own follow-up, a swing of the mace arcing with a twisting motion that gathered trailing shade-stuff behind it. Fascinating. He did not know of many materials able to withstand the abyss's touch enough for such an attack, and was not left long to ponder it before the magic thudded into his guard.

Silenos slid back, body shunted in spite of its mass. He heard popping as the substance of his keratin lance yielded to the necromantic assault, though a glance showed that the weapon was still intact. Somewhat.

It was time, he thought, to begin the secondary level of their battle—the psychological. There was a single critical weakness inherent to all casters that Silenos had discovered, and that was the *ego*. His kind were prone to thinking themselves infallible, invincible. Their arrogance reached the point of delusion. It was almost as if they actually believed themselves to be his equals, that the innate superiority enjoyed by House Shaiagrazni's foremost prodigy was somehow to be shared.

A ridiculous misconception, but a useful one. He put it to work shortly.

"It was all a plan, you know," Silenos noted, thrusting forward with his own lance and jerking the motion short. He'd spent some time studying the clumsy, barbaric science of melee combat, and learned well. It was beyond him to internalize the thousand minuscule skills and habits that made a true expert in the area, but he did not need to. Simply seeing the way Galukar and others fought had been enough to give him some inspiration.

Muscular tweaks, alterations to the mobility of his joints and a dozen other differences all added up to make his body fundamentally move differently and, more importantly, counterintuitively to the eyes of a more experienced fighter. It was no substitute for that same experience, of course, but it was something of an equalizer.

Where the Dark Lord had expected to turn Silenos's hand and make his stab go wide, it instead twisted in and bit down on his armor's pauldron. Steel would have been mangled beyond recognition—even were it made thicker than his entire torso. Whatever that black metal was, it was clearly made with magic. Silenos began to hypothesize.

The blows came back to answer his, faster by no small margin. He blocked what he could, and soaked the others with his greater size and physical prowess. There were advantages to sheer mass after all, though the Dark Lord seemed eager to test them. His every mace swing left another crack across the master-crafted keratin, sending shivers to visibly excite the air in shock waves racing dozens of meters around them. No undead came to help—none were able to even approach save the strongest of them.

Impossibly resilient metal forming his armor and mace—plus an unyielding potence of body to compound them. Silenos was rather certain this enemy made use of magic over kinetic energy: pressure, momentum, motion. Such abilities could imbue a substance with temporary power that held for as long as its wielder remained focused, and far exceeded the possible bounds of ordinary materials. Even ones made with other magics.

But it was not permanent, not like Vigor, and if Silenos was able to wound the Dark Lord—or distract him even—then there was every chance he'd find a brief opening.

However well-made the mundane materials of his body were, they would not withstand him. Not with Vigor empowering his fleshcrafting.

And so he spoke.

"Ado Mortascia is clever, but of course she never had any true chance of drawing Wudra onto my side of the conflict. I was simply banking on your fearing that she might to lure your forces to her. It was rather pleasing to hear how many you'd committed. I was resigned to lose Baird too in his feigned failure to delay you, but you actually failed to even kill him in the process of falling for my bluff, which only left my position the stronger. All your victories over the past weeks have been illusory, set up and knocked down to draw you into this battle, in this field, at this day. I've prepared the terrain quite well—even left my defenses imperfect and incomplete to ensure you'd take the risk of attacking."

It did not matter how true Silenos's words were; they merely needed to sound immediately, potentially plausible enough that the Dark Lord would consider them. Time spent doing that was time with his attentions divided. Silenos had found himself suffering in cases where he found his plans subverted by another, and what unbalanced him would surely work to unbalance this simpleton just as well.

No sign of distraction came, so Silenos pressed his enemy on the physical level. As they fought, he reformed his flamethrower into a more conventional cannon, raising the half-finished weapon to ward off a blow that threatened to bypass his guard and feeling a stab of satisfaction as his enemy fell for the bluff. Obviously the Dark Lord had gathered information on Silenos's weaponry, he would have been disappointed if he hadn't.

But however knowledgeable, however fast, there was only so much one could do to avoid a shot of near-hypersonic matter at point-blank range. The cannon was finished a moment later and spit out its attack like smoldering rock from a volcano.

A small explosion rang out where the slug crunched into the Dark Lord's breastplate, keratin and bone splintering to pieces on impact with his— apparently still harder—armor. Silenos's eyes were inured against such pressure and light, and the Dark Lord clearly had a considerable portion of even his current strength.

But he did not have his mass. Even as the projectile's energy failed to do more than damage his armor, its momentum proved enough to unbalance him. The necromancer's feet left the ground, and he hurtled backward as might a leaf caught by wind. Silenos saw him fall back, skull hitting the ground, body rolling. He came up in a crouch just as Silenos came down upon him to press his advantage.

The lance struck the mace, sounding out again and scraping the top layer of soil from the ground around them. Silenos took a step forward, forcing his enemy to retreat and capitalizing on his momentum as he swung and thrust more. He punctuated his attacks with periodic shots from his cannon, exploiting the enemy's newfound caution, driving him around.

For his part, the Dark Lord was hard to trap. Every boulder Silenos almost pinned him behind he turned and smashed aside with a quick, casual swing. Every trap he avoided, be it through agility or simple force. Clearly he was used to battling more physically powerful foes.

Well, there was no matter. Because Silenos was not as unused to using that power as he had been.

He was a surging tsunami, driving the Dark Lord like driftwood, chasing him and watching every place he tried to run. There were only so many times one man could evade a trap, only so much spatial awareness and skill could compensate for. At the end of the day, Silenos had the mass, the strength, the resilience. And he had a weapon capable of injuring even him to boot.

His cannon fired, this time filled with compressed nitrous that deliberately missed the Dark Lord by centimeters. The explosion at his back sent him shunting forward, straight into Silenos's thrusting lance. The meeting of keratin and metal was like nails on a chalkboard.

Once more the Dark Lord was sliding back, heels digging trenches, soil hissing and spitting as water was vaporized by the frictive grind of metal. He stopped meters back, just in time to duck another of Silenos's swings. This time he ducked right into a raising knee, catching the jagged barb Silenos had added to the tip right in his helmet. It scraped a chunk off, sending black flakes to rain away from him as he stumbled again.

A dirty, simple brawling trick. Learned from Baird. Sometimes it was the simplest tactics that were most effective—Silenos had seen that much watching him spar with his knights and grotesqueries.

The mace came flying for Silenos, and he weathered it as it rebounded from his head. His neck had been particularly reinforced in this new form, with the Dark Lord's strength and blunt instrument in mind. He stabbed again while his enemy was stumbling away, then the cannon rose once more.

A bluff, and one that sent the Dark Lord scrambling back into Silenos's next swing. Metal broke, limbs splayed, his opponent landed in a pile and scrambled back. Silenos chased him.

It was almost disappointing to be faced with so insubstantial an adversary—with Lilia and Galukar keeping the Entities at bay, there was no contest between them at all.

The Dark Lord was up as fast as ever, though slightly clumsier now. His armor seemed to be slowly surrendering to Silenos's assaults, resilience pushed past its limits by Shaiagraznian magic, wearer not far behind. And yet . . .

A confidence underpinned his motions that hastened Silenos to reengagement. Even still, he was too slow.

Silenos saw the Entities burst into reality between them, screaming, roiling infants wearing the entropic placentas of their own unexistence and sloughing them off into showers of decayed matter and discordant energy. They were wailing, convulsing faceless things whose forms he barely had time to even try to perceive before they too broke down. Consumed by the Dark Lord, all their magical intensity compressed and imbibed into his own.

He felt his enemy's power grow and realized in an instant that he had been hasty. This fight was only just starting.

CHAPTER FORTY-NINE

The Dark Lord was stronger. He was faster, and he seemed suddenly without all the fatigue and wounded sluggishness that had been causing Silenos's advantage to grow by the attack. He had made an error, and it seemed like that error was about to kill him. It took a very young and a very stupid caster to die. He could only hope his hasty precautions over the past few weeks would be enough.

Silenos raised his lance, missing the mace as it twisted unexpectedly low and thudded into his side. The impact hurt—more than the last few he'd taken, cracking the keratin with a jagged pop and sending the kinesis of his wound to permeate deep through the softer tissues below. He stumbled back, guard instinctually shifting to protect his wounded side just as the Dark Lord's mace came around for the other. This time it hit an already weakened set of armor, cracking that fully open, and caving in a rib beneath it. Blood rose up into Silenos's mouth as his knee buckled.

It shouldn't have been possible. He'd never heard of a creature able to feed off the magics of an Entity, let alone several. The closest he'd ever heard a caster getting was his own ritual to absorb from as part of a contract—and only he and Adonis had known about that. Whatever was happening now was beyond the scope of his predictions.

But not beyond killing him.

He fell back, too slowly. He guarded too weakly. He felt his combat form's anatomy slowly surrendering to the whittling blows of his enemy.

And then the Dark Lord disappeared, hurled to one side with a supersonic whipcrack shaking the air in his wake. A moment later, the sound of a cannon shot reached Silenos's ears. He looked to the side, and found himself truly surprised.

For descending from the skies was Swick the Swift's airship, repaired and battle ready.

God, did it feel good to be in the air again. Swick had barely even known how much he'd been dying, trapped down there on the dirt. Now he was free, now he was airborne, and the world was that much sweeter.

The wind was a gentle caress on his skin, the skies a refreshing blast of oxygenated air to infuse his every breath with energy. There was the same old thrill to flying he'd always felt, but stronger. Sharpened and intensified by years of neglect. He'd forgotten how life felt up here, after so long seeing it only through his fugue of alcohol. Now he remembered.

But he didn't have the luxury of dwelling on it for long because they were closing in on their enemy. Were it not for Swick's Vigor, he'd have been unable to pick anything out at all—unable to even remain on the deck of the ship's exterior with the speed they were moving. As things were, he could just make out the Dark Lord fighting against Shaiagrazni at the midst of some great battle.

Beside him, he just barely heard Felicia growl.

"That's the fucker, right?" she asked.

Swick had glimpsed the Dark Lord once or twice—always from a safe distance, of course. He nodded.

"Then ready these new weapons of yours. This one's for my brothers."

He hurried to do so, taking careful aim with Shaiagrazni's cannon and whispering a silent prayer of thanks to the insane fleshcrafter for being so preemptive in outfitting the vessel with it. It was a bigger weapon too, firing iron balls measuring a good half foot in diameter. He loaded one, packed the back of the weapon with blasting oil, gave the signal. Waited for his own.

They'd not had long to rehearse, and Swick could only hope their aim was on point. Fortunately, luck was behind them.

His ears shivered as the cannon fired, and the entire vessel trembled as if in fear of its own prow's weapon. A whipcrack rang out, sharp and sudden, and he heard a light popping as an air funnel formed and died all within a fraction of a second.

The Dark Lord was hundreds of yards ahead—perhaps as much as half a mile. But the impact caught him in less than a second, aimed more perfectly than skill alone could possibly have allowed and bowling the caster fully off his feet to grind a deep gouge out through the dirt underfoot. He stopped sliding and rolling only after he'd been driven twenty paces sidelong.

Of course that was not much of an alleviation on their current situation. For one thing, the ground was still covered in shambling undead as far as the eye could see—while Galukar and Lilia both fought tooth and nail against swarms of . . . something. Swick couldn't describe the things, seeing them only as physical anomalies in the periphery of his vision. They were powerful though, and barely being held at bay.

Right about then, Shaiagrazni collapsed from his wounds, and remained collapsed even while the undead around him started hurtling for his unconscious body with weapons raised and jaws wide.

Well, that made priority number one quite obvious: stop their strongest fighter from being cannibalized in his sleep.

"We're going low!" Swick called, not needing to glance over his shoulder to know the command would be heard, heeded, executed. Rigging rerigged, sails raised as a windbreak, ship prepared to turn its velocity downward, bleed the excess speed away, and strafe over the enemies.

It had always been among the deadliest maneuvers a skyship could perform, but its mastery and frequent use was half the reason for Swick's reputation. He felt the deceleration start all at once, then continue with a sluggish consistence as they arced downward. The undead were almost on Shaiagrazni—they were almost on the undead—the wind was a scream in his ears. He gave the order just as they closed.

Felicia was the one on catch-and-run duty, tethered to the deck and fast as anyone. She leaped overboard just as they came nearest to Shaiagrazni's form.

While she did, in the precious moments before she dropped down to grab him, the cannons fired. All of them, at once.

Powerful damned things that they were, he actually feared the ship might break apart from the recoiling force of their blasts. It held though, and he was able to enjoy the sight of scores—even hundreds—of undead coming apart into clouds of vaporized viscera and rapidly spinning limbs. The air suddenly smelled of rancid blood and that strange acrid scent that always came with blasting-oil detonations.

And Felicia was dropping down in the distraction, grabbing Shaiagrazni just as the ship tore past. Both of them were dragged in its wake, rope croaking in pain at the considerable effort of hauling so heavy a load with so much speed.

Then everything went wrong.

A fireball came for the ship, breaking against its hull—newly reinforced with that keratin stuff Shaiagrazni used in his grotesqueries—but detonating in the impact. It sent flames blasting out in all directions, hot and dense. They engulfed Felicia and Shaiagrazni.

Swick stared, fearing for one moment that he was about to see charred corpses where there'd been allies mere moments ago. He didn't, of course. Both Hero and near-Hero seemed fine—the explosion had been far enough, the energy diluted enough by distance, that even Felicia barely had a singed eyebrow. But the rope wasn't filled with Vigor, and that was on fire now.

More fireballs quickly distracted Swick from the fact, and he started barking orders again.

"Propulsion!" he roared. "Full speed, sails down, evasion in light arcs!"

It was a very important detail, that last feature. With the speeds a skyship could move, turning at anything but a shallow angle would incur huge changes in acceleration and deceleration to its mass. With something as heavy as it, such differences were catastrophic.

Skyships were very rarely destroyed by enemy fire directly. Mostly, when one heard about such a vessel falling in battle, it was because the idiot piloting it panicked under enemy fire and tore his own ship in half trying to avoid it.

Swick didn't intend to make that sort of mistake, new hull or not.

Within moments, their speed was picking up, fireballs left far behind and even heavy trebuchet stones or ballista bolts not much quicker in catching them. They cut wide arcs around the army, circling over them with a league-long turning radius to manage their acceleration. Even that looked like just about the limit of what some crewmen could manage, but Swick didn't dare any less evasion than this.

Besides, they had other things to focus on than just flight.

"Cannons!" he roared. "Load the starboard set with blastshot, port with solid shot. Fire at will!"

They were circling the enemy clockwise, which meant that starboard was facing the army. Swick had seen the Dark Lord's durability firsthand though, and he wanted to make sure that they had as many fortress-cracking solid shots prepared as was possible if he suddenly attacked again. Hence the loading pattern on their port side, allowing for such weapons to be brought to bear with only a turning of the vessel. It would have to do.

And it did. In moments, cannons were firing. All half dozen of the heavy things spitting out their devastation in long volleys, one coming every minute and a half. There'd not been long to drill on the way to the battlefield, but the Red Fingers were always quick to learn, and they'd been careful to put as much work as they could into mastering the weapons. Twenty hours or so made a lot of difference.

But the shells made more. Each one was only a thin outer skin of the bony substance used in Shaiagrazni's mass-produced projectiles, their interiors filled with blasting oil and smaller solid projectiles about as wide as a man's pinkie. Upon impact, they detonated. Detonated powerfully enough that Swick could *see* the concussion as it distorted air and sent refractive waves running through it.

And he could see the carnage better. Every cannon was a hundred, even two hundred dead or dying enemies. Within their first volley, they'd erased enough of them to man a smaller fortress.

But they had the ammo for a good few dozen more.

Swick left the boys to it, with orders to bring him back for any new concerns, and finally hurried to look at Shaiagrazni. Things had deteriorated there.

The rope was still intact, despite the turns. That was good but expected—he'd specifically chosen the thickest one they had, a hand-wide mass of fiber able to withstand over twenty tons before snapping.

When intact. It wasn't now though, and in fact it was still on bloody fire. Swick cursed, recognizing the flames as some form of magic. It wasn't a particularly hard deduction given their vibrant-green coloration, and ability to continue burning the rope despite being pelted at all times by winds in excess of a hundred miles per hour.

Still, the rope held. For now, and it was being pulled back in. A few more moments—a minute, maybe, at most—and Shaiagrazni would be on deck.

Swick heard the call an instant later.

"Captain! Come look!"

He sighed. Of course things weren't that easy. When the fuck had they ever been?

The Dark Lord was up, and turned to them. Swick's blood ran cold. He wasn't just facing them; he was *close*. He must've crossed the battlefield without their noticing, carefully positioning himself at a point where the vessel's turn left it nearer to the bulk of the forces, setting a trap with him as the killing instrument.

And it was too late to turn away.

Ahead, the air twisted and flashed vibrant crimson. Demonic energies, Swick recognized, were building, densifying, solidifying. The very atmosphere seemed to break down around them, conjuring a strong wind that sucked in everything nearby as the Dark Lord's power continued to congeal. Then it came on as a single wall, a deadly stormfront from which no escape was possible.

For an instant, Swick froze. Fear flashed through his mind, punching the thoughts out of him, dragging him to memories of a looming stony wall and a fiery descent. Then his mind hardened, he gathered his wits, and he started throwing out orders.

"*Slow!*" he roared instantly. "*Sails one-third down! Angle them at twenty degrees!*"

There was no hesitation, thank God, but he saw plenty of confusion. That was fine. Swick was almost confused himself. He started running. "*Everyone take cover!*" Swick hit the wheel, watching his men disappear down under the decks. Then the wave was on him.

It caught the sails first, snagging them, dragging with resisting air for a solid few seconds.

The hull groaned, screamed, cracks forming and running along it measuring farther from head to toe than a man. The entire vehicle trembled with the strain, and Swick knew instantly it would have been destroyed already were it not reinforced so well by Shaiagraznian magic.

He'd banked on that though. He'd banked on everything that was happening. Swick had flown a skyship for longer than perhaps any other man in living memory, survived more crashing incidents than perhaps any ever.

And now, he was stone-cold sober.

CHAPTER FIFTY

They burst from the wave of magic with a shudder, and Swick had to suppress a nervous laugh. He was almost in disbelief of his own survival—almost in disbelief that he could possibly have executed a plan so well.

Then he looked back, and the disbelief was crushed under the heel of cold, weighty reality. He just barely glimpsed Felicia climbing on board as the rope holding her and Shaiagrazni snapped, dumping the caster down to land among the enemy below.

She looked at him, apologetic, but Swick couldn't care less what expression was on her face. She'd fucked them all either way.

Down below, the New Dark Lord landed. If there was any consolation to the disaster, it was seeing his multiton body absolutely pulverize an entire row of undead, pinning and crushing them practically into juice as it came down atop them. That didn't last long, however, for the dust cleared soon, and the original Dark Lord was soon approaching with a mace in hand and murder dripping off every inch of his armored body.

He seemed to be taking his time, for some reason. Perhaps he had an enjoyment of the dramatic. Swick really couldn't say.

He, on the other hand, hurried.

"Into firing position!" he screamed, knowing all the while how useless it would be. The ship was facing away from Shaiagrazni now, and its back hadn't been outfitted by cannons. It would take precious moments to slow, precious more to haul the artillery around. Longer, in total, than the Dark Lord would need to kill even three Shaiagraznis.

And then the ranks of undead around him just melted, falling apart into puddles of hissing black sludge as someone stalked out from among them.

Sphera, Swick recognized, and a moment later Collin Baird was behind her—followed by the princess Ado and . . .

The vampire. Well, now was no time for grudges. She was annoying to fight, which meant she'd be annoying for their enemies to. He repeated the turning order, a shade more hopeful now, a lot more enthusiastic.

With a gesture, the princess Ado threw out a great wall of ice between Shaiagrazni and the enemy. She was powerful, Swick thought, because the structure was *big* even as it appeared near instantly. Five paces wide, four high, and a good few inches thick.

The Dark Lord didn't even bother to hit it, just kept walking and smashed the barrier to pieces with the sheer weight of his pace. Swick grinned, realizing he'd fallen for the trick hook, line, and sinker. Because it hadn't been meant to impede him, just block his line of sight. The moment he emerged through it, Baird's arrow—timed as perfectly as Swick had ever seen of anything—caught him right in the chink where breastplate met gorget.

It dug in, drawing out a trickle of blood and sending the Dark Lord back a step. The vampire was next.

She wasn't nearly as fast as Baird's arrow though, and the Dark Lord blocked her attack with a contemptuous flick of his wrist. The next block of ice came down from above him, forcing him to sidestep, and Swick saw him quickly backing off to the horde of undead at his back. Thinner, now, compared to when the battle had begun. But numerous enough. He reached them before the vampire reached him.

And then the undead started clawing at him, as Sphera grinned and gestured hundreds of the things to pile in and around him, climbing, biting, thrashing at the necromancer as they tore themselves apart in the attempt to destroy him.

Not a bad trick, Swick realized. Who'd have noticed a few hundred undead among thousands of times as many?

But it was hardly a damning move—Baird barely had a weapon able to hurt the Dark Lord; these creations certainly didn't. He shook them off like a dog casting water from itself, continuing the fight.

Baird's next arrow missed—or was dodged, rather—tearing through ranks of enemy undead far behind the Dark Lord and ripping them to pieces of flying limbs. The mace came for Hexeri, missing but clipping her shoulder. Swick winced, seeing the limb mangled instantly as she shot back. A third arrow, dodged again, and Mortascia dropped down a new wall. Thicker, this time, perhaps intended for actual defense.

The Dark Lord saw fit to grace this one with a true strike, and smashed the entire thing into crystalline rubble as if it were nothing more than air. Swick's stomach dropped out of him. They couldn't fight this thing. They couldn't even try.

Baird tossed his bow aside as the Dark Lord closed, drawing a pair of longknives and going low. He whipped up at the last second, cutting a nice circle across the enemy's arm, which did absolutely nothing for the strength of his armor. Baird danced around him for a few moments, actually competing with the necromancer's speed. Eventually though, his luck ran out. A fist struck his gut, and he shot high into the air only to fall back down with blood torrenting out of his mouth.

Ado Mortascia and Sphera were the only ones left. Both moved at once, conjuring a wall of ice and doing . . . something else. The Dark Lord broke this one, stumbling back as shadestuff burst out of the hollow inside it and soaked him. A normal man—plate or not—would have been eaten down to a puddle at such an attack. The Dark Lord merely continued on, armor hissing and damaged. But only slightly.

Swick knew, at that moment, that he was moments away from seeing the women die. And then the fireball came.

It was huge. Bigger than huge, it was *monstrous*. Like an entire palace engulfed in flame, but with no supporting fuel at the center. Nothing but a burning tsunami washing across the landscape and closing in on them all. The moment before impact, it compressed downward, becoming a writhing, twisting vortex of heat that homed in on the Dark Lord and impacted him hard enough to drive the necromancer back a few paces. The fire exploded apart from his mace's impact, reforming moments later.

It was the demon Xekanis. Prince Nemo's pet. And the very world was sizzling at its presence.

Do it, Xekanis, destroy him.

Xekanis was all too eager to obey, practically burning the very air as he leaped in to battle the Dark Lord. It didn't matter that his magic was, for once, the inferior party. It didn't matter that this was a demonologist who may be perfectly qualified to best him. He saw prey, and he attacked. A beast unchained, a guillotine left to fall.

Nemo had always known he would be like that. He'd always known his friend was only a single word away from being unleashed. He expected to feel something at the sight, but he didn't. Perhaps he'd already filled himself up with too much emotion.

Turning, he saw the twitching body of Silenos Shaiagrazni. Nemo felt tears well at the sight. Trembling, he forced himself to speak. For all the good it would do.

"I'm sorry," he whispered. "None of this . . . None of it would've happened if I . . . I'm sorry." Nemo looked away, too ashamed suddenly to even take in the sight of Shaiagrazni. "I'm sorry you got hurt. I'm sorry I couldn't be better."

Something shifted. Nemo blinked, stepped back, tried to look through the distorted sheets of his tears. The moisture of his eyes was so thick that he almost thought he saw . . . No, he did.

Shaiagrazni was rising to his feet!

It sent an instinctual, terrified jolt through Nemo's body to see such a mountainous tower of flesh right itself so effortlessly. Shaiagrazni, he knew, was the same man he ever was beneath it all, but there was something fundamentally intimidating about this body. Eleven feet high, broader than three men, covered with such a mass of armor he wondered whether it made up the majority of his weight. And moving *easily* despite it all, body propelled by such a primal physicality as to manage its own weight like some performing acrobat.

He couldn't move, and wouldn't have even if he'd been able. Shaiagrazni was unsteady for a few moments, remaining still as organic matter formed and re-formed around him—creating a lance across one arm, a cannon barrel in the other. Then he lurched forth.

Nemo winced, expecting a blow that never came. When he looked up, Shaiagrazni had already torn for the Dark Lord with a speed that seemed impossible for even half his mass. The ground exploded under every stride he took, legs coming down like battering rams, musculature driving him along. His enemy was looking away as he closed, lashing at Xekanis with some strange whip of black energy that tore chunks of flame out and left it to fall as liquid away from the demon's body. Nemo felt his eyes leak ever more with tears at the sight of his friend's agony, his voice unable to even escape as a cry.

Then the Dark Lord turned to Shaiagrazni, just in time to be bowled fully off his feet by a tackle strong enough to bring down castle walls.

For an instant, the two of them were held together. Bound by Shaiagrazni's pillar-thick limbs as they rolled, grinding out deep trenches in the dirt and flattening formations of undead. Then the shot rang out.

Even fifty paces back, it strained Nemo's ears, the snarl of Shaiagrazni's cannon. He saw the Dark Lord fly away with smoke hissing from his chest, clearly caught at point-blank range. He landed among his own creations.

He lost sight of him, stared, froze. Then the Dark Lord rose again atop a mound of shifting necrotic bodies. Mace in hand, magic ablaze, bearing down on Shaiagrazni. Something shifted to one side, and a grotesquerie slammed into the pile of undead. It broke apart, and bodies flew in all directions; some fell straight down, others flipped fully over the towering grotesquerie's head, some remained clinging to its body and trying to stab through its skin. So big was the creature that most failed, but the stronger among them irritated it at least. They bought the Dark Lord a precious distraction to scale it himself, bringing his mace down on its head.

The thing was dead before it hit the ground, and the Dark Lord was moving on to its master next.

Nemo was far from a fleschrafting expert, but he could see that Shaiagrazni was still injured—or at least fatigued. If he fought the Dark Lord directly now, the outcome would be far from ideal. Xekanis was still writhing in a heap, and Nemo couldn't bring himself to even reach his friend.

It was King Galukar and Lilia's ambush, coming just before the Dark Lord reached Shaiagrazni, that changed things.

CHAPTER FIFTY-ONE

Galukar swore his teeth were loose. It was novel. He hadn't been hit as hard as he had today in . . . well, ever. Ordinarily that might have been exhilarating. Today, it was just an obstacle to butchering the damned animal who'd turned his sons into monsters.

But he did not let the rage take him, not yet. He would hold it back, keep it chained like a hunting hound, and release it only when he knew victory was theirs. Galukar had no intention of surviving the day, but he had every intention of making sure the Dark Lord *didn't*.

When he swung, it felt like the release of something hard and tense. Something he couldn't name.

The Godblade didn't miss, but its connection was shallow and sour. Sparks flew as it etched a new scar into the Dark Lord's pauldron, target melting back and retaliating with his mace. Galukar blocked it, flying from his feet as the strength came unexpectedly greater than before. He landed hard, rolled up, and saw the foot coming just an instant before the ice appeared before it.

Princess Ado was certainly doing her best, but Galukar didn't actually notice the impediment slow his enemy's strike before heel met nose and filled his sinuses with metallic blood. Once more, he stumbled off.

Blood whipped around in great tendrils, for once making Galukar glad to see the unholy magic as it shielded him through the precious moments needed to counterattack. The Dark Lord was already pulling back, of course, focusing now on the vampire. She held her ground rather than flee. Had she done otherwise, Galukar knew she'd simply have been run down.

He and the vampire were both wounded, both badly. Galukar had been injured by the Dark Lord first, and now he'd collected a new set of scrapes and gashes from slaying his horde of demons. She was not much better.

With their strengths combined they could *last*, but it was an inherently uphill battle. And one made harder by the Dark Lord's bolstered power. Galukar fought with every inch of might he could muster, managing to last entire seconds before being cast aside with another rib broken. The vampire fell shortly after.

As he landed though, he found a sense of victory overtaking him. Because from the corner of his eye he saw Silenos Shaiagrazni approaching, body healed, wounds half closed, motions smoother and less clumsy than they'd been seconds before. He attacked the Dark Lord in just the way Galukar would have.

A surprise cannon shot to the back.

Galukar had seen great warriors fight; he had seen great casters fight. He'd never seen anything—anything at all—like this.

Shaiagrazni opened the battle first, great tendrils of flesh erupting from the carpet of ruined bodies at his feet. Their heads were barbed with keratin, and they shot for the Dark Lord like the undulating limbs of a kraken. The Dark Lord replied as he might have been expected to, mace thrashing out to deflect them, cracking the hardened tips and bursting the fleshy bodies like rotten fruit.

But this was not the New Dark Lord's only effort. While it still occurred, something more formed at his feet. Large, broad, reinforced. A cannon, Galukar realized. A cannon aimed in such a way that he was overlapping the sight line. He scrambled aside just in time for its fireball to miss him, ears ringing as something impossibly large tore through the air. Hundreds of undead came to pieces, perhaps thousands. Then the projectile hit something solid enough to stop it and detonated. It was like watching the sunset touch the ground, a great cascade of obliteration that scoured an entire acre of all habitation.

At the end, the Dark Lord still lived.

He rose up high, higher, higher still. Taking flight as if the defiance of natural law was too small a slight to even register beside his others. Shaiagrazni's body shifted, mass redistributing as wings shot outward, and he was soon following. Slower, but more confidently.

With a gesture, the Dark Lord tore something into the air before him. From it emerged a demon, snarling and thrashing, its flesh made of hemp rope and eyes burning with the color of jealousy. It shot down for its prey—a powerful one, this!—but failed to reach him before Shaiagrazni's answering stroke intercepted.

Spirits. Incorporeal undead. Wisps, wraiths—there was an abundance of names for them. Galukar had rarely seen the things. Usually they could only be produced by carefully creating the right circumstances. Apparently Shaiagraznian necromancy was not limited in such a way. The specters swarmed their demonic prey, sending it falling out of Shaiagrazni's path as sheer weight of numbers let the preternaturally strong spirit things tear into it despite the great weight of magic giving it strength.

Cannon arm raised, Shaiagrazni fired at the Dark Lord and clipped his shoulder. That armor was becoming damaged now, its protection compromised more with every shot. The Dark Lord closed for a melee.

He was forced to veer off, inky shadestuff cast out into a wall before him. Those precious moments' delay were time enough for limbs to explode out of Shaiagrazni by the dozen. Some with keratinous lances and cannons, like his main arms, others merely coated with armored gauntlets. Several reached out now and threw another sheet of shadestuff out. Galukar watched it wash over the Dark Lord, sizzling and eating at his armor. The mace came around, smashing Shaiagrazni in one of his numerous shoulders and tearing the offending limb entirely off.

One had been removed, scores more remained. A blast of energy came out, burning two more of Shaiagrazni's arms to desiccated slivers of ash. Demonic, Galukar thought, another foul trick in the Dark Lord's repertoire. But in a duel of dark magic, he doubted any could match the sheer versatility of his tenuous ally.

As if to prove the point, Shaiagrazni moved again. Limbs and torsos began liquefying on the ground below him, flying up to congeal before him into a great coiling mass. From it emerged . . . dark elves. Many, all attacking. For one moment, Galukar didn't understand.

Then he did. Shaiagrazni was resurrecting his enemy's slain soldiers? Such a psychological attack seemed unlikely to work on a man as unapologetic as the Dark Lord, but he supposed it was worth an attempt if nothing else.

But it didn't work, not even delaying the caster, who smashed through them and came for Shaiagrazni. That was when the mass of flesh erupted, revealing another jet of shadestuff that blasted the necromancer back. A perfect misdirection. Shaiagrazni pounced on it as eagerly as any creature had pounced on anything.

His lance tore a pauldron clear off the Dark Lord's armor, and while his guard was raised, a cannon shot blasted his guts at point-blank range. Scraps of black metal flew apart, and this time blood trickled from the injury. The damage was adding up, his defenses eroding, his strength failing. He backed away. Shaiagrazni closed in, mastery of the air clearly to his favor and used excruciatingly well as his assault became three-dimensional. Up, down, diagonally—his attacks came in from every way they could, and suddenly the disparity of skill seemed fully reversed against the Dark Lord's favor.

The Dark Lord's arm splayed out, a blast of demonic magic that lashed Shaiagrazni backward and bought him a moment. He used it to close, swinging his mace around in a crippling blow. Shaiagrazni blocked it, barely, flakes and chips smashing from his lance as he shot back. His enemy pressed the advantage, swinging one way and the other. Galukar turned to the vampire queen.

"Do something!" he snapped. "You must be able to."

But she just stared at him, clearly as perturbed by her lack as he was his own.

"They're too high, too fast, and too durable," she replied through gritted teeth. "Shaiagrazni is on his own."

He was, but even as the vampire said it, he started to push back the Dark Lord's advantage. Clearly, the armored caster was no undead because he wore the fatigue of his injuries openly in his slowed movements and weakened strikes. Shaiagrazni broke out from the pinning barrage with another cannon shot aimed for his head, then smashed the lance against his chest as he retreated. His other arms landed their own hits, smaller, scraping blows without his bodyweight behind them, but nonetheless grinding away the face of his armor and reaching precariously closer to the meat below it.

Galukar hadn't thought anything in the world could defeat the man who'd killed his sons. Now though, he knew better.

The Dark Lord faltered, breaking back into a retreat that Shaiagrazni intercepted with all the hesitation of a starved tiger. He closed in, raising above his enemy and blasting him downward toward the earth with his cannon. The Dark Lord pulled up just moments before impact with the ground.

Shaiagrazni did not.

Nine thousand pounds of flesh, bone, and armor plating smashed into the Dark Lord and drove him into the earth so hard that it was blasted into a crater. They churned it away, drilling down and not stopping until they'd formed a hole so deep Galukar couldn't even see the bottom. Debris was sent flying out in every direction, stunning stronger undead and ripping the weaker ones to pieces. By the time the air had finally cleared, they still hadn't emerged.

Everything fell silent, save for the undead. And somehow even *they* remained still, as if they were waiting to see whether they crumbled to dust at their master's death before attacking. Then, finally, after what felt like an age, movement in the crater.

Something shot out of it, landed, bounced, and rolled. A smoldering black thing of twisted plates and oozing blood. The Dark Lord. A moment later, Shaiagrazni emerged, landing just yards from him and looking down at the caster.

"You have given me considerable inspiration to improve my weaponry," the fleshcrafter announced, nonchalant as ever.

The Dark Lord shifted, slowly making his way up to his knees. Galukar stared, taking the sight in, waiting for the sense of victory. He felt none. Only the rage.

"*Murderer!*" he roared, sprinting ahead and forgetting all about his injuries and exhaustion. The Godblade was starved, and the Dark Lord's blood seemed a banquet enough to fix that. He'd closed only a few paces before the magic became visible.

It was subtle at first, then obvious. Thickening and deepening in its coloration until even a blind man would have spotted it. A roiling, boiling tempest of dark energy and unfathomable depth. Galukar almost hesitated. *Almost.* Then he charged on regardless.

The magic leaped outward as quickly and eagerly as a flame doused in oil. It slowed Galukar, sending out winds with force enough that even his preternatural strength was tested in marching through them. He strode on, managing another two paces before he stopped altogether. Then the winds intensified.

Galukar watched as the air twisted and imploded, falling into itself, coiling around some invisible epicenter and thickening to an almost liquid density. Then it all stopped at once. With a flash of light and a blast of magic, the world went pure, searing white.

CHAPTER FIFTY-TWO

Silenos didn't need to shield his eyes—he'd long since hardened the visual organs of his combat form against so mundane an attack as bright light— and so he had a far clearer view of what was happening than most present.

Granted, he'd have seen more regardless. Silenos was a master of magic, always and above all other things. And what was occurring before his eyes . . . Well, it was certainly magic.

There were some in House Shaiagrazni whose magic specialized more into the realm of manipulating and mastering Entities than Silenos himself, and he had no doubt any of those phenoms might have gleaned more from the sight than he. Nonetheless, he recognized enough. Reality itself was beginning to surrender. Similar to the existential disturbance inherent to any Entity's presence, Silenos thought, but . . . different. Less compressed, more localized. More deliberate.

Magic often caused bleed over into more tangible forms. Light, most commonly, but heat or pressure too. Silenos found none of that here—instead he saw, with his arcane sight, that the complexity of ethereal forces at work was such that it actually caused bleed into other forms of *magic*. Silenos did not see it, so much as extrapolate its presence through the magical disturbances emerging all around.

And they were many.

The ground trembled, crying. Literally crying, sobs and weeps escaping the cold dirt as though it were a living thing. Blood emerged instead of tears—all rather typical for manifestations of an Entity. But not a weak one.

Silenos looked around, finding much of the Dark Lord's army in ruins. Evidently, without the power of their master to galvanize and support them, the undead had been a poor match for so strong an assault as could be mustered by Galukar and Lilia at once. Let alone the skyship unleashing Silenos's cannon upon them.

They were still present though, and the undead did not halt their attack, not for anything. That so many still existed proved the Dark Lord was still alive. So Silenos turned back to the maelstrom of magic.

Just in time for it to warp further.

He recognized the warping of spatial fractals as it occurred, the schisming of a world. Then he caught the faintest glimpse of a silhouette. The Dark Lord's.

"Get back," Silenos commanded with no particular urgency. The fight was won.

"What is that?!" Baird snapped, bow already raised and body tense with adrenal activity. It seemed his default response to most things, though Silenos could hardly fault it given their past few months. If anything, it was impressive that he sustained it, every other word still left more blood drizzling down his chin.

"A closed isofractaline spatial-temporal schism," Silenos informed him. Baird stared, incomprehension twisting his features. Silenos resisted the urge to roll his eyes. "It is a gateway through time and space. Doubtless, an escape route for our enemy. That he is using it only now, when the battle has already extended beyond its final stage, means we have won. If it were for reinforcements, he'd have called on it much sooner."

There was more to it than that though. In all his haste to establish a foothold in the new world, Silenos had yet to even consider the magics of dimensionalism. It was . . . an avenue. A potential one, to investigate further at a later date.

"Where is the Dark Lord?!" Galukar cried, sounding somehow mournful to now be without the enemy who had come so close to killing him. Silenos stifled his irritation, the demanding cognition of his new situation making such things far too distracting to sustain, and replied.

"He's fleeing?!" the king snarled. Had Silenos been thinking clearly, he might have lied. Instead he just nodded.

"Then it's over," Lilia noted, seeming more fatigued than relieved. Perhaps there was some emotion-blunting effect inherent to her condition like other undead.

"Not until that fucker's dead," Baird scowled, though even he seemed content to leave that for the future, and oddly deflated at the end of the carnage.

Silenos tuned out the bickering morons as they began hurling one inane remark after another at one another. His concerns went deeper and further than the execution of a single wounded enemy, particularly now that he'd gained so much fuel for the designs of his new weaponry. He found himself strangely eager to begin work on them.

"Bastard!" came a roar. *"You won't escape me that easily!"*

Before Silenos could even consciously register King Galukar's voice, the giant imbecile had already sprinted for the distortion and disappeared through it. A silence fell upon the scene, all present staring. None, quite yet, comprehending.

"The absolute fucking twat!" Baird exclaimed, overcoming his shock first. "What the shit was that? Is he dead?"

Silenos felt his temper threatening to boil, and cursed his newly constructed emotional centers for the thousandth time.

"No," he growled. "He will simply have been sent to wherever the Dark Lord vanished."

"And if the Dark Lord's still there?!" the boy shot back, suddenly more fearful, not less, for the revelation. A curious one, Baird. His father's son without a doubt, and inheritor of all his views on monarchs and empires. But still worried for the death of King Galukar. Silenos would have to examine his brain when he died. He imagined the anterior insular cortex would be rather more developed than was average among humanity.

"Doubtless," Silenos replied, "he will be killed."

Baird blanched, as did others. Lilia in particular—which was a surprise even to Silenos. He found himself moving to speak quickly, almost surprised when his words were smothered by those of another.

"But . . ." It was a new voice, and Silenos turned to see a new face attached to it. A female one, tall for her sex and . . . Yes, Galukar's daughter if his cursory glimpse of her genetic structure was to be trusted. Almost certainly, in fact. "He can't." Her tone was a tight whisper, as disbelieving as it was despairing. "How can anyone . . . kill him?"

Silenos saw the faces around him slowly curdle and had to fight back a wave of amusement.

"King Galukar will not be dying today," he declared. "I shall save him. He is, after all, a useful asset, and the thought of having him owe a dark caster the debt of life is amusing beyond compare."

The eyes that hit him were not hateful, bitter, or vitriolic. Rather . . . amused? Silenos was somewhat unnerved, but had no time to inquire about it. He leaped through the distortion.

Familiarly, the world twisted and churned like dyed water being spun about in a vortex. Silenos was accustomed to breaks in reality and kept his wits about him, remaining coherent as he fell through the nothingness until, at last, his feet came down upon solid ground once more.

They were in a strange land that he did not exert the effort to analyze beyond its tactical significance—flat but rocky, with ample cover and steady ground. Silenos quickly found the Dark Lord standing over a beaten Galukar, Godblade to one side and new injuries worsening his fatigue.

Silenos considered calling out, but decided instead to announce his presence with a cannon blast. The sound hit his enemy only after he had been blown from his feet by the solid projectile, sent spinning and flying backward to crash against a rocky plateau and leave deep fissures racing across its face. Silenos was beside Galukar the instant later.

"Up," he commanded. The king stared at Silenos blearily, eyes unfocused and vacant with concussion. Silenos touched the imbecile's forehead. Healing a creature as potent as King Galukar was . . . frustrating. The magics that made his body so invulnerable against blade and bludgeon were indiscriminate in halting his fleshcrafting, but Silenos had no shortage of raw power to drive into the effort. Within moments, Galukar's wits had solidified as much as they might have in minutes or more by themselves. It was enough.

"You came through after me," the king gasped, seemingly disbelieving.

"You are lucky I did not come through to ensure the quality of your torture, you babbling simpleton," Silenos snapped. "Now up with you!"

The shifting of stone told Silenos he had worn out his grace period, and he turned to fire again. The Dark Lord was moving already, leaping from the cannon's path and leaving the great boulder at his back to break apart where supersonic matter met fragile stone. He disappeared behind cover. Silenos backed away, reloading, readying himself, not even risking a glance at Galukar as the man shambled along beside him.

"Can you fight?" he asked.

"Yes," Galukar growled.

"Can you?!" Silenos pressed sharply. A hesitation followed, and then a more reluctant answer.

". . . No, damn it."

"Then look like you can."

The king took good advice when it was handed to him, at least, and they backed off for the distortion. Ten meters separated them from it. Silenos had closed it down to five when the Dark Lord finally moved.

He'd been quick in encircling them, and even more subtle than fast. Silenos only saw him coming from one side by the flash of movement catching his eye. His cannon roared, the earth shivered, and the Dark Lord twisted from the shot's path again.

It was no use because Silenos had aimed for the ground. His explosive shot came apart in a great nitrous blast that engulfed the enemy and sent him staggering even with the near miss. Galukar was already moving, as well he should have been, but the Dark Lord was faster. Closing in before Silenos could reload again and swinging that great mace of his. It smashed into a shield of keratin, forcing him back as his heels split the stone underfoot.

He saw his enemy's wounds in the sluggishness of each attack, though the skill involved was still a step beyond his own. Silenos turned away another attack, another. He ceded ground despite his superior mass, waiting to see Galukar vanish through the distortion. Then he acted.

Instantly, Silenos reversed his retreat and thundered forth, driving the Dark Lord away with a lance thrust that sent sparks flying where keratin met steel. Weight was all at play now, and Silenos had more of that by far. His enemy was still stumbling when he turned for the distortion and dashed through it.

For the second time that day, the world fell in on itself around him. Silenos emerged at a stagger, coming two strides from the distortion before letting his head clear. He looked around, found all the faces of his allies tight with surprise and relaxing with relief. Opening his mouth to speak, he gasped as something wrapped around him from behind. A chain, dark metal and thrumming with magic. It went taut.

Tearing him backward into the distortion.

Epilogue

The distortion snapped shut, even as Silenos was through it. He realized that its destination, this time, was different. A foolish oversight. The Dark Lord had more control over his construct than Silenos had considered. That lapse may now cost him his life.

But why did I?

Silenos was . . . no, not wrong, but lying to himself. He hadn't overlooked this possibility; he'd simply dismissed it. Why? Why had he saved Galukar, knowing it may well sentence him to death in his place? What had possessed him to do what he had done?

He searched for his answers, and found none. Around him, enemies emerged.

The Dark Lord's forces had been decimated nine times over at the last battle, and Silenos saw it reinforced that he had no great reserve of servitors to unleash upon him. Still, the entities closing in were . . . potent.

The tall, lithe beings Baird knew as fomors were among them, numbering perhaps a dozen. Two lichs of power enough that Silenos had no doubt they had been near to Heroes in their own lives accompanied them. Fourteen in all. Alone, he'd have beaten them.

But they were not alone. The Dark Lord seemed to have regained his breath and steadiness as he stood among them, while Silenos's own wounds throbbed. His odds of withstanding whatever fight was coming were slim.

Oddly enough, he felt a strange strength at that. Born from the very same sort of defiance that had so inconvenienced House Shaiagrazni in the past. Now he knew, he supposed, what it was to be a weakling.

"Have you nothing to say?" Silenos asked his enemy, speaking more to buy time than for any genuine interest. He was actually surprised when the Dark Lord's head tilted, hand raising up to gesture his minions into stillness.

Slowly, the Dark Lord's gauntleted hands came up. The tension in his servants told Silenos that this was no opportunity to strike, and so he remained quiet and watched as latches came undone and air hissed from impossibly tight seals. The black helm—now battered and lumpen where it had been impacted by too many blows—was lifted. Below a crop of curled hair emerged, black. Below that came bronze skin, and eyes bronzer still. An aquiline nose, thin lips, slim jaw, and high cheeks. Lined, worn by age. Maturer, without a doubt, than the last time Silenos had seen them.

But so very dreadfully familiar.

"Hello, Silenos," said Adonis, speaking with the same voice he'd used all those years ago when he was still Silenos's apprentice in House Shaiagrazni.

Silenos remained silent.

Ian B. Urns is the coauthor of the Author's Nightmare series, originally released on Royal Road. He writes dark fantasy stories with all the action, humor, and horror he can cram in. Having penned six novels thus far and developing his skills with each new book, he hopes to continue expanding into other genres. Urns lives in the United Kingdom, where he avoids natural light and eye contact with other living things.

A. C. Erinle is the coauthor of the Author's Nightmare series, originally released on Royal Road. A Nigerian novelist who favors character-driven fantasy and world-building, he has penned several books now, sharpening his writing skills with each one. He spends his free time frolicking in nature and otherwise enjoying life, before marching back into his Writing Hole. His stories are dark, but they never fail to be optimistic. Erinle currently resides in Lagos.